DARCY'S
TEMPTATION

DARCY'S TEMPTATION

A Sequel to the Fitzwilliam Darcy Story

REGINA JEFFERS

Ulysses Press

Published in the United States by
ULYSSES PRESS
P.O. Box 3440
Berkeley, CA 94703
www.ulyssespress.com

ISBN: 978-1-56975-723-9
Library of Congress Catalog Number 2009902007

Editors: Jennifer Privateer, Lily Chou
Editorial Associates: Abby Reser, Kate Kellogg, Lauren Harrison
Production: Judith Metzener
Cover design: TG Design
Cover illustration: Image thanks to the Art Renewal Center®
    www.artrenewal.org

Printed in the United States by Bang Printing

10 9 8 7 6 5 4 3 2 1

Distributed by Publishers Group West

This book is dedicated to all those
who believe true love is the most compelling of tasks.

"Sonnet 42"

That thou hast her, it is not all my grief,
And yet, it may be said I loved her dearly;
That she hath thee, is of my wailing chief,
A loss in love that touches me more nearly.
Loving offenders, thus I will excuse ye:
Thou dost love her, because thou knowst I love her;
And for my sake even so doth she abuse me,
Suffering my friend for my sake to approve her.
If I lose thee, my loss is my love's gain,
And losing her, my friend hath found that loss;
Both find each other, and I lose both twain,
And both for my sake lay on me this cross:
But there's the joy; my friend and I are one;
Sweet flattery! Then she loves but me alone.

—William Shakespeare

PREFACE

Every woman dreams of her one great love—the man who inspires an emotional response with just a glance across a crowded room. A romance novel must, by definition, exist purely for the advancement of the hero's love affair with the heroine; yet, the reader must want the hero to win the woman's love. To be believable, there must be a connection beyond the sexual appeal; there must be some conflict, which is character-driven. The characters must have believable reasons to be drawn together, as well as to be frustrated by their desires.

The main characters should respond realistically to the emotional conflict. They should have "fatal" flaws and exhibit a sense of vulnerability. The heroine should possess some insecurities and doubts to make the reader embrace her as a viable character. The hero should be honest and live by a strong moral code. He must embody all the qualities the heroine desires in a man. Often, he will easily make decisions for others, and he may not be in tune to the feelings of other people. In traditional historical romances, a gap must exist between the hero and heroine—socially, financially, and emotionally. She must win him over.

Jane Austen's greatest love story—that of Elizabeth Bennet and Fitzwilliam Darcy—has lasted for two hundred years because of its perfection in the manipulation of the situations commonly found in Regency England. Jane Austen created characters who were the perfect fit for each other, but who were not pulled together purely by physical desire.

In *Darcy's Passions,* I followed Austen's original plot line to tell the story of Fitzwilliam Darcy's journey to find love with Elizabeth Bennet. I tried to be true to Austen's plot although I made no attempt to mimic her style; I would consider that an insult—how could I think of copying *perfection*?

My hope in this sequel to *Darcy's Passions* was to have Darcy revisit some of the internal conflict he felt when he first met Elizabeth Bennet. I debated long and hard about whether to use amnesia as part of the plot line. I wanted my readers to know Darcy and Elizabeth belonged together no matter what journey they took to find each other.

In addition, I planned to explore the relationship between Georgiana Darcy and Chadwick Harrison. Harrison, an abolitionist, must face the dangers associated with a strong political agenda. His trials and tribulations must intertwine with those of the Darcys. His and Georgiana's relationship must mirror that of Darcy and Elizabeth.

I created a secondary love affair for Kitty Bennet and Clayton Ashford. At the end of *Pride and Prejudice*, Jane Austen indicated Jane Bingley and Elizabeth Darcy would help Kitty find herself. Later, Austen shared what she perceived to be Kitty Bennet's future: Kitty would marry a clergyman.

Darcy's Temptation begins the day after *Darcy's Passions* ends—on New Year's Day. It continues the saga of Darcy and Elizabeth through the first year of their marriage. I loved telling the new story line, but, in the beginning, I found it a bit daunting to create new scenarios to establish the characters for readers not familiar with *Pride and Prejudice, Darcy's Passions,* or any other of the many Jane Austen rewrites. I added a twist from *Darcy's Passions* to drive this story forward. In *Darcy's Passions,* Fitzwilliam Darcy briefly met Elizabeth Donnelly. He fancied her until he found her given name to be "Elizabeth," and then he was lost once again to his memories of Elizabeth Bennet. Elizabeth Donnelly reappears in Darcy's life and tries to reclaim his affections.

It was important to keep the main characters of Darcy and Elizabeth fresh while manipulating the secondary story lines. I tried to balance bringing the readers up to date while entertaining them with the new stories.

I continue to give my thanks to my many students and co-workers who offer their encouragements. Will Davis, who started this process with a "challenge" eighteen months ago, continues to be a vocal supporter, and Brooke Stegall is a phenomenal sounding board. My love, as always, goes out to my son Josh, a brilliant young man in his own right.

Regina Jeffers
Indian Trail, North Carolina

CHAPTER 1

"We have all a better guide in ourselves,
if we would attend to it, than any other person can be."
Jane Austen, *Mansfield Park*, 1817

The light streaked across the room through the slit in the heavy drapes, piercing his eyes, and Fitzwilliam Darcy reluctantly abandoned his dreams of Elizabeth Bennet. Ever since he met her in Hertfordshire over a year ago, the woman possessed his every thought—both waking and sleeping. This particular dream held real possibilities: Elizabeth Bennet lay beside him in bed, her legs wrapped across his body; she smiled her signature enigmatic smile, and Darcy rolled toward her to cup her face in his hands. "I love you, Fitzwilliam," she whispered.

"You are bewitching." He returned her smile and lowered his head to kiss her lips.

Elizabeth wrapped her arms around his neck and pulled her body closer to his, and Darcy felt himself becoming aroused by her nearness. "Fitzwilliam," she whispered as she kissed along his jaw line. "I have something special to tell you; I hope you will be pleased to know I am with child."

The news ricocheted through his body. "A child, Elizabeth—you are with child? My heir—an heir for Pemberley grows within you. Everything. You are everything, I do so love you, my Lizzy."

The dream moved to the next level as he caressed her tenderly and kissed the woman he loved more than life. The kiss grew deeper and deeper, and Darcy could feel her passion grow under his touch. She brought magic to his life and love to his home.

"Fitzwilliam," the voice crept into his subconscious. The arm draped across him lightly rubbed his abdomen, and his back felt the warmth of her body as it snuggled close to his form. He forced his eyelids open to meet the new day, while he instinctively clasped her arm to his body and held it close to him. A smile flitted across his face as the realization of his dream lived in the woman laying behind him in his bed.

"Umm," he moaned as he loosened her hold on him so he could turn to face her. "Are you awake already, my Love?" Darcy moved the curls from her face. "It's very early," he whispered to the air.

"I was dreaming about you," she mumbled, fighting to return to sleep.

He kissed her forehead. "I dreamed of you, Elizabeth Bennet Darcy, since I saw you first in Meryton."

"Do you mean when I was only tolerable?" A hint of a smile turned up the corners of her mouth as she gave over to being awake.

"Will I never live down that remark?" Darcy teased as his kisses moved down the side of Elizabeth's face.

Elizabeth kept her eyes closed although she now felt fully awake. "Maybe in twenty or thirty years."

"We will add your 'last man in the world I could be prevailed upon to marry' to those phrases we wish to forget." Darcy found her upturned mouth and kissed it tenderly.

"Our child will wonder why his parents once were so foolish." Elizabeth's free hand snaked around his waist and caressed the small of Darcy's back and down his hips. Instinctively, his hand reached a similar point on her body as he pulled her closer to him.

"Our child will know his parents married for love." He kissed along her neck and across her shoulder blade.

"Then you are truly happy, my Husband? A finer lady would not please you more?"

Darcy's hand cupped her face. "Remember, my Love, I am sick of civility, of deference, and of officious attention; I desire only the liveliness of your mind."

Elizabeth's smile and the desire in her eyes encased him. "At the moment, Mr. Darcy, I doubt my mind has anything to do with the warmth I feel coming from your body."

"You are correct, Mrs. Darcy; I believe my *frivolous sensibilities* are lost to you alone." Darcy kissed her passionately, his tongue searching her mouth.

"I love you, Fitzwilliam."

Her words created an immediate need in him, and Darcy's hands began to search the intimate points on her body. Lost to loving her, he groaned, "Lizzy."

"You know that is the one word which drives me crazy. I love the way you slur the *z*'s; it tells me how much you desire me." Her voice came out in gasps as his assault of her body continued. "Say it again, please."

"I love you, Lizzy," he whispered in her ear.

"That is perfect—absolutely perfect."

Darcy lay back in the tub, relaxing in the hot water. Thoughts of Elizabeth clung to his memory; never had he felt so satisfied with his life. So many years Darcy played the role of the dutiful son—lived his life taking care of others. He never trusted anyone else to address the concerns of his estate or to protect and provide for his sister Georgiana. Yet, Darcy always felt *cheated* by his life. He never allowed himself his own moments of happiness. Until he met Elizabeth Bennet, Fitzwilliam Darcy did his duty but ignored his dreams and his desires.

Elizabeth's presence created a quagmire for him from the beginning. A full gamut of emotions possessed him during those months—fear, bewilderment, elation, depression, devastation, happiness, and satisfaction. Now, he could not remember a time when he did not love her and when Elizabeth was not his wife. Yet, in reality, they had only been a couple for three months.

A smile turned up the corners of his mouth as visions of Elizabeth appeared behind his closed eyes. When he first dreamed of her, Darcy only saw her fine eyes or her enigmatic smile. Those images flitted in and out of his subconscious, often distracting and befuddling him because Elizabeth, by his early assessment, lacked all the qualities he *wanted* in a wife. As time progressed, thoughts of Elizabeth's vivacity, as well as his respect for her, grew, and Darcy began to picture her as a part of his life. He often fell asleep with visions of Elizabeth Bennet standing on the steps of Pemberley or walking with him and Georgiana through his estate's parkland. Those dreams of Elizabeth lasted many months, and Darcy feared he would never know the living, breathing Elizabeth Bennet.

Finally, he won her heart; then his dreams took on a more intimate nature. He dreamed of Elizabeth in his bed and the pure pleasure of taking her. However, none of those dreams came close to the actual act of touching and feeling Elizabeth in his embrace. He so needed her in his life. Darcy abandoned all the "restrictions" of love; they shared love as it should happen between a man and a woman—natural desire and respect. He knew not how other gentlemen treated their wives, other than bar talk, which he considered to be the alcohol and false pride speaking. He spent his time with Elizabeth trying to please her before he took his own pleasure, and Darcy welcomed her coming to him when she desired him. Such love could not be contained by the proprieties of the time.

"Do you plan to stay in your tub all day, my Husband?" Elizabeth's voice held strands of amusement as she stood looking at the muscular frame of the man she loved.

"I could not get you out of my mind," he said before submerging. When he came out of the water, he called, "Would you hand me a towel?"

Elizabeth's eyes traced his frame when he stood. "Maybe I should help you dry off." Her voice betrayed her real thoughts.

"As much as your offer pleases me," he began, "we still have a house full of guests." Darcy took the towel she offered and then stepped forward to kiss her lips gently. "Mmm, so tempting." He could not take his eyes from hers. "I swear, Elizabeth, when we rid ourselves of these guests, I will never invite another to my house. I want the pleasure of loving you all day—every day."

"Fitzwilliam, you are so not what I once thought. How could I ever think you to be so proper?" She snickered as she lightly touched the expanse of his chest and dabbed the water dripping from his hair. "I will wait for you in the sitting room," Elizabeth said with a hesitation. "We will go down to breakfast together."

"I will only be a moment." He kissed her cheek while she caressed his chest. As she started to walk away from him, Darcy grabbed his robe and quickly cinched it while he crossed the room and caught her arm. "Elizabeth." She turned to look at him, and he cupped her face in his hand. "Do you have any idea what effect you have on me?" His eyes searched her face, praying she would understand him.

"You have a like effect on me, Sir." Elizabeth went on her tiptoes to nibble on his lower lip.

Both of them found their breath coming in short gasps before they even touched each other. "We are coming back to this room for an early afternoon nap; we are both very tired today after staying up so late last evening." He nearly whispered the words because she never released him from her eyes.

A hint of a grin fell upon her face. "I am exceedingly tired today, Fitzwilliam; we may need to spend several hours *resting*, but for now I will be waiting in the sitting room, my Love."

Darcy released her arm to let Elizabeth leave, but it took several moments for him to move.

Henry finally appeared. "Are you ready, Mr. Darcy?"

Elizabeth sent his man in to help him dress.

"Yes, Henry, I am."

As they descended the staircase to breakfast, Darcy took her arm in his, but his eyes rested again on Elizabeth's face. "I never thought you could be more beautiful than you were on our wedding day, but being with child becomes you, Mrs. Darcy."

Elizabeth blushed with his attention. "From tolerable to beautiful—that is quite a change of heart, Mr. Darcy," she teased.

"I was always open-minded, my Love," Darcy returned the taunt.

"Oh—definitely," she returned, "how could I have ever doubted you?"

"Ah, the newly announced parents have risen for the day," Mr. Gardiner called as they entered the room.

"Yes, Uncle, we took longer coming down this morning, but we could all use a few extra minutes' sleep after our joyful evening." Elizabeth walked to him and offered up an affectionate embrace.

Darcy asked from the side bar table, "May I fix you a plate, Elizabeth?"

"Yes, Fitzwilliam, but please remember my delicate constitution." She moved to greet her aunt also.

"I doubt Mr. Darcy is likely to forget the delicacy of her condition any time soon," Jane Bingley teased as she carried her husband's plate to the table and returned for one of her own.

"That is true, Mrs. Bingley. Your sister will have to go some to top this gift." Darcy's eyes fell on his wife when he said these words. "Only twins could outdo this one."

"Twins!" Elizabeth exclaimed. "May I deal with only one heir for Pemberley at a time, Sir?" Her tone told everyone his familiarity in front of her family members did not offend her.

"Listen to the two of you," Charles Bingley laughed. "Could anyone at this table ever think Darcy to be so happy? Mrs. Darcy, he is a changed man."

"I told him something similar just a few minutes ago." Elizabeth's eyes sparkled, and Darcy's eyebrow shot up, anticipating her remark. "He is not so proper, after all," she teased. Visions of his body brought a flush to her cheeks.

"Well, I do not know about that," Bingley chuckled. "But he does seem to have found contentment."

"My wife is an exceptional woman." Darcy crossed to place the plate on the table; then he kissed Elizabeth's hand and held the chair for her as she took her place at his table. "Would you like tea, Madam?" He bowed slightly to indicate his attention to her needs.

"May I have chocolate instead?" She grinned with all his regard.

While the others found Darcy's devotion to Elizabeth amusing, he, meanwhile, whispered in her ear, "Anything, Elizabeth."

Georgiana Darcy and Kitty Bennet entered the room together. Kitty anticipated the appearance of Clayton Ashford, the young man who captured her attention the previous evening. Mr. Ashford received a living from the Darcy family; he attended the New Year's Eve dinner out of respect for his benefactor, but Ashford found himself quickly involved in the celebration of Mrs. Darcy's announcement of an heir for Pemberley. Besides being happy for the Darcys, Ashford realized an heir would bring a sense of stability to the many tenants and businesses, which depended on this great estate for their existences. Of course, his own existence depended on the Darcys' continuing good standing.

Kitty Bennet's attendance at the dinner proved to be an unexpected pleasure for Ashford. Her hand in his during the dance set gave Ashford his first sense of endearing contentment. He did not know what true effect her presence had on him for he had not acknowledged those thoughts of her yet; however, their relationship invited further possibilities.

The object of his attention now filled her plate while distractedly looking for Mr. Ashford to enter the room. When he appeared, a singular thrill shot through her as he wished the room a "Happy New Year," but kept his eyes on Kitty's face to judge her reaction. She offered him a simple "good morning" and a nearly invisible nod to the vacant chair beside her own, in hopes Ashford would join her.

Georgiana Darcy, on the other hand, knew this day would bring her a deprivation of Chadwick Harrison's attention; therefore, she did not anticipate the day, as did Kitty. Mr. Harrison took an interest in Miss Darcy, but he promised Elizabeth he would not declare his intentions until after Georgiana's next birthday. As Mr. Darcy's only sister, Georgiana held high expectations of a good match, and Mr. Harrison must prove himself to her brother before asking for her hand in marriage. Harrison's presence at Pemberley this last month allowed Georgiana to get to know him, and her regard for this stranger grew quickly. Today, he planned to return to Hines Park, his estate; it would be some time before they would see each other again.

When Mr. Harrison entered the breakfast room, Georgiana (unlike Kitty, who readily met Mr. Ashford's eyes) dropped her glance, fearing she might betray her feelings for the man, not only to him, but also to herself. Therefore, Harrison chose the seat next to Mr. Bingley and across from Georgiana rather than the empty one next to her. Although he promised Elizabeth Darcy he would not approach Georgiana at this time, Harrison would not miss the opportunity to talk to her and savor the last of their interactions.

"Good morning, Miss Darcy," he said with more interest than necessary. Harrison did not know whether Georgiana was aware of his arrangement with her sister, but he wanted her to know his interest did not wane.

"Mr. Harrison—I hope you slept well." Georgiana allowed her eyes to rise to meet his briefly.

He leaned forward to speak to her alone. "I did; thank you, Miss Darcy. It was certainly a momentous evening, was it not?"

Georgiana let her smile rest on her brother and Elizabeth. "I am so happy for Fitzwilliam. He deserves such elation in his life; my brother put his world on hold to run this estate and serve as my guardian. I could wish him such pleasure for the rest of his days." Georgiana's voice held the pride of and respect for her brother.

"I hope to replicate his accomplishments," Harrison offered. "Hines Park is not as large as Pemberley, but soon I hope it reflects some of the lessons I learned here, and then I, too, may think of starting a family of my own." Harrison's words bordered on impropriety, but he felt a need to let Georgiana know his dreams could be found in her.

She offered him a hint of a smile, which was more than he could expect to receive under the constraints placed on him by the Darcys. Yet, it held possibilities; he could set his dreams based on the softness of Georgiana's countenance.

Knowing when her birthday fell, he emphasized, "I would hope to have everything in place by late summer."

"You will be missed, Mr. Harrison." Kitty said the words Georgiana could not, and Georgiana shot her new friend a "Thank you" when no one looked at them.

Darcy called from across the table, "When will you depart, Mr. Harrison?"

"I planned to do so early this afternoon, Sir. Hines Park is only a little over a two hours' journey."

"I am sure you are anxious to see your home again," Jane Bingley added.

"I am, Mrs. Bingley; yet, I will miss the new friendships I formed at Pemberley." Again, he hoped Georgiana would understand his double meaning.

"I wonder where Anne and Edward could be," Elizabeth expressed her thoughts out loud. "You do not suppose Anne is feeling poorly again."

Georgiana assured her, "I saw her this morning; she and Edward were going to take a short walk through the gardens before they joined us. I am sure they will be here soon."

Almost as if on cue, Edward and Anne entered the room. "Edward, we began to worry," Darcy called out to his cousin.

"Anne wanted some fresh air before breakfast." Edward led Anne to a seat next to Mrs. Gardiner and leaned down to speak to Anne privately. "I will fix you something."

Anne barely whispered, "Just some toast and some tea."

Edward spoke to Anne as one might coax an obstinate child. "Will you not try something a bit more than that? Please do it for me."

"For you," she agreed and then caressed his cheek.

Darcy joined his cousin at the side bar table. "How is Anne really doing, Edward?" Darcy whispered as he shot a quick glance at Anne de Bourgh.

"She was under our aunt's scrutiny so long Anne sometimes must be coaxed into vibrancy." Edward's face showed his love for the adolescent-like woman.

"I would never, I fear, think of Anne as vibrant." Darcy's words held regret he had for never helping Anne escape Lady Catherine's control. "However, Edward, I am sure with your love she will be just that."

"Thank you, Darcy."

"For what?"

"For understanding I truly love Anne." Edward's words sounded as if he had not been able to convince others of his regard for his cousin.

"We always were more than cousins, Edward. I sincerely pray for your happiness." Edward gave Darcy a grateful nod and returned to the table to join Anne.

"Mr. and Mrs. Darcy." Clayton Ashford stood to take his leave. "I am afraid I must depart. I thank you for sharing your evening and your home with me."

"We were pleased you could be here," Elizabeth offered. "You must come again soon. Would you be free tomorrow evening for dinner?"

"I would, Mrs. Darcy. I thank you for the invitation. May I also ask your permission to announce your good tidings of an heir for Pemberley at this week's services? I know the community will rejoice with the news and offer their prayers."

"I have no objections, Mr. Ashford. Do you, Fitzwilliam?"

"You are welcome to be our town crier, Mr. Ashford."

"Mr. Ashford, I will walk out with you." Elizabeth stood. "I think I must inform key staff members at Pemberley before they hear our news from a tradesman in Lambton."

"Mr. Ashford, may I have the coach brought around to return you to town?" Elizabeth and Mr. Ashford stood in the main entryway.

"No, thank you, Mrs. Darcy. I prefer to walk. I bid you farewell until tomorrow evening." With that said, he pulled on his coat and departed down the lane toward Lambton.

Elizabeth worked her way to the study. She stopped before entering the room to ask one of the maids to have Mrs. Reynolds and Hannah come to her.

"Enter," Elizabeth called at the light knock on the study door.

15

"Mrs. Darcy, did you wish to see us?" Mrs. Reynolds felt some agitation at being summoned to the study.

Elizabeth came from behind her husband's desk to greet them. "Yes, Mrs. Reynolds, please will the two of you come to join me?" Elizabeth gestured to the chairs.

Both ladies took the seats she offered, but the unusual situation bothered them. "Mrs. Darcy, have we done something wrong?"

"Oh, Mrs. Reynolds, is that what you thought? I apologize for giving you the wrong impression. On the contrary— because Mr. Darcy and I value your service to me and to the estate, we felt it appropriate to tell you something before the news spreads through the community via Mr. Ashford." Both women took on the look all women have when their suspicions are about to be confirmed. "Mr. Darcy and I hope to welcome our first child in late July."

"Oh, Mrs. Darcy," Hannah squealed. "I am so happy to hear this. I suspected as much by the way you picked at your food lately. This is great news."

As tears welled in her eyes, Mrs. Reynolds could barely contain herself. "Mrs. Darcy, you are to let me take on things; you are not to let Pemberley be a concern. The Master must be beside himself with happiness."

"He does seem quite content with the prospect, Mrs. Reynolds. I wanted you two to be aware. Hannah, I will obviously depend on you in a personal manner. I will need additional clothing and some personal care in choices of food. Mrs. Reynolds, we must prepare a nursery. Yet, all these little things were never my concern in bringing you here. You are a part of the Pemberley family, and you have an interest in what happens within our lives. Mrs. Reynolds, you may tell other staff members as you see fit."

"This will be great news; the staff and the tenants waited for a long time. It has been over seventeen years since Pemberley knew such happiness. Master Fitzwilliam will have an heir for the estate. Pemberley will survive." Mrs. Reynolds's eyes misted again with tears. She and Hannah stood to take their leave. "Bless you, Mrs. Darcy. Everything will finally be happiness at Pemberley."

Elizabeth felt a bit overwhelmed with Mrs. Reynolds's reaction. She knew how important giving Darcy an heir must be, but she never suspected her time would bring forth such emotions. Recently, she came to understand the great responsibility her husband assumed when he took over Pemberley after his father's death. Elizabeth also now possessed a better idea of how many people depended on Darcy and the estate for their subsistence, yet sometimes she still could not conceive how she fit into the picture. Carrying Darcy's child gave Elizabeth a new acceptance of what all he and this estate meant to hundreds of people at Pemberley, but also to those in Lambton and at Kensington Place. She married into responsibility. Immersed deep in these thoughts, Elizabeth seated herself behind Darcy's desk to pen a letter to her parents.

1 January

Papa and Mama,

It is New Year's Day at Pemberley. We had a glorious celebration last evening with a few close friends. Although our party was small, our joy at being in our own home could not be expressed. Mr. Darcy gave up celebrating the Festive Season at Pemberley after the deaths of his parents. Opening up the estate once again told him this was a beginning; his previous sadness could be no more. You will be happy to know Jane and Mr. Bingley, along with Kitty, arrived safely. Having my dearest sisters with me renewed my energies.

Mr. Harrison will end his stay with us today and return to Hines Park; his astute insights will be greatly missed. Colonel Fitzwilliam and Anne de Bourgh are with us for a few days before they travel on to his father's estate. They will officially announce their engagement at his parents' anniversary party. We will all travel to Matlock to join in their celebration. Uncle and Aunt Gardiner and their children are happy to visit her family and friends in Lambton, as well as spend time with us. Mr. Darcy enjoys Uncle Gardiner's company; I believe my dear Fitzwilliam misses his father's counsel, and my uncle serves that purpose of a more mature voice in his life.

Georgiana and I successfully orchestrated the tenant celebration at Pemberley. The steward, Mr. Howard, claims we created goodwill between the tenants and the Darcy family. My regard for Mr. Darcy's caring nature grew during this celebration. Hearing his tenants tell of the many ways he served them gave me great pride in having married such a man. It is amazing to me he knows all their names and all their histories; he treats them exceptionally well. It bothers me I ever so misjudged him. Georgiana continues to open herself up to new possibilities; I hope she and Kitty will become good friends.

When Jane and Mr. Bingley return to Netherfield, I request Kitty be allowed to stay with me here at Pemberley. I am in need of my sister's help because Mr. Darcy and I shall become parents in late summer; having Kitty with me would give me great pleasure during this time. Fitzwilliam plans to secure tutors for Kitty while she is with us. Of course, Mama, having Kitty here will expose her to eligible young men. In fact, our new vicar already shows an interest in her.

I must close now as our guests await my return. I miss all my dear family and pray to see you soon.

Your loving daughter,
E. D.

Elizabeth also wrote to Charlotte.

1 January

My dearest Charlotte,

I will write more at a later date, but I must tell you my happy news. Mr. Darcy and I expect our first child in late July. Because I know Lady Catherine will likely be displeased when she learns of this, I wanted you and Mr. Collins to know before she did. She is likely to learn soon for Colonel Fitzwilliam and Miss de Bourgh are guests in our home. I am sure Anne will write to her mother. I realize you rejoice in my happiness even if Mr. Collins's position prevents your saying so. You are as always in my thoughts.

Elizabeth Darcy

She closed both letters with wax and pressed the Darcy seal in each before writing the directions on the outside. Elizabeth moved from behind the desk to stand by the glass doors leading to the gardens; she stood there for several minutes before Darcy found her. He watched her before approaching; if she ever realized how many times per day he took pleasure in just looking at her, Elizabeth might become uncomfortable around him. Darcy could give himself no greater satisfaction than to memorize her form. "There you are, my Love," he said as he came up behind her and encircled her waist with his arms.

Elizabeth leaned back to feel the warmth of his body. He heard her emit a light moan as he kissed the side of her neck. "I was just enjoying the view."

"Pemberley in the spring and early summer must resemble Heaven because I know of no place more beautiful. I cannot wait for you to see it; you will love it as I do."

"I already love it, Fitzwilliam." She turned to face him directly. "I was just thinking about how much a part of my life you and Pemberley have become. I wrote my parents about our unexpected gift and asked for Kitty to stay with us; as I did so, I felt guilty for not being homesick for Longbourn. How is it I lived at Longbourn for over twenty years and at Pemberley for less than two months, but it is Pemberley of which I think when someone says *home*?"

"I do not know how to explain it because I feel as such, too. When my mother died, so did life at Pemberley. Now, with you here, it lives again. It is no longer just a fine *house*—it is my *home*. We, obviously, belong together—our *fatum*."

"I do so love you, Fitzwilliam." Her arms snaked around his neck, and Elizabeth leaned in to rest her head on his chest. For some time, Darcy held her there, stroking her hair and feeling how she melded into him. Finally, she agreed they must rejoin their guests. "Fitzwilliam, before we go, may I ask you a couple of things?"

"Of course, Elizabeth."

"First, I would like to employ tutors for Kitty while she is with us. She is not as shallow as is Lydia, and Jane and I wish to help her become less provocative."

"I have no problem with the idea. I realize making a good match may depend on such training for your sister. It is our duty to help her find an appropriate mate."

Elizabeth smiled at him. "Thank you, my Love. Secondly, I have been thinking about your teaching me about Pemberley. Should not Georgiana also be made aware of how to run the estate?"

"I am not sure what you mean, Elizabeth."

"I realize with the jointure Pemberley is mine until my death if something happens to you, but I would want it to also belong to Georgiana—at least, as long as she wants to be here. I would feel uncomfortable if I made decisions for her family's estate without her input. Plus, do you not think it would be to her advantage if she knew about estate business, in general? When she chooses to marry, no man would be able to fool her into believing his worth is more than it actually is. Some men would object to her knowing their business, but a man who respects our sister for herself rather than her thirty thousand pounds would not."

"I see. So you believe I should approach my sister on this idea?" Deep in thought, Darcy finally released her and took a few steps toward the window.

"I wish you would, Sir, if you believe it has any merit." As Darcy always saw Georgiana as needing protection, Elizabeth seemed tentative about how he would react to such a proposal for his sister.

"Let me think about how it might be handled. Georgiana's natural instinct is not as adventurous as is yours, my Love; she may not see such knowledge as being part of her realm."

"Georgiana simply wants your respect for her worth. I believe she would welcome an opportunity to learn about Pemberley."

"Mr. Harrison said a few days ago I was blessed to have two progressive-thinking women in my household," Darcy added as he turned back to embrace his wife once more.

"Did he now?" Elizabeth teased, knowing she was serious with him too long. "What did he mean by *progressive*, do you suppose?" She went up on her tiptoes to brush Darcy's lips with hers.

Darcy's passion quickly rose just being near his wife. "I hope my sister is not *progressive* in the same way as you right now, my Love."

"Oh, do you believe, Sir, there is more than one meaning for the word?"

"Certainly." His hands began to caress Elizabeth's back as he kissed her neck. "*Progressive* may mean 'improving,' which seems appropriate for my sister. She improves each day under your influence, Elizabeth."

"And what of me, Sir? How may you consider me to be *progressive*?" Her challenge offered him a warning of choosing the right words. "Do you see your wife as too *forward-moving* and too *liberal*?"

"Not at all, Madam." Darcy found an interest in the curls that draped down from her hair. "Your *progressive* nature means you are *dynamic* and *spirited*. You consume my mind."

Elizabeth laughed with a cackle, which began deep within her. "Fitzwilliam, I admit you handled that quite well. I always took delight in your ability to twist the English language to prove your point."

A full smile overspread Darcy's face. "Truthfully, my Love, our verbal swordplay was one of the first things that attracted me to you. I used to say things to provoke a response just to hear you address me directly."

"Fitzwilliam Darcy, you did not!" She seemed shocked by this disclosure.

"I am afraid, my Dear, I did." His eyes twinkled, realizing her reaction to his words.

Elizabeth relished his early attempts to win her attention. "Tell me, Sir, when did you so manipulate me?"

"Do you recall Miss Bingley's litany of qualities of an accomplished woman?"

"Of course, how could I forget? She wished to let me know I could be found wanting." Elizabeth shifted her weight, indicating she still felt limited when she recalled the words.

"Oh, my Love, do not even begin," he cautioned. "I know how you think. You want for nothing. It is Miss Bingley who lacks any real worth." Darcy saw her shoot him an incredulous stare. "Do you not recall to Miss Bingley's list I added extensive reading to improve one's mind? Caroline never reads unless forced to do so. I knew you were a voracious reader. I assumed you would understand my reference."

"You forget—I thought you hated me then."

"That still amazes me, Elizabeth; I could not take my eyes from you. You played havoc with my emotions that evening, my Love. You stood beside Mr. Bingley as we played cards. When you offered your attentions to Charles, I said something to provoke you to draw your attention to me—to force you to look in my eyes." Darcy caressed her jaw line with the back of his hand.

"It could not be so. Why did I not see your desires?" Elizabeth shook her head in disbelief.

Darcy chuckled; how often they misunderstood each other in those early days of their relationship took on comic effects in hindsight, although his misery at the time nearly destroyed him. "Do you remember my comment of knowing only a half dozen women who were truly accomplished? I knew you would never let that comment go by."

"It seems, Sir, you knew me better than even I did." Elizabeth kissed him tenderly.

"If I knew you as well as I should have, it would not have taken us so long to find each other." Elizabeth saw the remorse drift into his eyes.

"None of that, Mr. Darcy." She massaged the frown lines in his forehead. "We agreed we went through all we did so we could be happy now. Do not remember the bad; it never existed."

Darcy drew Elizabeth near where he could feel the contours of her body next to his; her warmth brought him comfort. "As long as you never consider leaving me alone again, Elizabeth."

"How could I ever leave you, Fitzwilliam? You possess my heart." Her kiss this time made him want her, and Darcy's hand searched the neckline of her dress, running his finger along the top of her breast. She finally broke the embrace. "My goodness, Sir, you are *dynamic*, or is that *progressive*, today?"

He began to laugh. "We will continue this later, Madam, in our room."

"I am anticipating the pleasure, Sir. Let us rejoin our guests now." She took his proffered arm to leave the room.

"I said it before, but we will invite no one else to our home, Elizabeth. Believe my words." They both knew the irony of their relationship. They needed close family and friends to sustain them, but solitary interludes held a real appeal.

CHAPTER 2

"Happiness in marriage is entirely a matter of chance."
Jane Austen, *Pride and Prejudice*, 1813

———◆◆◆———

"I plan to ride into Lambton, Charles. Are you in the mood for a brief outing?" Darcy asked when he entered the drawing room.

"I would enjoy such a time, Darcy. Let me change." Charles Bingley missed the interactions he and Darcy once shared.

"Fitzwilliam, would you post the letters I wrote?" Elizabeth asked as she joined the others.

"Of course, Elizabeth. Where are they?"

"I left them on the tray for Mr. Howard's attention. Thank you, Sir." Elizabeth's voice held an intimacy only Darcy recognized. Her "thanks" seemed innocent enough to the others in the room, but even something this simple held sexual tension for them. Their passions always rested just below the surface so when she said, "Thank you, Sir," Elizabeth also allowed her eyes to drift up his body, and Darcy arched an eyebrow when she rested her attention on his countenance.

He winked at her when she pursed her lips. "I will retrieve them, Madam." Then he offered his wife a seductive smile as he left.

Elizabeth held images of him in her mind as she picked up her needlework and joined her sister and aunt. "Aunt Gardiner, where are the children?" Elizabeth asked as she abandoned those images to the mundane activities of daily life.

"Your uncle took them for a tour of the grounds."

"I am pleased Mr. Darcy asked Charles to join him for a ride today. My husband missed Mr. Darcy's counsel," Jane confided.

"It would be natural, Jane, being such good friends for so long." Elizabeth had no idea whether Darcy felt the same as Charles; they never discussed it; she supposed he held similar feelings as Charles Bingley.

"Since our marriage, Charles had only Mr. Hurst and our father for male companionship."

Elizabeth found this amusing. "Mr. Hurst is certainly not a conversationalist, and our father, though quite capable, usually cannot be bothered to do so."

"That was Charles's plight of late. We met Sir William one evening a fortnight ago, and I did not think I would ever get Charles to leave his conversation with the man."

"Well, I am sure our husbands will enjoy whatever men discuss when not with women." Elizabeth allowed Darcy held thoughts of which she was not privy; this realization bothered her for some reason, although she tried to pass them off. "Where are Georgiana and Kitty?"

"Miss Darcy and Miss de Bourgh are in the music room with the colonel," Mrs. Gardiner offered. "I believe I saw Kitty in the garden earlier."

"Mr. Harrison packs for his journey," Jane added.

"Let us have some tea." Elizabeth put her needlework away. "Now as we are alone," she took on a conspiratorial tone, "I am dying to know what each of you think of my new home."

Sipping her tea, Elizabeth turned to her beloved sister. "Well, tell me, Jane, do you not love Pemberley?"

"Elizabeth," Jane looked around the drawing room, "Aunt Gardiner and I spoke of the splendor of Pemberley yesterday. It is a magnificent estate and definitely lives up to its reputation."

"Then you approve?" Elizabeth asked as if someone might object.

"As for me," Mrs. Gardiner teased, "the most perfect thing about Pemberley is seeing you with Mr. Darcy, Elizabeth. To see you so happy at last is most gratifying."

"Thank you, Aunt. I still worry about how to make Pemberley my own, but Fitzwilliam's love makes the transition easier. Could either of you ever think both Jane and I could be so blessed?"

Mrs. Gardiner smiled. "Mr. Bingley could not be more amiable, and he matches our Jane perfectly. Mr. Darcy is more complicated, Elizabeth, but from the time I met him last August, I knew his devotion to you would create a perfect world for you two. You are both of a solitary nature; so as Mr. Bingley fits Jane, Mr. Darcy fits you."

"It amazes me I once found him to be disagreeable," Elizabeth mused. "Now, I admit I cannot stand to be away from Fitzwilliam for very long."

"Our Lizzy met her match, Aunt," Jane laughed.

Elizabeth enjoyed the humor at her expense. "Mr. Darcy captured my heart."

Bingley and Darcy rode easily; Bingley found the company pleasurable, while Darcy preferred riding when he had things on his mind. Reaching Lambton, Darcy turned to his friend. "Bingley, I hope you will not be offended. I want to speak to Mr. Spencer about Elizabeth's condition. Mrs. Darcy had a recent accident, and I want to be sure everything is well. I shall not be long, though."

"Of course, Darcy. I would like to find something special for Jane. Shall I meet you in half an hour at the Royal Crown?"

"We will have something to drink before returning to Pemberley. Thirty minutes it is, Sir."

Darcy posted the letters and walked briskly to Mr. Spencer's house. He asked the housekeeper to see the doctor.

"Mr. Darcy." Mr. Spencer suspected he would see Darcy today. "I see your wife spoke to you, Sir."

"She has, Mr. Spencer. Now, I would like your learned opinion of Mrs. Darcy's condition." Darcy took the seat Mr. Spencer offered.

"Well, Mr. Darcy, I believe your wife has as good of a chance for a complete delivery as does any other woman. Her recent accident should cause no long-term problems. Mrs. Darcy suspected her condition prior to the fall. She did all the right things during the fall. Mrs. Darcy protected the baby; she is a very smart woman, Sir."

Darcy found a new respect for his wife. "My Elizabeth is remarkable."

"Mr. Darcy, your sister was the last *life* brought into Pemberley's world. Since Miss Darcy's birth, you knew nothing but death in your home. Mrs. Darcy will change that for you. Of course, I cannot guarantee a live birth, but I have no reason to think otherwise."

"Are there any precautions of which I should be aware, Mr. Spencer?"

"I warned Mrs. Darcy about the terrain surrounding Pemberley, but your wife is healthy. She needs to be cautious but not frightened of her everyday activities."

The next question brought Darcy some discomfort. "Mr. Spencer, what of my private relationship with my wife?"

"Mr. Darcy." The man stood to come to sit across from him. The doctor knew it cost Darcy a great deal to open himself up to these questions. "There are many misconceptions about intimate relationships between a man and a woman when she is with child. I hear old wives' tales, which suggest the baby will see the gentleman's manhood and refuse to enter the world. These are ridiculous to a man of science such as I. Normal relationships are acceptable, Mr. Darcy, until your wife's lying in. Be aware of her abdomen as the baby grows. Place no extra weight on her as she expands, but there is no reason to abstain from your wife's attentions. Keep her life as normal as possible, but do so within reason, and your chance of an heir will be in your favor."

"You must think me a foolish husband, Mr. Spencer." Darcy shifted uncomfortably in his chair.

"On the contrary, Mr. Darcy. I wish the husbands of many of my patients cared as much for their wives as you do for Mrs. Darcy. You, obviously, want what is best for her and are willing to accept some discomfort to have accurate information."

"Mr. Spencer, I would do without an heir for Pemberley if it meant carrying my heir would put Mrs. Darcy's health in danger. I want nothing to happen to her. Please remember that when you are called upon regarding the delivery of our child. Mrs. Darcy is to be your priority."

"I understand, Sir. Thank you for explaining your feelings to me. I will convey your wishes to the midwife you choose."

Darcy expended as much emotionally as he could afford on this matter; he stood to leave. "Thank you, Mr. Spencer, for addressing my concerns." With polite farewells the men separated. Spencer stood in disbelief at how much Darcy changed since meeting Mrs. Darcy. Pemberley, in the doctor's opinion, would never be the same.

"I hope you have not been here long, Bingley," Darcy offered as he slid into the chair across from his friend.

"No, Darcy, I just arrived. May I order something for you?"

"Some tea would be nice." Bingley motioned for an additional cup to be brought to the table. The locals scrambled to meet Darcy's needs. His presence in Lambton created a buzz of activity; many in the area owed their existence to the estate. "Did you find something for Mrs. Bingley?"

"I bought her a new handkerchief," Bingley began. "I resolved after our conversation the other day, I would let my

Jane know of my devotion to her whenever I can. Do you not think little 'gifts' appropriate, Darcy?"

"Bingley, I learned my lesson about offering advice on your and Mrs. Bingley's relationship." Darcy chuckled lightly, a bit embarrassed by his own admission.

Charles laughed; Darcy once tried to keep Bingley and Jane apart. "I am asking your advice, Darcy."

Darcy knew Bingley still lacked self-confidence in most of his interactions with others; Charles handled conflict with retreat rather than surety. "Bingley, I believe any woman responds to spontaneous examples of affection from the man she favors. Shower Mrs. Bingley with gifts or simply express your devotion to her when the opportunity arises. Do not worry about Mrs. Bingley's regard for you. Obviously, if it did not diminish in the months you were apart, it is not likely to do so now."

"Do you believe that to be so, Darcy?"

"I most certainly do, Bingley."

"My fear is we are too close to Longbourn for our marital felicity. Mrs. Bennet appears at our door regularly, and Jane's kindness will not allow her to rebuke her mother." Bingley paused and looked a bit uncomfortable with his next thoughts. "Mrs. Bingley is not willing to abandon Netherfield yet, but if things do not change soon, I will try to convince her. If that were so, would you help me find something closer to Pemberley? I would like Jane to have access to Mrs. Darcy; her family is important to my wife."

"Mrs. Darcy would certainly welcome such a change, as would I. We spent little time together since our respective engagements."

"Male companionship has been lean at Netherfield. Even going shooting became an ordeal." Bingley looked uncomfortable again.

Darcy tried to assure his friend. "When you are ready to

change, Charles, it would do me well to serve you once again. In the meantime, I will be aware of any land which may come available."

"Darcy, are you as content with marriage as you seem?"

"Bingley, Elizabeth's presence creates such satisfaction. Pemberley was never so alive; you should have seen her and Georgiana at the tenant's celebration. I could not be prouder of either of them. When I chose Elizabeth as my wife, I chose her obvious beauty but also her wit, her intelligence, her compassion, and her devotion. I need a woman beside me who will help me transition Pemberley into a new age. Elizabeth is that woman for me."

"Your words sound as if you plan for your estate, and Elizabeth plays a major part in that plan."

"I do. Some will judge me poorly, although I know you will not be one of them. Elizabeth is learning the estate's business. I will not have a dependent—Elizabeth will be my partner. That lifestyle works for the two of us. I do not advocate it for everyone, but it is what I need. Elizabeth fills in the areas which I cannot." Darcy's matter-of-fact statements persuaded Bingley to their truth.

Bingley offered his friend a light chuckle with the irony he saw in the situation. "You once told me duty to your family's name outweighed your need for affection in a choice for a wife. Luckily, you found both in Mrs. Darcy."

"Your wife's sister certainly captured my heart, Bingley." Just dwelling on Elizabeth brought a gamut of images to Darcy's mind, and a hint of a smile formed on his lips. "Speaking of our wives, maybe we should return to Pemberley. I imagine Mr. Harrison is ready to depart."

"Mr. Harrison, you will be missed," Elizabeth turned to her guest. "Your stories of the Americas were very entertaining, Sir."

"Mrs. Darcy, you never lack for hospitality and generosity. You welcomed me as a member of your family during the most holy of days. I am blessed to earn your friendship." He bowed to Elizabeth respectfully.

Elizabeth appropriately dropped her eyes before acknowledging his praise. "Mr. Harrison, you are welcome at Pemberley anytime, Sir." Darcy stood beside his wife and sister as they bid the man farewell.

"Mr. Darcy, your counsel was most enlightening." Harrison finally turned his attentions to Georgiana. "Miss Darcy, I look forward to seeing you again." He wanted to embrace her—to hold her—but instead he offered Georgiana a loving glance and a proper bow before leaving in his coach for Dove Dale.

Walking back to the drawing room, Elizabeth instinctively encircled Georgiana's waist with her arm. "Mr. Harrison will return soon, Georgiana. Mark my words." Elizabeth held concerns for Georgiana's gentle disposition. Although she knew Harrison expressed a desire to know Georgiana better, Elizabeth's wariness at his honest entreaty held trepidation; yet, she did not wish to belie the man until she knew for sure. Her qualms lay only with protecting Georgiana. Miss Darcy held back tears while smiling at her new sister.

"I will wait," Georgiana whispered, knowing she could open up her thoughts to Elizabeth without fear of censure. Their relationship created the female bond Georgiana always desired. Since Elizabeth entered Fitzwilliam's life, Georgiana found herself able to express her innermost thoughts. Elizabeth caught Georgiana's eye and nodded without further comment.

Later that afternoon, Darcy and Elizabeth reclined leisurely across their bed, having spent themselves in passion. He brushed his lips across hers playfully. "Mrs. Darcy, your husband loves you most ardently."

"I am pleased to hear it, Sir," she murmured. "I would hate to think my affections were not returned."

Darcy bent to kiss her tenderly and then withdrew enough to lock eyes with her. "What bothers you, Elizabeth?"

"What makes you think there is something wrong, my Love?"

"Elizabeth, do not try to hide what bothers you; are you feeling unwell?" He stroked her hair from her face.

"It is nothing, really—something quite innocent that Jane said. She commented on how often Bingley missed your company, and I kept thinking how much I used to depend on Jane's understanding; but since we are together, I think of nothing else but your presence. I felt guilty for abandoning my sister. Add that to my earlier thoughts of Pemberley being my home now, and I judged myself to be a poor daughter indeed."

Darcy pulled her to him, allowing the curves of her body to linger beside his muscular frame. The truth she offered held levels of pain for her, and he tried to be sensitive to her needs. He stroked Elizabeth's hair, realizing the depth of her "confession." Elizabeth needed him for himself, and she needed him above all others in her life. "I can remember nothing before there was you in my life, Elizabeth." He whispered the words close to her ear. "Sometimes life brings two people such as you and I together. How do we explain to others we need only each other to experience happiness? When you accepted my love, we became joined as few are. It does not make you a poor daughter; it makes you my joy and my delight."

Elizabeth asked tentatively, "Do you miss the company of your gentlemen friends such as Mr. Bingley?"

"I found Bingley's company today a pleasant way to spend my time until I could return to your arms. I need only you in my life. I teased about having no future guests in my house, but there was truth in my words. You consume me and fill me, Elizabeth." Darcy took the kiss this time to a deeper, more passionate level as if he had to possess her.

Darcy found Georgiana at the pianoforte in the music room. "Fitzwilliam," she spoke in surprise upon seeing him enter the room. "Is there something the matter, Sir?"

"I was concerned for your well-being," he began, "as is your sister Elizabeth."

Georgiana blushed with his attention. "I am fine, Sir, I assure you."

"I wish you peace and contentment, the kind I found with Elizabeth." Darcy took his sister's hand.

"I understand your caution, Fitzwilliam; I am not disappointed, nor am I angry about your choice on my behalf." Georgiana touched his cheek tenderly. "If anything," she continued, "I am more confused about what I should or should not be feeling."

"Elizabeth and I only desire your future happiness. We asked Mr. Harrison to wait because we want to give you time to know yourself better. As a young woman, many changes will occur in the next year. At least, that is what Elizabeth says happened with her and her sisters. We simply wish to make that transition easier for you. Elizabeth assures me this is what is best for you at this time."

"I am thankful to have Elizabeth with us," Georgiana looked at him closely. "I never knew how much I needed her type of love in my life."

Darcy chuckled lightly. "That is a sentiment I easily share."

"You really chose well, Fitzwilliam." Georgiana returned his steady stare. "When the time comes, I hope to be as wise."

"Speaking of my lovely wife," he cleared his throat, "Elizabeth made another suggestion of which we both hope you will agree."

"You have my attention." Georgiana shifted a bit uncomfortably.

"It is nothing of which to be concerned." Darcy noted her shift. "As you know, I have a plan for Pemberley's future, one which involves Elizabeth as an active partner in running the estate. The times change, and I must learn to change with them. Elizabeth agreed to become familiar with the management of the estate and our other properties. Even in London, she studied the books and the finances on the Darcy holdings."

"I knew you offered some liberty in this matter, but I never realized you involved Elizabeth to this extent."

"Many of my gentlemen friends would be shocked if they knew of my doing so, but I care not. I will do what is necessary to keep Pemberley a viable part of this community. It is my duty to our parents to maintain Pemberley in its glory. Elizabeth knows my desire for the estate. I, as you also know, gave Elizabeth a jointure; if something happens to me, she will continue on with my vision."

"Fitzwilliam!" Georgiana gasped. "I am amazed you chose to trust Elizabeth with so much responsibility. It is unheard of."

"It is a change," Darcy said calmly, "but do you not agree it is necessary?"

"Of course, I agree," she assured him. "Elizabeth will blossom under your tutelage. She is so perceptive about what needs to be done, and she possesses the courage to see things through."

"I am gladdened by your assurances," he said, taking her hand in his, "because Elizabeth believes you, too, should become familiar with the estate. She wishes you to join her in this endeavor."

"Me!" Georgiana's voice cracked.

"My Dearest One." Darcy caressed her chin line. "You will live in a world foreign to what we have now. Cities are infringing on the estates, and the life we know in Regency England will never be the same again. Elizabeth believes it would be to your benefit to know how an estate should be run. A man, who values you as a learned woman, will accept your knowledge and welcome your ideas. If not, maybe the man is not an appropriate choice."

"Fitzwilliam," she stumbled through the words, "you and Elizabeth trust me that much?"

"We do." Darcy held her eyes, trying to relay the truth of his words. "Elizabeth wishes you to help her with Pemberley if, Heaven forbid, I meet an untimely demise. She wishes not to make decisions for your ancestral home without your input."

"Oh, Fitzwilliam," she said, flushed with excitement, "I am overwhelmed by your confidence in me. I will try not to let you down. I mean, I may let you down, but I will try not to do so."

"Then you are pleased with the idea?"

Georgiana's arms snaked around his neck as she hugged him closely. "The fact you and Elizabeth value me gives me a purpose."

"Then you will join us with Mr. Howard tomorrow afternoon." Darcy stood to leave. "I encourage you to ask questions of Mr. Howard, Elizabeth, and me when you need to do so."

"Thank you, Fitzwilliam." Georgiana's eyes sparkled with delight.

The lessons started the next afternoon as Darcy requested. To his satisfaction, both Georgiana and Elizabeth asked astute questions and offered insights he and Mr. Howard did not consider. "Do you really believe punishing Mr. Jenkins for poaching a deer when his family is hungry is the best way to resolve the problem?" Elizabeth asked.

"If we do not, then all the tenants will help themselves to the game on the estate. Soon there would be no game left," Mr. Howard confided.

Georgiana asked, "Is there not some way to share the game? Mr. Jenkins was only trying to take care of his family—he was not trying to make a profit from the kill. None of us believe it was a malicious action; he did what any of us in this room would do in a similar situation."

Darcy sat behind his desk, fingers clasped and listening to the conversation. "I believe I hear you saying Mr. Jenkins's punishment does not meet the crime."

"Exactly," Elizabeth chimed in.

Darcy cautioned, "Then what do you propose? Please remember I must discourage the other tenants from following suit."

Elizabeth paced the floor several times before turning back to her husband. "Obviously, Mr. Jenkins owes the estate for the deer. Is there not a disagreeable job for him to do as repayment? The job should be one nobody wants to do. Mr. Howard, can you not think of something?"

"I suppose so, Mrs. Darcy. Maybe something to do with the waste pots."

"That would resolve one of the issues," Darcy summarized. "But there seems to be a bigger problem."

"Fitzwilliam," Georgiana's voice came out small, "I have an idea, if I may."

"Of course, Dearest One," he encouraged her.

"It seems every year the estate has an abundance of some sort of game. Some years it is the deer. Other years it is the rabbits. When there is an abundance, the animals destroy prize vegetation. Why not have a controlled kill of the animals in plenty to regulate the population? We could offer the animals to the tenants on an equal basis. My first inclination is to give them the meat, but it might be better for their self-respect if the tenants pay the estate, either with money or physical labor. They could clear away the brush, plant gardens, repair walls—whatever Mr. Howard needs."

"Interesting." Darcy leaned back in his chair to consider his sister's suggestion. "It would resolve several areas of concern. What do you think, Mr. Howard?"

"The animals are often killed anyway, but are done so indiscriminately," he mused. "We could better balance the natural habitat. I am unsure how to go about this, but I would be pleased to pursue it if you like, Sir."

"Let us, you and I, look into it, Mr. Howard," Darcy set forward once again. "Where might we use the staff we already have in place in an efficient manner?"

"Yes, Mr. Darcy." Mr. Howard picked up the account ledgers for the estate. "Is there anything else, Sir?"

"No, thank you, Mr. Howard." The man bowed to each of the family members and then exited. Darcy came from around the desk. "Well, Georgiana," he teased, "I see I can retire tomorrow as Master of Pemberley."

"Do not tease me, Fitzwilliam. I was shaking throughout that exchange." Georgiana held out her hands to show him how they twitched.

Elizabeth came to sit beside her. "Georgiana, you were very mature in your thinking. I was quite impressed."

Georgiana still seemed unsure. "Were you, Elizabeth?"

"Exceptionally so." Elizabeth squeezed the girl's hand. "You and I will make a formidable pair." Elizabeth looked up and winked at Darcy.

"You were very insightful," he added. "Tomorrow, if the weather permits, I would like for the three of us to ride out and begin to examine the estate together."

"Yes, Fitzwilliam." Georgiana stood and straightened her dress. "I think I will go practice for a while. I promised Anne we would work on some music together. She wants us to play when she and Edward announce their engagement."

"Then we will see you later, Sweet One," he said as Georgiana exited.

Darcy's attention now turned back to his wife. "Do not look so smug, Mrs. Darcy." He pulled Elizabeth into his arms. "No one likes a prideful woman," he whispered into her ear as he kissed the side of her neck.

"Nor a prideful man," Elizabeth added as she allowed her lips to lightly brush against his.

Darcy breathed in deeply. "Wait here," he told her as he crossed to close and lock the study door.

"Mr. Darcy?" Elizabeth allowed her voice to rise in anticipation.

Darcy returned to her embrace, basking in the warmth of her affection. "Yes, my Love?"

An inviting smile convinced Darcy that lifting Elizabeth into his arms and sitting her on his lap would receive her approval. Cradling her there, he first traced her lips, then along the line of her dress, with his fingertips. "Do you love me, Elizabeth?" he murmured in her ear.

She captured his lips with a demanding response. "How could you think otherwise?"

Darcy slid his hand up her leg and became intoxicated by the small gasps Elizabeth emitted. The touch of his hand brought a quick rise in her desires; his touch left her wanting more intense sensations.

"Fitzwilliam," Elizabeth could barely speak his name as shudders ran through her body. "You are incorrigible, Sir," she stammered.

"And you are too tempting, my Love." Darcy slowly removed his hand from her leg.

Yet Elizabeth was not finished with him; she began to kiss along his chin line. "Would you like to join me on the floor?"

"I may need more encouragement," he teased.

Elizabeth stood briefly, turning to lean down and kiss his upturned face, kissing him deeply and passionately while enticing his lips apart. She withdrew reluctantly, but her mouth hovered above his. "I will ask you again, Sir, if the floor has not some appeal for you?"

Darcy swallowed hard, trying to refocus. Then, instinctively, he stood long enough to lower them both to the floor. "I love you more than life, Lizzy."

At dinner that evening, Mr. Ashford returned to Pemberley. Kitty Bennet boldly placed him across from her at the place settings. Ashford felt more comfortable being in the company of those gathered at Pemberley than previously. The pleasure of again seeing Kitty Bennet haunted his thoughts most of the day, and being allowed to take her hand when going into dinner nearly undid his composure. Pockets of conversation broke out about the table. Georgiana and Jane discussed a book they both read. Elizabeth and her aunt and uncle entertained the Gardiner children. Bingley felt it his duty to chaperone the interchange between his wife's sister Kitty and the young vicar Mr. Ashford. Darcy spoke extensively to his cousins Edward and Anne.

"Have you finalized your travel plans, Edward?"

"Anne and I will travel to my parents' estate at the end of the week. My parents' anniversary party will be the night of the next full moon. Anne and I will formally announce our engagement that evening as all our dear family will be in attendance. You and Elizabeth will attend, shall you not, Darcy?"

"Unless something would happen with Elizabeth's delivery, I see no reason we could not attend." Darcy caught his wife's eyes with a promise of continuing passion.

"I do not wish to change your mind, Darcy. You are one of my best friends, as well as my cousin, but I must remind you Lady Catherine will, obviously, be in attendance."

"I appreciate your concern, Edward, but I welcome my aunt's presence on your behalf."

Anne whispered, "I hope my mother is as gracious."

"Do not concern yourself, Anne." Darcy lightly touched her hand. "Even Lady Catherine should see Edward's love is the best choice you could make."

Anne dropped her eyes rather than respond, but all three knew Lady Catherine's fury was not easily assuaged.

"Darcy," Bingley called out to get his friend's attention.

"Yes, Bingley?"

"Have you heard Mr. Ashford's plans for a village school?" Bingley's eyes lit up. "It is fascinating."

"Really, pray tell, Mr. Ashford." Darcy leveled one of his looks on the man, and the vicar shifted uncomfortably in his chair.

"Of course," Ashford stumbled a bit at first, "that is, if you approve, Mr. Darcy."

Darcy nodded at Ashford's acknowledgment of his position in the community.

"Many of the larger villages establish a village school to educate the children of the area. If a community wishes to grow and to prosper, it needs citizens who are at least minimally educated. How can you, for example, get your tenants to understand the need for a balance between nature and agriculture if they know nothing about the need to conserve the land or to rotate the crops? I believe a school will benefit the community, and I seek your support in this endeavor, Mr. Darcy." Ashford did not break his gaze as he engaged Darcy, a fact Darcy admired in the man.

"You certainly have enough books you could donate to the school." Bingley liked the idea.

"If we choose to open such a school," Darcy guarded his words carefully, "I am sure some books could be procured for it. Mr. Ashford, why do we not plan on meeting later in the week to discuss what you envision, and then we will decide what we can or cannot support."

"Thank you, Mr. Darcy. We appreciate the opportunity to speak to you on this matter." Ashford played the humble card.

Kitty started to say something, but the look both Bingley and Ashford shot her told Kitty this was not the time. Darcy would decide without encouragement from her, but Kitty thought if she got the chance she would ply Elizabeth on Mr. Ashford's behalf.

As conversations resumed, Edward turned again to Darcy. "When shall you arrive at my parents' estate?"

"Elizabeth, Georgiana, Kitty, and I will travel to Nottingham and stay with Lord and Lady Pennington for a few days prior to arriving at Matlock. We will come a day or two before the party, depending on Pennington's availability."

"I have not seen Lady Pennington in some time," Anne added.

"Elizabeth and I met them by accident when we were in London. Her Ladyship took quite a liking to my wife. Plus, it will do Georgiana and Kitty well to socialize with other young people at the Penningtons' and at Matlock."

Edward confirmed, "I will convey your plans to my mother and father."

"I wrote to Lord Pennington earlier today to request the honor of joining them prior to the party. I should hear from him before you and Anne leave us." Despite his early protest to the contrary, Darcy liked playing host to those he loved.

When the men rejoined the women after dinner, Georgiana and Anne played numerous songs to the delight of everyone. Elizabeth gifted them with two vocals before returning to her seat beside Darcy.

"That was beautiful, Elizabeth," he whispered to her as he kissed the back of her hand.

"You are prejudiced on my side, I believe, Sir." Elizabeth touched his cheek tenderly.

"The first time I heard you sing at Lucas Lodge, the clarity of your voice sliced through me. I stood with my eyes closed, taking in your joy for life. I was deeply disappointed when you chose not to continue."

"Then you offered to dance with me."

"Which you promptly refused," Darcy reminded her.

Elizabeth took his hand in hers. "I do sorely wish we were more reasonable in those days."

"As long as we are never apart again." Darcy massaged the inside of her wrist with his fingertips, an action she always found to be exceedingly erotic.

"I plan to grow old with you, my Love." Elizabeth squeezed his knee and slid her fingertips up the inside of his thigh when no one looked on. His quick intake of air brought a sly smile to her face.

CHAPTER 3

"From politics, it was an easy step to silence."
Jane Austen, *Northanger Abbey*, 1817

———◦◦◦———

Mrs. Reynolds and Mrs. Gardiner joined Elizabeth in what would become the baby's nursery. "This room has not been used since Miss Georgiana was born," Mrs. Reynolds said, touching some of the delicate items found there.

"Much of it is dated and not usable," Mrs. Gardiner added. "Some items are rotting, unfortunately."

"I do not mind the fact some items are dated, but I would prefer quality to quantity. My tastes tend to be less ornate than what I see here." Elizabeth walked around the room, lightly touching the items, very much as she did that first day back in London at Kensington Place.

"So, where do we start, Elizabeth?" her aunt asked. "Do you have a vision for the nursery?"

"I really have no idea; this is not an area in which I excel." Elizabeth sat down in frustration. "However, I cannot just ignore the need to have things as I would like them to be. It will be the place where my child will spend a great deal of its time."

Hearing their voices, Kitty came through the open door. "What a lovely room," she gushed. "Will this be the nursery?"

"That is what we planned, but I have no idea where to begin." Elizabeth looked about in disbelief.

"Well, I would start with the drapes on that window. That heavy fabric blocks all the light. Something lighter, maybe in yellow—would be better." Kitty walked about the room, moving items here and there.

Mrs. Gardiner smiled at Elizabeth, who nodded to Mrs. Reynolds. "Kitty," Elizabeth began, "do you have other ideas about what we might do in here?"

"Of course, if it were my child's nursery, I would remove this dark carpeting. I saw a rug in an East Wing guest room, which would work perfectly in this room. The pattern was more playful. I would keep the crib, naturally, but a new mattress is needed. I would trim it with lighter colors—white lace and yellow ribbons. I love this little brush, though. It is exquisite." Kitty's excitement grew as she envisioned the necessary changes.

"Ladies, it sounds like we need to put our Katherine in charge of the renovations in this room. Would you like that, Kitty?" Elizabeth came to stand in front of her younger sister.

"Do you mean it, Elizabeth?"

"I would like for you to check with me or Mrs. Reynolds first, but you may move items in some of the unused rooms, add paint, order some new fabric or other needed items."

Kitty's pleasure showed. "You are trusting me with your child's nursery?"

"Remember Mr. Darcy has discerning tastes—nothing ostentatious," Mrs. Gardiner cautioned.

"I promise, Aunt Gardiner. I will make wise choices."

"Then we should try it." Elizabeth spoke with more confidence.

Kitty spun her sister around in circles. "How can I ever thank you, Lizzy?"

A few days later, Darcy sent for Kitty to come to his study. Although Darcy always treated her well, he still intimidated Kitty; she never abandoned her original opinion of the haughty, prideful gentleman. "Did you wish to see me, Mr. Darcy?"

"Please come in and have a seat for a moment." He came around the desk to sit across from her.

"Have I done something to displease you, Sir?" Kitty felt like a schoolgirl being reprimanded.

Darcy laughed. "Is that what you thought? I am sorry if you were concerned. I heard from your father, and he approved of your staying with us at Pemberley. I spoke to Elizabeth and she is very pleased with your suggestions for the nursery. She feels your talents lie in art or design, and I promised my wife I would secure tutors for you to enhance that talent, as well as to improve your studies. Mr. Thompson will come to you three days per week. He will supervise your drawing lessons and teach you languages. We have an extensive library at Pemberley of which Elizabeth and I would like to see you take advantage. Elizabeth says you are familiar with the pianoforte, but playing music is not to your taste."

"Mary's talent far exceeds the rest of us on the pianoforte," Kitty reasoned.

"There are two instruments available for your practice at Pemberley. I am afraid Georgiana and my cousin Anne are occupying the newer one quite frequently as they practice their duet, but my cousin Miss de Bourgh will be leaving soon. Either way, please avail yourself of some practice time." Darcy outlined what he expected of Kitty while she resided in his home.

"Yes, Mr. Darcy, thank you." Kitty tried to look contrite. She knew Mr. Darcy offered her something her father could not give her—an exemplary education and a chance to "better herself." She realized to escape the stigma created by Lydia's elopement, she would need to tend to her lessons more diligently.

"There is one other thing. Elizabeth says you need some new items for my uncle's anniversary party. I ordered two new day dresses and two gowns. If you take a coach into town later today, Madame Schlater at the emporium will help you choose appropriate material and take your measurements." Darcy watched her countenance carefully as he revealed this information. He took great interest in her reaction, and a smile turned up the corners of his lips as the realization played across Kitty's lips.

"Mr. Darcy," she exclaimed as tears welled in her eyes. "I will do my best to make you proud of me."

"Kitty," he said, taking her hand to help her stand. "Elizabeth assures me I will approve of all of your actions, and I never doubt my wife."

Kitty curtsied, trying to remember to act properly, but she nearly skipped from the room. Her exuberance reminded him of Georgiana, and Darcy allowed his smile to grow as he watched her exit.

In late afternoon, Darcy and Elizabeth worked in his study when a light knock came at the door. Darcy called, "Come," without looking up, but Elizabeth smiled as Kitty entered.

"Lizzy." Kitty came to where her sister sat. "I came to tell you I found the most perfect fabric for the drapes for the nursery when I was in Lambton today. I had the man give me a snippet of the material for a sample. What do you think? We would layer the window coverings, using this pattern, a white eyelet, and a sheer panel, and then carry this pattern onto the crib and table dressings. We could even paint a contrasting pattern on the wall." Kitty's voice sparkled.

"I love this color, Kitty. Fitzwilliam, would you like to see?" Elizabeth walked over to show him the sample.

"Actually, I like the muted colors. It is an excellent choice, Kitty. I am very pleased," Darcy offered as Kitty beamed with excitement.

"Thank you, Mr. Darcy," Kitty gushed. "This was a perfect day, and I owe it all to you. I rode into Lambton under the Darcy livery, and people took notice. You arranged new clothes for me, and Mrs. Schlater's ideas were absolutely heavenly. I know I am going on and on, but I cannot remember a time I was so happy. You and Elizabeth are so kind to do these things for me."

"You are most welcome." Elizabeth hugged her sister while Darcy sat back and enjoyed the family scene. "Remember, Mr. Thompson is coming tomorrow, Kitty."

"I will remember, Lizzy. By the way, Mr. Darcy, may I find something by John Wesley or Samuel Johnson in the library, or even Sir Joseph Banks will do?" Kitty asked.

"Those are heavy topics, Kitty," he cautioned. "But I believe you will find all three available. The books are organized by the author's last name. Help yourself."

"Mr. Ashford quoted from all three on New Year's Eve. I thought I might want to read the whole thing."

"I see." Elizabeth's eyebrow shot up. "At least, you have *motivation*."

"I am too happy today to let even your teasing, Lizzy, bother me." Kitty offered a pretend pout before making her curtsy and exiting.

"You are right, Elizabeth; she is not Lydia," Darcy laughed. "One moment Kitty is a playful, giggling schoolgirl, and the next she is designing rooms with ease. I am anxious to see her vision for the nursery come to life. There are men and women in London who are paid well for designing rooms for those with money."

"I do not wish to tempt my sister with information such as that."

"I would not want Kitty in London alone, either, but if her talent proves itself, she could make herself a small fortune from just our connections. It could give Kitty a better chance for an appropriate match."

"I will keep it in mind," Elizabeth mused. "I do so worry about her."

"Just like Georgiana, Kitty will become a fine lady, with more to her than just what a tutor may teach her. My sister blossoms with your guidance; Kitty will also," Darcy assured her.

In a little over a week, the Darcys found their household greatly reduced in number, bringing the immediate family a return to normalcy but also a profound sadness. Edward and Anne left for Matlock a week after New Year's.

"We will see you at the anniversary party." Darcy shook his cousin's hand. "Please give my regard to my aunt and uncle."

"Wishing you a safe journey," Anne added quietly.

"I am pleased you shared our holiday." Darcy bowed to Anne. "You are always a welcome addition to our household." With that, he handed her into the coach, and Edward followed.

Elizabeth moved up to stand beside Darcy, snaking her arm around his waist. Standing together long after the coach was out of sight, they watched it depart. Elizabeth looked up at Darcy. "What of your thoughts, my Love?" she asked, finally securing his attention.

"I was pondering how much Anne suffered at her mother's will. If we married, her suffering would have continued for I do not have Edward's patience. My disposition would be a disaster for my cousin." Darcy finally looked at Elizabeth, but his mind was elsewhere. "I should have done something for Anne before now, but I feared giving her any attention would encourage Lady Catherine's plans. I protected myself, but I let Anne, literally, fade away."

Elizabeth cupped her husband's cheek and locked his eyes with hers before she spoke. She realized Darcy paid dearly emotionally when he expressed his anxieties. "Anne and Edward shall work this out, Fitzwilliam. Anne recognized your inability to help her; in fact, I always felt her refusal of you, as a mate, was her first step at independence. She allowed herself to love Edward and plan a life with him rather than accept the predicted outcome."

Darcy took Elizabeth's hand and kissed her palm.

"Like the two of us, all Anne needed was someone to love her for herself. Edward is that man. In many ways, he is a better man than you, my Husband."

Darcy's eyebrow shot up. "Pray explain yourself, Mrs. Darcy."

Elizabeth traced a finger along his chin line. "Edward is the only person I ever saw who treats you as an equal. All others, including our Mr. Bingley, cower in your presence. Edward gives you support and guidance without continual censure. You are much more complex—even difficult at times."

"Difficult, am I?" he teased.

Elizabeth laughed. "Exceedingly so."

"Then how came you to fall in love with me instead of my cousin? You had your chance at Hunsford. The colonel spoke fondly of you there."

"I prefer a challenge." Elizabeth winked at him, but she quickly realized she offended Darcy so she shifted her tone. "Fitzwilliam, do you remember when I refused you, and I accused you of a desire to offend me and to insult me with the wording of your proposal? You told me of your regard although you said it was *against your will, against your reason, and even against your character.*"

"Reminding me of one of the worst moments in my life offers me little solace, Elizabeth!"

"But that is just it, Fitzwilliam." Her eyes lit up. "I tried to not love you, the same as you tried to not love me. Yet, we fell in love against our will, our reason, and our characters. We are meant to be together, as are Edward and Anne. You complete me."

Despite the fact they stood before the house where everyone could see, Darcy pulled Elizabeth into his arms and held her there, her head resting against his chest. When he finally released her, he whispered, "It frightens me how much I need you in my life; I depend on your goodness and your love for my happiness."

"I love you, Mr. Darcy." Elizabeth gifted him with a brilliant smile as she teased his sensibilities.

Darcy touched her chin with the tip of his index finger. "And I you." He smiled before taking her hand to lead her back to the house.

Two days later, the Darcys lost Bingley and Jane, as well as the Gardiner family. "Must you go so soon, Jane?" Elizabeth nearly pleaded.

"My uncle and my dear Charles both agree we should take advantage of the dry weather and milder temperatures," Jane reasoned. "We will travel together as far as Hertfordshire, assuring safety in case we need each other."

"I know it is best, but I do so miss your company."

"You have Mr. Darcy now, Lizzy. He is your family as Charles is mine." Jane's practical nature showed.

Elizabeth countered, "That does not mean I miss you less, Jane."

"We will return in the spring when the weather permits."

"Your stay must be an extended one then. I am told Pemberley in the spring must resemble Heaven itself; we will enjoy it together. I should be quite pleasingly plump by then." Elizabeth's playful attitude returned.

Their aunt entered to check on Jane's progress in packing. "Our husbands wish to leave soon."

"It is my fault. I hoped if I delayed the packing, I might be able to spend another day with my sister and you."

"Elizabeth," Mrs. Gardiner said, taking her hand, "we all know Mr. Darcy will be able to fill your time when we leave. Besides, you have Kitty and Georgiana now."

"But it does not keep me from needing you," Elizabeth protested.

"Your uncle and I will return before your confinement; we would not want to miss such a happy occasion. He and Mr. Darcy already discussed how they might entice the bigger fish from the lake."

"Men!" Elizabeth laughed.

"They are strange creatures," Mrs. Gardiner added.

Darcy, Elizabeth, and Georgiana spent several hours each day with estate business. Georgiana rode her favorite horse while Darcy took Elizabeth out in a curricle or a phaeton; he would not let her ride the horse he bought her when they first came to Pemberley. "It is too dangerous now you are with child."

"Yes, my Husband," Elizabeth agreed, yet she playfully rolled her eyes when Darcy looked away.

The women as before added a new dimension to how Darcy looked at his estate. His decisions did not waver, nor did his resolve, but he reviewed issues and problems with different perspectives, often hearing Georgiana's and Elizabeth's voices in his head. The ladies developed a new respect for him; Darcy held direct responsibility for the well-being of everyone on the estate, as well as indirect influence on the surrounding community and Derbyshire itself.

"At age three and twenty Fitzwilliam assumed control over all this." Georgiana gestured to the landscape rolling out in front of them. "Plus, he became responsible for me at the same time. When I look at all he learned from the time he was eighteen to the time of our father's death, I am surprised he functions in such an exemplary manner."

Elizabeth slid her arm around Georgiana's waist and acknowledged, "If I knew what Fitzwilliam faced every day, I could have seen past his preoccupation with being right; our journey to find each other could have been more pleasant."

"I doubt that could happen," Georgiana offered as they waited for Darcy to rejoin them.

Elizabeth looked at her in surprise. "Really?"

"Fitzwilliam had to go through the pain to know your love could save him. Because he has always been in charge, my brother needed you, Elizabeth, to show him what he *wanted* was not what he *needed*."

"You are growing up too quickly, Georgiana," Elizabeth chuckled. Hearing Darcy return from the trail sprawling in front of them, Elizabeth turned back toward him. "Did you find the problem with the stream?"

"A large tree tumbled across the opening. I'll have Mr. Howard send some men out here to cut it up."

"I'm glad it is that simple," Georgiana added.

Darcy came to them. "Are you ladies ready?"

"We are, Sir," Elizabeth said as she took his arm. As he handed her into the curricle, Elizabeth touched his cheek tenderly. "You amaze me, Fitzwilliam. I should have been wise enough to see the man you are and to trust the depth of your love and affection. Thank you for teaching me to be happy."

Her words brought Darcy instant desire. As Georgiana rode away in front of them, Darcy caught Elizabeth's hand in his. "Do you think we could be alone for a while once we return to the house?"

Elizabeth watched the passion turn his dark eyes onyx. She knew that look, the one he reserved especially for her. "Definitely," she laughed, "most definitely." She leaned over and kissed him, letting her lips lightly brush his. "I can think of nothing more pleasurable."

Two days before the household left for Nottingham, Mr. Ashford called upon Darcy to discuss the prospect of the village school. The men sequestered themselves in the library for several hours, and the discussion often became heated, but when Clayton Ashford exited the room, he had a promise of support from his benefactor. Feeling the elation of his "victory," Ashford readily accepted Elizabeth's invitation for dinner. Kitty Bennet's entrance to the drawing room brought Ashford even greater pleasure.

"Elizabeth, I think I will take a walk in the garden before dinner," Kitty said after making her curtsy to Mr. Ashford.

"Maybe Mr. Ashford would care to join you." Elizabeth gave Kitty a slight glance.

Ashford offered Kitty a bow. "It would be my honor, Miss Bennet."

They walked for a long time in silence, the tension thick. "You will leave for Nottingham soon?"

"In two days, Sir," Kitty's voice trembled; she could not look at him for her nerves controlled her racing heart.

"How long will your family be away?" His voice betrayed his thoughts.

"Elizabeth says we shall be gone a fortnight. I have lessons prepared for that long." Kitty took a seat on a bench and motioned for Mr. Ashford to join her there.

"The Darcys arranged a tutor for you then?"

"Yes, Sir, Mr. Thompson comes to me three days a week. We are working together on drawing and the languages. I practice with Miss Darcy on the pianoforte. Mr. Darcy opened his library to me. You will be happy to know I chose a piece by Samuel Johnson to read; I did so at your recommendation. Perhaps when I finish it, we may discuss some of Mr. Johnson's ideas." Kitty turned slightly so she could speak to Ashford directly.

"I am flattered, Miss Bennet, and I look forward to being able to discuss your reading with you." Ashford's eyes sought hers. For a reason he could not verbalize, having her attention became instantly important.

A silence followed where neither knew what to say. "Did I tell you my sister and Mr. Darcy are allowing me to design the baby's nursery?" Kitty blurted out.

"You must be excited they trust you with such a responsibility." Ashford tried to convey the pride he felt in knowing her by his tone.

"Elizabeth and Mr. Darcy have been most kind. They even ordered additional gowns for our trip," Kitty gushed with excitement.

Ashford let his eyes drop from hers. "Then you anticipate several gatherings?" he asked tentatively.

Kitty noted for some reason her leaving bothered him, and she wanted to know more. "The Penningtons plan multiple gatherings, as do those at Matlock. I assume Georgiana and I will meet many new acquaintances." As Kitty relayed this information, she watched Ashford closely.

Each of his statements came out as questions. "You are anxious to go?"

"Such opportunities come rarely to those such as I, and I have nothing here or at Longbourn to make me regret going." Kitty hoped she gave Ashford the opening he needed.

"Miss Bennet," he stumbled with the words, "I think any young lady should experience what life has to offer; yet, if you will so allow it, I would like the opportunity to call on you upon your return."

Kitty's heart skipped a beat. "Mr. Ashford, I would gladly accept the possibility for your attention upon my return."

Ashford wanted to take her into his arms and feel Kitty Bennet's closeness, but propriety, as well as his place in the community, would not allow such diversions. Instead, he whispered, "Thank you, Miss Bennet."

Kitty answered as she could by taking his arm to return to the house, but Ashford's closeness did not escape her sensibilities. Although she knew Clayton Ashford for less than a fortnight, Kitty enjoyed his company more than anyone she ever met. She desired his companionship, yet she also worried her interest in Mr. Ashford had its roots in her profound loneliness of late. Since Lydia's patched-up wedding, many in Meryton avoided her company. Until she came to Pemberley, she was unsure she could overcome the stigma Lydia's foolishness left on her family. She did not want to mislead Mr. Ashford with a romance built on his willingness and her loneliness. The fortnight of her journey would give Kitty time to reflect on this amiable young man.

Not as large as Pemberley, Lord and Lady Pennington's estate was still a stately property. Kitty found the great hall and oak stairway fascinating. Alabaster was used extensively throughout the house, and the mantelpieces displayed hewings of fine woodcarvings. "Mama would be struck silent," she whispered to Elizabeth as they entered one of the public rooms.

Elizabeth laughed lightly at her sister's naïveté. Elizabeth was Mistress of Pemberley for less than three months, but her perspective changed once she married Darcy.

"Darcy, my Boy." Lord Pennington came forward to meet them. "We are most excited to have you with us." He embraced Darcy. "Ah, you brought your beautiful bride. Welcome, Mrs. Darcy; and Georgiana, my Child, look how you have grown!" His jovial nature encompassed them all. "And who might this be?" Lord Pennington's attention turned to Kitty.

"This is Mrs. Darcy's sister, Catherine Bennet, Your Lordship," Darcy made the introductions.

"Your Lordship." Kitty dropped her eyes and made an appropriate curtsy.

"Evidently, beauty runs rampant in your family, Mrs. Darcy," Pennington teased as Kitty blushed. "Her Ladyship will join us in a moment."

"Her Ladyship will join you now," Lady Pennington said as she stepped through the door. The Darcy party offered the obligatory bows.

"Mrs. Darcy," she exclaimed, "it is so good of you to bring our Fitzwilliam to visit so soon."

"I assure you, Lady Pennington, the visit was my husband's idea."

"If so, my dear, it is because you gave him contentment at last." Lady Pennington gestured to chairs for all of them.

"Elizabeth would never consider me to be amiable," Darcy mocked his wife. "In fact, just a few days ago she called me *difficult*."

Lady Pennington laughed at Darcy's playfulness. "Are they this way all the time, Georgiana?"

"Often much worse," Georgiana added to the mirthful tone. "They seem to like to look into each other's eyes often."

"It appears, Mrs. Darcy," Darcy said, turning to his wife, "we are to be attacked on all sides." He actually laughed out loud, something he rarely did.

"I will expect you to defend me, Sir," Elizabeth added happily.

Lady Pennington smiled at their good humor. "It is nice to see Fitzwilliam happy at last." Then her Ladyship nodded toward Kitty. "This is your sister, Mrs. Darcy?"

"Kitty is one of my sisters; I am one of five daughters. If you recall, my eldest sister is married to Mr. Darcy's friend, Charles Bingley."

"And your other sisters?" Lady Pennington asked. "Are any others married?"

Elizabeth shot Darcy and Georgiana a quick glance of panic, not sure how to respond. It was Georgiana who found her voice first. "Elizabeth's youngest sister Lydia is married to an officer in the regulars who is stationed in the North. In fact, you may remember him; his father was our father's steward." Elizabeth could not believe how calm Georgiana appeared, considering her history with the nefarious Mr. Wickham.

"Do you mean George Wickham?" Lord Pennington asked, but the frown on his face indicated his disapproval.

Kitty dropped her eyes; a reminder of Lydia's shame followed her even here in Nottingham. The thoughts of Clayton Ashford's countenance brought her hope.

"My sister Mary is at home with my parents," Elizabeth changed the subject. "We asked Kitty to remain with us at Pemberley. Would you like to share our news, Fitzwilliam?"

"Kitty will stay with us for Elizabeth carries an heir for Pemberley." Every time he said the words, Darcy felt a tightness in his chest, as if saying the words finally made them real.

The look on Lord and Lady Pennington's faces showed their pure delight. "Oh, Mrs. Darcy," Lady Pennington laughed excitedly, "my cousin Lady Anne would be so pleased her beloved Pemberley would be so blessed. Is this not exquisite news?" She turned to her husband.

"A heir for Pemberley will be most welcomed. Congratulations, Darcy." Lord Pennington shook Darcy's hand.

"I must warn you," Darcy added quickly, "cigar smoke makes my wife very ill."

"For her Ladyship, tripe would send her into fits," he laughed. "Well, I am sure you would like to freshen up. A servant will show you to your rooms. We have another guest, a Captain Rutherford, staying with us. He is out riding right now. I am sure you will like him, Darcy; he is an acquaintance of Edward's. The captain will attend the party with us."

"I look forward to meeting him." Darcy stood and took Elizabeth's hand. "We will see you once we freshened our things."

Going up the stairs behind the maid leading the way, Elizabeth caught Georgiana's hand and mouthed the words "Thank you" to her.

When they reached their rooms and were out of earshot, Georgiana told Elizabeth, "It felt good to be able to vocalize about Mr. Wickham; it is my way to rid myself of his ghost. I hope, though, I did not embarrass you, Elizabeth."

"I do not want to publicize Lydia's actions, but I agree with you. Trying to hide her connections will only amplify them. Acknowledging Lydia's marriage and then moving on seems the best way to handle the situation."

"If Fitzwilliam did not save me, Lydia's fate could be mine. I cannot judge her."

At dinner, Captain Rutherford joined the party. "Are you not on duty?" Kitty asked without thinking.

"I am on extended leave," the captain assured her.

The captain, though not as tall as Darcy, still offered a strong and powerful profile. His hazel eyes and angular nose made him rather young looking. His blond curls lay close to his head, giving him a halo-like quality.

As anticipated by the Penningtons, Georgiana Darcy became the object of his attention that first evening. Attractive and distinguished, Rutherford offered Georgiana much of his time. The captain's smiling eyes helped Miss Darcy overcome her natural shyness around strangers, and she managed to hold up her end of the conversation.

"I understand you recently met Chadwick Harrison, Miss Darcy," Rutherford said as he sipped his wine after dinner.

"Mr. Harrison was my brother's guest at Pemberley for several weeks."

Rutherford mused, "How did you find Mr. Harrison?"

"Mr. Harrison was very amiable." Georgiana flushed in remembrance.

"He was a favorite of yours then, Miss Darcy?" The offhanded remark caught Georgiana off guard.

"Any person Fitzwilliam prefers is one of my favorites, Captain." Georgiana did not like the turn of the conversation. "Are you familiar with Mr. Harrison, Sir?"

The captain sounded mysterious. "Only by reputation."

"Then you will get the opportunity to meet Mr. Harrison," Lord Pennington added. "I understand the Earl invited Harrison to the party."

"Really?" Kitty looked knowingly at Georgiana. "I, for one, am most anxious to reacquaint myself with Mr. Harrison."

"Mr. Harrison will be at the party?" Elizabeth chimed in.

Lord Pennington assured her, "Yes, Mrs. Darcy."

"Then we shall all be happy to renew our acquaintance." Elizabeth guarded her words more than did Kitty.

"Did Mr. Harrison tell you about his time in the Americas?" Rutherford tried to sound casual, but even Darcy began to notice the captain's interest in Chadwick Harrison.

"I would suspect, Captain Rutherford, if you want to know about Mr. Harrison's time in America, you should go straight to the source itself. My family is not of the nature to discuss the business of others of our acquaintance." Darcy's eyebrow shot up as a visual sign to his loved ones to follow his lead in dealing with the captain.

"Of course, Mr. Darcy," Rutherford seemed embarrassed. "I was just interested in something I heard."

When the gentlemen withdrew, Elizabeth moved to sit next to Georgiana while Lady Pennington showed Kitty many of the portraits in the family gallery. "What was your private opinion of Captain Rutherford, Georgiana?" Elizabeth asked when they were finally alone.

"I do not know, Elizabeth. Earlier during the meal, we spoke of music and books. I found him congenial and very entertaining. In fact, I looked forward to speaking to him more. I felt comfortable, which you know is difficult for me, But—then…."

Elizabeth seemed concerned, "But what?"

"The captain seemed to press me for my opinion of Mr. Harrison. Although he said nothing of a negative nature about Mr. Harrison, there was something, which bothered me. It was a feeling I could not identify; I felt a need to protect Mr. Harrison."

"Of course, your previous connection to Mr. Harrison may account for your protective senses," Elizabeth teased Georgiana as much as she knew the girl's sensibilities would tolerate, "but I, too, felt uncomfortable with the captain's questions. Even your brother sensed something was amiss. Just be aware of what you say to the man."

"Maybe it was just curiosity on the captain's part. I am sure others know Mr. Harrison's political preferences. He does little to hide his opinions."

"You are probably correct." Elizabeth patted her hand. "Rumors spread quickly in a rural community. The elder Mr. Harrison's death and his son's taking over the estate are sure to arouse interest in the man." The ladies agreed on the surface, yet both refused to speak their concerns about Captain Rutherford.

For the rest of the week, Captain Rutherford continued to show deference for Georgiana Darcy. He never returned to the subject of Chadwick Harrison, and, in reality, Harrison's presence appeared to be the least of Miss Darcy's concerns. She and the captain walked through the gardens together and joined each other in the music room. The captain played the violin very well, and the two often practiced together. Kitty joined them, but the captain was obviously taken with Georgiana.

"What do we know of Captain Rutherford?" Darcy asked his wife, seeing his sister join the man in the estate's gardens once again.

"He is in his mid-twenties, I believe." Elizabeth came to stand beside Darcy at the window. "Like Edward, he is the second son of an earl, out of Leeds or thereabout. He earned a substantial fortune in the Navy, having taken several enemy ships. His older brother, according to Lady Pennington, is the sickly sort so it is likely the captain will eventually inherit the family estate. Her Ladyship says the property is smaller than most of the estates in the Derbyshire area, but it has been run well and is profitable."

"It amazes me," Darcy said as he came behind Elizabeth and encircled her in his arms, "how you women can evaluate a man's worth just by looking at him."

"I thought you wanted me to share what I knew." Elizabeth feigned being offended; therefore, Darcy distracted her by kissing along her shoulder blade while undoing the upper buttons and ties of her dress.

"I did want to know," Darcy said, kissing her neck and behind Elizabeth's ear, "but the depth of your knowledge," he returned to her shoulder blade as he eased her dress down her arms, "never ceases to amaze me."

Elizabeth turned in his arms to face him; she captured Darcy's mouth with hers. By now, he loosened her gown nearly to her waist, and Elizabeth allowed it to drape down over her arms, exposing her corset and chemise.

"It amazes me, my Husband, how quickly you can do this to my gown," she laughed, but Elizabeth barely withdrew from his mouth.

"You inspire me." Darcy captured her face in his hands as he deepened the kiss Elizabeth offered.

When he released her mouth, Elizabeth gasped, "If you call me Lizzy, then I am yours, Sir."

"I love you, Lizzy," Darcy kissed her again before carrying her to their bed. "You are my imagination—my every dream come to life."

CHAPTER 4

*"I do not want people to be agreeable,
as it saves me the trouble of liking them."*
Jane Austen in a letter to her sister Cassandra

No one in the Darcy party nor the Penningtons wanted to leave for Matlock, but the time for the anniversary celebration drew near. Bringing tidings for the Matlocks' anniversary and to openly acknowledge Edward and Anne's engagement offered pleasant possibilities, but the shadow of Lady Catherine's censure for Darcy's choice of a wife and Anne's choice of a husband loomed greater than life.

"I am not anticipating this gathering," Darcy told his wife as they dressed for the journey.

"Surely, your aunt will not spoil her daughter's engagement party and her brother's anniversary party." Elizabeth hoped for small civilities, although she was all too familiar with Lady Catherine's meddlesome ways.

"Elizabeth, we both know predicting either your mother's or my aunt's actions is impossible."

Much to their chagrin, Lady Catherine already resided at Matlock when they arrived, but Darcy and Elizabeth avoided her through much of the afternoon.

Late in the day, Elizabeth descended the staircase of Lord and Lady Matlock's mansion, looking for her husband. As she reached the bottom and turned toward the sitting room, Lady

Catherine de Bourgh exited into the foyer, and Elizabeth found herself face to face with Darcy's disapproving aunt.

"Lady Catherine." Elizabeth started and quickly added a curtsy.

"Miss Bennet." Lady Catherine's disdain radiated in her voice.

Elizabeth did not want a confrontation, but she would not back away from one. "It is Mrs. Darcy now your Ladyship." Elizabeth returned Lady Catherine's glare.

With an indignant sniff, Lady Catherine snorted, "Others may address you as such, but I will never recognize such an unholy union."

"Your recognition was not sought, your Ladyship," Elizabeth made her own displeasure known. "My husband would surely welcome it, but our union will survive your censure. Now if you will excuse me, I will speak to Fitzwilliam." Elizabeth started past the woman, but Lady Catherine's voice stopped her.

"Your presence at Pemberley taints my sister's memory, Madam."

Unfortunately for his aunt, Darcy stepped into the hallway at that moment. "Lady Catherine, if you have something to say to me or to my wife, please step into the study." He offered Elizabeth his arm as he led her to a nearby settee. Elizabeth felt his anger in the stiffness of his arm.

Lady Catherine did not appreciate being so dismissed; her anger and her folly increased as she followed Darcy and Elizabeth into the study. Darcy closed the door behind his aunt and joined Elizabeth in the seating. He did not acknowledge the fact Lady Catherine still stood in the middle of the room. Finally, Lady Catherine seated herself across from them.

Darcy's eyes left Elizabeth's face, and he leveled an intense stare on his aunt. It was the kind of stare he used in difficult business dealings. Even Elizabeth feared approaching him when he looked as such, but Lady Catherine did not flinch. Elizabeth nearly admired the woman for it. "Your mother, my sister, would not be satisfied with your matrimonial situation, Fitzwilliam; you chose against your duty to your family. You dishonor your mother's memory in both your choice of a wife and your denial of Anne." Undaunted, Lady Catherine squared her shoulders and waited for Darcy's response.

Darcy took Elizabeth's hand, and she realized he stroked her wrist with his fingertips. How Darcy maintained his composure, Elizabeth did not know; her own stomach twisted and turned, and she knew she paled.

"My mother always wished for Georgiana and me to be happy. She married for love, and I believe my marriage to Elizabeth would please her for I am truly happy. As for Anne, I would think you would wish the same for her. Edward truly cares for Anne."

Lady Catherine rolled her eyes in disgust. "Your mother would never accept the dishonor you brought to Pemberley. It will suffer with Miss Bennet as its mistress."

Darcy knew if he allowed himself to react to Lady Catherine's accusations as he wished to do, she would win, and he would never give his aunt the pleasure of such a victory. Therefore, Elizabeth felt his grip on her hand tighten as she, too, struggled not to let her countenance change. "Again, you misspeak, Aunt. Elizabeth won the hearts of the tenants with her compassion and her charity. I fear if I spoke out against her, I would have a riot on my hands. The future of Pemberley is more secure than ever; Elizabeth carries my child, an heir for Pemberley. Mrs. Darcy makes Pemberley a home rather than just a fine country estate."

"So you do not intend to at least acknowledge your lack of caution put the Darcy name in jeopardy?" Lady Catherine fixed her gaze on Darcy, while totally ignoring Elizabeth.

Darcy fought to keep his voice even in his response. "I will not acknowledge that remark with a reply. I am the Darcy family now." He purposely lifted Elizabeth's hand to his lips for a kiss.

"Well, I see, Miss Bennet, you succeeded in capturing my nephew with your arts and allurements." Lady Catherine shifted her attention to Elizabeth in hopes of breaking at least one of them. "You attained a position far above what you deserve, but your lack of breeding will betray you to society. Society will not be easily fooled by your *charms.*"

Elizabeth's slight pressure on Darcy's hand let him know she intended to respond on her own. She spoke quietly, but her voice held a strength Darcy recognized. "Lady Catherine, you are correct; I lack the breeding to purposely insult my loved ones and call it civilities. I also lack the breeding it takes to meddle in another person's life to the point of putting my own happiness above his. If others choose to act as you do in such situations, I will be pleased to be excluded from their company. Yet, if my husband chooses to forgive your interference in his life, I will once again offer you my respect and begin our relationship anew."

Lady Catherine's distaste for such a situation became evident as a sneer formed upon her mouth. "I will never seek your respect, Miss Bennet."

Darcy's contempt played through his response. "Miss Bennet is Elizabeth's sister Mary. My wife's name is Mrs. Darcy, and you will address her as such, or you will not speak to her." Then he turned to his wife before standing and offering his hand, palm up. "Are you ready, Elizabeth?"

As they started to exit, Lady Catherine's demanding voice called out. "Wait, I am not finished with you, Fitzwilliam."

Darcy paused only briefly to look at Elizabeth before they exited together, her hand on his proffered arm. "I thought I heard something, Mrs. Darcy, but I must be mistaken." He gave her an amused look as his eyebrow shot up. Elizabeth pursed her lips and gifted him one of her enigmatic smiles. They were on the staircase before either of them took a breath.

As the extended party all sat down to dinner that evening, all went well. Lady Catherine completely ignored Darcy, Elizabeth, and Kitty. She did direct a few simple comments toward Georgiana, but more out of curiosity over Captain Rutherford rather than to offer her niece any form of civility. When the men retired to the study, Lady Matlock and Anne kept Lady Catherine company while Elizabeth, Kitty, Georgiana, and Lady Pennington moved to the far end of the drawing room to talk about gowns for tomorrow's ball. The time passed quickly in quiet splendor. As the men rejoined the ladies in the drawing room, both Darcy and Elizabeth assumed the impasse of the last few hours would be the order of the evening, especially considering their earlier confrontation with Lady Catherine.

Darcy moved to sit with Elizabeth, taking her hand in an intimate grasp. Edward retrieved Anne from her mother's side and brought Anne to sit across from Darcy and Elizabeth. The conversation began anew with the colonel sharing a story of their youth. "Darcy pulled Anne's hair, causing her bonnet to slip to the side. Anne turned to grab the bonnet and ended up stepping ankle deep in the mud." They all laughed at the colonel's retelling. "Anne was so angry she chased after Darcy, tearing the hem of her dress. My aunt was furious."

"My mother pretended to be angry," Darcy added. "She took me to task with her words, but under the surface she fought back the laughter."

"My sister would never laugh at Anne's mistreatment by her son." Lady Catherine's words brought an icy silence to the room as she came forward to tower over them. "Lady Anne would be appalled then by Fitzwilliam's treatment of Anne; she would be horrified at how he continues to mistreat my daughter by denying my sister's wish they marry. Instead, he takes up with a woman of little or no consequence and brings shame to this entire family by bringing a child by her into this world." By now Lady Catherine's words reverberated in the silence of the room.

Darcy and Edward both jumped to their feet. Anne protested, "Mother!" while Elizabeth buried her face in her hands.

"Be quiet, Anne!" Lady Catherine snapped. "You should, at least, Sir, send the child away and not mark this family with the corruption of the ancestral name of Darcy."

"That is enough, Madam!" Darcy's voice boomed through the room, and even Lady Catherine retreated a few steps. "You will not speak of my wife in those terms."

"Lady Catherine," Edward tried to intervene, "Anne and I love each other. Please be happy for us and let Darcy's choice be just that—his choice. My cousin has never been so happy."

"Anne," Lady Catherine looked past Edward, "you are not well; you should return to your room to rest."

Automatically, Anne rose to follow her mother's orders, but Edward's hand gripped her arm, holding her in place. He never took his eyes from Lady Catherine as the control for Anne came to a head. "Anne is feeling perfectly fine, are you not, Anne?" Edward's words demanded a like response from his intended.

Anne's voice came out shaky, but there was a sense of resolve in her manner. "I will remain with Edward."

"You will not control my daughter at your whim, Sir. You prove you care nothing for Anne for you jeopardize her health with your actions!" Lady Catherine's challenge echoed through the room.

"It is you, Aunt, who made Anne an invalid." Edward's words pierced the air, and Anne steeled herself, knowing the confrontation loomed. "You browbeat her into submission, but I will not tolerate your doing so any longer!"

"This is your fault!" Lady Catherine turned back to Darcy. "Your denying your mother's wishes means I must give my daughter to this—this—!"

"This what?" Lady Pennington took a step forward to join those surrounding Lady Catherine.

Lady Catherine's anger now consumed her, and she no

longer guarded her words. "Anne deserves a fine estate of her own. Instead, all she receives out of this marriage is Edward's title as a son of an Earl. Anne brings her wealth and bloodline to the marriage. What do you bring, Colonel?"

"He brings the kind of love to protect me, Mother." Anne grasped Edward's arm for support.

"I withdraw my consent, Child."

"I am no child. I am of age, Mother; I do not need your consent." Anne swayed against Edward, and he placed his arm around her shoulders to brace her.

"Catherine," the Earl now intervened, "although you are my sister, and I normally offer you some latitude in your opinions, Edward, whom you deem unworthy of Anne's regard, is still my son. I will not tolerate your censure of him. You will leave my house tomorrow morning; you are no longer welcome here!"

Lady Catherine began to protest, "I never!"

"That is just it, Catherine. None of us in this room ever stopped your censure, and we allowed you to hold court over everyone else. We will no longer tolerate such behavior. Please leave us immediately."

Lady Catherine looked about her; no one in attendance gave her encouragement. In fact, Matlock, Darcy, and the colonel all literally turned their backs while the rest of the room dropped their eyes and refused to look at her. As if by consensus, everyone began conversations with those in close attendance, ignoring the old woman who stood mouth agape. "You will pay for this insult!" she barked before exiting the room.

Darcy immediately dropped to his knees in front of Elizabeth. "My Love, come with me," he whispered in her ear. Elizabeth stood as he led her from the room. "We need fresh air," he continued as he retrieved their outer garments against the cold. Darcy wrapped a pelisse around her, pulling a shawl from the shelf to give her extra protection. Elizabeth still covered her face with her hands so Darcy led her gingerly to the gardens.

"Elizabeth," he began once they were clear of the house. "Elizabeth, please, do not shut me out."

Elizabeth did not know why she still cried, but the agitation of her mind was painful. So much went awry; all of her family's mistakes hit Elizabeth full force. "Fitzwilliam, I am sorry." Elizabeth scrambled to his embrace, needing the solace only he gave her.

Darcy lifted her chin to kiss her lips lightly. "Sorry for what, my Love?"

"Everything you gave up for me!" The sobs began again.

He wiped away the tears with his handkerchief. "I received so much more of value in return."

Elizabeth nearly wailed. "I made you the laughingstock of the *ton*; I cost you your position in society!"

"Elizabeth, I was never part of the *ton*; they tolerated me because of my family's wealth, but I was always on the outside looking in. Do you not remember my actions at Meryton and at Netherfield? I hung on the outskirts of each group, listening and nodding, but not interacting. I hate each time I must be in large groups; I am never at my best. I become invisible, but you, Elizabeth Darcy, looked past my coat of invisibility; you saw me when I was not there." Darcy locked eyes with her. "I do not need the *ton*. I do not need Lady Catherine. I need you—without you, I am nothing again."

Elizabeth clung to him, desiring the strength of his devotion. Being held by Darcy created an intimacy Elizabeth needed. "I love you, Fitzwilliam."

He traced her chin line with the back of his hand, and their eyes locked in an intimate moment. "I love you, my Lizzy."

Elizabeth whispered to him, "You do not play fair, Sir."

"I prefer to use all my advantages, Mrs. Darcy." He kissed her gently again.

When she spoke, Elizabeth's voice sounded shaky. "Then you do not regret aligning yourself with someone such as me?"

"Elizabeth, I sought your attention for nearly a year; desperation and depression were regularly my company. Each night I dreamed of your loving me, of having your eyes light up when I entered a room. I dreamed of your desiring me as much as I desired you. Now, all those dreams come true in you. Aligning myself with you is the answer to every dream I ever held; how could you doubt how much I love you?"

"But what of Georgiana? Have I not ruined her reputation as well? We prepare for her coming out, but I darken your sister's chances."

Darcy laughed lightly. "We both know if Georgiana had her way, her coming out would be postponed indefinitely. She rejoices in your current condition not totally for our sake. I suspect your confinement gives my sister joy for her coming out will need to be delayed another season. Georgiana will be accepted no matter what our situation. People in the *ton* respect money. Georgiana comes from money—she will succeed remarkably. Plus, under your tutelage my sister develops a confidence she never possessed. I am sure she would never question my choice in marrying you."

"My brother's right, Elizabeth." They both spun around to find Georgiana standing tall and majestic in her confidence. "My aunt's bitterness should never make you question your worth to Fitzwilliam or to me. You touch our lives in so many ways; you cannot suspect we have any regrets. You brought life to Pemberley."

Elizabeth continued to sob throughout this exchange, but now the tears were those of joy rather than despair. She rushed to Georgiana's arms. "Thank you, Georgiana."

Offering them comfort, Darcy now moved to encompass both women in his embrace. "A man of lesser fortune would be wealthy to have the two of you in his life."

After several minutes, Darcy encouraged them to return to the house. "Would you object to my foregoing the rest of the evening with your family and returning to our rooms instead?" Elizabeth pleaded for privacy.

"I will go with you," Georgiana offered. Elizabeth nodded, and Darcy agreed.

Elizabeth caressed his cheek as they parted. "Thank you, Fitzwilliam."

"I shall not be long, my Love. See to her, Georgiana," he whispered to his sister before they ascended the staircase leading to the guest rooms.

"Fitzwilliam, how is Mrs. Darcy?" asked Lady Matlock when he reentered the room alone.

"Georgiana is with her. My wife begs your forgiveness for leaving the gathering early." Darcy's breeding took over his reactions. He moved to Edward's side. "How are you dealing with this?"

"The prospects of returning to Rosings any time soon does not play well on my disposition at the moment."

"Then you and Anne will extend your stay at Matlock?"

"Indefinitely," Edward added while viewing Lady Pennington's civilities to Anne. "Anne will need to recoup her resolve before facing our aunt again."

"Do not stay away from Rosings too long, Edward. Her Ladyship will plot to keep the property upon your marriage; you must be there to prevent her deceit. Would Anne consider an earlier date for your marriage? It would resolve some of your issues."

Edward shook his head in disbelief. "You are probably right, Darcy. The depth of Lady Catherine's evil amazes me. How can she be the sister of your dear mother and my father? How can she abuse her daughter in the name of love?"

Darcy leaned in to share his private beliefs. "Do not allow Lady Catherine to stay on the estate. Place her in London or better yet in Vienna or Paris. Keep her away from Anne. Our aunt will never stop until she has her way in this family."

"I fear you are correct, and that grieves me so. I will speak to my father; his support will lend viability to the solution. Now, if you will excuse me, Anne needs me as Elizabeth needed you."

"Of course." Darcy bowed to his cousin.

Edward and Lady Pennington helped Anne to her feet and led her toward her quarters. Captain Rutherford, thankfully, made a quiet exit when the ruckus started. The Matlocks and Lord Pennington conferred privately in the corner.

Darcy scanned the room, finding Kitty huddled in a chair in the corner. Her eyes were down, but he could see sobs shook her retracted shoulders. Until of late, Darcy had very little interaction with his wife's sister, his earlier opinions of Kitty Bennet tied closely to those he knew of Lydia. Darcy watched Kitty and Lydia as they chased after the members of the –shire stationed at Meryton, and he thought them to be quite silly and lacking in common proprieties.

Now, he saw his wife's sister as a young woman hurt by his aunt's words. What Lady Catherine said to him and to Elizabeth affected Kitty as well, so Darcy moved to sit beside her. He slid his arm around the girl's shoulders, and Kitty surprised him by collapsing against him and allowing her tears to flow freely now. For a moment, Kitty reminded him of Elizabeth. "Miss Bennet—Kitty." Darcy brushed her hair from her face as he spoke to her softly, encouraging her to trust him.

Finally, Darcy made out some of her words between the sobs. "Mr. Darcy—thank you for loving Lizzy—I was wrong—I do not want to be like Lydia—we brought you such mortifications—can you forgive us?"

"Kitty." Darcy pulled the girl closer. "It is I who should apologize to you; it is my family who crossed the line of civilities tonight. I am sorry to see you suffer."

Kitty pulled herself upright and looked Darcy in the eyes. He saw the shift of her shoulders, obviously, a Bennet trait. "Mr. Darcy, I am ashamed I once believed you to be prideful and haughty."

"It seems your sister's earliest opinions of me permeated the whole family," he laughed lightly. "But I was just thinking something similar; I used to believe you to be very much like your youngest sister. Now, I see traces of my Elizabeth in you." Darcy cupped Kitty's chin when she started to drop her eyes again.

"Lydia brought much shame on our family. Our Uncle Gardiner paid dearly to save her foolish name, as well as ours. In Meryton, some people no longer speak to Mary and me. I hoped in coming to Pemberley, I could leave that behind."

"Reputations are not something we can buy, Kitty; you must earn them with exemplary actions, and even then, some of lesser consequence, but more wealth, will set themselves in judgment. You must know in your heart your actions speak of your purity."

His words did not bring Kitty the comfort Darcy hoped. Her tears flowed again, and after several awkward moments, she finally confessed, "But I once allowed Mr. Denney to kiss me!" She blurted out her confession without much forethought.

Darcy gently brushed the tears away with his already damp handkerchief. "What you allowed was not the end of the world, although I would never encourage such actions. Yet, what liberties Lydia allowed Mr. Wickham showed her lack of regard for you and all your sisters. I know if Mr. Denney demanded more of you, you would never participate, especially if you knew it could hurt your whole family."

"Of course not, Mr. Darcy," Kitty exclaimed a bit too loudly. She dropped her voice after looking around to see if anyone noticed. "I was just curious what it would feel like."

"And how did it feel, Kitty?" Darcy wondered about the workings of the young female mind.

"Mr. Denney's beard scratched my face, and his breath smelled of port and cigar smoke. It was not what I expected; my novels describe a more pleasant experience." Kitty felt foolish for having believed such romantic notions.

Darcy chuckled again at Kitty's naïveté. "Do you know Elizabeth kissed me several times before we were married?" A short gasp told him Kitty never expected Elizabeth allowed him such privileges. "Of course, we already set a date for our marriage when this occurred. However, I know from my friend, Mrs. Bingley did not allow him more than the holding of hands."

"Jane would never cross the line of propriety." Kitty did not appear surprised by this news.

"As I see you to be more like Elizabeth—more passionate—more feelings in your interactions, I share this with you so you see there is no true standard. Do you see Elizabeth as any less proper than your sister Jane?"

"Most certainly not! Elizabeth is all what a lady should be!"

"Both Mrs. Bingley and my Elizabeth did what was best for them—they neither hurt their family and both have a clear conscious. That is what you see when you look into their faces—the purity of their actions and the purity of their hearts. Do you understand what I am trying to tell you?"

"Lydia hides her actions with too much face paint and too many ribbons on her bonnet," she said with some conviction.

"Quality—not quantity—is the standard."

Kitty looked about sheepishly. "Mr. Darcy, may I ask you something else?"

"Of course, Miss Bennet."

"Mr. Ashford, before we left Pemberley, asked if he might call on me when I returned. Would you speak to him on my behalf?"

"Do you wish for Mr. Ashford to make such calls?" Darcy seemed amused.

"I reflected on it for the past several days. I would like to get to know Mr. Ashford better." Kitty hoped she did not seem too forward for Darcy's standards.

"I will speak to Elizabeth tomorrow, and we will determine what is best for your future. I must say Mr. Ashford seems like a sensible young man." Darcy's approval brought Kitty joy.

"Thank you, Mr. Darcy."

"Are you ready to retire for the evening? If so, it would be my honor to escort you to your room." Darcy offered Elizabeth's sister his arm.

Kitty stood and took his arm, happy to be accepted as part of his family. At the top of the stairs, she turned to him one last time. "May I be allowed one last question?"

Darcy's smile showed no annoyance with Kitty's entreaties. "Certainly."

"When you first kissed Elizabeth, what was it like?"

The laughter came easily this time, and Darcy half teased her when he said, "Of course, your sister had no beard, and she did not smell of cigars or port, so my experience was more pleasurable than the one you described."

A pout took Kitty's lips. "Do not tease me, Mr. Darcy. I really want to know."

"Very well, Miss Bennet." He started by looking away and visualizing the moment. "Your sister just agreed to be my wife. Elizabeth tilted her head to look up at me, and I knew I could do nothing else. It was exciting, breathless, and exhilarating— all the things one would expect when two people are in love, but it was more than that; it was as if I was coming home—it was where I belonged. I guess it was very much like those novels of which you are so fond."

"I knew it had to be better than Mr. Denney. Mary said all kisses are purely to lead to sins against God's will." Kitty's astonishment showed with the enthusiasm in her tone.

"Your sister Mary is more devout than most of us, but I will share one more insight. If there is a Heaven on earth, mine lies in your sister Elizabeth. Now, we spoke beyond what a married man should say to his wife's sister; I will see you in the morning, Kitty."

Kitty dropped him a curtsy before giving Darcy a large smile and heading to her room. Darcy chuckled in watching her go. *I hope my child is a son,* he thought. *Another female in my household may be more than I can handle.*

With that, he returned to his rooms. Georgiana left when she saw him come in. "I gave her some chamomile tea to help her rest. Elizabeth says she waits for you to join her before she sleeps."

The description he just offered Kitty of their first kiss came back quickly to his mind's eye. "I will go to her soon."

Once alone, Darcy stayed in the sitting room, exhausted by the pretense he played. He did not know how long he sat there staring at the dying embers in the fireplace.

"Will you not come to bed, my Husband?" Lost in his own thoughts, Darcy jumped at the sound of Elizabeth's voice.

"How can you still want me there after the public humiliation my family caused you tonight?" Darcy could not take his eyes from the woman he loved.

Elizabeth, likewise, sought assurances from him once again. "How can you still want to be there after the mortifications my family cost you?"

In a second, Darcy crossed the room and violently pulled her to him, grasping her so tightly Elizabeth could hardly breathe. "My Love, do not leave me."

"I can go nowhere—you are my everything, Fitzwilliam. My life lacks purpose without you there."

Darcy kissed her, demanding Elizabeth's love, branding her as his; he never felt such need to possess her. Once he thought he might never know her love, but now he fully understood the depth with which Elizabeth loved him. He could not lose her; Elizabeth must continue to love him.

"Let us go to bed. I need you where nothing comes between us."

Darcy picked her up; Elizabeth snuggled into his chest. "My dearest, loveliest Elizabeth," he spoke softly into her hair, "with you, I am finally home."

Chadwick Harrison, like many of the Matlocks' neighbors, arrived at the estate in the late afternoon. Nearly a month had passed since he last saw Georgiana Darcy, and the man missed the sweetness of the woman, but when he found her, a naval officer kept her company.

"Mr. Harrison," Georgiana said, looking up from the pianoforte when he entered the music room, "it is pleasant to see you again." She stood and made her curtsy, but the woman emerging in her never took her eyes from Harrison's countenance.

Harrison made her the proper bow. "Miss Darcy, you are looking well. I have not seen them yet, but I assume your family is in health." Georgiana shot the captain a furtive glance. All those present at last night's fiasco pretended no such confrontation occurred. The captain, the only other person in the room at the time of Lady Catherine's attack on her family members, chose to ignore the issue in deference to his allegiance to Lord and Lady Pennington.

"They are, Sir. My family wishes to renew its acquaintance with you." Georgiana offered Mr. Harrison an endearing smile. Turning to the officer she added, "May I introduce Captain James Rutherford."

"Captain Rutherford." Harrison made the man an obligatory bow. "I am pleased to meet any friend of Miss Darcy's."

"Mr. Harrison," the captain acknowledged the man with a like bow. Sensing Georgiana wished to speak to Mr. Harrison privately, the captain excused himself. "Miss Darcy, I hope you do me the honor of a dance set this evening."

Georgiana felt uncomfortable. For the past several days, she accepted the captain's attention, but now with Mr. Harrison in the room, she no longer wanted the captain's regard, but she saw no way out. If she refused the captain his dance, Georgiana would have to sit out the rest of the evening, and Georgiana wanted to dance with Chadwick Harrison. "It would be my pleasure." She smiled briefly at Rutherford before he exited.

Georgiana moved from the instrument bench to a settee, and Harrison followed her there. "Has your time at Hines Park been productive, Sir?" Georgiana asked politely once they were seated.

"It has, Miss Darcy. I am anxious to speak to your brother during the evening; I have questions to which I hope he has answers. Plus, I wish to extend a dinner invitation to your family while you are in the area."

"I would enjoy seeing your estate, Mr. Harrison." Georgiana dropped her eyes before they met his.

"My estate is progressing. I would like your opinion of it. I value your opinion, Miss Darcy." Harrison hoped to say more, but his promise to Mrs. Darcy prevented that. The sexual tension made them uncomfortable, and they fought valiantly against the emotions trying to surface. When Harrison first met Georgiana Darcy there was an instant attraction, but in his first estimation, he considered her to be naïve. His weeks at Pemberley proved his initial opinion to be in error. Miss Darcy possessed an independent spirit hidden by the beauty of her face. Harrison found during those weeks with Georgiana he could socialize without the pressure of mating or remain silent without censure. This contradiction confused him at first; now he welcomed it.

Noticing they were actually alone, the couple fell silent. Finally, Harrison said, "I missed my conversations with your family, Miss Darcy. Hines Park is sadly without the fulfillment I found at Pemberley." Harrison looked around to make sure no one could observe or hear him. "Miss Darcy." she turned to look at him as he lowered his voice. "Please excuse my impropriety when I tell you I missed you."

"Mr. Harrison," Georgiana said, blushing deeply, "although I cannot accept your lack of proper manners, I do accept your words most willingly."

Harrison said nothing else; he wanted to tell Georgiana he loved her, but he made progress; therefore, he turned his attention to other matters. When the time came, Harrison knew Georgiana Darcy would, at least, listen to his plea. "How long have you known the captain?"

"Only about a week—he is an acquaintance of my guardian Colonel Fitzwilliam; the captain is a guest in the house of my mother's cousins, Lord and Lady Pennington. When I first met him, I thought you two were familiar because the captain asked me many questions about you."

"Did he now? What did the captain want to know?" Harrison's interest peaked.

"Nothing in particular which I recall—the captain just wanted to know my opinion of you." Georgiana felt somehow she betrayed Mr. Harrison.

Although concerned about the captain's questions, Harrison did not want to alarm Georgiana. "I hope, Miss Darcy, you were able to offer the captain a good report on my behalf."

Georgiana laughed lightly, and Harrison's heart skipped a beat. "I found several good things to share with him." Georgiana looked at Harrison and smiled. He thought he could spend the rest of his life sitting on this settee with this woman.

"Like the captain, I hope you save at least one dance set for me this evening."

"I will look forward to it." Georgiana's voice broke with anticipation.

Harrison knew he treaded the line with his words, but he also implored, "Would I be too forward if I ask you to double my pleasure this evening and not only consider a second set with me but a place by my side when we go in to dinner?"

"My brother may object," Georgiana offered, "but I will save you the set before dinner is served, but that means I must dance with others first."

Harrison would not take pleasure in watching Georgiana dance with the captain and others, but the prospect of sharing her company over dinner allowed him tolerance. "I understand, Miss Darcy."

Knowing they should spend no more time alone, Georgiana suggested they find Kitty. "I am sure Miss Bennet will want to save you a dance set this evening, as will my sister Elizabeth."

CHAPTER 5

"Every man is surrounded by a neighborhood of voluntary spies."
Jane Austen, *Northanger Abbey*, 1817

Harrison walked about the ballroom, wanting desperately to spend the evening in the presence of Georgiana Darcy, but for this first set he chose to dance with Kitty Bennet while Georgiana accepted the hand of Captain Rutherford.

"This is an agreeable dance," Georgiana said as she and the captain made their pass the first time.

"It is, Miss Darcy," Captain Rutherford responded. "Were you able to renew your acquaintance with Mr. Harrison?" the captain asked as they came together to proceed down the line.

"Mr. Harrison is an amiable man."

"Really? You said as much before." The captain's remark came too quickly.

Georgiana seemed surprised by the captain's tone. "Would you not think so, Sir?"

Captain Rutherford could not respond immediately for they parted to each side. When the form brought them together again, he said, "Mr. Harrison's opinions are considered controversial by many. I assumed your bother would be concerned with your knowing the man."

His words brought an evident perturbation to Georgiana's countenance. The captain's words were calculated to have an impact on the young *girl*—to serve as a warning. She did not respond as they came together again and again, and Rutherford thought Georgiana would remain silent through the rest of the dance and maybe the rest of the set. Yet, the man underestimated the young *woman* standing in front of him.

Georgiana Darcy might have accepted the captain's words at one time with little or no comment, but that was before her brother showed Georgiana her worth. So as she came forward to meet the captain at the end of the first dance, she reprimanded him, "If you are referring to Mr. Harrison's dislike of our government's policy condoning the impression of others in deplorable conditions, I take offense."

"Offense, Miss Darcy?" the captain asked, incredulously.

"I know little of the life of those of whom Mr. Harrison speaks, but I do know some men relegate women to positions of no consequence. If a man would treat women thusly, how would he treat men of different circumstances?"

The dance ended on a sour note for Georgiana Darcy, and her agitation became evident as Darcy stood with his wife watching the revelers.

"Should I separate Georgiana from the captain?" he whispered in Elizabeth's ear.

"Your sister is capable of responding to Captain Rutherford's words without your assistance, my Love. Trust her."

"She seems disturbed."

"Georgiana's response shows more resolve than agitation. I suspect the captain just heard a bit of Darcy philosophy." Elizabeth looked at her husband with amusement.

"Darcy philosophy?" He smiled at the woman he loved.

"Yes, the Darcys are committed to those to whom they affect; it is a characteristic quite out of step with much of society. Thankfully for me, you, Sir, gave me your affection." Elizabeth's eyes met his.

"I do choose to seek my comfort in your arms," Darcy whispered once again. They stood a bit too close even for a married couple, but their devotion to each other demanded as such. "I love you, Mrs. Darcy," he said under his breath, and Elizabeth made a point of squeezing his hand in response.

The second song of the dance set ended, and Captain Rutherford returned Georgiana to her family.

"Captain," Darcy began, "you dance well for a man used to the rolling motion of the sea." It was a comment so uncharacteristic of Darcy that both Georgiana and Elizabeth turned to look at him.

"My land legs do me as well as my sea legs," the captain laughed. "I am also quite comfortable on horseback."

"I do not believe I heard you say upon which ships you sailed," Darcy's statement came out as a question.

"I changed ships several times," Rutherford offered. "At another time, I will be happy to share my experiences with you. Now, if you will excuse me, Sir—I asked Miss Andrews for the pleasure of the next set." Rutherford made Darcy and the ladies a quick bow before exiting.

"An unusual man," Elizabeth commented as the captain took his leave. Darcy did not say anything, but his expression told Elizabeth he held similar thoughts.

"Do you think I might have the honor of your hand for this next set, Elizabeth?" Darcy asked finally.

"It would be my pleasure, my Love," Elizabeth said, smiling up at him, "but maybe your sister would prefer your company." Elizabeth shot a quick glance at Georgiana.

"No, please, Elizabeth," Georgiana stammered, "you and Fitzwilliam should dance. It is such a beautiful evening; please enjoy it."

"Are you sure, Georgiana?"

"Yes, I am quite content to sit here for a few minutes."

"Would you do me the honor then?" Edward stepped forward. "Anne would prefer to talk to my mother, and I am in an excellent mood." The man beamed with pleasure.

"Edward." Georgiana took his arm. "It has been too long since we danced, and I can think of nothing more pleasant."

"You are growing up too fast." Edward touched Georgiana's cheek. "How have you changed so much?" Edward marveled at Georgiana's new confidence.

"That is easy," Darcy interjected. "My sister and my wife conspire against us all."

"The truth is, Colonel, my husband encourages impudence from both his sister and me." Elizabeth's eyes sparkled when she looked at Darcy.

Edward laughed out loud. "You are an unusual trio. I was so involved with my issues with Anne and Lady Catherine, I took little note of the changes happening at Pemberley."

"Love happened at Pemberley." Darcy smiled. "We became a family again."

Edward looked on in amazement at the transformation of Georgiana Darcy. As one of her guardians, he took pride in the young lady standing up with him. "In case others do not have the merit to tell you, Cousin, you are splendid this evening." Georgiana's eyes flickered with excitement.

"You made my evening, Sir." Georgiana smiled at the man who gave her guidance through the years. "I hope Anne realizes the jewel she earned in her choice of a husband."

For Georgiana, waiting patiently for the set before the evening meal seemed interminable, but finally the opportunity to dance with Chadwick Harrison arrived. When he claimed her hand to lead her to the dance floor, the intensity between them could not be denied. When they lined up across from each other, their eyes found only one another.

"Miss Darcy," Mr. Harrison said as he wove his way through the other dancers, "you are magnificent this evening." He dropped his voice so only Georgiana could hear.

She circled the gentleman opposite her, but Georgiana smiled shyly at Mr. Harrison. "You must not speak so boldly, Sir." Georgiana's words offered him a reprimand, but her tone told Harrison she accepted his remarks.

"I apologize," Harrison offered as they passed again.

"Accepted, Sir." Georgiana graced him with a knowing smile, and when they took hands once again, Georgiana heard Harrison gulp for air.

Finally, he found his voice. "You seemed out of sorts earlier, Miss Darcy." Harrison hoped what he perceived in Georgiana's face displayed her contempt for Captain Rutherford. Harrison could not suppress the jealousy he felt when Georgiana took the captain's hand.

"You are mistaken, Mr. Harrison, I found my cousin's attention quite pleasant." Georgiana flirted by feigning innocence.

"Miss Darcy," Harrison said as he took Georgiana's hand for the second time in the dance, "you know I do not speak of the good colonel."

Georgiana blushed, and Harrison's heart took flight. "The captain spoke too freely for my tastes."

"May I ask the source of your irritation? I would not want to make the same misstep." His voice teased Georgiana's sensibilities.

They parted, weaving their way through the form. "Unless you speak of your own beliefs, you would not be discussing what the captain chose as a topic."

Harrison's interest in Rutherford suddenly took a different course. "Am I to assume my sentiments were a point of discontent in your conversation?"

Georgiana dropped her voice once more. "The captain warned me against being swayed by your opinions." Her eyes darted around the room to see if others heard her.

Harrison realized the captain upset Georgiana so he put his own present concerns aside. "Perhaps you misunderstood the gentleman." He gritted his teeth as he said the words.

"Perhaps," Georgiana agreed, but neither of them thought so.

When they went into dinner, Chadwick Harrison escorted Georgiana to the table, finding his way to the Darcy party with whom he was most familiar and with whom he recently spent most of his time.

"Mr. Harrison," Darcy greeted him, "how pleasant to see you again, Sir. How goes life at Hines Park?"

"Progress comes steadily to Dove Dale; I hope you and your family will be kind enough to join me for dinner while you are in the area." Harrison pressed his cause. "I am anxious for your input, Mr. Darcy, if you can spare the time." Harrison then turned his attention to Elizabeth and Kitty Bennet as they approached. "Ladies, you look well."

"As do you, Mr. Harrison," Elizabeth acknowledged.

"Being at home once again renewed my energies, Mrs. Darcy."

Darcy took Elizabeth's hand to lead her to their seating. "Mr. Harrison requests we dine with him some evening before we return to Pemberley."

"That would be pleasant, Fitzwilliam," Elizabeth replied. Neither expressed their concern about exposing Georgiana to Mr. Harrison's attention so soon; that would be a subject for their private chambers.

Darcy placed Georgiana close to Mr. Harrison but not next to him. He still wanted his sister to explore other possibilities prior to committing herself. Harrison sat to Darcy's left, where Darcy could monopolize the conversation with the man, but her brother's efforts only amplified Georgiana's interest.

When the meal finished, the Matlocks announced the engagement of their son Edward to Anne de Bourgh. The guests had the opportunity to publicly acknowledge the couple's union. The absence of Lady Catherine de Bourgh became a minor scandal, but many in attendance were familiar with the situation prior to their coming to the Matlocks' anniversary party.

Anne and Georgiana played for the gathering; they rehearsed two songs to dedicate to Edward. The colonel beamed as he watched both women closely. Georgiana became a young lady of wealth; Anne became the woman to whom he gave his heart. Now, he must remove Anne from Lady Catherine's control in order for him to finally achieve happiness. These songs were symbolic of how far they had all come, but how far they still had to go.

"Anne," Elizabeth offered, "your gift of music was so special. Edward is blessed to find such an accomplished lady."

"Thank you, Elizabeth." Anne dropped her eyes. "The pianoforte is a new love of mine, and Georgiana indulged my interest and helped me perfect these pieces. Edward gives me so much; music is of little consequence in the realm of things."

Elizabeth did not let her comments die. "Miss de Bourgh, in my limited experience, men appreciate when a woman gives gifts of little consequence."

"Actually, Mrs. Darcy is correct. The memory of your gift, Anne, will remain with me forever." Edward kissed the back of Anne's hand, while she blushed profusely.

When the meal ended, Mr. Harrison led Georgiana back to the dance floor for their second and final dance set of the evening. "Miss Darcy," he began softly so others could not hear, "your performance on the pianoforte tonight was incomparable, as are you."

"Mr. Harrison," she laughed lightly, "your flattery is too much for a woman of my position to willingly accept." Georgiana knew she should not encourage Harrison's veiled declarations, but his words made her heart jump and her breathing labored.

"Again, I must apologize." The man could not hide his regard for Georgiana. "Your presence makes my tongue say things my mind knows I should not."

When they progressed down the line, hand in hand, Harrison noticed the color rising in Georgiana's being. "I do sincerely beg your forgiveness, Miss Darcy," he whispered. "I would not wish to lose your favor simply because I am too happy at this moment to control my mirth." Harrison worried he overstepped his bounds.

"It would be difficult for you, Sir, to lose my favor." Georgiana said the words while looking Harrison directly in his eyes.

Her boldness offered him all he needed for the evening. Georgiana accepted his advances and returned them within the bounds of propriety. Some day Harrison dreamed of abandoning all forms of propriety and making Georgiana Darcy his own. "That is all of which I may wish," he said softly while allowing his eyes to return once more to hers in an intimate exchange.

Several days later, Darcy escorted his family to Hines Park for Mr. Harrison's dinner party. Edward and Anne accompanied them. Harrison played the good host, offering up the best of seasonal fruit and game birds for their enjoyment. Darcy and Harrison spent some time reviewing the changes made at Hines Park since Harrison took over as its master.

"I like the renovations you made in the house, Sir," Darcy assured him as they met in Harrison's study.

"I would prefer to use the entire house, but it is more economical to use just the two wings I showed you while I repair the last wing."

"An estate needs constant repair; your plan appears prudent."

"Beside the farm land, I plan to breed horses. The stable and bloodlines present at Hines Park were part of my father's passion. I must play to my strengths."

Darcy took a sip of the port Harrison offered him. "Your father's love of superior horses was well known. My Cerberus was once his—that common knowledge should do you well."

"Then you believe my efforts will prove well for the estate?" Because of Darcy's tendency to present a noncommittal face, Harrison felt unsure of Darcy's approval.

"Your initial steps prove sensible." Darcy stepped to the window to look out over the grounds. "You must remain observant, especially through the spring, to all the little details. Is your steward capable?"

"Although quite elderly, Mr. McAlyn is efficient. I considered finding a successor for him, however. At least, I should find him an apprentice."

Darcy turned back toward the man. "I will speak to Mr. Howard. Possibly he knows of someone who would serve your purpose."

"I remain indebted to you, Mr. Darcy." Harrison offered him a bow of respect.

"We should join the others."

Harrison stammered, "Mr. Darcy, before we do just that, may I speak to you of a private matter regarding your sister?"

"Mr. Harrison," Darcy said, setting his stiff jaw line, "Mrs. Darcy explained to you my thoughts regarding my sister's attentions."

"I understand, Sir. I would be offering false statements if I said I had no interest in Miss Darcy, but that is not of what I wish to speak." Darcy's eyebrow shot up in surprise. "I am concerned about Captain Rutherford."

"Captain Rutherford? Really?" Darcy exclaimed. "May I inquire upon what grounds you object to the captain? Please say it is more than jealousy for my sister's time."

Harrison chuckled. "You recognize my dream of spending more time with Miss Darcy, and I will admit the captain's attention to your sister did not go unnoticed; yet, it is his questioning of her regarding my political and social beliefs of which I speak."

Darcy came to sit across from Harrison. "Go on, Sir. You have my undivided attention."

"On two occasions of which I am aware, the captain questioned Miss Darcy about my beliefs regarding slavery issues."

"By what means have you found out this information regarding my sister?" Darcy's protective intensity arose.

Harrison stammered, "From Miss Darcy herself. I noted her agitation when she danced with the captain. When I asked out of concern for her well-being, Miss Darcy confided what was said."

"Although I am not comfortable with my sister keeping confidences, Mr. Harrison, I am appreciative of the trust she placed in you by expressing what bothered her to someone. I noted the captain's effect on Georgiana after the first set, but I was unable to ascertain the situation." Darcy's own agitation showed.

"May I speak freely, Mr. Darcy?" Harrison asked, and Darcy nodded his affirmation. "The captain, as I said, asked Miss Darcy if you objected to my company because of my views. Your sister graciously came to my defense. From what I know of Captain Rutherford, he has strong ties to those who oppose emancipation for slaves."

"And you, Sir, have strong ties to those who wish to push emancipation through Parliament." Darcy's statement became a question.

"Mr. Darcy, from the first time I met your family, I openly professed my belief. Although England passed the Abolition Act nearly five years ago, the institution of slavery still has not been entirely abolished. I stand behind my beliefs, and I am willing to face those who think otherwise. What I am not willing to do is place your sister in a like position. My purpose in this conversation is to make you aware that your family's association with me could bring Miss Darcy some censure and, Heaven forbid, some danger." Harrison automatically dropped his voice when he said the words.

"Danger!" Darcy snapped. "I will not tolerate Georgiana being placed in such a position!"

"Neither shall I, Sir. I will withdraw my interest in your sister, at least temporarily. What I ask of you, Mr. Darcy, is to make yourself more aware of Captain Rutherford and his asso-

ciates; I assumed you would want to know the situation."
Harrison seemed repentant. "I wish, Sir, I could change this for
your sister."

Darcy sat for several minutes contemplating the innuendos
associated with Harrison's information. "I appreciate your offer
to withdraw from my family; however, I doubt my sister would
tolerate such actions, but I will ask you to curtail meeting with
Georgiana or others within my household until I have in place
protection for them and adequate information."

"I will do as you ask, Mr. Darcy." Harrison accepted the
terms willingly. "Now, we should rejoin the others before they
suspect something to be wrong."

Consumed by his thoughts, Darcy rose. "I assume you are
right, Sir. I thank you for your counsel, Mr. Harrison."

After dinner, when the gentlemen rejoined the ladies, Georgiana stirred when Chadwick Harrison reentered the room.
Almost invisibly, her eyes suggested he join her on the settee.
Looking casual, the man did just that as he turned his attention
first to Elizabeth, ignoring Georgiana.

"Mrs. Darcy, I hope Hines Park meets with your approval."

"It does, Sir; it reminds me of Netherfield Park in size and
style, does it not, Fitzwilliam?" Elizabeth sensed Harrison and
Darcy had a new understanding, and she hoped to determine
what it could be.

Darcy added without much enthusiasm, "They are comparable."

Kitty joined them. "Mr. Bingley and my sister let Netherfield in our home county of Hertfordshire."

"I found Netherfield to be a fine estate for Mr. and Mrs.
Bingley," Georgiana joined the conversation. "As a young
couple, the estate could grow with their family." Georgiana
chose her words wisely; Harrison understood her sentiment
perfectly well.

"Of course, nothing can live up to Pemberley or to Rosings
Park," Harrison added thoughtfully.

"Mr. Harrison," Edward asked, "I notice a framed letter from Olaudah Equiano and a copy of his book predominantly displayed in your study. Did you know him, Sir?"

"I met the man only once; I was barely ten at the time. It was shortly before Equiano's death, and I was on a trip with my mother's brother to the Peak District. Equiano gave a reading from his book, convincing my uncle and many other listeners to purchase it. That is the copy you see in my study. Equiano not only wrote the book, he also published it himself by subscription, getting people to advance the money up-front. Later, when I realized the atrocities of the slave trade, I framed my uncle's letter and took steps to preserve the book as a reminder of the social injustices it represents."

Anne joined Edward on his settee. "You seem quite vocal about your beliefs, Sir."

"I do not mean to offend, Miss de Bourgh," Harrison sounded apologetic, "but it is a topic about which I feel passionately. The thoughts of nearly five hundred Africans crammed below deck and living in squalor, chained together as animals, plays heavy on my senses." Harrison heard Kitty Bennet gasp, but he noted an acknowledgment of his views by Georgiana Darcy's shifting of her weight toward him as if in alignment with his words.

"Then Mr. Wilberforce's Abolition Act has made an impact on slavery?" Edward wanted to clarify his point.

"The law for which Mr. Wilberforce fought eliminated slavery on *British* ships; it has not affected the slave trade on *foreign* ships or in the British colonies." Harrison tried to mute his feelings and to answer responsibly. "Of late, there has been little political movement for emancipation, and even Mr. Wilberforce is feeling the frustration of the situation. It is my understanding the man intends to resign his Parliamentary seat of Yorkshire for the borough of Bramber."

"Then even Wilberforce believes it to be a fruitless cause?" Edward's intense interest in politics controlled the conversation.

"William Wilberforce's health has been less than perfect for some time, and being in his fifties, the man needs to refocus his energies, but he has not abandoned the fight. He will introduce a Slave Registration Bill soon. By registering the slaves, he hopes to prove whether the African slavers are still bringing in workers in the colonies." Harrison knew the conversation made Darcy and several of the women uncomfortable. "However, I monopolized the conversation too long. Let us speak of something more pleasant, Colonel Fitzwilliam. Please tell me about your wedding plans."

"We originally planned a wedding in late June, but my commission is not complete until that time so I am afraid we will settle for mid-July." The colonel's voice faded. Harrison cared little for wedding plans, but after his earlier conversation with Darcy, he knew he must avoid the concept of slavery.

The evening ended on a pleasant note with Georgiana and Elizabeth combining their talents for several songs. His wife's voice always brought Darcy contentment, and he smiled at Elizabeth as she sang.

"You are beautiful tonight," Darcy whispered to her when Elizabeth returned to sit beside him.

"You always say as such, Sir." Elizabeth squeezed Darcy's hand.

"Your face has been all I have seen since those early days in Meryton. It is what I see in my dreams each night." Darcy brought Elizabeth's hand to his mouth to kiss the back of it. "I love you, Elizabeth."

His unexpected words of devotion took her by surprise, and Darcy watched as her eyes welled with tears. "I do not deserve you, my Husband," she said under her breath, "but I am thankful each day you never gave up on us." Her eyes rose to meet his in a loving gaze of pure devotion.

In their room that evening, Darcy took Elizabeth in his arms. The fire burned down, and they sat quietly staring into the dying embers. Elizabeth traced his jaw line with her fingertips. Without warning, Darcy took her hand and kissed her palm and the inside of her wrist.

"You seem troubled, my Love."

"I had an unusual conversation with Mr. Harrison." Darcy and Elizabeth shared everything; trying to hide thoughts rarely worked so he easily confided in her.

"Mr. Harrison's after-dinner discussion with Edward took on a unique focus," Elizabeth admitted.

Darcy shifted his weight so he could speak to his wife directly. "Mr. Harrison is concerned for Georgiana's safety due to his interest in her. He feels Captain Rutherford could be a problem; Rutherford opposes all Mr. Harrison believes. The captain has on several occasions questioned Georgiana about Mr. Harrison's beliefs."

"Is that what played out on the dance floor the other evening?" Elizabeth recognized the exchange as being similar to the one she and Darcy had over George Wickham.

"Evidently. Mr. Harrison offered to withdraw his attentions from Georgiana until I confirm whether the captain should be allowed to be in her company."

"Mr. Harrison's integrity continues to impress me," she added absent-mindedly.

"How so?"

"Just as you once considered helping me find an appropriate match so I might be happy, so does Mr. Harrison offer to withdraw from Georgiana. Do you not see why I view the man as having integrity?" Elizabeth stroked Darcy's face once again.

"How did you know I considered finding you another mate?" Darcy asked in disbelief.

"Your sister likes to relate our courtship to Kitty," Elizabeth teased.

"I must speak to Georgiana." Darcy pretended to be upset, but his smile told Elizabeth his love for her never stopped. "But what should we do about Captain Rutherford?" He brought the conversation back to the issue at hand.

"Of course, we must learn more of the captain. Is it possible he simply opposes Mr. Harrison's views without a strong compunction to cause harm?"

"I suppose it to be so," Darcy mused. "Yet, if the captain's allies are more aggressive, we need to know that also."

"Certainly, Fitzwilliam." Elizabeth snuggled into Darcy's shoulder once again. "We will protect Georgiana together."

"You said earlier you did not deserve me; it is I who has grown from knowing you, my dearest Elizabeth." Darcy kissed her forehead and pulled his wife even closer.

"I will be happy to return to Pemberley," Elizabeth said dreamily. "I miss our home."

"Do you consider Pemberley your home?" Darcy asked, stroking her arm and listening to the regularity of Elizabeth's breathing.

"Wherever you are is my home. Elizabeth traced Darcy's lips with her fingertips. "But I admit to no longer thinking of Longbourn as my home; I belong to you and to Pemberley."

Darcy tilted Elizabeth's chin to seek her mouth with his. The depth of the kiss increased as Elizabeth edged even closer to him. "You are stunning." Darcy's breath came out in short bursts.

"My love for you cannot be expressed in words, Fitzwilliam." Elizabeth kissed him again as her hands interlocked behind his head, pulling him down to her.

In the middle of the night, Darcy felt Elizabeth touch his face. "Fitzwilliam." She whispered close to his ear. "Fitzwilliam, wake up."

Darcy rolled toward her but fought to stay asleep. "What is it, my Love?" Darcy slurred the words.

"The baby," she said to his face, "it moved. The quickening began." Elizabeth's words held her delight.

Darcy's eyes shot open as what she said zigzagged through his subconscious. "Lizzy? When?" He reached out to touch Elizabeth's abdomen.

"Just now," she giggled.

Darcy kissed Elizabeth deeply. "You are my one true love," he whispered.

"Feel, Fitzwilliam." Elizabeth took his hand and pressed it to her lower stomach.

The fascination went across Darcy's face. "What an extraordinary sensation!" he teased. "To think that is our child." Darcy's eyes encompassed Elizabeth as he bent to kiss her once again.

"Our child likes the feel of your hand, Sir," Elizabeth clasped his hand to her as the child moved sporadically, "as do I."

Darcy laughed. "It is so soon," he thought out loud. "I did not think the quickening would begin for another few weeks. At least, that is what Mrs. Reynolds told me."

"So our child has a mind of his own." Elizabeth snaked her arms around Darcy's neck and pressed herself to him.

"*His* own?" Darcy taunted. "Do you believe it to be a boy?"

"I cannot know," Elizabeth said, kissing Darcy's neck, "but the child will be loved. That is of importance."

"Conceived in love to live with love." Darcy deepened the kiss he planted on her mouth, needing to feel Elizabeth's desires. "I love you, my Lizzy." His mouth captured hers again and again, wrapping her in his love and satisfying a hunger he knew only when in Elizabeth's presence.

The Darcy party prepared for the departure from Hines Park. Hannah and Henry supervised the placement of the luggage for Darcy's coach. Anne and Edward, with Mrs. Jenkinson, left earlier.

"Miss Bennet and Miss Darcy." Mr. Harrison stood and made a bow. "May I have the pleasure of showing you the gardens before you depart?"

Kitty did not particularly want to see the gardens; she thought only of returning to Pemberley and seeing Clayton Ashford again, but she saw Georgiana give her a fleeting glance so Kitty knew her response. "That would be most pleasant, Mr. Harrison," she said, and smiled at the man. "You will join us, will you not, Georgiana?"

Georgiana dropped her eyes, unable to look at Harrison without betraying her thoughts. "I would enjoy it," she said softly.

Harrison led both girls through the maze of hedgerows and beech trees to the garden's center fountain. Kitty graciously pretended to admire some plantings far enough away from Harrison and Georgiana to allow them to speak freely but close enough to maintain propriety.

"Miss Darcy," Harrison spoke anxiously, "please forgive my rashness, but I fear we have only a few moments." He looked about nervously.

"Speak what you will, Sir." Georgiana swallowed hard as she lowered her voice.

"I spoke to your brother about Captain Rutherford." Harrison saw confusion come into her eyes. "I cannot explain now—the captain is dangerous. Please trust me, Miss Darcy. That is all I can tell you at this time."

"You spoke to Fitzwilliam?" Georgiana's eyes darted to where Kitty stood.

"I wanted to be sure you are safe." Harrison's urgency enveloped Georgiana. "I *must* know no harm comes your way because of me."

"I do not understand, Sir."

"It is complicated; just do not believe the captain, please, Miss Darcy," Harrison pleaded with her. "You must trust me on this."

Georgiana's response came at last; her eyes rose and looked deeply into the man's. "I trust you, Mr. Harrison," she whispered. "I trust you with my life."

The intensity between them stood thick among the overhanging branches. Their eyes never left each other. Georgiana knew what Harrison thought at that moment; the desire streamed from him; she felt he undressed her with his eyes. "Georgiana," his voice caressed her as if his hands actually touched her face.

"Chadwick," Georgiana returned his familiarity as a hint of a smile turned up the corners of her mouth. Again, no words came, but meaning and understanding held them together.

Suddenly aware of the change in their situation, Kitty Bennet loudly cleared her voice. "Please, Georgiana," Kitty coaxed as softly as she could, "your brother is coming this way."

The words reached Georgiana's senses; bewildered, she turned to Kitty.

"Mr. Darcy walks this way," Kitty cautioned Georgiana.

Georgiana thanked Kitty with a nearly imperceptible nod and then let out a soft laugh before saying to Mr. Harrison, "Did you learn of the local well dressings, then, Mr. Harrison?"

Harrison, too, snapped to a more acceptable form of address. "Unfortunately, Miss Darcy, they lacked much of what you and your sister accomplished at Pemberley."

By that time, Darcy came to greet them. "Ladies, your sister wishes to return to her home soon," Darcy said to Georgiana and Kitty. "Are you ready to join her?"

"I am sorry to delay your departure," Harrison politely begged Darcy's pardon.

"It is I, Mr. Harrison, who took too much of your time." Georgiana knew Harrison would not complain.

"I am not seeking to apply blame," Darcy stated. "Elizabeth tires easily now, and she wishes to depart soon. That is all I wish to imply."

"Then we must leave you, Mr. Harrison." Kitty judiciously took his arm to return to the waiting carriage.

Darcy offered his sister his own arm, and she gave him an appealing smile. "You appear very content, Georgiana." Darcy looked closely at his sister.

"Like Elizabeth, I am content to be returning to my home." Her words hid the fact that from now on, her dreams would be associated with this garden and this estate.

CHAPTER 6

"Husbands and wives generally understand
when opposition will be in vain."
Jane Austen, *Persuasion*, 1817

———◦◦◦———

For a week the Darcys enjoyed their return to Pemberley without interruptions of their time or their peace. Without houseguests, they could set their own schedules and their own interests. Darcy, Elizabeth, and Georgiana returned to regularly scheduled time to deal with estate business. The ladies did not ride out as did Darcy and Mr. Howard, but they did address issues with the tenants.

"Do you not think we should also set up a regular schedule for visiting the tenants?" Georgiana asked as they sat in Darcy's study, enjoying an unusually sunny early February day.

"You are probably correct," Elizabeth said. "The tenants need to know we care for their needs, and regularly going among them would help relay that concept. My only concern is as my time comes due, the need for the visits shall fall on your shoulders, and I would not want you to feel the burden of that responsibility alone."

"Elizabeth, I would enjoy being a part of helping the tenants. It is an area of which I am passionate. In the past, Fitzwilliam would never tolerate my going among them, seeing me as too fragile. Until there was you, my brother considered me too delicate to be involved in the estate. I do not know how you changed his thinking, but I would welcome this as an area of the estate business in which I could be of service."

"Of course, Kitty or even someone from the household staff could help during my confinement, I suppose," Elizabeth offered. "If you are sure, Georgiana, then we should look into how we want to approach this endeavor."

"I am sure, Elizabeth." Georgiana allowed her eyes to meet her sister's. "It is important to me."

They continued to work on a tentative schedule for nearly an hour before breaking for some afternoon tea. "We will consult both Fitzwilliam and Mr. Howard," Elizabeth added as she closed the journal in which she recorded her notes. "We will start our visits at the beginning of the week then."

"Thank you, Elizabeth," Georgiana said as she handed her sister a cup of tea, and they moved to sit across from each other.

Elizabeth looked out the study's windows. "I am looking forward to my first springtime at Pemberley," she said wistfully.

Absent-mindedly, Georgiana confided, "I am pleased to be here and not in London this year."

"Will you not miss the society London offers?"

"I shall miss some of the concerts, but not the pressure of London's society toward perfection. I feared being found wanting." Georgiana's ease in speaking to Elizabeth began when they first met and continued as Elizabeth accepted Georgiana's feelings as legitimate. The young girl needed someone such as her brother's wife in her life, and although Elizabeth was only a few years older than Georgiana, she took on a "motherly" role. "I shall not miss delaying my coming out for the sake of your confinement." Georgiana gave Elizabeth a huge smile.

"Your brother said as much several days ago," Elizabeth teased.

Georgiana gasped, "Did he really?"

They sat in companionable silence for several minutes before Georgiana got enough nerve to broach a subject, which had come to life since her meeting with Chadwick Harrison. She began cautiously, "Elizabeth, may I ask you a very personal question?"

"Of course, Georgiana."

"You and Fitzwilliam have an unusual connection; how did you achieve such openness in such a short time?" Georgiana leaned forward as if to hear the "pearls of wisdom" she expected from Elizabeth.

Elizabeth actually cackled with mirth. "Oh, Georgiana, if you are looking for me to give you such secrets, I am afraid I have none in my possession." Elizabeth saw disappointment flit across Georgiana's face. "Please believe me," she added quickly, "if I possessed such wisdom, I would gladly share it with you. You know how dramatic the changes were for your brother, but mine were much more subtle. Of course, I owe it all to my husband."

Georgiana seemed puzzled. "To Fitzwilliam?"

"Your brother, when he spoke to you of your hopefully finding a man who would not be intimidated by your intelligence, he spoke of a man like himself." The puzzling look on Georgiana's face amused Elizabeth.

"Does Fitzwilliam believe I should seek a man like him? I am sorry, Elizabeth, but my brother's moodiness would sorely play unfriendly on my nerves." Georgiana laughed uneasily, fearing she said too much.

"I agree," Elizabeth joined in the mirth. "I believe your brother and I were destined for each other. We serve in perfect complement to one another."

"But how did you achieve that complementary relationship? That is what I would like to know."

"The relationship must be based on absolute trust; you can hide nothing from your mate. Your brother opened himself up to me shortly after I accepted his advances, but it took me longer to achieve such emotional honesty. He expressed his vulnerability in telling me about your parents' love, his shyness, his vision for Pemberley, his intimate thoughts, and his constant need of assurance of my regard. Sometimes I felt overwhelmed, sometimes I felt protective. Your brother needed so much from a relationship; I often thought I could not satisfy everything he required of me.

"Fitzwilliam wanted me to share everything. I assume because he took care of everything for so long, he needed someone with whom he could entrust some of those responsibilities without worrying about the outcome. Why did we fight so violently before my fall? It was because your brother still held vestiges of total control. Like our courtship, each of us needed my accident and recovery to reach an understanding. We found relief only in sharing—an intrinsic need of being a part of each other.

"The biggest change for me came the day I realized your brother meant more to me than anything else in the world. I no longer thought of my parents and sisters as 'my family' or Longbourn as 'my home.' Fitzwilliam became everything I needed and wanted in life. I can honestly say I remember little of my life before your brother. It is as if I did not exist until he loved me."

Georgiana asked seriously, "So where do I go from here?"

"You must not rush things. Find a man who really listens to you and values your true self. That is not an easy task, but you will be happier than you can imagine. Do not settle for less, Georgiana. If you want my secret, that is it. Fitzwilliam allows my confidence to grow while still being my constant joy."

Georgiana asked quietly, "Are there many men like my brother?"

"I cannot say," Elizabeth laughed. "I think, however, what you really ask is Mr. Harrison that type of man?"

Georgiana blushed and diverted her eyes. "I still prefer his company to all others."

"Time will give you the answers, Georgiana," Elizabeth added softly. "I know it sounds trite when I say be patient, but it is the key. Do not rush into a relationship." The women sat together for some time, sharing the connection in silence before returning to their duties.

Kitty Bennet kept herself busy with the renovations for the nursery. At first, disappointment found her when Mr. Ashford did not appear upon her return to Pemberley. However, she learned by accident he traveled to Kympton to administer to the needs of the curate, who took ill. Although she desperately wanted to see him again, knowledge of Mr. Ashford's caring nature sustained her.

So, on an early February afternoon, Mr. Ashford took Kitty by surprise when she espied him walking up the lane to Pemberley. She stood in the nursery watching his stride and mannerisms as he approached the house. Kitty wondered what it would be like to have Clayton Ashford kiss her. Would it be as Mr. Darcy said—like coming home? The cleric seemed nervous, but confident at the same time, and she saw the glint of a smile slip into the corners of his mouth when he looked up at the house. A warmth crept into her being, and Kitty found she had to sit down and gulp for air. "Why do I react this way when I think of Mr. Ashford?" she said out loud.

The light tap on Darcy's door announced the presence of Mr. Ashford; the vicar entered the master's study. He had been a guest at Pemberley a few times already, but this time the situation held a difference—a yearning and a need for something intangible. Studying his employer, Ashford thought Mr. Darcy did not look surprised to see him.

"Good afternoon, Sir," Darcy stood and acknowledged the man, "it has been several weeks since we saw you, Mr. Ashford."

"I have been in Kympton. Old Mr. Matthews took ill. I planned to call upon you before now, Mr. Darcy." Ashford shifted uneasily as he took the seat Darcy offered.

"What brings you here this afternoon, Mr. Ashford?" Darcy took his usual seat behind the desk.

Fearing he might lose his nerve if he did not speak quickly, Ashford went directly to the point. "I came today, Sir, to seek your permission to call upon your sister Miss Bennet with the ultimate goal of asking her hand in marriage." Ashford gasped for air, trying to clear his dry throat after looking into Darcy's formidable eyes.

"I assume you made your intentions known to Miss Bennet." Darcy amused himself with Ashford's nervousness.

"I have, Sir." Ashford remained in all seriousness.

Darcy teased, "And she is willing?"

Ashford swallowed hard. "I believe so, Sir."

"I would act in Mr. Bennet's stead, but, of course, I would seek his consent." Darcy smiled knowingly. He hoped Mr. Bennet was not as hard on Mr. Ashford as he was initially on Darcy. After a few moments of excoriating silence, Darcy added, "Mr. Ashford, may I speak openly?" Darcy, too, sounded serious.

Ashford sat forward, giving Darcy his full attention. "Certainly, Sir."

"Our Kitty will not be an easy woman to love, but she will be a jewel for the man who helps her find her true worth. Unfortunately, my wife's mother is a foolish woman who taught her younger daughters that beauty is more important than substance. The result was the youngest daughter ran off with an unsuitable match. We arranged her marriage to save the rest of the family.

"As you may imagine, I do not share this information easily, but if you choose to align yourself with Miss Bennet, you inherit some of the baggage. The other daughters rose above the standards taught by Mrs. Bennet. Mrs. Darcy and Mrs. Bingley are exceptional women. Mary Bennet is one of the most devout young ladies one could hope to meet; only Lydia selected poorly. My wife and Mrs. Bingley chose to bring Kitty into our fold. Now that you know her background, Mr. Ashford, do you wish to withdraw your interest in Miss Bennet?" Darcy held the man with his intense gaze.

"Of course not, Mr. Darcy," Ashford stammered, "but it does explain my initial reaction to Miss Bennet. The batting of the eyes and the pursing of her lips nearly drove me away until I looked beyond those exaggerations." Darcy chuckled at Ashford's earliest evaluation of Kitty Bennet. "Yet, the more I looked into her eyes, the less chance I had to withdraw. Is that not a mark of a man in love, Mr. Darcy? In Miss Bennet's eyes, I saw the man I want to be."

Darcy actually laughed out loud this time, shocking and embarrassing Ashford. "I am sorry, Mr. Ashford, your words brought me back to my early days of admiring Mrs. Darcy. I am afraid Elizabeth's *fine eyes* haunted me for many months before I admitted loving her. At least, you eliminated the torture I felt at the time, Sir."

"Then you hold no objections, Mr. Darcy?" Ashford seemed hopeful.

"None whatsoever, Sir," Darcy assured the man. "I will write to Mr. Bennet and inform him of my decision and seek his consent."

Ashford stood and bowed. "Thank you, Sir."

"Why not join us for dinner, Mr. Ashford?" Darcy offered. "You may renew your acquaintance with Miss Bennet."

"I would enjoy that, Sir." Ashford smiled with gratitude.

Darcy added, "I will send Miss Bennet to you in the library, Mr. Ashford."

Although he need not distrust the vicar, Darcy sent a maid to sit in the library with Kitty and Mr. Ashford. He wanted no more scandal, especially not in his own household.

"Mr. Ashford," Kitty spoke his name as she dropped a curtsy.

He rose to his feet and bowed politely to her. "Miss Bennet, it is pleasant to see you again." Ashford's eyes searched her countenance to observe her reaction to him.

"Please have a seat, Mr. Ashford." Kitty motioned to a chair near the fireplace as the maid moved to one in the corner of the room. "I understand you were in Kympton, Sir." Kitty tried to sound casual.

"I was, Miss Bennet." Ashford continued to stare at her. "I hope your trip to the east was pleasant."

"It was pleasant to spend time with my sister's new relatives, but I am happy to once more be at Pemberley." Kitty wanted to hint she missed him.

Ashford knew he had no right to ask Kitty his next question, but his jealousy overruled his reason. "Did you find pleasant dance partners for the ball?"

"Miss Darcy and I found agreeable company, Sir. Mr. Harrison attended the celebration." Ashford continued to smile at her. "Do you find something amusing, Sir?" Kitty asked incredulously.

"Nothing, Miss Bennet." He realized she avoided his question. "I just wanted you to know I missed your family's companionship."

"You were missed as well, Sir." Kitty dropped her eyes, afraid to see how he would react to her boldness.

Ashford tried to steady his voice. "Miss Bennet, I spoke to Mr. Darcy."

Kitty could not look at him. "To Mr. Darcy?"

"Miss Bennet," Ashford found his voice again, "as I told you before you left for Nottingham, I would like for us to spend time together to learn more about each other. If you agree, after an appropriate time, I would extend my hand to you in marriage. That is, if you are willing to accept my interest."

Kitty swallowed hard, keeping her eyes downcast, not knowing whether she possessed the nerve to give him the assurance he sought. "Mr. Ashford, my family missed you, but I wished to return to Pemberley specifically to see you again."

Ashford's heart went soaring; she accepted his advances. "Then we have an understanding, Miss Bennet?" Ashford moved to sit beside her on the settee.

"We have an understanding, Mr. Ashford."

For the next hour, Kitty Bennet and Clayton Ashford talked of nothing and of everything at the same time. "Are you enjoying redecorating the Darcys' nursery, then, Miss Bennet?" he asked to find out more about the vivacious girl seated beside him.

"I discovered the most attractive pattern in a little shop in Lambton," Kitty bubbled with excitement. "Mr. Darcy even approved it. It is fine and delicate enough for the infant, but it will serve well as the child grows."

"I would be interested in seeing it sometime." Ashford reached out and touched the back of Kitty's hand with his fingertips, allowing his hand to linger next to hers.

Kitty's eyes drifted casually to where Ashford's hand rested on the settee's cushion. With the slightest of grins playing across her face, she slid her hand under his cupped one, smiling largely when he clasped hers and pulled it to his lips for a gentle kiss to the back of it.

"Mr. Ashford," she gasped.

Ashford expected her to withdraw from him, but instead Kitty squeezed his hand and gifted the man with another of her smiles. "Tell me about your position here in Lambton, Mr. Ashford."

Elizabeth happened by the library and observed the scene between her sister and the young vicar. She started to enter the room and demand to know what was going on; instead, Elizabeth sought Darcy's advice. "My Husband," she called as she entered his study, coming to stand in front of Darcy's desk, "what do you know of our Kitty and Mr. Ashford?"

"Mr. Ashford asked my permission to call on your sister with the intention of offering her his hand." Darcy smiled with amusement.

"She already holds his hand." Elizabeth rolled her eyes. "How long have you known about this, Sir?"

"Actually, for only a few days," he confided. "I assumed Kitty shared her feelings with you previously, my Love."

"Do not look so smug, Sir," Elizabeth offered a pretend reprimand. "What do you know?"

Darcy came from behind his desk and led Elizabeth to a chair. He seated himself across from her. "I became aware of the seriousness of the matter the night of Lady Catherine's vituperation. Georgiana escorted you to our rooms; Edward and Lady Pennington took care of Anne. The others spoke quietly among themselves. When I returned to the drawing room, I realized no one considered poor Kitty's feelings. My aunt's attack on your family connections also hit your sister."

"Poor Kitty." Elizabeth looked pained by the memory. "I did not even think to see to her needs. She was always so foolish. I thought Kitty would ignore Lady Catherine, except for the fact your aunt dampened the night's social hour."

"You are mistaken; your sister sobbed quite uncontrollably for awhile."

"Thank you, Fitzwilliam, for helping her. I hope Kitty did not distress you; she is very much like Lydia, I am afraid." Elizabeth blushed with shame for her family.

"That is another mistaken assumption on your part, my Love." Elizabeth looked at Darcy in surprise. "I believe Kitty is very much like you."

"Like me? What did Kitty share with you?"

"There were many issues I could not address, but the gist of the conversation dealt with the subtle censure both Mary and

Kitty received by some in Meryton because of the rumors of Lydia's rushed marriage. Compound that with Lady Catherine's speech and the secret Kitty once let Mr. Denney kiss her, and your sister was quite distraught." Darcy found the look of surprise on Elizabeth's face endearing.

Elizabeth exclaimed, "She allowed Mr. Denney what?"

"It seems Kitty read too many novels about romance, and she wondered about having a man kiss her. Luckily, Mr. Denney's beard scratched her face, and the man smelled of port and cigars. She found it most unpleasant from what I understand."

Elizabeth found the idea of Kitty confessing this to her "very proper Mr. Darcy" to be exceedingly amusing, and she laughed out loud. "What else was said?" She wiped away the tears of joy streaming down her face.

Darcy, not sure he liked being a source of his wife's entertainment, answered a bit haughtily, "Your sister thought herself to be no better than Lydia. I could not allow that so I explained how she must face the world with the knowledge of a pure heart. Then she confessed Mr. Ashford might be calling on her, and she would be interested in receiving his attentions. Naturally, when the young man did just that this afternoon, I gave him my permission, pending your father's consent. I posted a letter to Mr. Bennet a while ago. Do you have some objections to Mr. Ashford, Elizabeth?"

"How will the man react when he finds out about Lydia and Mr. Wickham?" Elizabeth looked worried.

"I took the liberty of sharing some of the details with Mr. Ashford. I thought a man of the cloth would be discreet, but because of his position, he had to know to what his interest in Kitty might lead. I would not want him to turn away from her once he began the relationship. That would be devastating for Kitty; she must know of his acceptance of Lydia's shortcomings." Darcy took on a businesslike manner.

"You are quite the Cupid, my Husband." Elizabeth smiled

at him. "Do you believe Mr. Ashford to be a suitable match for Kitty, then, Sir?"

"Mr. Ashford has a respectable income, and he is quite taken with her already. He speaks of *her fine eyes.*" Darcy watched as the reference to their earliest days together brought joy to Elizabeth's face.

"You tease me again," Elizabeth suggested lovingly. "We are quite a pair; your sister speaks to me of love, and my sister speaks to you of the same subject. When did we become the *older sages* of relationships?"

"Now it is I who is being teased," Darcy laughed. "Are Mr. Ashford's intentions acceptable to you, Elizabeth?"

"He would make my sister an excellent match, Sir. Thank you for taking care of Kitty. You amaze me with your magnanimity; I am blessed by being loved by you." Elizabeth stood to leave, but her words moved Darcy, who strode over to her purposefully.

He spoke softly into her ear, "It is I who does not deserve you, my Love." Darcy caressed Elizabeth's cheek. "I told your sister when I first kissed you it was like coming home." His gaze intensified.

Elizabeth snaked her arms around his neck, toying with a curl along the line of his shirt. "In that case, Sir, let me say, welcome home." Darcy kissed her passionately, and she deepened the kiss, again and again.

Although it was late morning, Elizabeth still sat at her desk penning letters to family members and to other social obligations. She did not notice Darcy at the door for several minutes. He watched her bite her lower lip and twirl a single strand of her hair as she worked her way through her correspondence. Darcy's smile spread as he leaned back against the doorframe. "You are beautiful," he finally said.

Not expecting him, Elizabeth jumped when she heard his

voice. "I thought you were out of the house, Sir." Elizabeth smiled, realizing he returned to find her.

"I thought I might show you a part of the estate today." He seemed to have a purpose. In reality, Elizabeth had several tasks she wanted to complete today, but the look of eagerness on Darcy's face forced her to place her items to the side for his benefit.

He helped her dress for the weather. "I hope you do not mind a short walk." Darcy tightened her fur-lined pelisse around Elizabeth's body. "I will need to find you a larger pelisse soon." He patted her stomach lightly.

"Do not make fun of my blossoming figure, Sir," Elizabeth spoofed.

Darcy took her hand as he led her from the house. "I would never make such a mistake, my Love."

They walked for nearly a mile, mostly uphill behind the estate. "Much farther, Fitzwilliam?" Elizabeth usually did not tire easily, but her current condition made her more susceptible when climbing inclines.

"Only around the bend of the road, my Love," Darcy coaxed her along.

Elizabeth took a deep breath and pressed forward to reach their destination. Coming around the curve of the road, which would only be accessible by foot or horseback, Elizabeth froze. Nestled among the pin oaks and Spanish chestnut trees was a small lodge, probably used by hunting parties.

"Fitzwilliam, it is wonderful," Elizabeth stammered.

"Let me show you inside," he encouraged her.

The place had a masculine feel to the furnishings, but the workmanship possessed a level of elegance not evident in most hunting lodges. Elizabeth stood in awe, looking around the room. "Exquisite," she mumbled. "I had no idea this was on our property."

Darcy stepped back to let Elizabeth explore the lodge's

several rooms. Finally, it struck her. "Why is there a fire burning in the fireplace, Fitzwilliam?" She turned to give him an enigmatic smile.

"I missed you of late, my Love," Darcy said as he encircled Elizabeth in his arms.

Elizabeth taunted, "You see me every day and every night."

"In a house like Pemberley, we are never truly alone. I needed time with you, Elizabeth."

"How long may we stay here?" Elizabeth laughed. "I could be yours forever and never tire."

"I brought us some food in a picnic basket, several warm blankets and a fur rug for the floor, plenty of firewood, and a change of clothing. May we stay the night, Elizabeth?"

Elizabeth rushed into his arms. "Do you mean it?"

Darcy clutched her to his chest. "Elizabeth, we need time together; the demands of Pemberley will increase with the spring plantings. We need to find time for us." Darcy, as usual, reasoned their escape. "I need you in my life, Elizabeth. I need to know you love me."

Elizabeth felt contentment in his arms. "Of course I love you, Fitzwilliam. I feel such a sense of acceptance when I am with you."

Darcy experienced warmth and protectiveness when he held Elizabeth. Ironically, as much as they both resisted loving one another, now they depended on the other for their true happiness. The strength of Darcy's devotion held her to him as he bent his head to kiss the one person who completed him.

"Let us spread out the food and enjoy the meal," Elizabeth told him. "We can put the bearskin rug in front of the fire and sit together. I cannot believe we have a whole evening with no interruptions. Thank you, Fitzwilliam, for arranging this."

"I told only Georgiana and Mr. Howard where we are, and I told them we are not to be disturbed unless there is a true emergency."

Looking around the rooms, Elizabeth noticed the bed-clothes turned down in anticipation of their use. She shot Darcy a quick glance and a raised eyebrow, and he feigned innocence while putting a new log on the fire.

"Come and sit with me, my Love," Darcy called to her. He leaned back against the hammock; Elizabeth came to sit between his legs. "I wanted to take you on a picnic to the stream," he told her, "but the weather is still too cold for that. I hope this does not disappoint you."

"Heavens, no," Elizabeth gushed. "A picnic would give us only a few hours of pleasure. This promises us a complete evening."

Darcy took her in his arms and kissed her tenderly. "I love you, my Elizabeth," Darcy whispered into her ear. "I dreamed of having you in my life for so long, and now my dreams are real."

Elizabeth shifted her position to rest her head in Darcy's lap, smiling up at him engagingly. He began to remove the pins from her hair, allowing her locks to loosely drape across his legs, and he felt a rush of desire for her. The woman resting on his lap cared about him for himself. Elizabeth cared not for his wealth or his position; she would be happy to be in his arms even if they lived in one of the cottages. The realization of Elizabeth's devotion brought Darcy the contentment that so eluded him for years.

His eyes traced the lines of her face, and he stroked her chin line with the back of his hand. She closed her eyes and allowed her husband's closeness to take her to that special place in her mind where only she and Darcy existed.

"Why do you smile?" Darcy asked, amused at seeing the corners of Elizabeth's mouth turn up.

"I dreamed of your touch." Elizabeth tightened her eyes to sustain the image. "You and I were dancing at Netherfield, but there was no one else there. We circled, and all I could see was you. I felt your eyes on me; you undressed me and made love to me without even touching me—all the while we were dancing."

"Could we not dance, unclothed?" His voice held another level of amusement, and Darcy traced her jaw line again.

Elizabeth's eyes shot open. "Dancing unclothed!" she exclaimed. "You are incorrigible, Sir."

"I just modified your dream and made it my own." Darcy gave her a look of innocence.

"Come lie next to me," Elizabeth suggested. "There will not be dancing, but I can promise part of your dream will come true."

"Be still my heart," he teased. Then he took Elizabeth's face in his hands and kissed her passionately. He lay next to her and began to unlace the ribbons of Elizabeth's dress. "We are such stuff as dreams are made of," [1] Darcy whispered in her ear.

"Dreams are the true interpreters of our inclinations." [2] Elizabeth laced her fingers into Darcy's thick hair and pulled his mouth to hers. "I hope, Sir, to make our dreams come true." With that, she explored his mouth with hers.

The passion came sweet and unbridled. For a while, they slept in each other's arms, legs untangled. Darcy's breath came relaxed and even against Elizabeth's cheek. She felt the pleasure of his warmth and reached out to stroke his chest. "My Husband?" Elizabeth kissed the indentation of his neck.

"Again?" Darcy teasingly asked as he rolled toward Elizabeth and scooped her into his arms.

"That is what happens when you give me yourself without restrictions." Elizabeth now kissed his chin line and earlobe. "Umm, you are delicious," she laughed gently in his ear. "Again," she said, as if a command.

"Yes, my dearest Elizabeth," Darcy pulled her hips to his body. "With you, my dear, love is a symbol of eternity. It wipes out all sense of time, destroying all memory of a beginning and all fear of an end." [3] Their kiss became more passionate; he deepened it and increased Elizabeth's desire. "Lizzy," he began.

"Finally, you call me Lizzy," she teased again.

★ ★ ★

Elizabeth sat in Darcy's study, making a list of supplies she and Georgiana would take to the homes of the tenants. They sectioned off the property so they could efficiently visit an area every few days. If the weather became a problem, the ladies could vary the section, traveling the better roads in the carriage. The list completed, Elizabeth sat back, leisurely lounging in Darcy's chair. She liked working at his desk, touching her husband's things and smelling the hint of his favorite scent, strongly masculine in every way. She closed her eyes and inhaled deeply, letting the hint of a smile cross her lips.

"Are we still dancing, my Love?" Darcy's resonant voice asked.

Elizabeth kept her eyes closed while offering him her signature smile. "My Husband, have you not heard the best things happen in the middle of a dance; a person can do things naturally he would not do elsewhere?" Elizabeth opened her eyes to find Darcy standing directly in front of her. She stood and slid her arms around his waist. As she moved in closer, Elizabeth whispered, "Dancing, in your case, can lead to romance."

Darcy bent to kiss her lips lightly. "You, my Love, are so tempting. Keep dreaming, my Elizabeth; I find your dreams very inviting."

"What brings you here, Sir? I thought you rode out this afternoon." Elizabeth ran her hands up the muscles of his back.

He led her to a nearby chair. "I have news I need to discuss with you, Mrs. Darcy."

"Is something the matter, Fitzwilliam?" Elizabeth noted the seriousness in his voice.

"I have some initial information on Captain Rutherford."

"What of him?" Elizabeth reacted to Darcy's tight-lipped manner. "Should we be concerned?"

"I am still unsure of Captain Rutherford, but his father is a vocal force in Leeds. I received a response to my inquiries. It seems some of the Earl's tenants threatened to leave him because of their poor conditions."

"Lady Pennington swears the estate is very profitable," Elizabeth protested.

"If the profits are made at the distress of others, I am concerned. I would not want Georgiana in such a place." Darcy played with the ring on Elizabeth's hand. "It is reported the Earl had a man whipped to death for poaching a deer on the estate. Can you imagine our sweet, sensitive Georgiana in such a situation?"

"Do you remember her punishment for Mr. Jenkins's crime? What a contrast in judgment!"

"The captain associated with more radical factions at Oxford," Darcy continued. "The Earl owns lands in sugar cane, and the captain's uncle is quite influential in Dutch interests in the West Indies."

"That still tells us nothing about whether the captain is likely to be a danger to Mr. Harrison or to our family." Elizabeth shifted her weight to move into Darcy's embrace. Something told her instinctively things were not right, and only his embrace could ease her concern.

Darcy tightened his embrace of Elizabeth. "That is the quagmire, my Love. I feel I must go to Hull to find out for myself about what dangers the captain presents."

"Fitzwilliam, no," she gasped as she pushed herself away from him far enough to see his face.

"Elizabeth, I must know if Georgiana is in danger." His voice demanded she agree.

"How long will you be gone, my Love?" Elizabeth said at last; she fought back the tears.

"I asked Hannah More to meet with me, and she agreed." Darcy stroked Elizabeth's arm and kissed her forehead.

"Are you familiar with Miss More?"

"My father met Miss More on several occasions. The first time I was a mere child; she was a guest at Sir Charles and Lady Margaret Middleton's home in Kent. Lady Catherine arranged the introductions. I believe that is where Miss More met Thomas Clarkson. When I was nearly seven Miss More and Mr. Wilberforce holidayed in the Peak District. They planned the early abolition movement during that trip. My father met with them twice; he chose not to be actively involved in their campaign although he never openly supported slavery."

Elizabeth grasped at straws. "Why can Miss More not come here?"

"She is nearly seven and sixty years of age, and her health is poor. Miss More cannot come to me; I must travel to Hull. She promised to answer all my questions." Darcy knew Elizabeth worried about such a separation.

"Can you not send Mr. Howard?" Tears flowed down her cheeks.

"Elizabeth, you know that is not possible." Darcy lifted her chin to kiss her mouth. "I do not wish to go, but I must protect my sister."

Elizabeth fought back the tears. "How will I sleep without your arms around me?" she asked him innocently.

"How may I survive without you nestled close to me?" Darcy answered her.

"When will you leave?" Elizabeth reluctantly accepted his need to protect Georgiana.

He said quietly, "Tomorrow."

"Tomorrow," Elizabeth whispered as her tears returned once again.

CHAPTER 7

*"Silly things do cease to be silly if they are done
by sensible people in an impudent way."*
Jane Austen, *Emma*, 1815

———◦◦◦◦———

The morning Darcy left for Hull, Elizabeth grieved before his carriage even departed Pemberley's grounds. Against propriety, she embraced him in the courtyard while he waited for his luggage to be secured. He clutched her to him, and Elizabeth rested her head on his chest. He stroked her hair and whispered endearments as he supervised the proceedings. "Elizabeth," he encouraged her to withdraw, "I must leave, my Love."

Elizabeth knew her very public display of affection would be the talk of the servant quarters this evening, but feeling bereft of Darcy's warmth before he even left the grounds, she cared not. "Fitzwilliam, please do not go," she pleaded.

"There is nothing of which to worry," Darcy cautioned her. "I stay with Lord and Lady Pennington in Nottingham this evening. Perhaps they may tell me more about Captain Rutherford than we already know. I travel to Hull tomorrow. I swear to be home within the week," he reassured her.

"But Fitzwilliam," she began, "do you not feel it, too? Surely if I feel it, you do also. Something is amiss." Elizabeth's words held her fears.

Darcy reached out and caressed her cheek and then lightly kissed her lips. "It pleases me you will so miss me, my dearest Elizabeth."

"How may I survive without you? It is not fair; you make me depend so dearly upon you, and then you leave me, Sir." Elizabeth nearly pouted.

"I shall think of you every moment, my Love. I cannot imagine my life without you as my wife. I shall hurry back to once again be in your arms." Darcy lifted her chin and lightly brushed her lips with his. Then he quickly got in the carriage, rapped on the roof with his walking cane, and left.

Yet, he could not leave without looking back at her, standing in the circular carriageway, tears streaming down her face. Darcy ached at having to leave. He spent nearly a year earning Elizabeth's love and leaving her side, even for a few days, seemed an incomprehensible act.

Elizabeth watched the retreating coach. The distance between them increased by the second until only silence remained. Reluctantly, she turned toward Pemberley, finally entering the foyer. "He is gone," she said to Georgiana when they met in the drawing room.

"Fitzwilliam will return soon. He loves you, Elizabeth; my brother will not tarry in Hull." Georgiana smiled at seeing Elizabeth so distraught.

"I know I am being foolish, Georgiana, but I feel I may never see Fitzwilliam again." Elizabeth sat down in Darcy's favorite chair, touching the arms of it as the emptiness overtook her heart. "Please be safe, Fitzwilliam," she whispered.

Darcy spent the night at Lord and Lady Pennington's estate. "We are pleased you are back so soon, Fitzwilliam," Lady Pennington told him over dinner. "Why do you travel to Hull tomorrow?"

"I have important business."

"What kind of business could take you from your bride so soon?" His Lordship asked in an amused manner.

"May I be discreet?"

"Of course," Lord Pennington said quickly and then dismissed the servants in the room.

Darcy waited patiently until only they remained. "I travel to Hull because it came to my attention your former guest Captain Rutherford has on more than one occasion questioned my sister regarding our family's interest in Mr. Harrison. Harrison believes the captain to be a dangerous individual."

Lady Pennington gasped, "This cannot be, Fitzwilliam!"

"I hope you are correct, Lady Margaret. Yet, I must find out what others know of the captain. If he simply opposes Mr. Harrison's views, I want to know. If the captain has more aggressive ideas, I must be aware of those also."

"How is Mr. Harrison a factor in Georgiana's future?" Lady Margaret asked.

"Harrison spent nearly a month at Pemberley learning how to run Hines Park. He expressed an interest in Georgiana, but Mrs. Darcy insisted the man wait until after Georgiana's next birthday to openly express his intentions. Elizabeth feared we knew too little of him."

"Your wife is very astute," Lord Pennington remarked, and Darcy nodded in agreement.

Darcy returned to his retelling. "Mr. Harrison has very strong beliefs about the slave trade; he sold off his father's holdings in the Americas because of his beliefs. Although I am not so politically inclined, I admire Mr. Harrison for his fortitude and his integrity. Yet, I do not wish to place my sister in danger."

"Then you believe Georgiana returns Mr. Harrison's interest?" Lady Pennington inquired.

"Elizabeth believes as such, and she has Georgiana's confidences. They are quite close."

"Then we, too, will make ourselves more aware of Captain Rutherford's associates," Lord Pennington stated.

Darcy asked, "Then you know little of him?"

"An acquaintance from Leeds recommended the captain,

with the understanding he was also familiar to Edward," Lady Margaret shared. "We know his father, although not well. He has a reputation for being quite ruthless; we were pleasantly surprised to find the son to be so amiable."

"The apple does not fall far from the tree," Darcy said with a degree of irony. "Could the captain's appearance be a façade?"

Lord Pennington answered, "Anything is possible."

"May I ask your Lordship if you think of anything of which I should be aware, you will send word to me at Pemberley?"

"Then you will not return here after you leave Hull?" Lady Margaret asked.

"Under the circumstances, I believe it best if I go to Leeds to ascertain what I can of the captain and his father the Earl," Darcy mused.

Lord Pennington agreed thoroughly, "You are correct, my boy."

The evening finished with the three of them sharing every conversation they had with Captain Rutherford. Darcy departed early the next morning for Hull, concerned more than ever with his sister's safety and the mystery surrounding the "amiable" Captain Rutherford.

North of Hemswell, Darcy's coach came to an abrupt halt along an isolated stretch of road. At first, he knew not what happened, but as Darcy opened the coach door, a long gun greeted him, and he immediately knew the precarious position in which he found himself. His coachman and a postilion stood with their hands raised as three armed men moved them gingerly away from the coach.

"There be no killin' if ye do what we say," one of the men called out. Another of the men began to rummage for valuables and weapons found upon the coach, tossing trunks along side of the road.

"Take what you want, but leave my men alone," Darcy ordered the man holding the gun on them.

"Ye stand back," the man ordered and leveled a gun at Darcy's face.

Darcy stepped back, allowing the man access to the coach. The belongings could be replaced; a man's life could not. Once the robbers took what they wanted from the coach, they motioned for Darcy to move off toward the woods.

Darcy demanded, "You have what you want. Leave us alone."

"We think ye oughter be askin' for mercy," the man laughed.

Darcy realized quickly the robbery might not be the whole purpose of this detainment. He edged back; in the past he might take a chance, but with Elizabeth and the baby in his life, he took a more cautious approach. "What else do you need from me?" he asked softly.

The man asserted, "Ye be askin' too many questions."

"Questions about what?" Darcy began to look around, trying to determine what should be his next course of action.

The third man warned, "Aye'm not done w'ye."

Out of the corner of his eye, Darcy saw the coachman take a step to the side; he tried to warn the man with a nod of his head, but it was too late. The coachman lunged at the shortest of the attackers, and the melee began. The postilion died instantly, a bullet to his head. Darcy saw it, although he had no time to focus on the act, for he struggled with two of the men. The blows came hard and fast; Darcy fought valiantly, but the men's combined strength proved too much for him.

As if in slow motion, Darcy felt the robber's fist strike him under the chin. His jaw jammed shut, and the blood spurted from Darcy's mouth as he bit his own tongue. The blow spun his head around, forcing him to turn awkwardly in place; losing his balance, he found himself falling backwards. When his head hit the rock, the pain immediately came, and the blood gushed from the gash. He tried desperately to raise his body from where it lay, but try as he may, all Darcy could do was to roll to his side.

He saw the men shoot the coachman and climb onto their horses to retreat, but he could make no sense of what else happened. A fourth well-dressed man bent over him. "You will not need these items." The man hissed as he took Darcy's walking stick and diamond stickpin. "Nor this." The man ripped the ring bearing the family crest from Darcy's finger.

"No," Darcy moaned loudly, trying to resist the man's thievery.

Then the filcher strode to the horse awaiting him. Mounting, he looked back at Darcy lying on the ground and tipped his hat to him. The man's blond, tight curls glistening in the late afternoon was all Darcy could decipher; riding tall in the saddle, the man took the lead. The rest became a haze, and Darcy lay without moving. "Elizabeth," he whispered as his eyes closed—"my dearest Elizabeth."

When the Donnelly coach came upon what was left of Darcy's chaise and four, Darcy had lain along the road for nearly twenty hours. He moved very little, the blow to his head keeping him from being mobile. He expected to die there along this deserted path on more than one occasion during those first few hours, but somehow he maintained his hold on life.

"Miss Donnelly," the steward said, coming to the window of the stopped coach, knocking on the window with a gloved hand.

"Yes, Mr. Lansing." The lady turned to her faithful aide.

"Madam, evidently there was a robbery."

The lady gasped, "Is anyone hurt?" She could see the clothing strewn on the ground.

"Two people are dead, Madam, but Walton reports they found a gentleman. He is injured, obviously losing a substantial amount of blood."

"Should I attempt to go to him?" The woman looked uneasy at this possibility.

"Madam," Lansing began again, "the scene is too much—far too much for a lady of your delicate nature—a lady such as yourself should not be exposed to such sights."

"What must we do, Mr. Lansing? I must perform my charitable duty; we cannot leave the gentleman to die. Should we not bring the man to safety?"

The man seemed relieved his mistress made the suggestion first. "Walton and a footman could wrap the gentleman in a blanket, but that would mean placing him on the floor of the coach. Would that be acceptable, Madam? We could leave the window of the coach open. It might be a bit uncomfortable, but otherwise the gentleman could pay with his life." Mr. Lansing knew his mistress's preoccupation with cleanliness.

"Of course, Mr. Lansing." She took a handkerchief from the sleeve of her dress. "I will be able to endure what is necessary to save the man's life." Her hand shook and her lip quivered with the thought of the man's dirty body lying within the coach.

Mr. Lansing handed her a bottle of smelling salts. "In case you are feeling poorly, Madam."

"Bring the gentleman to the coach. Also, retrieve as many of his belongings as seem appropriate," she ordered at last.

"Yes, Madam." Lansing bowed as he left.

A footman and the lady's coachman carried the man's body between them, supporting his long limbs under his knees and shoulders. It took them several attempts to wrestle Darcy's body onto the floor of the Donnelly coach, where he lay like a freshly caught fish. Before they wrapped his body in the blanket spread on the floor of the coach, Miss Donnelly ascertained the injured man to be a man of consequence, but dried blood and dirt covered his face, obscuring his identity.

"We return to the estate, Walton," she told the coachman. "We will get the gentleman a proper doctor; the local villages have no one to attend him."

"Yes, Madam." The coachman replaced his gloves. "The

new doctor arrived two weeks ago; I am sure he will be pleased to be of service to you."

"Remind Mr. Lansing to speak to the doctor before he enters Darling Hall," she instructed the coachman.

"I will do so, Madam. We will begin immediately." The coachman closed the door. Once they loaded the gentleman's luggage onto her coach, Miss Donnelly covered her mouth with the handkerchief to block the man's repugnant smell and pulled her feet closer to her body; then she rapped on the roof of the coach to start for home.

The movement of the coach roused the man somewhat. "Elizabeth," he moaned from his parched lips. For a moment, Miss Donnelly thought the stranger called her name, but he did not open his eyes nor did he move on his own. Instead, the man's body rocked back and forth with the movement of the carriage. It took Miss Donnelly nearly an hour and a half to reach her estate. The journey with the invasion of her private space by the man's body seemed interminable for the lady. She fought back the unladylike involuntary spasms her stomach demanded; she shielded her eyes from the sight of his badly beaten body, and she silenced her ears to his moans of pain. As much as possible, Miss Donnelly treated the man as if he did not exist.

Reaching Brigg, the Donnelly coach turned for Darling Hall, the family estate. Since the demise of her parents, the estate belonged to Elizabeth Donnelly. No male cousins existed for several generations, and Miss Donnelly's parents had the foresight to provide her with an additional legal binding—a sort of codicil. The estate belonged to her until the time of her death. However, if Miss Donnelly chose to marry before her eight and twenty birthday, she would inherit an additional fifty thousand pounds. Of course, the second option would be society's preferable choice, as well as hers. Although not grand in scale, the estate could provide an adequate living if handled properly. Unfortunately, of late, it experienced several monetary losses, and Miss Donnelly secretly sold off artwork, furnishings, and tapestries to pay the taxes and to meet her extravagant expenses.

In appearance, Miss Donnelly's beauty seemed an asset in attracting men, and the estate served as a second means of securing an appropriate mate. The woman possessed excellent manners and correct opinions; yet, she did not stir interest with social circles and the *ton*. She had peculiar habits, which many men could not tolerate even in a woman with wealth and beauty as her "selling" points.

Arriving finally at Darling Hall, the footman and coachman unloaded Darcy's body. "Mr. Lansing, place the gentleman in the blue suite and have Mr. Logan fetch the new physician. Tell the stable staff to clean the coach thoroughly. If necessary, remove and replace the upholstery within the coach. The fulsome smell of the gentleman's body must be obliterated; I will not tolerate the man's presence and his blood and his body fluids soiling my coach. I want all his clothing washed properly; if the items are stained beyond repair, burn them. Once the physician tends to him, please have the gentleman cleaned properly. Of course, you know what to do with his bedclothes."

"Yes, Madam," the steward bowed.

"Although the man is injured, I will not tolerate his bringing his dirt into my house," she demanded. "Tell Julian to clean these steps once again."

"I will speak to him, Madam."

"Finally, tell Mildred I wish a bath immediately."

The man smirked when his mistress looked the other way. "I am sure she prepares one as we speak."

Irritated, she said, "You are dismissed, Mr. Lansing."

"Yes, Madam." The steward made his final bow.

Miss Donnelly entered the drawing room of Darling Hall. Before she took a seat, the lady walked about the room, touching the various items, inspecting them and looking carefully at her glove after each touch. When she came to the figurines along the mantelpiece, Miss Donnelly frowned and reached for the bell cord. "Did you ring?" The housemaid curtsied when she entered the room.

Miss Donnelly did not answer; she simply stood with her gloved index finger extended. "I will address it immediately, Miss Donnelly, and I will speak to the new maid regarding her duties," the servant stammered.

"Do so or both of you will be seeking new positions," the mistress threatened.

The older woman dropped her eyes. "Yes, Madam."

"I expect this to be cleaned thoroughly by the time I return," the lady demanded before exiting to her chambers.

Nearly three hours later, the steward found Miss Donnelly at her embroidery in the newly cleaned drawing room. "Miss Donnelly." He tapped lightly at the door before entering.

"Yes, Mr. Lansing," she spoke as the man entered the room. "Has the physician seen the gentleman? What news does he give about the man's health?"

"The physician came and went, Miss Donnelly. The gentleman, as we suspected, lost a good deal of blood. The doctor says with the blood loss and his head injury, the man is likely to sleep several days. Mr. Addison fears some mental functions may be affected. I placed Conrad in the man's room to observe his progress and meet his needs. The staff is cleaning the gentleman and his room. Mrs. Lewis cleaned his clothing as you specified."

"Thank you, Mr. Lansing. I may try to visit the gentleman later."

"Yes, Miss Donnelly."

For five days Fitzwilliam Darcy lay on the fine bedclothes of the blue suite at Darling Hall. He had no visitors, including Miss Donnelly, attended only by an old servant named Conrad. The physician called daily; the servants cleaned the room daily; the steward James Lansing reported to his mistress daily.

To say Miss Donnelly did not visit the gentleman would be a fabrication. The first night he lay unconscious on the pillows of the blue suite, Miss Donnelly's curiosity got the best of her judgment. So, in the middle of the night, she left her bedchamber and stole down the dimly lit hallway to the man's room. She knew the rest of the household slept, and she would go unnoticed.

Conrad snoozed on the pallet in front of the fireplace. Miss Donnelly knew he would not stir unless she did something foolish. With a gloved hand, she gingerly turned the door's handle and slipped into where the man slept. All day long she wondered what he looked like. His body she recognized in the coach to be physically pleasing. Could his countenance, once smeared with blood and dirt, prove as attractive?

Taking the candle to light her way, Miss Donnelly tiptoed to where the gentleman lay. It took only seconds for her eyes to adjust to the shadows lying across his face. A slight gasp of excitement slipped from her lips before she allowed herself a smile of recognition. She met him only once in London. She attended a private party at the home of Mr. and Mrs. Albert Hurst, friends of a distant cousin. It was a little over a year ago, shortly after Christmas. They spoke cordially to each other several times during the evening, and she thought the man seemed interested in her; but shortly after their introductions, he withdrew within himself, and the evening ended on a sour note. The man reclining on the pillows in her blue suite was Fitzwilliam Darcy.

"Miss Donnelly, you sent for me, Ma'am?" Mr. Lansing entered the study.

She looked up from the letter to which she attended. Miss Donnelly took the time to blot the ink and seal the letter with wax before she acknowledged the man standing in attendance to her. "Have a seat, Mr. Lansing." She pointed to a high-backed chair placed at an angle to the desk.

The man leaned back in the chair, glad to have a moment to rest. "Is there a problem, Miss Donnelly?"

She took a folded piece of paper from the drawer and slid it across the desktop to Lansing.

He leaned forward, removed his gloves, and picked up the page while eyeing the estate's mistress. Inside the folded paper he found fifty pounds. A knowing smile overtook his face. "Miss Donnelly, how generous of you."

"It is my way of thanking you for helping me save my cousin Frederick's life." The lady nodded, knowing he would understand the subtext of this conversation.

"Your cousin Frederick." He repeated the words as if committing them to memory.

"Yes, my cousin Frederick—the one we found on the road and brought back to Darling Hall so he and I might marry." The corners of her mouth turned upward.

Lansing's eyes sparkled with mischief. "The cousin to marry so you inherit the additional fifty thousand pounds left in your parents' will—that cousin."

Her voice took on a conspiratorial tone. "As my steward, you are well aware of my parents' wishes. I will be eight and twenty in four months; should I not consider the offer of my cousin's hand?"

"I agree; marriage to your cousin would seem a viable solution to your problem. Should I review the papers we found in your *cousin's* possession in the coach?" Lansing picked up on her tone.

"I believe most of my cousin's papers were lost or burned in the attack."

Lansing wiped his mouth with the back of his hand, and Miss Donnelly snarled her nose in disgust. "I apologize, Miss Donnelly," he said as he slid on his gloves once again.

She fanned her face as if the saliva he left on the back of his hand spread danger.

Trying to divert her quirky ablutions, he continued, "Again, Miss Donnelly, you are very generous. Why so much?"

"I assumed you might need to remind key staff members my cousin Frederick resided with us for three weeks. He went to Hull on business and to obtain a license for our marriage. He was attacked upon his return. Do you remember all those details?"

Lansing thumbed through the paper and folded it once again, sliding it in his jacket pocket. "I remember it all clearly, Miss Donnelly." He stood to leave. "I remain your faithful servant."

The afternoon Darcy finally opened his eyes, no one he recognized seemed to be about. The only person in the room, a servant who identified himself as Conrad, insisted the gentleman not move or leave the bed until someone could fetch the physician.

"Sir, my name is Mr. Addison. I attend you."

Darcy pushed himself up in the bed. "Mr. Addison, could you tell me where I am and why I am here?"

"You were robbed from what I understand, Sir." The doctor examined Darcy's wounds. "You are at Darling Hall near Brigg. Miss Donnelly brought you here."

"Miss Donnelly?" A question seemed appropriate.

"I am new to the area myself, Sir. Miss Donnelly owns this estate," the doctor added as he finished his examination. "Your wounds heal nicely; you should be able to return home soon,

Mr. . . . I am afraid I do not know your name."

"I am . . . I am . . . I cannot remember my name. What is my name?" Terror spread across Darcy's face; he looked beseechingly at the man.

"It is all right, Sir," Mr. Addison tried to allay Darcy's fears. "This is common after a wound such as yours; a brief memory loss makes sense. You have been here for five days, and you were lying on the road for possibly several days before that time. Your body suffered a great shock. Such an injury would cause some confusion. I am sure Miss Donnelly can answer your questions; she had her men retrieve your belongings. Possibly there is some form of marking among your things."

He allowed the physician to push him back down on the bed. "When may I see Miss Donnelly?"

"I will tell her steward, and he will address your concerns to Miss Donnelly," Mr. Addison assured him. "I need for you to take it easy, Sir. It is likely you will experience dizzy spells for a few days. I want Conrad here to bring you some broth and to gradually increase your food intake so you might regain your strength."

Darcy felt the chaos of the situation. "You will send for Miss Donnelly?"

"I will do so, Sir. I will call upon you again in a few days." With that, the physician exited the room.

Darcy found himself alone again. Where was he? Who was he? Who was Miss Donnelly? There were too many questions to which he had no answers. He lay back on the bed, trying to forcibly remember some of the details of his life.

He waited for Miss Donnelly to appear, but the lady did not come. "Where is she?" he spoke to no one in particular.

"The mistress does not think it to be proper for her to enter a gentleman's bedchamber," Conrad, the servant, informed him as he tended to the serving tray.

"Then send me her steward," Darcy demanded. "He can relay the information, or give me paper and pen and I will address Miss Donnelly in writing."

"A lady could not receive a letter from anyone but her husband or her intended," Conrad reasoned.

Darcy's frustration showed; he wanted to leave the bed, but every time he tried to stand, he was beset with incoherent dizziness. "Someone help me," he moaned as he forced himself to sleep.

After breakfast, Darcy and his friend rode to her estate. As usual, tender words of his worth greeted the other gentleman. Darcy, on the other hand, received a cold welcome; yet, he did not care what her mother said or did. His eyes searched Elizabeth's face, trying to see what she must be thinking about him after being so chastised by his aunt. Before her mother had time to tell Darcy of his aunt's calling upon the family, his friend said, "It is a beautiful day. May we take a walk and enjoy the weather?"

Soon five set off together; his friend and Elizabeth's eldest sister lagged behind, allowing the others to outstrip them. Little discourse occurred between the three remaining; her younger sister was in awe of the "haughty Mr. Darcy." Darcy and Elizabeth each formed a resolution to speak what had not been said before.

When they reached the path leading to a neighboring lodge, her younger sister asked to be excused, and then they two walked on in silence for a few moments. He tried to get the courage to approach her when Elizabeth found her voice, "Sir, I am a very selfish creature, and for the sake of giving in to my own feelings, care not how much I may be wounding yours."

What was she saying? She did not care if she hurt his feelings? He was devastated; he was too late. His aunt's rebukes combined with his earlier insecurities showed Elizabeth she wanted nothing of him.

"I can no longer help thanking you for your unexampled kindness to my poor sister."

She did not speak of his aunt's attack, but she knew about his involvement in her sister's marriage. Now, as was customary, Elizabeth would be obligated to marry him.

"Ever since I have known it, I have been most anxious to acknowledge to you how gratefully I feel it. Were it known to the rest of my family, I should not have merely my own gratitude to express."

There it was—the dreaded word "gratitude." He did not want Elizabeth's gratitude; he wanted her love. What could he say to her now? He never wanted her to know of his part in the wedding. Darcy stopped and turned toward her. Elizabeth stopped, too, and they faced each other for a few infinitely long seconds. Without planning to say so, her words of "gratitude" drove him forward. "I am sorry, exceedingly sorry, you have been informed of what may, in a mistaken light, have given you uneasiness. I never wanted you to know; it was not done to make you feel an obligation to repay. I did not think your aunt was so little to be trusted."

Elizabeth glanced up briefly at him; the tension was so thick. Both knew what needed to be said, but neither could broach the subject. She tried to explain how her youngest sister's foolishness let the news of his attending his worst enemy's wedding slip out. Then she said, "You must not blame my aunt. My youngest sister's thoughtlessness first betrayed to me that you had been concerned in the matter, and, of course, I could not rest till I knew the particulars. Let me thank you again and again, in the name of all my family, for that generous compassion which induced you to take so much trouble, and bear so many mortifications, for the sake of discovering them. It truly befuddles me why you would put yourself through all that trouble."

She left him the opening. She could not understand why he troubled himself with the man he hated most in the world. How could he overcome such mortifications? Darcy loved her; that is why. His sister demanded it; that is why. "If you will thank me, let it be for yourself alone. That the wish of giving happiness to you might add force to the other inducements, which led me on I shall not attempt to deny. But your family owes me nothing. Much as I respect them, I believe I thought only of you."

Silence enveloped them; he wanted her to say something or do something to let him know if he overstepped the limits. Yet, she was never silent, he thought. If he offended her, Elizabeth's temperament would be to reprimand him. Dare he believe she would willingly listen to him? When he looked closely at her downcast face, he saw her embarrassment but not her disdain. He could contain it no longer, and he added, "You are too generous to trifle with me. If your feelings are still what they were last April, tell me so at once. My affections and wishes are unchanged, but one word from you will silence me on the subject forever."

Now he waited, frozen in time, forgetting even how to breathe; his eyes searched her face, anticipating her answer. An eternity passed as he waited; finally, Elizabeth raised her eyes to his. "Sir," she said the words slowly as if to convince herself as much as him, "my feelings . . . my feelings are so different from what they were last April. My sentiments have gone through a full array of emotions since the period to which you allude; I willingly receive your present assurances. The fact you still seek my love gives me great pleasure."

The conviction with which she said the words made the dream real, and he slowly lifted her hand to his lips and kissed it tenderly. "My Love, I have imagined this moment so many times, but never once did I feel such contentment and exhilaration at the same time." Transfixed, they stayed that way for many minutes, fighting the urge to smother each other with kisses. "You are beautiful, my Dearest One." Elizabeth started to drop her eyes, but he lifted her chin with his finger. "If you plan to drop your eyes each time I tell you how much I love you, my Dearest, you will forever be looking at the floor. You need never to look down again." She rested her hand on his chest; he wondered if she felt the faint trembling and the erratic beating of his heart. He closed his eyes, and her nearness consumed him. "My Love, you have stolen my heart; I cannot live without you. Please say you will be my wife."

"I can think of nothing more perfect than our matrimonial felicity. Being forever known as your wife would be my happiest desire." His breath caught in his throat; Elizabeth was finally his. Now so close he

could feel her breath on his cheeks, his arms enveloped her as she offered her mouth for their first kiss.

"I have been waiting for you," he whispered into her ear. The passion in his voice made her body tremble, and he instinctively moved in closer to support her. He dreamed of this moment for over a year; the pure pleasure of tasting her lips and holding her at last radiated through his body.

★ ★ ★

Elizabeth looked at the clock once again. How many hours would it take for her husband to return to Pemberley? The night without him lasted forever. She tossed and turned, trying to find a comfortable place to sleep; yet, the bed was the same one she shared with Darcy. The difference lay in his absence. How had she come to so depend on him for her existence? She needed Darcy as she needed air. She sat at her embroidery, but her mind drifted to the man she loved. Elizabeth felt him today, and the feeling brought her little comfort. She put her needlework down and walked to the window to look out over the grounds of the estate, the home he loved. Darcy wanted her here with him.

Hugging herself and trying to still the fear creeping into her heart, Elizabeth whispered his name, "Fitzwilliam," before closing her eyes, hoping to capture his image. "I miss you, my Husband," she mumbled to the emptiness of the room. Elizabeth swayed, thinking of his arms around her and the endearments Darcy offered when he held her near. Finally, she turned back to find something to pass the time. Maybe she would write a letter to Jane; sitting at Darcy's desk would ease her longing. She crossed behind the furniture, striding purposely to the door when suddenly a pain—a sharp, penetrating pain —brought her to an abrupt halt. She clasped the back of her head, swooning from the pressure radiating through her.

Images of Darcy flashed before her eyes as flames of a candle flickering in the wind. "Fitzwilliam," she screamed as the blackness overcame her.

The smelling salts pulled at Elizabeth's consciousness. "Mrs. Darcy," she heard Mrs. Reynolds's voice. "Can you hear me, Mrs. Darcy?" A cool cloth gently touched her face, teasing Elizabeth's eyes open, blinking several times to force her senses to respond.

"Elizabeth?" Georgiana's face appeared above hers. "Elizabeth, are you all right?"

Elizabeth fought hard to make clear her immediate thoughts. "Where is Fitzwilliam?"

"My brother is not here. Do you know what happened, Elizabeth?" Georgiana tried to lift Elizabeth's head from the floor.

"Georgiana, we must find Fitzwilliam." Elizabeth pushed herself up as the urgency rushed into her voice.

Georgiana tried to assure her. "My brother is in Hull, Elizabeth."

"No," she demanded. "He needs me. I heard him call my name. Please believe me; Fitzwilliam needs me." She clutched at Georgiana's hands. "We must go to him; we must help him."

"You fainted, Mrs. Darcy." The housekeeper supported Elizabeth to her feet as the mistress stood gingerly. "Mr. Darcy is away, but he will return in a few days." Mrs. Reynolds helped her to the nearest chair.

The panic set in; Elizabeth looked at each of them with eyes enlarged by the fright. "Do you not understand? Fitzwilliam needs me. He is in pain. I felt his pain. Please help me, Georgiana," Elizabeth pleaded.

"My brother is fine, Elizabeth." Georgiana took her hand.

Elizabeth sat down dejectedly. How could she make them understand? All her reason told her Darcy would return in a few days, but something of her fear remained. She looked about, finally forcing a smile to her face although the feeling of dread did not leave the pit of her stomach. "Of course, Fitzwilliam is well," she said the words, trying to convince herself of their truth. "I do not know what happened."

"Shall I send for Mr. Spencer, Madam? Is it the child?" The woman's loyalty to Pemberley caused her to think of the heir Elizabeth carried.

"No, I am fine; there is no need for Mr. Spencer. I just overextended myself once again. I assure you I am well." Elizabeth strained to persuade them of her health while still feeling an emptiness only Darcy's presence could fill. "Please, I will be fine; I simply need a few moments to recover my balance."

"Let me help you to your rooms, Mrs. Darcy," Mrs. Reynolds suggested.

Elizabeth stammered, "Maybe I will lie down for awhile."

She allowed the Darcys' trusted housekeeper to help her to her sitting room and bedchamber, and although she put on a happy face, she could not escape the apprehension that clutched at her heart. As she lay across the bed, clasping at the embroidered pillow, Elizabeth allowed her eyes to close. "Stay with me, Fitzwilliam," she whispered. "Do not leave me; come home to Pemberley. I am here, my Love." Tears welled in her eyes, and silent sobs soon racked her shoulders.

For the next few days, Elizabeth forced herself to go through the motions of being Pemberley's mistress. She and Georgiana visited several of the tenants; she had fittings for new dresses. Now, with her condition, Elizabeth needed additional items, but her heart did not participate in these activities. Her heart wanted Darcy home; then everything else would be important once again.

Elizabeth stood for hours watching the lane leading to Pemberley, knowing Darcy would return sometime in the next couple of days. She wondered why she had no word from him;

Darcy would send an express, but Elizabeth heard nothing. So, her eyes searched the lane, watching for Darcy's coach to return. "Please, Fitzwilliam," she whispered to her reflection in the window. "I need you here, my Love."

CHAPTER 8

"It is not time or opportunity that is to determine intimacy;
it is disposition alone."
Jane Austen, *Sense and Sensibility*, 1811

On the sixth day of Darcy's absence, an express post arrived. Elizabeth assumed it was "from" her husband, but then she realized it was "for" her husband. She took the letter into his study, debating whether she should read it. Finally, she reasoned Darcy planned for her to act in his stead so she broke the seal and set down at his desk to read the missive. Immediately, Elizabeth's hands began to shake and she gasped, holding one of Darcy's handkerchiefs to her mouth to stifle the sound.

21 February

Mr. Darcy,

I assume the delay in our meeting resulted in your finding the information you sought elsewhere. I am sorry you were unable to come to Hull; I anticipated seeing the man you became; I possess fond memories of meeting your esteemed father. We all found his insights helpful, especially in our early years.

What did this mean? Fitzwilliam went not to Hull after all. How was that possible? The dread she experienced the last few days made it hard for her to swallow.

In case you still need my help in seeking information on Captain James Rutherford, I enclose a separate list of details regarding the man. Some of them are quite interesting, as I am sure you will agree. I look forward to meeting you one day soon.

Hannah More

Elizabeth flipped quickly to the second page to peruse the information contained within. She still felt confused. What did all this mean? Her husband never met with Hannah More as he planned, and she heard nothing from him. Her mind raced with what to do next. Without thinking, she rang for one of the maids.

"Yes, Madam," the woman appeared instantaneously.

"Have Mr. Howard attend me at once," Elizabeth demanded.

"Yes, Madam."

She returned to her reading.

> *Captain James Rutherford*
> *second son of Earl of Leeds*
> *attended Oxford for one year*
> *school suspended his education for undisclosed reasons*
> *served two years in navy*
> *recently dismissed from his position*
> *ruthless treatment of his subordinates*
> *made moderate fortune while in the service*
> *took inordinate chances to achieve a bounty*
> *many men lost lives under his command*
> *reportedly highly in debt*
> *known to be intimate with questionable associates*

Mr. Darcy, I hope these facts serve your purposes. – H. M.

Elizabeth's eyes scanned the paper again; she could barely breathe. Darcy had not arrived in Hull—that was apparent from Hannah More's letter. Plus, Miss More's correspondence indicated some serious facts about Captain Rutherford, all of which she needed to discuss with her husband.

Mr. Howard's appearance at the door interrupted Elizabeth's thoughts. "Mr. Howard, I need for you to go to Hull as soon as possible. Mr. Darcy did not arrive as expected; I fear something bad happened. I will write out a note to Miss More while you make arrangements."

"Of course, Mrs. Darcy," Mr. Howard's concern came at once. "I will take some men with me; we will leave within the hour."

Georgiana appeared at the door of the study. "Elizabeth, I was told there was an express. . . . " Georgiana's words froze in the air, seeing Elizabeth's distraught look. She rushed to her sister's side. Kneeling in front of her, Georgiana begged, "Elizabeth, what happened?"

Elizabeth handed Georgiana the letter, unable to answer out loud. Georgiana snatched the letter and read it quickly. "My Goodness!" Georgiana exclaimed. "What do we do?"

"Mr. Howard took several men; he left for Hull moments ago," Elizabeth answered as if not comprehending. "I gave him explicit directions to send word immediately." They sat in complete silence for a few minutes, each engrossed in what they thought. "Georgiana, where could Fitzwilliam be?" she whispered the words.

Georgiana knew Elizabeth needed a reasonable answer, but, try as she may, she could offer her sister no solace. "My brother must be all right." Georgiana said the words as much to convince herself as Elizabeth. "He had trouble with the coach, or Fitzwilliam took his business elsewhere. Anything could happen." Georgiana's words poured out. "But nothing is wrong." Tears misted her eyes.

Elizabeth reached out and pulled Georgiana to her. "Oh, Georgiana, what will we do?" The fear of losing Darcy encompassed her; sobs of anguish smothered her.

Georgiana allowed her own tears to flow. "Fitzwilliam is all right," she repeated. "My brother is all right; he will be home soon."

Over the next three days, Elizabeth and Georgiana rarely left the house. They stood for hours watching the lane heading to Pemberley, hoping Darcy's coach would appear.

"Fitzwilliam has been gone ten days," Elizabeth said out loud, although she spoke to no one in particular.

"He will return soon," Georgiana responded.

They had multiple conversations of a similar nature since receiving the letter from Miss More. One moment they felt absolute despair at the possibility Darcy may never come home; the next moment they knew he must be safe.

The solitary figure of Clayton Ashford traveled the lane to Pemberley on a regular basis to visit with Kitty Bennet, but today he struggled with what he must do. "Mr. Ashford," the maid announced.

"Show him in," Elizabeth answered from behind Darcy's desk. With her husband away, it was the only place she felt his presence. She could not dare to think of his absence from her bed so she focused on the study from where he did all his work.

"Mrs. Darcy." Ashford made his bow upon entering the room.

"Good morning, Sir. I am afraid my sister has not come down to breakfast. You are a bit early today." Elizabeth offered the vicar half a smile.

"I did not come to speak to Miss Bennet," he said solemnly. "I came to speak to you, Mrs. Darcy."

Elizabeth froze, afraid of what he might mean. "Mr. Ashford, your tone tells me this is not a social call."

"Mrs. Darcy, please come and sit with me." He ushered Elizabeth to a nearby chair.

Elizabeth stammered, "You frighten me, Sir, with your seriousness."

"There is no way to say this without bringing you hurt." He heard Elizabeth gasp. "An urgent express came this morning from Mr. Howard. He asked me to bring you his news for he feared you might require my comfort upon hearing it."

"It is Fitzwilliam, is it not?" Elizabeth's eyes searched Ashford's face for the truth.

Ashford took her hands in his. "Mr. Howard writes he found Mr. Darcy's carriage north of Hemswell. A robbery obviously occurred. The road is one not often traveled, but, evidently, looters stripped the coach of anything of value, including Mr. Darcy's personal belongings. The coachman and postilion were both dead. There was no sign of Mr. Darcy, however. Mr. Howard and the men organized a search of the surrounding villages and woods. He plans to question those he finds about what they may know. Mr. Howard made arrangements to ship the bodies home for a proper burial."

"Fitzwilliam is not dead," Elizabeth said softly.

"Mr. Howard writes he hopes to know more over the next few days." Mr. Ashford expected Mrs. Darcy to break into tears, but instead she stared off as if seeing images.

"My husband is not dead." She reached out to lightly caress the cleric's cheek. "Fitzwilliam is alive."

"Mrs. Darcy, we sincerely hope you are right, but Mr. Howard's letter does not offer much hope. You must be prepared to face the possibility of Mr. Darcy's untimely demise." Ashford knew people often denied their hurt in such situations. "Would you like me to pray with you, Mrs. Darcy?"

"Mr. Ashford, I do not wish to seem unrepentant, but my prayers are already answered. I knew as much for several days if I just listened to my heart. I felt Fitzwilliam's pain, but of late I felt his peacefulness. He may be hurt, but my husband is not dead. He speaks to me in my dreams."

Ashford pleaded, "Mrs. Darcy, please let me help you."

"I will not hear of it, Mr. Ashford." Elizabeth leveled her best Darcy stare on the man. "If my husband were dead, there would be a body. If Fitzwilliam lives, I am content to wait for his return."

"If it is acceptable, I remain at Pemberley in case you, Miss Darcy, or Miss Bennet may need my services?" Ashford looked a bit confused by her insistence.

"You are always welcome, Mr. Ashford." Elizabeth actually smiled. "Thank you for coming to us today." She stood, the enigmatic smile flitting across her face. "You are most welcomed."

"Miss Bennet," Ashford spoke softly to Kitty, "your sister seeks comfort where none may exist."

"Elizabeth is the strongest and the most realistic of us," Kitty assured him. "If she believes Mr. Darcy is alive, I do not doubt her. I never saw two people so in love—so connected— if my sister says Mr. Darcy speaks to her in her dreams, I would believe her if I were you, Sir."

"Do you truly believe such a love can exist?"

"Many would tell you such a love could only exist in the pages of a novel, but there is not a woman alive who does not believe in the possibility of finding her great love. My sister is fortunate to be loved by Mr. Darcy."

"What of you, Miss Bennet?" Ashford suddenly felt inadequate. "Do you wish for such a love, too?"

"I want a husband who treats me with respect and listens to my simple ramblings without tiring of me. Mr. Darcy once told me when he kissed Elizabeth for the first time, it was like coming home. Any woman would wish to affect her husband as such."

During this, Kitty did not realize Ashford moved closer to her. When she turned her head, Ashford's mouth was only inches from hers. "Miss Bennet," he stammered, "please forgive me." He caressed her jaw line.

Kitty whispered, "For what should I offer forgiveness?"

"For this." Ashford lowered his mouth to hers. The kiss lasted only a few elongated seconds, but the tantalizing tingle both felt when he withdrew stayed with them. Their eyes locked, and their breathing came in short bursts. "Katherine," he whispered as his thumb stroked her cheek. "I want to be the man you love."

Kitty thought of the difference in the kiss she described to Mr. Darcy earlier and the one she just experienced. "Clayton," she offered him a teasing smile, "I never knew you were so romantic."

"You bring out the best in me." Ashford gifted her with a smile of his own.

Kitty held back a sigh; Clayton Ashford confused her. Was he shy? Evidently, that was not an accurate estimation. His piety could be questioned at times also. The man, obviously, cared for her, but Kitty could not be sure of her own feelings although she would not let him know. Mr. Ashford could be her last chance. He was a good man, a gentle man—a gentleman—and she would learn to love. At least, he was amiable.

She said at last, "You seem very pleased, Sir."

"You do please me, Miss Bennet."

Kitty worried she might be seen by Ashford as being too forward. She did not want Lydia's reputation to follow her so she said, "We should really stop this, Sir."

Her caution bothered him; Ashford nodded his agreement and looked away in disgust. "I apologize for overstepping the bounds of propriety, Miss Bennet. Hopefully, you will see it in your heart to forgive me." Humiliated by his actions, he turned his back on Kitty and stepped away from her.

Suddenly, Kitty realized Ashford felt ashamed of what had happened. His shoulders hunched forward, withdrawing inward with his censure. Not wishing to lose this thoroughly delightful moment, she came up behind him, touching his shoulder. He turned to look at her hand on his arm, not sure what it meant. Kitty looked up into his eyes. "Did I do something to offend you, Mr. Ashford?"

"It is I who offered offense." He looked saddened by what he had done.

"You offered me no offense. It seems I might be a bit susceptible to you," she teased, but blushed from her own forwardness.

Ashford tried to reason with himself before he spoke again. Having her touch his arm sent shards of longing through him. He knew as the spiritual leader of the community he should not be acting as such, but Kitty Bennet's presence was of all he thought. "When I heard the news of Mr. Darcy," he choked out the words, "I realized I could lose you, Miss Bennet, before I ever knew the pleasure of kissing you. It was a thoroughly selfish idea, which I tried desperately to resist, but even I could not ignore your words of desiring a great love." Ashford's eyes searched Kitty's face for her reaction to his words. "Please tell me you could learn to love me."

"I do not have to learn to love you, Mr. Ashford. I already do." Kitty said the words as if she meant them, trying to convince herself as much as him. The words brought the desired response from Ashford, as they visibly shot through him, he crushed her to him, holding her head to his chest and whispering words of endearment.

"Katherine, my beautiful vivacious Katherine," he whispered into her hair. "You gave me the greatest gift a man could receive."

Kitty sighed, thinking this man's depth of feeling scared her and exhilarated her at the same time. One moment he took on a serious mien, and the next he violated propriety, and as the community's religious leader, his violating propriety seemed almost amusing. Obviously, he wanted only her assurance she could love him. That, Kitty could easily do. *The man loves you,* she told herself. *He needs you; you will learn to need him, too.*

Sounds of others in the hallway forced them apart, and Ashford moved away to the window to conceal the emotional ride he just took.

"Mr. Ashford," Kitty hissed. He looked back over his

shoulder at her. Kitty knew what she would say to convince him—what he wanted to hear. "You are home, Sir," she smiled at him before taking a seat and working on her embroidery.

Ashford looked at her in amazement and offered a soft laugh. "You are incredible, Miss Bennet," he mumbled in hushed tones, "absolutely incredible."

★ ★ ★

Darcy woke from the dream with a start; he still felt the woman's breath on his cheek. "I have been waiting for you," he whispered.

He wondered, "*Waiting for whom?*" The dream seemed so real; he could feel the erratic beating of his heart and the nearness of the woman. "Elizabeth," his mind said to him, and the image disappeared. He wished he could see the woman's face in the dream. Darcy knew her name, but he wanted to see her face, then the question of who he was could be answered. If he could remember the woman in the dream, he could make sense of his life once again.

This was Darcy's world: He slept often, always dreaming of the same woman—always hearing her words of endearment—always feeling her touch him. When he did not sleep, he fussed with the servant, frustrated that the man would not help him escape the room in which he found himself. He saw no one besides the servant, and Darcy came to realize until he could leave the room on his own, the mystery of whom he was and where he was would remain. So, he set about forcing himself to get stronger. Determined, for the next three days, he ate the food brought to him; he tried walking a few steps each day, compelling his body to respond to his will.

On the fourth day, Darcy, with Conrad's help, made his way to an upstairs sitting room, and then he awaited the appearance of Miss Donnelly. When she entered, the woman made him a quick curtsy. "I am happy to see you up on your own, Sir." She smiled at him, and Darcy had a flittering image of having seen her before. "You worried us, Sir."

"Hopefully, you will forgive me for not rising." Darcy looked at the woman more closely.

"Of course, Sir." Miss Donnelly took a seat across from him.

He stared at her, trying to see something familiar in the woman. "Thank you for opening your home to me. It was most generous of you."

"I am confused," the lady said. "Why would I not open my home? Soon it will be *our* home."

Darcy now saw the woman smile at him in an enticing way. "How may this house be *our* home?"

"Oh, your condition is worse than Mr. Addison led me to believe." Miss Donnelly feigned shock.

Darcy demanded, "Then are you telling me you know who I am?"

"Of course I do!" She brought her fan to her face and began to strum the air. "This is so stressful."

"Madam," he tried to control the volume of his speech. "I have lain in that bed for nearly ten days not knowing anything about my life. I beg you, if you can speak on this matter, do so."

"Very well." Miss Donnelly dropped her eyes. "I hoped you would recall these details on your own, but I see it is not to be. My Goodness, where should I begin?"

"My name would be an excellent beginning."

"You are my cousin Frederick Donnelly, and we are engaged to be married." Miss Donnelly looked him directly in the eye while indicating the ruby ring on her gloved hand.

"We are engaged?" Darcy asked, trying to comprehend the situation in which he now found himself.

"Yes, Sir, we are. That is why I could not come to your

room during your illness; it would not be proper." A slight blush overtook her face.

Darcy stammered, "May I ask your given name?"

"Elizabeth Mavis Donnelly."

"Elizabeth," he murmured, but the feeling he experienced the last few days when he dreamed of the passionate woman did not surface; only confusion reigned.

Darcy wanted answers. "How did I come to be on the road?"

Elizabeth Donnelly continued to spin her story. Over the past week, she concocted what she thought to be a believable one. When Miss Donnelly met Fitzwilliam Darcy in London all those many months ago, he was single. If she "rushed" him into the marriage, even if he recovered his memory, he would likely not abandon her. And, if he did, she would not object. She would have her inheritance, and, besides, she hated men— hated the filth they brought into *her* house. Their hands covered in dirt. She would want no man to ever touch her unless he wore gloves. The thoughts sent a shiver through her.

Darcy saw her shiver, thinking the woman seemed reluctant to answer him. "Is there a problem, Madam?"

"No, Sir," she tried to cover her thoughts. "I just remembered the conditions in which we found you—they were so deplorable!"

Darcy did not answer; he simply nodded an understanding of the woman's sentiments, yet something about her bothered him.

"You decided to travel to Hull on business and while there secure a proper license for our ceremony. Then when you did not return in a timely manner, I worried for your safety as not returning would be uncharacteristic of such an honorable man—so I set out to follow you. We came across your carriage along the road. My household staff was dead, and you were injured. I had Mr. Lansing gather what we could, and we brought you here immediately. Needless to say, your health was my first concern. I am sure the coach has been looted by now."

The woman's recitation seemed a bit too rehearsed, but Darcy could not decipher what he should address next. Things did not seem right; yet, he could not imagine why she would purposely lie to him. "How long has our marriage been planned?" he asked suspiciously.

"Not long, in reality," she responded sweetly. "We are cousins, as I explained previously, although not close relatives. My parents died nearly three years ago; your older brother claimed your family's fortune, and a previous indiscretion," she wrinkled her nose in disgust, "caused your father to disinherit you. As you have the title, and I have the estate, I am sorry to say ours is a marriage to benefit both of our situations; however, I hope we can find a mutual affection for each other." The woman tried to entice him with her manners and her words.

"*If we marry*," Darcy stressed the words, "I would hope for a civil relationship." He did not offer the woman words of encouragement.

Trying to ply her womanly charms, she smiled at him. "I know this is difficult, but I hope we can continue our agreement once you regain your strength. Although ours is not a bond of love, it could be so in time. Prior to your attack, we came to an understanding of our relationship."

Darcy sipped his tea, barely removing the cup from his lips. "You are most generous, Madam." His words and manners took on a haughty tone. "If you have no objections, I believe I exhausted myself already. I beg your leave to retire to my chambers."

"Of course, Frederick," Miss Donnelly concluded. "I hope to see you again later then." With that, the woman rose, made a proper curtsy, and promptly left the room.

Darcy looked after her. Something did not seem right, but he could not determine the source of his concern. Perhaps his recent memory loss left holes he simply needed to fill. Perhaps the woman tried to deceive him. Either way, at the moment, he could do little but wait and see how things developed.

"Elizabeth Donnelly," he rolled the words over in his mouth, but they did not seem to fit.

Conrad helped him back to his room; the effort consumed Darcy's thoughts until he once more entered his chamber. He hobbled to the dressing area. "Are these my items, Conrad?" He tried to sound nonchalant.

"Yes, Sir, Mr. Lansing brought them in when you arrived." Conrad busied himself in turning down the freshly made bed.

Darcy picked up the handkerchief embroidered with the initials "F.D." Could it be he was really Frederick Donnelly? The name felt foreign. He clasped the handkerchief in his hand and made his way to his bed. "Conrad, when did you first know of my being a part of this household?" Darcy used the older man's shoulder for support as he lowered himself back on to the bed.

"When Mr. Lansing brought you here." Conrad strained under Darcy's weight.

The news did not totally shock him, but Darcy tried to hide his reaction. "I was not here prior to that time?" he said as casually as he could.

"I cannot say for sure, Sir; I was away taking care of me sister, she be ill, Sir—gone for over a month." Conrad pulled the bedclothes up as Darcy shifted his weight to get more comfortable.

"So, I could have been here prior to the robbery?"

"Yes, Sir, you could have. Would you like for me to ask some of the other staff?" Conrad seemed concerned.

"If you could do so discreetly," Darcy said, again trying to play down his urgency, "I would be most appreciative."

"I will do me best, Sir." Conrad retreated to the other side of the room. "Try and rest now, Sir."

"Thank you, Conrad," Darcy acknowledged the man's efforts; then he turned over in the bed and welcomed his dreams.

"Wait," he called to her. She walked ahead of him in the garden.

"Can you not keep up, Sir?" She turned around and walked backwards, smiling broadly at the man she loved.

Darcy increased his pace to overtake her. The sound of her laughter brought him such joy; he could not wait to take her in his arms. Just as he came near, Elizabeth stumbled, literally falling into his waiting arms.

"I believe I have you at a disadvantage." Darcy's desire dripped from his mouth as he pulled her closer. "You belong to me, Elizabeth." He bent to gently kiss her lips.

"What do you intend to do with me, Sir?" Elizabeth's words lightly brushed Darcy's cheek.

"Love you—love you forever," he whispered the words into her ear.

"I love you, my Dearest One." The woman's hands found a home in his thick, dark hair. Delightful sensations coursed through him as Darcy's lips returned to claim her mouth.

He gasped, "You are magnificent."

The woman in his dreams, obviously, held a connection to his previous life, but Darcy could not justify his feelings for the passionate, vivacious lady of his imagination and the reserved, calculating woman who served as his current benefactor. *Could these be my fantasies—my hope for a more loving relationship? Could I possess some repressed feelings for Miss Donnelly, which are playing out in my whimsy?*

Darcy asked Conrad to fetch him paper and ink. He decided he would record his thoughts and questions. A journal would not be his answer; he simply needed a way to organize his musings. For example, why did he not ask Miss Donnelly if someone informed his father and brother of his injuries?

Should he not write to them if for no other reason than to allay their fears of his demise? Even an indiscretion would be *forgiven* in the face of danger. Where was his father's estate? What was the nature of his reported indiscretion? Did he have marketable skills such as law or trade or the military? Where did he attend school? The number of questions grew by leaps and bounds. Darcy would record his questions and then seek the answers.

"Mr. Donnelly," Conrad spoke the name as he carried in the evening meal, "I hope you are ready for something to eat. Would you like to move to the table, Sir, or would you prefer the tray brought to the bed?"

"The table—thank you, Conrad." Darcy laboriously pushed himself up in the bed. "I need to move, if you would be so kind as to offer me your shoulder once again."

"Happily, Sir."

Moving steadily toward the straight-backed chair, Darcy forced his body to react. "In case I have not said so," he said, gritting his teeth with the effort of moving, "your continual concern for my recovery is most appreciated, Conrad."

"You are most kind, Sir," the servant offered. "I have something I found for you, Sir." He helped Darcy lower himself into the chair and situate himself in front of the dinner tray.

Darcy breathed heavily with the movement. "What would that be?"

"Old Mr. Donnelly had this, Sir." Conrad brought out a walking stick. "I asked Mr. Lansing if we might use it for you; Miss Donnelly consented; I thought it might help steady you, Sir."

"Conrad," Darcy began, "how may I ever repay you?" He took the stick, fingering the fine carving of its handle. "It is a magnificent accessory."

"I am sure there are many other items from the old master, which will be of use to you when you marry Miss Donnelly."

Darcy looked closely at the man. "So, I am intended for Miss Donnelly?"

"That is what Mr. Lansing confirms, Sir." The man set out the food items for Darcy.

Darcy asked suspiciously, "What do the other servants say?"

"That is just it, Sir," Conrad lowered his voice. "The others say the same thing—nearly word for word. No matter who I ask, the story is the same, and the wording is the same. No one changes even the wording of the story. Do you not think that odd, Sir?"

"Quite odd." Darcy guarded his reaction. "What was said?" He sipped the soup.

"Everyone said you were here three weeks. You and Miss Donnelly are to marry. You went to Hull on business and were attacked when returning to the estate. Those were the words, Sir."

"They are the same as what Miss Donnelly provided me," Darcy mused.

Conrad tried to busy himself about the room before he responded. "I cannot tell you, Sir, how this bothers me."

Darcy put down the soupspoon and turned to the older man. "May I ask why you addressed me as Mr. Donnelly today?"

"I have been instructed by Mr. Lansing to do so."

"Mr. Lansing is Miss Donnelly's steward?" The statement came out as a question.

"Yes, Sir. He has been the estate's steward for three years—since old Mr. Donnelly's passing." Conrad stoked the fire as he spoke.

"Conrad, what can you tell me about Miss Donnelly?"

"I have been with the estate for over twenty years. Miss Donnelly was six years old when I came here. The old master and his mistress were likeable people, they treated us very well. Miss Donnelly is more severe than were her parents. She is very explicit about the estate being clean. The current mistress becomes upset if items are not cleaned several times a day. She allows Mr. Lansing free reign in running the place. It fell on hard times of late, and the mistress was forced to sell off several of the estate's items to meet expenses. Of course, Sir, you heard none of this from me."

"I will keep your confidence," Darcy stammered. "You gave me much upon which to reflect." Darcy finished the meal, and, with Conrad's help and the use of the walking stick, he made several trips up and down the hallway between his chambers and the top of the staircase.

Now, each trip Darcy made down the hallway outside of his room, he became more aware of his surroundings—the estate's furnishings and its overall condition. "It seems to me," he began one afternoon as he sat with Miss Donnelly in the same upstairs sitting room, "the estate is in need of some very badly needed repairs."

"Really, Frederick, whatever can you mean?" Miss Donnelly continued her act of submissiveness.

"There are places up and down this hallway where flooring, doorframes, and window frames should be replaced. The wood has rotted. Why has your steward not addressed these issues?" Darcy's voice demanded an answer.

Miss Donnelly said simply, "I do not like the mess such repairs would create in my house."

"Well, we will have no such foolishness once we are married. In fact, I wish you to send Mr. Lansing to me later today. We must address the repairs immediately. Please tell him to bring the account books also; we must make the estate a viable place once again."

"Is this really necessary, Frederick?" Miss Donnelly's disdain showed.

"Of course it is necessary. You should have seen to it prior to now. This is, at least, an area in which I feel I may be of use to you. Although I do not remember many specifics of my life prior to my attack, some things must come from instinct."

Miss Donnelly snarled her nose with the possibilities. "I still do not see where there is such a need for immediacy."

"I will broker no denials, Madam," Darcy demanded. "As soon as I am able, I want to ride out across the estate to survey the land."

"I suppose you insist on this issue also." Sarcasm crept into her voice. "Must we deal with the tenants and the land ourselves? Mr. Lansing is quite capable of addressing these issues."

"As your husband, I want to bring more than a title to our marriage."

"However, I ask no more of you than that."

"Well, I will not hear of it," he snapped. Now that he escalated the conversation to a case of wills, Darcy quickly added without warning, "What is my title? Exactly where is my father's estate?"

Miss Donnelly flustered as Darcy settled his attention on her. "Does it matter if you have been disinherited?" she stammered.

"Certainly it matters. If all I have to bring to this marriage is my title, I must know what I may give to you and to any children we might have," he said adamantly. "Who knows— maybe my brother will die before I do, and then everything my father has will be mine after all. It has happened in more than one family."

"Well, your title is of little significance to me," Miss Donnelly cooed.

Darcy quipped, "Madam, I appreciate your generosity, but I insist on knowing of what we speak. If I have no title to give you, you would be better off seeking another. I would gladly release you from your commitment to me in such a case."

"Frederick, I do not wish to be released from our engagement." Her mind raced, trying to come up with a logical solution. She tried to think of an area greatly displaced from her own home. "Your father's estate is in Hertfordshire." In reality, Miss Donnelly knew little about Hertfordshire; she only knew it to be far removed from Darling Hall. "Your father is a Lord, my dear." Her speech became sugary.

The word "Hertfordshire" shot through Darcy, forcing a sense of familiarity. "Hertfordshire, is it? I wish I could remember something of it."

"Do not let it trouble you, Frederick; we never have to face your father again. We will concentrate our efforts on Darling Hall." Miss Donnelly shifted her weight to take a prominent position once again. She rose to take her leave, and Darcy forced himself to his feet also. "I will bid you adieu, Sir, until later." She made him a curtsy.

Darcy extemporaneously took her gloved hand and brought it to his lips. He kissed it lightly. "Do you always wear gloves, Madam?" He tried to analyze her words by looking deep in her eyes.

Feigning demure feelings, she dropped her gaze. "I am afraid my mother demanded I do so. I was never able to break the habit."

"Obviously, I would prefer to take your hand," Darcy weighed his words. "Next time, please do not wear them." His voice held intimate promises.

Miss Donnelly flushed with color. "Frederick, I will try." Flustered, she quickly left the room.

CHAPTER 9

*"There seems something more speakingly incomprehensible
in the powers, the failures, the inequalities of memory,
than in any other of our intelligences."*
Jane Austen, *Mansfield Park*, 1814

Elizabeth Donnelly sought the safety of her own chambers. Shaken by the scene she just experienced, she gasped for air. "Can I do this?" she mumbled as she secured the door behind her. "I must be careful," she chastised herself. "Now, I must let Mr. Lansing know a few discreet staff members must mention Hertfordshire. How much will that cost me?"

She forced herself to sit down and draft more specific details of her story. "Whom do I know from Hertfordshire?" It was some time before she remembered once meeting Sir William Lucas at St. James. The man, a pompous imbecile, insisted on introducing her to his inferior connections. At least, it was a name she could casually include in future conversations. She supposed she would have to tolerate the repairs Mr. Darcy mentioned. If she declined, he might become suspicious. She needed to let Mr. Lansing dispose of another of her mother's tapestries to cover the cost of the items. *I cannot let Mr. Darcy know what is happening with the estate. Once we are married, we can let Darling Hall and move to his estate, or I can secure a nice living from him as part of a divorce. Some women would not want a divorce, but I care not if it would let me stay here and live as I wish.* Her thoughts ran the gamut of her emotions.

Darcy had similar thoughts. Every time he considered Miss Donnelly's story a fabrication, some element of it rang factual and made him question whether the whole thing might be true. "Hertfordshire," he mulled the word over in his mind. What did he know about Hertfordshire? Elements of the word held an unstated reality, but he could recall no specifics of it. Could he really be from an estate in Hertfordshire? If only he could remember....The beautiful woman and *Hertfordshire* held an unknown actuality. If he could just connect them somehow...

Sunday brought the day of Darcy's redemption; in a few hours he would be free of Elizabeth. As much as he rejoiced at his being able to return to himself, his friend was despondent about the loss of her sister's company, and he found he, too, would feel the deprivation of Elizabeth's presence if only he would allow himself the luxury of admitting as much. Reliving the last few days as he dressed for church services, he acknowledged Elizabeth's power over him escalated to the point of distraction, and he felt obliged to struggle against his feelings. He could not—would not—entertain a design on her. His prayer on this particular Sunday was to rid himself of the good opinion he formed of her. Putting distance between himself and Elizabeth could ease his distress; therefore, he resolved during the night to pretend business in town and to leave Hertfordshire.

Waiting on the ladies in the main foyer, Darcy paced with a renewed strength of resolve. His friend, on the other hand, anticipated the pleasure of escorting Elizabeth's sister to the morning's services. As he contemplated how he could tell his friend, without offending the man, he chose to leave Hertfordshire, the sisters stood at the top of the stairs looking down at the gentlemen. Elizabeth's sister, still a bit pale, was dressed in royal-blue muslin, amplifying her blue eyes.

Darcy thought he heard his friend let out a low moan, but he could not be sure it was not his own response he heeded; for a few paces behind her elder sister, taking a supportive role, stood Elizabeth. The image hypnotized him. Elizabeth was perfectly beautiful and perfectly insensible to the fact. Only moments before, he silently professed his desire to be away from the brilliancy of her eyes, and now he could not force his regard from her countenance. Clothed in a simple dress of muted rose trimmed with red stitching, which complemented her hair, Elizabeth had no idea what inducements she created in a man of such esteem.

His friend sprang up the staircase to attend to her sister's needs, taking up a position by the woman's side and allowing himself the pleasure of bracing her unsteady motion. Pausing to give her sister distance and some moments of growing affection, Elizabeth nearly giggled with delight at seeing his friend's actions single out the woman.

Shortly, Elizabeth began her descent, and Darcy discovered himself compelled to meet her and offer her his arm. A bit embarrassed by his behavior, his gentility took control of his actions as he offered the incomparable Elizabeth his hand. She did not expect his chivalry, but propriety allowed her to permit him to do the proper thing.

Irritated with his sisters for being fashionably late once again, his friend said, "Why do we not take the ladies in my carriage? My sisters may come with my brother Albert in his."

Darcy knew the folly of such an action. Two single gentlemen in possession of good fortunes escorting two single ladies to local church services could be viewed easily by society and by the ladies themselves as a declaration of the gentlemen's intentions. He wanted to say as much to his friend, but the slight pressure of Elizabeth's hand upon his wiped the idea away. He resolved to leave Hertfordshire in the next few days, and that would hinder any hopes she may be contemplating. He would allow himself the pleasure of her company one last time.

In the carriage, they found companionable silence. Both ladies kept their eyes down as Elizabeth fussed over her elder sister's comfort. The gentlemen stared out the coach's windows, but Darcy's mind was anywhere but on the scenery; Elizabeth's lavender—her lush eyelashes—the flush of color on her cheeks—the shift of her shoulders— all these things consumed his being.

Alighting from the carriage, the ladies entered the church ahead of the gentlemen; his friend grabbed Darcy's arm, delaying their entrance momentarily. "Thank you for allowing me this deception. My sisters will take great offense, and we shall hear their rebukes this afternoon, but for me this will be well worth it."

Darcy tried to cover the deepest regard he held for Elizabeth. With a straight face, he said, "Although we should not allow decency to fall to the wayside, I do enjoy being in your company, and, by the way, is this adventurous enough for you?" Darcy winked at his friend good-humoredly.

"You are a faithful friend." The man shook Darcy's hand enthusiastically. "Let us find seats close to the ladies; I am afraid my attention may not be on the sermon today."

Darcy felt guilty for deceiving his friend, but how could he admit to the man his feelings for Elizabeth. He had not even vocalized to himself the disorder her presence afflicted upon him.

Over the next fortnight, Darcy's recovery became more evident. His strength returned. Only his mental clarity remained in question. Along with the return of his strength came a resurgence of his serious mien.

"Must you ride out today?" Miss Donnelly showed her abhorrence for the situation.

"I must, Madam," Darcy stated matter-of-factly. "I expect to examine the farms on the estate today. Do you hold some objections?"

"No, Sir," she tried to cover her dislike of the activity. "You will freshen your clothing before you make an appearance for dinner." Miss Donnelly snorted with contempt.

"A gentleman always makes an appropriate presentation," he replied in a haughty manner. "Please do not remind me of my obligations; there are many things about my former life I do not remember, but if my father is a Lord of the realm, I am sure he would raise me with proper manners."

"I meant no offense," the lady apologized. Miss Donnelly did not like playing the role of the submissive female, but to save her estate, she would do what was necessary. Besides, at age seven and twenty her options were limited.

"Accepted," Darcy snapped. He made a quick bow and exited the room.

He walked toward the stables. He asked the groomsman earlier to prepare a mount from the estate's horses. Seeing Mr. Lansing waiting surprised him.

"Mr. Lansing, I need no one to escort me across the estate."

"I understand, Mr. Donnelly, but Miss Donnelly requested I do so. I would not wish to disappoint the mistress." Lansing's face held a plastered-on smile.

"You may accompany me, but I will decide what I see; you will not *handle* me. Is that clear?"

Lansing's smile became a smirk. "Perfectly clear, Mr. Donnelly."

"And remove that condescending look from your face. I will not tolerate such attitudes when I am the new master of this estate," Darcy ordered. Using the mounting block, he swung up into the saddle and galloped away from the steward.

"Many of the farms are in deplorable conditions," Darcy told Miss Donnelly over dinner. "I spoke to several of the tenants, and they expressed a concern in how Mr. Lansing metes out punishment for poachers and how he does not address their questions about repairs or developing their crops. I was very disappointed about these reports."

Miss Donnelly queried innocently, "Where was Mr. Lansing during this?"

"I sent him away; how else would the tenants open up to me?"

Trying to stall for the proper response, Miss Donnelly poured Darcy a cup of tea. "I noted no deficiencies in Mr.

Lansing's handling of the estate."

"Well, I will have different standards of performance for Mr. Lansing when I take over the estate."

"When you take over the estate?" Miss Donnelly seemed surprised by his remark.

"Of course." Darcy's words held no room for question. "As your husband, your property comes under my auspices."

"But it is my estate," the lady argued.

"Unfortunately, the law does not see it that way." Darcy sipped his tea. "I had an epiphany of a sort today. While riding the land, I recalled my father teaching me what to do when inspecting the estate. At least, I believe it was my father. That is what flashes of my memory said—my father taught me the delights and responsibilities of being a man of property. I vaguely remember accompanying him on the spring inspection of his farms and holdings."

Miss Donnelly tried to control her apprehension. If she married Darcy, she would receive an additional fifty thousand pounds. Her marital prospects were few, but turning over the control of Darling Hall to an outside person went against her beliefs. She needed the funds, she needed a husband; for that she created an "illusion," and now she could not escape her own lies. "I am happy the experience brought you some memories. I am sure you will return to us completely very soon."

"It is my prayer," Darcy replied tentatively. "It is as if I live in a parallel world."

"Is it too soon for us to set a wedding date? I do not wish to rush your recovery," Miss Donnelly tried to sound concerned, "but our living in the same house and unmarried is a major break in propriety. Your attack postponed what we originally planned as a speedy engagement."

"I understand your sensitivity to the situation. I was here nearly a month, was I not?"

"A month since your attack," she corrected. "You were here three weeks prior to your fateful journey to Hull."

"Ah, yes, I did not count those days," he mused. "Then I suspect we should address a date. Would you consider another month as too long?"

"It is longer than I would prefer," Miss Donnelly tried to tempt him with a perfect fluttering of her eyelashes.

"Yet, I would want to be fully recovered, at least, physically. A month should serve that purpose well."

"Of course, Frederick, a month will be soon enough." She took another sip of her tea and became lost in her thoughts of how she would manage this situation for another few weeks.

★ ★ ★

Ten days passed since Elizabeth received word of Darcy's attack. Mr. Howard returned from Hemswell, but no news of Fitzwilliam Darcy followed. No one saw him, and no one knew of his whereabouts.

"I am sorry, Mrs. Darcy," he stumbled across the words with feelings of inadequacy. "I searched a ten-mile area around where we found Mr. Darcy's coach. I found people who took the wheels, the metal trim, and the seating cushions, but I do not believe any of them knew of Mr. Darcy. They all were poor peasants who simply took what they could from an abandoned coach."

"Mr. Howard, you did all you could." Elizabeth offered him forgiveness for failing in his journey. "At least, we know Mr. Darcy is alive somewhere."

"If you say so, Madam." Mr. Howard tried not to give her false hope.

"I say so." Elizabeth gave him a warning look. She would accept no negative thoughts when it came to her husband's life.

Each day, Elizabeth and Georgiana visited the tenants. The time Elizabeth spent in the poorer homes gave her a sense of comfort; her efforts would make Darcy proud. She and Georgiana took charitable baskets of food and assorted supplies. The foundation they established at the Christmastime celebration made it easier for the tenants to welcome them. Most knew of Mr. Darcy's disappearance, but the fact both Mrs. Darcy and Miss Darcy still made their duty calls told the tenants Pemberley would continue even if the Master did not return.

"I promised Fitzwilliam I would keep Pemberley alive." She and Georgiana traveled back to the estate's main house. "It is one of his *passions*; I cannot let it die."

"Elizabeth," Georgiana said, her eyes misting over, "I am so frightened."

"I cannot tell you the last time I dreamed." Elizabeth spoke to the air, not looking at anyone. "When Fitzwilliam first left, I dreamed of him each night; it gave me solace. Yet, since the day I dreamed of his pain and later his peacefulness, I cannot bring an image of his face to my dreams. It is as if Fitzwilliam Darcy ceased to exist—where did he go, Georgiana?"

Georgiana began to sob, and Elizabeth took the girl in her arms again. "Elizabeth, if my brother is well, he will come back to us. We have to believe that." The sobs racked the girl's shoulders.

"I stand for hours in the gallery looking at his portrait; I pray to have Fitzwilliam home again—no matter what the circumstance," Elizabeth nearly pleaded.

"My brother would say beware the prayer the devil answers." Georgiana tried to tease to break their somber mood.

"There could be nothing worse for me than living my life without Fitzwilliam." Elizabeth could not give up the longing so quickly. "He had a plan for you and me to live out our days at Pemberley. The child I carry will inherit this estate, and I will not let your brother's dream for Pemberley die."

"Elizabeth." Georgiana bit her bottom lip. "Shall you ever forgive me?"

Elizabeth looked shocked. "Forgive you—for what?"

"If I showed no interest in Mr. Harrison, my brother would not have gone to Hull to learn how to protect me. I promise to never see Mr. Harrison again!"

"Oh, Georgiana, you did nothing wrong!" Elizabeth hugged Darcy's sister again. "If it were not this situation, something else would take him away. It is part of our journey. I seriously believe that."

"Do you?" Georgiana gasped.

Elizabeth tilted the girl's chin so she could look directly in her eyes. "Your brother loves us; he will come home to us. As far as Mr. Harrison goes, let both your head and your heart decide. Do not blame him for what happened to Fitzwilliam."

"What would I do without you in my life, Elizabeth? Thank God Fitzwilliam gave me you."

Another week passed; Elizabeth went through the motions of normalcy. She addressed the books each day with Mr. Howard; she rode out regularly with Georgiana to make tenant visits; she approved Kitty's renovations to the nursery. These were all things she would do if Darcy were home. She summoned her mantle of confidence as she went about her duties as the Mistress of Pemberley.

Elizabeth's charitable activities included the new village school. Along with Mr. Ashford and Kitty's help, she chose books from Darcy's library to be donated for the school's use. "Kitty, please write to Papa later today and ask him for some of our old schoolbooks and the books we read as young girls. If he will send them, I will have staff go to Longbourn to bring them here." Elizabeth handed her younger sister a book for the donations.

"Oh, yes, we have so many books at our home, Mr. Ashford."

Ashford asked, "Your father is a reader, then?"

Elizabeth began to laugh. "Our father, Mr. Ashford, could enter his library and never come out again if not for the demands of society."

Georgiana entered with books of her own. "Here is a copy of Goldsmith's *The Vicar of Wakefield* and Mrs. Radcliffe's *The Romance of the Forest* and *The Children of the Abbey*. Of course, some people may not approve of Mrs. Radcliffe's offerings," she teased. Georgiana added her contribution to the stack of books.

Elizabeth picked up the Goldsmith book and fingered it delicately. "Is there something wrong, Elizabeth?" Kitty asked.

Elizabeth's eyes welled with tears. "We talked about those books, Georgiana, the day my aunt and I came here for tea. Miss Bingley and Mrs. Hurst were here. Do you remember?" Elizabeth took a seat, unable to stand any longer.

Georgiana came and knelt in front of her. "Of course, I remember. You protected me from Miss Bingley; you were everything Fitzwilliam promised me you would be."

"We went into the conservatory; I chose the yellow box-wood rose." Elizabeth's voice seemed distant.

"My mother's favorite plant." Georgiana swallowed hard.

"Do you know Fitzwilliam brought every yellow rosebud from the conservatory to Kensington Place for our wedding night?" Tears streamed down her face. "In the conservatory I told him yellow was my favorite color of flowers, and although some say yellow represents jealousy, I believe it demonstrates a constancy of spirit—like the sun, it lasts forever. I preserved some of those roses in the books at Kensington Place." Elizabeth broke down, "How can I go on without him?"

"We are all together; you do not have to be without Fitzwilliam. He lives within you; your child will keep my brother alive for us until he comes home again." Elizabeth allowed Georgiana to take her to her room; the girl offered endearments along the way.

Mr. Ashford looked at Kitty; she, too, cried. Immediately, he was in front of her. "Do not be sad, my loveliest Katherine. I cannot bear it."

"What if Mr. Darcy never comes home?"

The man pulled her to him so Kitty could rest her head on his chest. "It is a quandary, and although initially I thought there was little hope, I believe Mr. Darcy will come home to Pemberley. There is too much love for him in this house for God to allow Mr. Darcy to never return."

"Do you really believe this?" Kitty's voice came out small.

"Great loves never die, my Katherine." He stroked the back of her head. "Your sister and Mr. Darcy have a great love." He lifted her chin to look deeply in Kitty's eyes. "Some day we will write the story of our own great love."

Kitty wanted him to kiss her again, but he already broke with propriety by taking her into his arms. Instead, Mr. Ashford slowly traced her jaw line with the back of his hand before releasing her. "Come, Miss Bennet." He briefly took her hand to lead her outside. "I am in need of a walk in the garden."

"I think I would prefer seeing the boxwood rose in the conservatory," she teased.

Ashford stopped short and turned back to her; a smile overspread his face. "Any flower which so inspires love is definitely to be seen."

"Mrs. Darcy, I am sorry to disturb you," Mr. Howard called as he entered the study.

"What may I address for you, Mr. Howard?" The stress of her deprivation became more obvious the last few days.

"Some of the tenants are stirring up trouble. With Mr. Darcy gone, some want to return to the old ways of planting. They are gathering at the Jefferson farm. What do you want me to do?" Mr. Howard fidgeted with his hat.

Elizabeth came around the desk. "Tell Mr. Shepherd to

hitch up the small coach; I will go with you to Jefferson's. I am in no mood to hear their complaints today."

"Yes, Mrs. Darcy." Then the man was gone.

"If the Darcys want to be fixin' with the crops, let them come here and do it themself." Jefferson spoke loudly so all could hear.

Unfortunately, about that time Elizabeth stepped around the corner of the building. "I am here, Mr. Jefferson. It seems you have a complaint you wish to address."

Jefferson scooped the hat from his head as a sign of respect, but he did not back down. "I be beggin' your pardon, Mrs. Darcy, but my complaint lies with Mr. Darcy."

"Mr. Darcy is not here, and I am, so your complaint is mine to address." Elizabeth came forward to face the man.

"We be thinkin' the four-crop rotation be a waste of land." Jefferson could not back down in front of his friends.

Elizabeth knew what happened in the next few minutes would affect how Darcy's plan for his estate would be fulfilled; she chose her words carefully. "My husband is a learned man. You who have been on the estate for years know him to be as kind as he is intelligent. He rejoices at the birth of each new baby and grieves at the loss of each passing. He loves this estate. It is more than his ancestral home; it is his passion—his compulsion. He loves this land enough to suffer the censure of society to teach both his sister and me how to run the estate. He does not just want the knowledge of a future heir to the land to be his only hold on it. Mr. Darcy traveled all the way to Scotland to learn about the best way to save the land from depletion. The four-crop rotation is successful elsewhere, and it will be successful here. However, Mr. Jefferson, if you so object, we will release you from the obligation you have to this estate, but please understand if you choose to leave, you may *never* return. I will not help those who do not believe in my husband's dream for Pemberley. I will gladly divide your land among your neighbors. So, what will it be, Mr. Jefferson?" Elizabeth stepped in closer as she knew Darcy would to make a point.

Jefferson began to fidget under her stare, and Elizabeth fought back a smile of triumph. "Well, Mrs. Darcy, we meant nothin' by it. We just want to be sure we be havin' a home."

"Mr. Darcy's heir is on its way. Pemberley is growing stronger each day. If you believe in my husband's dream for Pemberley, then follow Mr. Howard's orders. If not, tell Mr. Howard, pack your things, and leave the estate forever. Mr. Darcy's dream lies in this land and this child, and I will broker no complaints in those areas." Elizabeth turned on her heels and left the men mumbling apologies as she left.

Once they returned to the coach, Elizabeth let out the breath she held. "You were brilliant, Mrs. Darcy," Mr. Howard gushed in admiration.

Elizabeth slumped back against the coach's seat. "I wish Fitzwilliam was here. He would know how to handle these things so much better than I."

"You are wrong, Mrs. Darcy; you did exactly what Mr. Darcy would have done. He would be proud of how you took on this task. When he first shared his plan, I scoffed, but Mr. Darcy knew you were the right person for this estate. Pemberley lives through you, and I do not just speak of the heir you carry."

Elizabeth blushed at his words. "I hope you are right, Mr. Howard."

Elizabeth decided to take tea in the lower drawing room. She sat with her feet propped up on a hammock; no one else came into the room, and, in a few minutes, she drifted off to sleep. Unusual for her, a nap came as the confrontation with Jefferson drained her of her energies.

Elizabeth knew he waited for her. Compelled, she slipped carefully out of the bed she shared with her eldest sister, Jane. Grabbing her pelisse, she crept quietly down the stairs, unlatched the door, and hurried through the mist surrounding Longbourn. She cut across the open field and entered the tree line leading to the hill behind the estate. The morning mist rose slowly, and she felt as if she walked through a cloud. Why she came she knew not, except Elizabeth knew Darcy waited for her—needed her—loved her.

Then a familiar figure filled her senses. Darcy turned to pick up Cerberus's reins and began to mount. He wore his breeches, an open-neck shirt, boots, and a greatcoat. Elizabeth felt her heart flutter with anticipation. She loved this man with every ounce of being in her body. He turned at the sound of her approach, and their eyes locked, peering into each other's souls. As if in a trance, they moved forward; only a lover's embrace could satisfy their needs. Without a word, Darcy encircled her with his arms, clasping her to his body; she felt his warmth radiating through her, filling her with the love only he could give. The sun danced behind them as he whispered her name into her hair, "Elizabeth."

"Fitzwilliam." She laid her hand upon his chest and welcomed his nearness. Their hearts beat wildly as they envisioned the happiness awaiting them.

"Dearest Elizabeth," he said, lifting her chin to look into her eyes. "What are you doing here?"

She nibbled on his lower lip. "I could ask you likewise, Sir."

"I could find no sleep for images of you. I sought my release by riding here to assure myself this was not a dream, and I find a living, breathing Elizabeth."

"Fitzwilliam, you have no fear of finding yourself alone ever again." She stroked the stubble of his beard. "For you, Sir, stole my heart, and only you may be rid of it. It is at your whim."

Darcy brushed his lips across hers in an inviting tease. "We should not be found together like this," he said unwillingly.

"'Tis true. My father might be required to defend my honor on my wedding day," she said, bestowing a full kiss upon his faintly trembling lips. His arms enveloped her as she moved closer for a long, tender moment.

As they separated, Elizabeth's fingers gently traced his lips; he caught her hands and kissed her fingertips. "I will await you at the church," he smirked as she turned to leave.

"Do not forget to bring my heart," she taunted him over her shoulder.

"Elizabeth," he called.

Turning slowly and giving him an enticing gaze, she said, "Yes?"

"You did not answer my question. Why came you here this morning?"

"Did you not will it, Sir?" She laughed and walked briskly back to the house. Still feeling the tantalizing tingle of Darcy's kiss on her lips and the intensity of his stare on her back, Elizabeth left him on the crest of the hill. In a few hours, she would be his forever.

Brisk footsteps brought her to a waking state once again, and Elizabeth had just straightened her dress when Lady Catherine strode confidently into the room. Elizabeth staggered to her feet and made a quick curtsy to the elderly woman. "Lady Catherine," she spoke haltingly.

"Miss Bennet," Lady Catherine snapped.

Elizabeth set her jaw line. "Lady Catherine, my name is Elizabeth Darcy, and I insist you call me as such, or we can end this conversation before it starts."

Lady Catherine turned and walked over to a seat. "May I?" She indicated the chair.

"Certainly." Elizabeth gestured toward the chair. She already dealt with one crisis today; dealing with Lady Catherine on top of everything else could be more than she could handle. Elizabeth smoothed the front of her dress before taking a seat herself.

"I will come to my point quickly." Lady Catherine kept a prim and proper attitude. "My nephew met with a tragic act, and although his body has not been found, he has been gone nearly a month, and he has not returned home. We must assume he is no longer alive." Elizabeth tried to interrupt—to protest—Darcy's aunt's words, but a raise of Lady Catherine's hand indicated she was not through. "I understand from my daughter, who should be Fitzwilliam's rightful wife, you are with child."

"My husband told you at Matlock I am with child. Our baby is due in July." Elizabeth knew not where this conversation led.

"You told my nephew you expect a child in July, but I know better. I have proof *this child* you carry will come in June because it is not my nephew's heir, but is instead the offspring of a militia officer. You, Miss Bennet, are no better than your youngest sister."

Elizabeth gasped. "Lady Catherine, how can you say such lies? The child belongs to Fitzwilliam Darcy!"

"You may sway the opinion of others, but I am onto you. You will leave this house immediately, or I will expose your deceit to the world," Lady Catherine demanded.

Upon hearing the commotion, Georgiana entered the room. Seeing Elizabeth's distress, she rushed forward and stood by her, taking her sister's hand. "Lady Catherine, what are you doing here?" Georgiana's voice cracked with emotion.

"I come, my dearest niece, to restore this property to a true Darcy, to you."

Georgiana shook her head in disbelief. "Lady Catherine, even if my brother never returns to us, he left a jointure for Pemberley in Elizabeth's name. Fitzwilliam wanted Elizabeth to be here. His plan for this estate revolved around Elizabeth and his child."

Lady Catherine offered her cut. "That is precisely my point, Georgiana. The child does not belong to Fitzwilliam. It is the bastard child of a militia officer; I heard rumors of such from Mr. Collins."

Georgiana flushed with anger and then squeezed Elizabeth's hand. "Aunt, I will not tolerate such lies about my sister in this house. You would never speak as such if my brother were here."

Lady Catherine continued as if everyone agreed with her. "I will send the Colonel to take over the estate. As your guardian, he will run it until you come of age, and then it will be yours."

"Lady Catherine." Georgiana steadied her voice as she stared vehemently at her mother's eldest sister. "That would be a futile effort. Even if you successfully forced Elizabeth from this estate, when I came of age I would deed it back to her. I plan to marry and move away from this land. Pemberley belongs to Elizabeth. That is what Fitzwilliam wanted, and that will be my resolution. Now, if there is nothing else, I will ask you to take your lies and leave this house! It belongs to Elizabeth and to me, and neither of us cares to welcome you here again! Good day, Madam."

With Georgiana's help, Elizabeth rose to her feet; she and Georgiana locked arms and exited the room. They never looked back, but they heard servants scrambling as Lady Catherine scattered them in her wake.

The emotional day played havoc with both women. They entered the music room although neither of them planned to play. They held each other tightly, while tears came to them again. "Oh, Elizabeth, I am so sorry you suffer at my family's hand."

Elizabeth used her knuckles to force the tears from her face. "It is my family as well; Mr. Collins is my cousin. It just proves what Kitty feared—people in Meryton still speak poorly of our family even after your brother bought Lydia her respectability. How could Mr. Collins repeat such lies?"

"Mr. Collins says what my aunt wants to hear. Would it not be a miserable existence to depend on another's favor as such?" Georgiana reasoned.

"You have the same kind of goodness as my dearest Jane." Elizabeth squeezed Georgiana's hand. "However, I feel no sympathy for the man. He deserves all the groveling, which is forced upon him by your aunt." Elizabeth led Georgiana to adjoining chairs. "Can you fathom what Lady Catherine said?"

"If she were successful, Lady Catherine would be able to alleviate two of her vexations. She would drive you from Pemberley, and she would separate Anne and Edward by sending him here to be my guardian."

Elizabeth nearly laughed. "Lady Catherine is a pathetic creature, although I admit to loathing when she comes near me. Thank you for defending me against her. After my early confrontation with Mr. Jefferson about the crops, I had little left to fend off Lady Catherine's attack."

"Although I wish with all my heart my brother would return, I am glad he did not witness what just happened. I am sure he would have done our aunt bodily harm." Georgiana fought back her laughter. "Could you not see my brother physically removing Lady Catherine from the room?"

"In Matlock, Fitzwilliam restrained his contempt for Lady Catherine's accusations." Elizabeth, too, found humor in the images. "However, in the *comfort* of his own home, I doubt if restraint would be a word in his vocabulary." Elizabeth took Georgiana's hand once again. "You have become quite the force with which to face; your brother would be happy you finally found your voice."

"Do you believe so, Elizabeth?" Georgiana seemed timid once again.

"Fitzwilliam's dream for you was to move past your disastrous encounter with George Wickham and to become a strong, confident woman. He is a man who believes women cannot be treated as chattel—they have a voice to which men must sometimes listen. Your brother dreams of giving you a life in which you are valued as a person—not as property. That is why he went to Hull—to secure your future. He would be so proud of you."

CHAPTER 10

"Good-humoured, unaffected girls will not do for a man who has been used to sensible women. They are two distinct orders of being."
Jane Austen, *Mansfield Park*, 1814

Fitzwilliam Darcy continued to recover from his wounds. A slight limp remained, but his strength returned. His tall, muscular physique once again filled out his waistcoat and breeches. A handsome man, Darcy's presence filled a room. Along with his return physically came a more pronounced haughty manner. "Should we not consider an invitation for dinner for some of our neighbors or at least the local cleric?" Darcy asked as he and Miss Donnelly sat down to dinner.

"I prefer not to associate with my neighbors." Miss Donnelly spoke without guarding her words.

Darcy looked incredulous. "Not associate with your neighbors? I understand a desire for solitude, but one cannot ignore society's demands for proper behavior!"

Miss Donnelly rued her words. She did not want Darcy to mix with others from the community until after their marriage. Too many people knew her family and their relatives. Her ancestors were in the area for three generations. At Darling Hall, she could control what information he learned about his past, but she could not be sure of what others might say to him. "Many of my neighbors possess country manners. Do not expect the local gentry to offer much toward polite society." Miss Donnelly took a smug demeanor.

"Pardon me, Madam, what did you say?" Darcy shook his head as her words interlaced with the shadows of his memory.

"Is something the matter, Frederick?"

"Not exactly—I am afraid your words seemed familiar in their phrasing." Darcy's countenance twisted in the effort to remember.

"Shall I call for Conrad to come to assist you, Sir?"

"No—no, I am fine." The color returned to his face. "I apologize if I startled you." He shook his head to clear the last vestiges of the memory. "We were speaking of country manners. I concur—country manners are greatly lacking in a sense of decorum and can often be viewed as vulgar. Yet, we must persevere if we are to establish ourselves in the community."

"But Frederick," she started to protest.

"No, Madam," Darcy stopped her short. "I will not hear of it. We will become the standard bearers of fine society in this area. I am a Lord's son and will act as such."

"Frederick, do you not think we should at least wait until after we are wed?" Miss Donnelly tried to delay his wishes.

"Again, I hear your concern, but we cannot hide. Although our being in the same household is unusual, I think people need to see we hold ourselves to a higher standard. It will keep the local tongues from wagging, and we must officially announce our engagement. I suggest within the fortnight."

Miss Donnelly knew from the tone of Darcy's voice and his manner of speaking she would not be able to change his mind. She would need another diversion. She did not answer Darcy but simply lowered her eyes and nodded in affirmation.

"Then it is settled. You will take care of the invitations tomorrow. Shall I speak to the household staff?"

"No, Frederick, I shall handle it," she mumbled.

"Very good, Madam." He stood to take his leave so he politely took her hand. "I thought I suggested you dispense with wearing gloves when we are within our own home."

She stammered, "I would prefer not to do so."

"It is not a choice," Darcy demanded, pulling one of the gloves from her hand.

"No, please do not do that," Miss Donnelly's voice rose in volume as she tried to push his hands away.

Darcy forcibly caught her wrist. "Miss Donnelly, this is unacceptable. No woman of the *ton* wears gloves all the time. If you are to be my wife, you will do what I tell you to do." He jerked the glove from her and pulled her hand to his mouth to kiss the back of it. Miss Donnelly gasped with horror. "Was that so terrible?" he smirked.

Miss Donnelly looked at the ungloved hand, which Darcy still held in his two hands. "I . . . I am sorry," she mumbled. Then she dislodged her hand from his, gathered her skirt, and ran toward her rooms. She screamed for the servants to bring her hot water immediately.

Darcy stepped into the hallway, watching the woman retreat. Her absurdity brought a smile to his face. "There goes my blushing bride," he chuckled.

Elizabeth Donnelly forced her hands into the water once again. "Bring me another bar of soap," she ordered the maid.

"But Miss Donnelly," the maid protested, "your hand bleeds from so much hot water and soap already."

"Do as I tell you," she shrieked.

The maid ran from the room. "Yes, Miss Donnelly; right away, Ma'am."

Darcy made his way to his chambers. "Good evening, Conrad," he addressed the servant as the man scrambled to remove Darcy's boots. "It seems I upset Miss Donnelly."

"So I heard, Sir." The servant had an amused look.

"I am afraid Miss Donnelly will see some more changes. My father evidently raised me to oversee an estate, and it is my intention to make Darling Hall the jewel of the area."

"Yes, Sir," Conrad's smile became larger. "But Miss Donnelly will not be easy to please."

"Unfortunately, neither will I." Darcy smiled insolently with self-satisfaction.

"Miss Donnelly, I am not happy with how Mr. Lansing is running this estate. It is my decision, when we marry, that I shall find an appropriate replacement."

"Frederick, I cannot release Mr. Lansing. He has been with the estate for nearly ten years; he is one of my most loyal servants."

"If the man is incompetent, his loyalty is of little use to us," Darcy insisted, as he seated himself behind the desk. "If you are uncomfortable with the task, I have no qualms in completing it."

"Frederick, you are changing everything about Darling Hall. It is too much, Sir; I must protest."

He laughed lightly. "You may protest all you wish, but as your husband, I will have the final say. Darling Hall will grow in its greatness."

"Sir," she started, but decided against continuing the argument. Darcy sat down to address the estate books, and Miss Donnelly went to find Mr. Lansing.

"You sent for me, Miss Donnelly." Mr. Lansing joined her in the drawing room.

"Please have a seat, Mr. Lansing." She pointed daintily to a chair across from her.

He slid into the chair. "Is there a problem, Ma'am?"

"Mr. Lansing, Mr. Donnelly is not happy with your work. He asked me to inform you after our marriage, your services will no longer be required."

Lansing began to laugh, lightly at first and then fully engaged. "Miss Donnelly, this is absurd; you and I both know there is no Mr. Donnelly. How can Mr. Donnelly release me from my position?"

The woman stood and began to pace the floor. "Mr. Lansing, if my intended decides to replace you, I have no choice but to do as he says."

Lansing crossed the room to stand in front of her. "Miss Donnelly, we have an *understanding*. Part of that understanding is I keep your secrets, *and* I keep my position as your steward."

"I know what you say is true, but I must go through with the wedding. We both know the estate needs the money. What can I do?" Her eyes beseeched him.

Lansing placed her gloved hand in his. "Come, Miss Donnelly," he said placatingly, "let us have a seat and reason out the situation." Lansing led her to adjoining chairs. Once they were seated, he continued, "Let us summarize the situation and draw more logical conclusions."

Miss Donnelly took on a defeated position. She began this farce on her own, but the complications made her wish for a way out. "Mr. Donnelly wants us to invite our neighbors to dinner. You know I cannot let that happen; too many people know my family for that to occur. Now, he is speaking of releasing you and other staff members. If I marry him, I become his property."

Lansing knew he sat in the catbird seat—she would do what he said. "Let us examine the options. First, you could abandon your plan and tell *Mr. Donnelly* who he really is. Of course, I do not imagine *Mr. Donnelly* will be too happy to know you kept him from his family. His censure would, at a minimum, be carried over to other members of the *ton*, and you would lose your social standing in London and the community."

"That is not an option I choose," she stammered.

"You could marry your Mr. Donnelly, and then let me go. I, unfortunately, know of your deception and even have several of Mr. Darcy's personal items in my possession. I would be forced to confront you in public, and you would be back to option one. Of course, I must assume Mr. Darcy's family would gladly reward me for my honesty." Lansing sat back in the chair, leisurely slouching against the cushions.

His words forced Miss Donnelly to examine his expression. Incredulously, she exclaimed, "You could not?"

"I could," he stated matter-of-factly. "A third option would be to move up the wedding date. Once you have Mr. Donnelly's name, do you really care if he leaves you? Your parents' will says *to marry;* it says nothing about heirs or living together."

Miss Donnelly latched onto his words as a way out of her predicament. "How do I convince Mr. Donnelly to move the date? He is quite adamant about waiting."

Lansing began to smile; he knew she would do what he suggested. "Hopefully, Madam, you will forgive my forwardness in saying the only way a man may be forced into a speedy marriage is to commit a compromising act."

He heard her gasp. "I cannot! You cannot suggest as such!"

"By your own report, *Mr. Donnelly* has made no advances other than to kiss your ungloved hand. If you are engaged, that would not be a *compromising* situation. Even if he were to kiss you, society would look the other way."

The color faded from Miss Donnelly's face. She swallowed hard before saying, "I am astonished you would suggest such a thing!"

"I do apologize; I overstepped my position as your adviser on estate matters. Option one is the honest thing to do." Lansing tried to look contrite, but a smirk overtook his face.

Miss Donnelly sat quietly for several minutes; then she turned her head to stare off in space. Finally, she said, "I would need a clergyman available to immediately perform the service. I cannot let Mr. Lunsford deliver the vows; he would spread the rumor of what happened. He tells his wife every transgression he knows of his parish."

Lansing restrained the laughter. "Do we know such a man?"

"I believe I know a person; I met him briefly in London. He has a living in Kent; his wife's father is Sir William Lucas, a man from Hertfordshire I met at the court of St. James. The cleric fawns and brags, but his services could be procured for this one time." Miss Donnelly's resolve took place. She still spoke to the air rather than to Mr. Lansing, as if she thought out loud. "I shall write him tomorrow. I am sure he will be pleased to perform the wedding of the aristocracy."

"Then what will you do to entice your cousin?" Lansing mocked.

She straightened her shoulders and finally looked at Lansing. "A lady would never discuss such things." Her words held bitterness.

Lansing stood. "A *lady* would never be in a position where this conversation would occur. By your leave, Miss Donnelly," he whispered. He overtly reached out and caressed her cheek in a mocking sign of affection before he exited.

Darcy sat in the drawing room with Miss Donnelly; the evening was warm for early March so a fire was not lit in the hearth. "Miss Donnelly, what do you think of Mr. Wordsworth's new volume?" Darcy asked, expecting a knowledgeable response.

"I am afraid, Sir, I have not read it." She barely looked up from her needlework.

Darcy looked up from the book. "What have you read lately?"

"Very little—I do not like to read," she mumbled as she concentrated on her stitchery.

"You do not like to read?" Darcy seemed shocked.

Again, she did not even raise her head. "No, Sir."

"How can you exist in the world without literature and poetry to temper your soul?"

Elizabeth Donnelly finally looked at him seriously. "It is of little significance. I read well enough to decipher Mr. Lansing's reports. That is all which is necessary for my existence."

"Then I assume you play the pianoforte or draw," he offered.

She laughed lightly. "I am afraid, Frederick, I have few talents associated with accomplished young ladies."

Before he thought about what he said, Darcy blurted out, "My sister is quite accomplished on the pianoforte. I bought her a new one for her birthday."

Miss Donnelly froze; her needle suspended in midair. "Your sister, Sir?" she nearly shrieked.

Darcy sat for a long time looking at her in bewilderment before he spoke. "Do I have a sister?" he whispered.

"No, Sir." Miss Donnelly swallowed hard, not sure if his memory suddenly returned.

Darcy's hands shook. "Then why did I say that? It seemed so logical and familiar at the time." His voice broke with a new fear.

"Possibly it is your brother's wife of whom you speak. She would be your sister in marriage." Miss Donnelly grasped at straws.

"Of course," he nearly stuttered. "That has to be it." His eyes cleared once more. "Somewhere, I discussed the qualities of an accomplished woman. I vaguely remember the conversation on the edges of my memory."

"That surely must be it," she assured him.

"I received a letter confirming the arrival of the cleric for whom I sent," Miss Donnelly told Mr. Lansing one afternoon. "He should be here by Saturday. I will press my cousin to be married as soon as I am sure of the man's arrival."

"What will you do?" Lansing asked offhandedly.

"I shall not discuss it with you," she told him as she closed the ledger in which she recorded expenses. "Yet, be assured I have a plan."

Darcy wondered about the life upon which he was to embark at Darling Hall. At times, he seemed so self-assured—he saw himself as the type who protected those he loved—a man who brokered for peace and serenity, a dutiful man who knew his position and his responsibility. He, obviously, knew something about running an estate, and Darling Hall could use his insights. He was a practical man—not one who sought recognition, but one who expected respect.

Although he could enjoy fine company, Darcy did not suppose he could tolerate those with false airs. Yet, as a Lord's son, he must give his dues to those of rank. As Lord Donnelly, Darcy knew he must be used to a superior wealth. Tradition and duty to family would be his mantle. He would marry Miss Donnelly, as he gave his word to her, and do the dutiful thing to create a viable estate and a home for his eventual heirs.

The suggestion of heirs brought Darcy to thoughts of Elizabeth Donnelly. Of late, he held profound concerns about the woman and his plan to marry her. Only two days ago, he forcibly removed her as she, literally, beat the household's elderly cook because the old woman spilled a bowl of sauce, which stained the rug in the breakfast room. Disciplining a servant as such made him wonder how she might treat their children, who regularly could be counted on to create similar messes. Add that to her lack of interest in the finer things in life, her obsession with cleanliness, her absolute trust in a man obviously not capable of meeting his responsibility to the estate, and her colloquial attitude, and Darcy began to consider whether his marriage to this woman would be advisable when balanced against her few attributes.

She certainly was not one most men would choose. She had no apparent talents, and Miss Donnelly had her quirks. In fact, she possessed only two redeeming qualities: a pretty face and Darling Hall. The thoughts of her in his bed offered repulsive images. *I wonder if she will take her gloves off then?* Yet, he knew men often took a mistress if the home bed did not fulfill their needs. Darcy could not imagine Elizabeth Donnelly would much care. "She has a repugnance for anything of an intimate nature," he once told Conrad.

What Darcy had trouble justifying was his nightly dreams. In those, he passionately romanced a different woman. Was she his fantasy to replace the "cold" Miss Donnelly? In his dreams, he took her deeply and completely, and the woman of his dreams returned his passion. She consumed him. Always the same woman, Darcy often woke feeling her breath on his neck or his heart racing from the heat of her kiss.

In addition to dreams of his "lady," he held realities of previous conversations. Some dealt with the qualities of accomplished women, his love of literature and music, his knowledge of an estate, and a history in Hertfordshire. These were fragments of his previous life, but Darcy could not put the puzzle pieces together to form a new whole. Where did the answer lie? Part of him wanted to be the dutiful son and possibly achieve his father's forgiveness. Marrying within the family and developing Darling Hall could earn him respect and honor. Part of Darcy wanted the relationship he found only in his dreams. Elizabeth Donnelly would never bring forth any such passion. Oh, but to find such a relationship would be unheard of in fine society.

He considered leaving, trying other options, but he possessed no funds of his own. He found himself fully at Miss Donnelly's whims. In some ways, he was no better than Mr. Lansing, at least in that regard. One moment, Darcy thought marrying Miss Donnelly was the most logical thing to do; the next he wished to run madly from the estate, warning all about the "crazy" world found behind the walls of Darling Hall. Could he go through with the marriage? Neither his dreams nor his reality could answer that question.

So, each night he welcomed the dreams of the unknown woman. She sustained him during his waking hours because the woman was the one constant in his life. The daylight hours brought him new realities, but the night brought a familiarity—a need he could not fill during the day. He saw her eyes—a pair of fine eyes—and an enigmatic smile, along with a raised eyebrow. Darcy felt the heat of her mouth on his—a love that devoured his reason. He imagined himself taking her into his arms along walkways, deserted paths, gardens, conservatories, and in his bed. She smiled at him, and he wanted her in a breathless desire. Darcy knew Elizabeth Donnelly could never meet such needs—not in a million years.

★ ★ ★

Georgiana Darcy first saw the familiar figure from the window of her bedchamber, and her heart leapt into her throat. She grabbed her pelisse and hurried down the central staircase.

"Where are you off to?" Elizabeth called to her.

"I believe I need some fresh air," she returned the call, but she did not stop. She was out the door and heading toward the rise behind Pemberley. When she crossed the second clearing, the figure stepped from a copse of Spanish oaks and pulled her within the secrecy the trees offered. "I feared you would not come." He looked deeply into Georgiana's eyes.

"Mr. Harrison, you should not be here; I should not be here," she stammered, feeling his closeness.

Harrison instinctively moved in closer. "I had to see you; I heard about your Mr. Darcy."

"Elizabeth is devastated; Fitzwilliam went to Hull, but he never made it to his destination." Georgiana dropped her eyes, not wishing to tell Mr. Harrison the real reason for her brother's botched trip.

"Miss More wrote to me; that is why I am here," Harrison told her. "I had to see for myself that you and Mrs. Darcy were all right. Would it be too much if I offered your sister my help until her husband returns?"

"What about Hines Park?" Georgiana's eyes did not leave his face.

"Indirectly, your brother's disappearance is my fault. I wish to be of service to you and Mrs. Darcy in some manner." By now, Harrison could feel the heat of his need for Georgiana Darcy.

"Elizabeth would never accept such self-censure from you, Mr. Harrison. She would offer you no blame in Fitzwilliam's disappearance."

He asked softly, "Would she accept my help?"

Georgiana could no longer look at the man without touching him. "You may come to the house and ask my sister yourself." Georgiana dropped her eyes.

An elongated silence hung between them. "Miss Darcy, please look at me," he whispered. Georgiana slowly raised her eyes to gaze lovingly on his face. "I like the man I see in your eyes." Harrison caressed her face. "A man could get lost in your eyes."

Georgiana's smile grew with the knowledge he was close to her after so long a separation. "Let me return to the house before you call on the estate. It is best if we are not seen together."

"I am happy you said *seen together* rather than *be together.*" Harrison offered her an unsure look.

"Definitely *seen together,*" Georgiana giggled. "I will greet you properly in my home, Sir." She turned to go, but in looking back, Georgiana impulsively mimicked his earlier caress and traced the outline of his lips.

CHAPTER 11

"What wild imaginations one forms where dear self is concerned!
How sure to be mistaken!"
Jane Austen, *Persuasion*, 1817

⸺◦◦◦⸺

Kitty Bennet waited for Mr. Ashford's daily visit but was surprised when a maid showed Lydia into the drawing room. "Lydia?" Standing immediately, Kitty gasped, "What are you doing here?"

Lydia Bennet Wickham untied her bonnet. "Well, is that any way to address me?" she protested. "Do not tell me you are taking on Lizzy's uppity airs. I came here to see you and Lizzy. Is that not acceptable?"

Kitty shifted nervously. "Of course," she began, "I am sure Lizzy will be happy to see you. Let me go tell her. Have a seat, Lydia; I will ask the maid to bring us some tea." Kitty started for the door.

"Are you not the be all and end all—that is right, Kitty, have a maid bring us some tea. I will have a seat and wait on you and Lizzy, but please hurry. My journey was long, and I would like some rest." Lydia strolled over to a chair and collapsed into it. "Well, Kitty, do not just stand there. Find Elizabeth."

Kitty rushed from the room. She knew Elizabeth would not be happy to see Lydia, especially an unannounced visit and with everything else going on at Pemberley. Truthfully, Kitty did not want to see Lydia, either. Kitty developed an identity separate from the flouncy, inconsiderate girl sitting in Pemberley's downstairs drawing room, and she definitely did not want Clayton Ashford to meet Lydia. He would see how poor her connections really were, and he would withdraw his affections from her. As far as Kitty knew, Lydia would mess up everything!

Georgiana Darcy rushed through Pemberley's front hallway, planning to be at the pianoforte when Mr. Harrison made his call on Elizabeth, but as she hurried by her brother's study, an ominous figure brought her to a complete stop outside the door. Mustering her courage, she stepped inside the room and addressed the man. "Mr. Wickham, why are you in my brother's study?" Her voice shook as she spoke, but Georgiana's countenance did not change.

A smirk overspread George Wickham's face as he made her a proper bow. "Miss Darcy, how nice to see you." He allowed his eyes to drift slowly down Georgiana's body.

His steady gaze created a momentary uneasiness in her, but Georgiana resolved long ago some day she would face Mr. Wickham full force as a Darcy. "I will ask you again, Sir, why I find you in Fitzwilliam's study? He will not be happy you assume liberties in coming here."

"Your brother is more than likely dead," he said as he stepped closer to her, "so any *liberties I may take* will be of little consequence to him." Wickham gave her a look of intimacy.

Georgiana took a step toward the desk, but Wickham moved in front of her. His smile told of a familiarity he should not be taking. "You certainly grew up, Georgiana; upon seeing you again, I regret leaving you so suddenly at Ramsgate." He reached out to caress her face, and Georgiana repulsively contracted, stepping back and closing her eyes to block out his presence.

"Mr. Wickham," Elizabeth's voice echoed through the study, and both he and Georgiana flinched with the sound.

"Miss Bennet," he stammered.

"You, Sir, know that is no longer my name." Elizabeth stepped to Georgiana's side and gracefully maneuvered the girl a few steps away from Wickham's presence. Then she stepped behind Darcy's desk. "To what do we owe the pleasure of your company today, Mr. Wickham?" Elizabeth's voice held true contempt.

"Elizabeth." Wickham offered her an affable smile. "Your mother wrote of your distress. Of course, I grieved at your loss as my sister and of the loss of my brother Fitzwilliam."

"I will kindly ask you to refrain from referring to either my husband or me in such familiar terms. I warned Lydia of that fact prior to my marriage to Mr. Darcy. I instructed Lydia to tell you, specifically, we would never welcome you in this house," Elizabeth asserted.

"Now, Mrs. Darcy, we cannot allow past transgressions to affect our current relationship. As I was just ready to explain to Georgiana, I came to make my apologies and to offer my assistance. My father served this estate faithfully for over twenty years. The least I can do is offer my help to you, my wife's sister, in her time of need." Wickham carefully avoided referring to Elizabeth or Darcy as immediate *family*.

Elizabeth laughed. "Can you really possess such gall to think I would accept an offer from you after the betrayal you offered to my husband?" During this speech Elizabeth's hands slowly pulled Darcy's desk drawer open enough to grasp the gun he bought her shortly after bringing her to Pemberley. Darcy took such delight in teaching her to shoot it. "Now, I will kindly ask you to quit this house and never return."

"Mrs. Darcy, surely you do not mean what you say." Wickham took a step toward the desk.

"I would not do that if I were you." Elizabeth pointed the gun at him. "At this range, I will not miss."

Wickham's eyes grew larger, and he stammered as he said, "Mrs. Darcy—Elizabeth—you must see the foolishness of this action." He tried to edge to the side.

Elizabeth cocked the gun. "If one lies down with a dog, he

is likely to get up with fleas. I do not choose to be bitten by fleas today, Mr. Wickham. Now, turn around and leave this house. I will not ask again."

Wickham offered her a smile while saying, "Of course, Elizabeth, I only thought to be of some service to you." He began to back away, but in order to exit the room, Wickham crossed Georgiana's path. The girl had not moved since Elizabeth placed her where she currently stood. Wickham could not give up his plan so easily, and, impulsively, he reached out to grab Georgiana's arm. When the girl screamed, Elizabeth fired.

In a blaze of smoke, the bullet grazed Wickham's left shoulder and lodged in the bookcase behind him. A curse filled the room as he advanced on Elizabeth, dragging Georgiana with him. Yet, before the smoke from the gun cleared, and before Wickham took more than a few menacing steps, he found himself held tightly in a stranglehold and the point of a stiletto resting beneath his chin. Mr. Harrison's voice hissed with anger as he tightened the hold. "If I were you, Sir, I would release Miss Darcy's arm immediately unless you would prefer to die on this spot."

Georgiana gasped, but Elizabeth calmly stepped from behind the desk and looked up at Mr. Wickham and smiled. "Mr. Harrison." She offered him a proper curtsy. "How pleasant to see you again." Her voice became sugary as she looked through Wickham as if he did not exist.

"I am sorry to intrude on your little party." His voice softened some from his initial appearance in the room, but Harrison had not loosened his hold on George Wickham.

"Mr. Wickham," Elizabeth said as she went over and removed his fingers from around Georgiana's wrist, "I will ask Mr. Harrison to let you live only because you are Lydia's husband." As she said the words, both Kitty and Lydia appeared at the door. "Lydia, your husband has a flesh wound to which you must attend," Elizabeth called out to her. "I will have Mr.

Howard and some of my men escort you two back into Lambton; I expect you shall want to return to Newcastle as soon as possible." Elizabeth's tone offered her younger sister no choice in the matter, and, for a change, Lydia did not protest.

"Mr. Harrison, will you show Mr. Wickham to the door?" Elizabeth never looked at the man again as she turned her back on Wickham and Lydia.

"Gladly, Mrs. Darcy." Harrison's voice was pleasant, but then he menacingly whispered in Wickham's ear, "If you touch Miss Darcy again—in fact, if I hear you even mentioned her name, I will finish this. Stay away from this estate forever. Do you understand me?" Wickham nodded his head in the affirmative as best he could under the restraint of the hold Harrison had on him. Harrison released the throat hold, but he pointedly placed the stiletto to Wickham's back. "This way, Sir." He motioned for Wickham to move to the door. Wickham, nearly doubled over from a lack of oxygen, gasped and rubbed his throat, but he moved past Lydia to exit the house. She chased after him, trying to help his progress, but Wickham shoved her away. As if by magic, Mr. Howard and two other riders appeared to follow the unhappy couple back up Pemberley's lane toward Lambton.

No one in the study moved until they heard the main door slam shut, and then Georgiana felt her legs buckle under her as both Elizabeth and Kitty rushed to her side. "Come, Sweetheart," Elizabeth spoke softly as she led Georgiana to a nearby chair. "Kitty, get her a drink," Elizabeth demanded quickly.

Georgiana smiled sheepishly, "Did you just shoot Mr. Wickham?" Her voice shook with glee.

"I believe I did." Elizabeth joined in the ambiguous laughter. Kitty looked at them both and began to giggle also. Within a few seconds all three stood together in each other's embrace, laughing playfully.

When Mr. Harrison returned to the study, he stood mesmerized by the scene. "I thought I might offer my assistance," he mused, "but I see you three are quite capable of handling situations in your own special way."

"Oh, Mr. Harrison," Elizabeth said as she came forward, wearing a look of utter abandon, "I must admit next to my husband, I was never so pleased to see someone as I am you today. How much you were missed—words cannot explain." She extended her hand, and he kissed it lightly as he bowed. Elizabeth took Harrison's arm as she turned him toward the drawing room. "Come, ladies," she called over her shoulder. "This house has been solemn too long. Mr. Ashford will be here momentarily, and I think we need the companionship of close friends. That is what makes Pemberley strong."

Within minutes, Mr. Ashford joined the group in the drawing room. As Georgiana and Kitty filled him in with the details of why he passed an obviously agitated man and woman walking toward Lambton and followed by Pemberley staff members, Elizabeth with her eyes indicated to Harrison for him to join her by the window.

"Mr. Harrison," Elizabeth began in hushed tones, "although I am truly happy to see you, may I ask why you came here today?"

Harrison mimicked her casual manner in case anyone watched them too carefully. "Mrs. Darcy, I received news from Hannah More regarding your husband's disappearance. I am astute enough after the last conversation I had with Mr. Darcy to realize he traveled to Hull because of what I shared with him regarding Captain Rutherford. I came to beg your forgiveness and to offer my assistance to you in any way I may be of service." His eyes searched Elizabeth's face for her reaction.

"You need no forgiveness from me; you did nothing. I honestly believe God sends us no more than what we can handle. At least, that is what my dear Fitzwilliam assured me after my announcement of delivering an heir for Pemberley. If Captain Rutherford was not the problem, another issue would take Fitzwilliam away. It is part of our life's journey."

"You are so wise, Mrs. Darcy; it is obvious why Mr. Darcy knew he needed you in his life." Admiration showed on Harrison's countenance.

Elizabeth blushed with his praise and then touched his arm lightly before adding, "I am going to offer you one reprimand, Sir, if I may."

"Of course."

"Please do not entice my sister to join you in the woods again," she teased.

Harrison chuckled lightly. "It was not my intention, but I will not lie and say I was not pleased to see Miss Darcy. I came to see if you would accept my help, but I held back knowing of my promise to you and your husband regarding your sister. Plus, I felt guilty about Mr. Darcy's disappearance."

Elizabeth smiled largely. "At least you sent her back to the house quickly."

Harrison allowed his eyes to drift toward Georgiana. "One of the hardest things I ever did." His lips turned up in the beginnings of a smile as he watched the woman who inspired him. Looking back at Elizabeth, he asked, "May I inquire as to why your brother caused such chaos today, or have I overstepped my bounds in doing so?"

"It is not something I readily share," Elizabeth hesitated. "Mr. Wickham spent a lifetime trying to exact revenge on my husband. He was once a favorite of the Darcy family, but he chose to let his jealousy control his fate. My husband's father educated the man and offered him a living. Instead, Mr. Wickham chose a more nefarious lifestyle—he took a settlement instead of the living. Then he came back to seek additional funds from my dear Fitzwilliam. Mr. Darcy refused." At this point, Elizabeth hesitated, not sure if she should share Georgiana's shame.

Finally, she began again. "Considering your admiration for my sister, I will tell you something of what happened, but she must trust you herself and tell you the specifics." Mr. Harrison nodded his agreement. "Mr. Wickham once played on Georgiana's innocence. That is why Fitzwilliam and I are careful about with whom she associates. She was not compromised, but Mr. Wickham is quite persuasive; he even once tried to entice me from Mr. Darcy."

Harrison looked a bit shocked, but he said nothing. Elizabeth continued, "The fact Georgiana faced Mr. Wickham today tells me how she matures." Harrison's eyes returned to Georgiana's face. "Mr. Wickham eventually compromised my youngest sister Lydia. Needless to say, I would prefer this did not become common knowledge." He nodded again, assuring her of his secrecy. "Mr. Darcy arranged Lydia's wedding in order to save her, my other sisters, and me. He did it because of his love for me, keeping it a secret and not wishing just my gratitude. Mr. Darcy is such an honorable man—the best man I have ever known."

Elizabeth let images of Darcy play across her mind. "Mr. Wickham's commission is a *gift* from my husband. It is a *long way* from here to Newcastle." Elizabeth laughed lightly. "Mr. Wickham saddled himself with the least of my sisters—my mother's darling girl whose head is filled with balls and military officers. I warned them before my wedding never to come here, but Mr. Wickham tried to take advantage of Mr. Darcy's absence to insinuate himself back at Pemberley. That is why I sent him packing."

"That is quite a story!"

"The truth is stranger than fiction," she mused. "Yet, it could make a great novel, could it not?"

"Maybe you could suggest it to Mrs. Radcliffe."

"I do not think it has enough drama for her taste—it would all have to take place in a darkened castle." Elizabeth allowed herself to laugh again.

Harrison returned to his mission in coming to Pemberley. "Then I will ask again, Mrs. Darcy, how I might be of service to you."

"Later today, if you would, I will ask you to ride into Lambton and be sure my sister and her husband have a room for tonight and tickets on tomorrow's coach. I cannot let Lydia suffer because of my disdain for Mr. Wickham," Elizabeth offered her plan.

Harrison bowed gently to take his leave. "That would be my pleasure, Madam."

Elizabeth touched his arm again to stop his withdrawal. "Would you stay with us for a few days? If it is not too much trouble, I would ask you to ride out with Mr. Howard and inspect the lands. I trust Mr. Howard, but it would do the tenants good to see someone—a man—who takes an interest in the estate. They know Mr. Howard to be an employee. I will ask Georgiana to ride out, too. If the two of you are with Mr. Howard, it will send a message to the tenants that Pemberley's future is in safe hands."

"Mrs. Darcy, how quickly you learned your husband's ways."

"Fitzwilliam's voice is always in my head. Let us rejoin the others. You may even sit next to my sister today," Elizabeth teased. "It will be your reward for your valiant efforts on her behalf."

"She is magnificent," Harrison verbalized his thoughts.

Elizabeth cautioned, "I have not changed my mind about your declaring yourself, Mr. Harrison. With my Fitzwilliam's departure, I need Georgiana more than ever."

Harrison dropped his eyes. "I know, Mrs. Darcy."

"Plus, you should know my husband and I are teaching Georgiana about the running of an estate. She will be a formidable mate for any man brave enough to choose her," Elizabeth taunted.

"If I believe in liberty for men of color, I certainly could not consider making my wife my *subject*. Miss Darcy's knowledge of an estate would not intimidate me nor would it intimidate any man who truly values a woman's ability. In the Americas, women work alongside their men; it is a liberating concept."

"Well spoken, Mr. Harrison." Elizabeth grinned largely. "Now, I am in need of some tea." They walked back toward the others. Harrison quickly claimed the seat next to Georgiana, fearing Elizabeth might change her mind, but Elizabeth took note of Georgiana's fragile condition after the scene with Mr. Wickham and allowed her husband's sister to glory in Mr. Harrison's attention to her.

★ ★ ★

Stress filled the day at Darling Hall. Miss Donnelly prowled the passageways, pacing the floors and possessing a foul mood. Fitzwilliam Darcy avoided her, going riding and shooting. He decided several days ago he would leave the estate soon; Miss Donnelly's temperament was too mercurial for his tastes. He decided he would beg his father for forgiveness rather than align himself with such a self-possessed woman. In fact, a little over a week ago, he addressed a letter to his father, pleading for just that—the right to come home and start anew.

Darcy stayed at Darling Hall for nearly a month. Now, he would wait for the response from his father and then bid Miss Donnelly adieu. She would not be happy with his decision, and Darcy dreaded the scene that would occur, but even a dutiful son had to consider the price he paid to please his father.

He remembered various facts in the past fortnight, but Darcy did not discuss them with Miss Donnelly. Her answers played down his recollections; however, the same ideas kept resurfacing nightly in his dreams. Darcy had not abandoned his thoughts of a sister. In fact, the name *Georgiana* rang clearly in his memory, and the girl in his dreams was too young to be his brother's wife.

He remembered a large estate, grieving for his mother's passing. His father grieved also to the point of distraction, often leaving his children alone. He felt a sister, but he could not recall a brother. As these memories resurfaced, he decided Miss Donnelly deceived him. He knew not why unless she simply did not have other options. The confusion caused by the memories and the lies deepened his anxiety each day.

As Darcy crawled in bed this particular evening, his own nerves frayed, he anticipated a return of his favorite dream— the dream of the woman who saw only him and who loved only him. The dream this evening was a new one, and he allowed it to overtake his senses.

More pensive than usual, his calmness possessed an intensity he knew not before. Finishing his ablutions quickly, he entered Elizabeth's bedroom to wait for her. He lit several candles and took a seat facing the door to her dressing room; yet, the door opened before he could settle his nerves completely, and she was framed in the backlight of the adjoining room. He remembered her being framed in a doorway at his friend's estate, boots and petticoat covered in mud. He actually thought her lovely then; now she was beautiful. With the light behind her, Darcy could see Elizabeth's perfect body through the gown. They looked at each other, entranced by the moment until she stepped slowly into the room, and the door closed behind her. Darcy could not stand to not be near her; so he rose and crossed to where she stood.

His touch of her skin sent a shiver through Elizabeth's body; he cupped her chin as he lifted it to kiss her lips—the kiss warm and tender. She moved in closer, encircling her arms around his waist and instinctively sliding her hands under Darcy's shirt and up the muscles of his back. He trembled as he kissed her again while slowly pulling her closer to him and letting his hands rest on her hips. Their breathing became shallow as the kisses became more intense.

Darcy scooped her into his arms and carried her to the bed, laying her gently against the pillows. She shifted nervously as his gaze grew in its eagerness. He removed his nightshirt and lowered himself beside her, kissing her repeatedly, his hands searching her body beneath her gown while his lips moved down her neck. Elizabeth reached out and pulled him to her; she would be his.

He felt her soft hands on his chest, and her lips caressed his chin line. Darcy moaned, knowing in moments she would give herself to him and, at last, be his forever. He allowed his hands to move down the curve of her back, and he pulled her hips to him. Unbelievably, she touched him intimately, and Darcy groaned with anticipation. His hands slipped her gown upward, desperately wanting the assurance of her embrace.

This dream was perfect. He felt it all—the heat of her breath, the warmth of her skin, the gloved hand caressing him. Darcy knew this could not be real, but he never wanted it to end. He cupped her chin with his hand to bring her mouth to his. "I love you," he gasped.

"I love you, Frederick," she purred.

The realization of her words and the encumbered feeling of her touch finally invaded his psyche, and Darcy violently pushed the woman from him while grabbing at the bedclothes to cover himself.

"Madam, what do you mean by being here?" he demanded.

Miss Donnelly stood before him, wearing nothing more than a silky nightgown along with wrist-length white gloves. Her appearance struck him as comical, and he fought the urge to start laughing.

"I desired your attentions." Miss Donnelly offered him a sugary smile. "May we not finish this?" She stepped closer to him to let him know her receptivity to the idea.

"I do not think so, Madam!" He put distance between them as he secured the bed linens around his waist.

Again, Miss Donnelly closed the distance between them. "But you told me of your love. You said, 'I love you,' not a minute ago."

"Madam, I assure you love is not the feeling I possess at this moment. You should not be found here," he tried to reason with her.

"We are to be married soon. We can anticipate our happiness," she argued.

Darcy's eyes took on a steel gray hue, his anger evident as he spoke to the woman still offering herself to him. "Miss Donnelly, *if* we marry, I will not be visiting your bed; even if we are alone forever, I shall not take my pleasure in you." His voice held a controlled resolve. "Now, I will ask you to leave my chambers."

"I will tell everyone you brought me here and compromised me; you will have to marry me." Miss Donnelly picked up her robe from the floor where she dropped it.

"If you tell people what happened this evening, I will deny it, and it will be your shame alone. As a female, your word will never take precedence over mine in a court of law, and I will take it that far if you insist on our marrying. What reputation you have will be ruined; your lifestyle is too idiosyncratic for the conservative farmer found in this area to believe anything you say. You will be left with no reputation at all. This is not a bourgeois neighborhood. Do I make myself clear!? You are eight and twenty and have no marriage prospects to date. Whom do you think the populace will believe? You invited me to Darling Hall; in fact, your carriage brought me to Darling Hall for all I know. I will swear you did so to ensnare me."

Miss Donnelly began to shake with anger and embarrassment. "You do not intend to marry me?" Her words hung in the air.

"I considered the matter, and it does not seem to be in our mutual interest to do so."

She started to continue her protest when she caught the movement out of the corner of her eye. Full of rage and mortification, Elizabeth Donnelly turned to see Conrad standing in the shadows. He rose from his pallet on the floor and stood mesmerized by the melodrama playing out in front of him. "You!" she screamed, pointing a gloved finger in his direction. "Why are you lurking about in Mr. Donnelly's room? Speak, man, don't stand there like a mute."

Her glare intensified as Conrad shifted his weight under her stare. He stammered, trying to compose an answer to an obvious question. Mr. Donnelly did not trust the household staff nor did he trust her. Before he committed an ultimate sin of speaking out unceremoniously to his employer, Darcy stepped forward, placing himself between Elizabeth Donnelly and his manservant. "Control yourself, Madam," he demanded in a harsh whisper. "You are making a scene. It is bad enough you entered my bedchamber uninvited; now you propose to complicate the matter by announcing to the staff your indiscretion. Have you no shame? You prove my point with this display. I assure you Conrad's silence in this matter, but if you do not leave now, your actions will readily become public knowledge. Now, I suggest you leave my room posthaste. We will never speak of this incident again. Do I make myself clear?"

Darcy's head remained only inches from her upturned face. A stranger coming upon the scene might think he stumbled upon a moment of intimacy between a man and a woman; however, Darcy felt nothing but contempt for the lady standing in front of him. He fought hard to keep that emotion out of his voice when next he spoke. "Conrad will escort you back to your room, Miss Donnelly. Have a pleasant evening." He placed his hand on her elbow to guide her toward the bedroom door, opening it precipitously. With a flick of his wrist, he motioned for Conrad to escort his employer back to her bedroom.

"I do not want that man near me," she demanded as she looked back at the truly stunned servant.

"Then I will summon your maid." Darcy pretended to pacify her. "Of course, that will add to your duplicity. I guarantee Conrad's loyalty to this estate and to your family; I cannot speak as such for the other servants. Now, do you still wish for me to summon your maid? I suppose if you insist, I could escort you wrapped in my bedclothes, but I do not see how that will nullify the situation. What shall it be, Madam?"

Shocked, she shrieked at the top of her lungs, pulled the gloves from her hands, threw them on the floor at her feet, and heavily stamped to her room. As instructed, Conrad followed at a respectful distance until she entered her chambers and slammed the door.

Miss Donnelly sat at the desk of her study. She had not seen Darcy all day. He took breakfast in his rooms. She must think of some way out of this mess; her mind raced, looking for a solution. If she could not seduce Darcy, he would not marry her; then where would she be? Her thoughts dwelt on the embarrassment of the previous night, and she was unaware of the maid's presence at the door.

"Miss Donnelly," the maid said, waiting for the mistress's attention before continuing. "There is a gentleman from Kent to see you."

Shaking the cobwebs from her mind, she said, "Send him in."

The short, pudgy clergyman entered the study and made Miss Donnelly an ostentatious bow. "Miss Donnelly, I am Mr. William Collins. Your request through my father Sir William

Lucas to officiate over your nuptials honored me. To marry the son of a lord is a rare distinction."

"Ah, Mr. Collins." Miss Donnelly made him a curtsy. "I forgot you arrived today." She tried to put on a face of confidence, but Miss Donnelly wondered what to do with Mr. Collins now that Darcy rejected her advances.

"Of course, I came as quickly as possible. My esteemed patroness Lady Catherine de Bourgh of Rosings Park kindly released me of my duties this week so I might attend to your needs. My curate will deliver my sermon to my flock at Hunsford tomorrow." Mr. Collins spoke quickly, trying to impress with his connections. "We may do the ceremony early Monday morning."

"Mr. Collins," she finally interrupted his speech, "my cousin and I wish to marry immediately. We were to marry previously, but armed highwaymen attacked Frederick, forcing us to postpone." Why she just did not admit there would be no marriage even surprised her.

"How awful," Collins gasped. "I assume your cousin is with health now."

"He is recovering quite well, thank you." She offered him a seat. "May I offer you some refreshments, Mr. Collins?"

"No, thank you, Miss Donnelly. Might I, however, meet your intended? I believe it is part of my responsibility as a spiritual leader to counsel my charges. Lady Catherine de Bourgh highly agrees this to be a part of my duties. In fact, she encourages it. I am currently providing such services to her daughter Miss Anne de Bourgh and her intended Colonel Fitzwilliam, who is actually the son of Lord and Lady Matlock."

Miss Donnelly thought she never saw such a pompous nincompoop in her life, but if she could still convince Darcy to marry her, she would tolerate anything. So, did it matter whether Darcy would visit her bedroom or not? That activity did not particularly interest her anyway. She would approach it as a business deal; Darcy would marry her, and she would give him part of the inheritance. There was still hope this could be resolved. About that time Darcy came down the main staircase. She quickly moved to the study's door and called to him. "Frederick, would you come here a moment? I have someone who wishes to meet you."

Darcy rolled his eyes at her request, but he did as she asked. He entered the doorway of the study and said, "Yes, Madam."

Mr. Collins jumped to his feet expecting to see a refined gentleman, but the surprise of seeing Fitzwilliam Darcy standing in the doorway froze the man in place. He knew from Lady Catherine and from his wife's family in Hertfordshire that Darcy had been missing for five weeks. To find him here in Brigg actually stifled Collins. "Frederick, this is Mr. William Collins. Mr. Collins, this is my cousin, Frederick Donnelly."

Darcy, much to Collins's surprise, did not change his expression. He made a quick bow before speaking. "Mr. Collins, welcome to Darling Hall. I am afraid, Sir, you caught me at an inopportune time; I must excuse myself. I am sure my cousin will entertain you nicely." Before anyone could respond, Darcy left the room and the house.

Miss Donnelly tried to cover her embarrassment. Obviously, Darcy's anger had not subsided. "My cousin is very busy with the estate," she stammered.

"Your cousin?" Mr. Collins's voice rose in disbelief. "That man is not your cousin!"

"You are mistaken, Sir. That man is my cousin Frederick Donnelly." She forced her voice to remain even.

"Madam," Collins said as he began to pace the floor, "that man is Fitzwilliam Darcy, the Master of Pemberley, the nephew of my esteemed patroness Lady Catherine de Bourgh. What kind of deceit are you trying to practice here?" His accusations hit Miss Donnelly fully, and she steadied herself with the back of the chair.

Repeating her earlier remark, she mumbled. "You are mistaken, Sir. He is my cousin Frederick."

"Madam, he is my cousin! Mr. Darcy is married to my cousin Elizabeth Bennet from Longbourn. It is an estate entailed to me upon her father's death. What makes you think I know not this man?"

Miss Donnelly whispered in disbelief, "He is married?"

"My cousin Elizabeth is with child," Collins added triumphantly.

"Mr. Collins," Miss Donnelly recovered quickly, "I will have my men bring my coach to take you back into town." She rang the bell for a maid.

"Miss Donnelly," he began to protest, but the woman left the room without even a by-your-leave. Within seconds, a staff member ushered him from the room and the house. Collins had no opportunity to speak to Darcy again.

CHAPTER 12

*"A lady's imagination is very rapid; it jumps from admiration to love,
from love to matrimony, in a moment."*
Jane Austen, *Pride and Prejudice*, 1813

Darcy rode the horse hard across the lands surrounding Darling Hall; agitation remained from the previous night. He had not slept after physically removing Miss Donnelly from his room. Her desperation meant he must be cautious. Having the foresight to have Conrad sleep in his rooms saved him last night. He would continue to do so. That would stymie her efforts to seduce him into marriage.

He pulled up the horse and dismounted. Looking back at the house from the rise to the left, he could see Miss Donnelly's coach leaving with the man he met in the study. This Mr. Collins was dressed as a clergyman so Miss Donnelly, obviously, had not abandoned her plans for marriage. The image of the woman standing in his room last night sent revulsion pulsing through his body. "She actually wore gloves to my bedroom," he muttered. "How could I even consider marriage to such a woman?"

Momentarily, Darcy thought of marrying Miss Donnelly and immediately having her committed for the mentally inept, but he knew that would mean being married until her death—even if she were no longer in the home. No, he simply wanted away from her—away from Darling Hall. The problem he faced was a lack of funds.

Darcy had nothing. Even the horse he rode belonged to the estate. If he took the horse, even with a promise to return it, Miss Donnelly would likely send the constable after him. That certainly would not get him back into good graces with his father, and his belongings left from the robbery were of little value for selling. Darcy's quandary—his escape from the situation in which he found himself—rested in a positive response from his father. He would simply delay his departure from Darling Hall until the fateful letter arrived.

The thing that shook his being, even more this morning than his confrontation with Miss Donnelly last night, was the dream in which he was lost to the woman. Darcy knew it was the same woman—the woman of whom he dreamed each night. Only last night, he finally saw her in the dream—not just felt her presence—actually saw her face. Next to him, the woman was petite and lilt, and his thoughts of her body next to his sent sensations coursing through him even now. If he could possess such a woman, then he thought he could feel contentment.

Mr. Collins's departure sent Miss Donnelly into a tailspin. She knew it would be only a matter of days before someone knew of her plans. What would she do then? Needless to say, Mr. Collins would send a dispatch to Mr. Darcy's real family, and then she would be found out. So, for several days she hid in her room, expecting Mr. Darcy and his loved ones to demand to see her. Yet, a week passed without notice, and she eventually returned to her usual routine, although she still avoided Darcy.

Had she known more of Mr. Collins she would know he did report seeing Mr. Darcy to his family. He told the person to whom he owed his living: Mr. Collins told Lady Catherine de Bourgh. Lady Catherine determined if her nephew wished to leave Elizabeth Bennet for a more appropriate match, then who was she to interfere. After all, her nephew demanded she stay out of his personal affairs, and, on this, she would honor his wishes. Therefore, no one knew of Darcy's whereabouts but his aunt and her faithful servant Mr. Collins.

★ ★ ★

First, Mr. Harrison came to the estate to help the ladies with the running of Pemberley. A few days later, Jane and Mr. Bingley reappeared. Finally, Colonel Fitzwilliam and Anne came to stay. Although Elizabeth appreciated their kindness upon her behalf, part of her wanted them to just go away. Darcy had been missing for nearly six weeks, and Elizabeth's nerves frayed with the effort to maintain her composure.

The end of March approached, as well as the end of Elizabeth's fifth month of pregnancy. Her girth expanded, and her need for Darcy's assurances multiplied with each additional pound added to their child's growth.

"Edward," she asked over tea, "why are you here?" Elizabeth knew the answer before she asked the question.

"I came to see how things at Pemberley progressed without my cousin here."

"May I translate for you, Colonel? Lady Catherine wanted you, as Georgiana's guardian, to assure I did not corrupt the Darcy line with my presence here."

The colonel blushed with her accusations. "You know my aunt too well," he chuckled. "Yet, I did want to see how you fared; you were always a favorite of mine, Mrs. Darcy, and I wanted promises you did not lose hope." With the kindness in his voice, the colonel undid her natural defenses.

"I miss Fitzwilliam," she sobbed, allowing herself the comfort of knowing Edward would not judge her for this display of femininity.

The colonel came around the table to take Elizabeth's hand. "It is a time when a woman would naturally feel the stress of everyday life; your taking on the running of this estate in my cousin's absence says he was a very astute man for having judged your real worth." Elizabeth collapsed into his out-stretched arms, tears flowing freely.

"I cannot go on without him," Elizabeth's voice broke with emotion. "It is not fair—three months is not long enough. Fitzwilliam and I wasted all those months fighting each other when we should have been together, building a future."

"He will come back." Edward stroked her cheek before using his handkerchief to dab away Elizabeth's tears. "If he is able, my cousin will return to you and to Pemberley."

The colonel's words, once she knew he spoke honestly, brought Elizabeth a new resolve. She squared her shoulders once again. "Thank you, Edward, I needed to hear those words from someone who knows my dear husband as well as I. As long as he is alive and safe, I will be happy."

★ ★ ★

During the week Miss Donnelly hid herself away in her room, Darcy took advantage of the reprieve to find out more about her, the estate, and her family. From the servants he learned of the demise of Miss Donnelly's parents and of the legal binding for her marriage, although the specifics regarding the additional bequest were not clear. He learned many of the staff left the estate with her takeover because of Miss Donnelly's temper tantrums and her fetish about cleaning. Darcy witnessed this firsthand. Reportedly, only Mr. Lansing could reason with her, but most felt he abused his power and lined his own pockets. As Darcy suspected, the estate had money problems, and Miss Donnelly sold off some family heirlooms to keep it afloat.

What was even more surprising, Darcy learned he was not at Darling Hall prior to his attack. He suspected as much for a long time, but now his suspicions regarding Miss Donnelly's deceit became truths. The question still remained why she did what she did, and, more importantly, who was he really?

Mr. Addison called one afternoon to check Darcy's progress. When he had the opportunity, Darcy questioned the man. "Mr. Addison, I understand you to say you are new to the area?"

Addison examined the wounds to see how they healed. "That is correct, Sir."

"Then you do not know Miss Donnelly's family?" Darcy tried to sound nonchalant.

"Darling Hall is one of the biggest estates in the area. I appreciate Miss Donnelly's support," Addison answered instead of responding to the question.

"I understand your candid remarks, Mr. Addison," Darcy assured him. "Yet, do you know whether the Donnellys have family in Hertfordshire?"

Mr. Addison put his medical instruments in his bag. "I cannot say for sure, but it would not seem so. From what I know of the family, they have deep roots in this area."

"It is just as I suspected," Darcy nearly mumbled, deep in thought. "I have memories of a different family from the one Miss Donnelly described to me. What should I do about this discrepancy?"

"May I ask what you mean?" The doctor seemed naturally curious.

"Miss Donnelly tells me I have an older brother who inherited my father's estate while I remember a younger sister, an elderly father, and I am the person in charge. Which memory should I believe, Mr. Addison?" Darcy looked confused.

The doctor asked kindly, "Do you dream, Sir?"

"I dream often of the family I described and of a woman I first thought to be a fantasy, but now I think she is real." Sharing his inner thoughts embarrassed Darcy.

"Memories and dreams are closely related. Your dreams are more reality than you realize, Sir."

Darcy shifted his weight uncomfortably; the images of the woman flitted across his mind's eye. "Again, I thank you, Mr. Addison; you gave me much to consider."

Based on what he already knew, when the post returned his letter sent to Lord Donnelly in Hertfordshire, Darcy took it in stride. He planned how he would face Miss Donnelly and demand the truth from her. Tomorrow would be the day he would confront her. Tomorrow, Darcy would learn her secrets.

★ ★ ★

Elizabeth sat at Darcy's desk going over the books for the estate when a maid brought in the post. At first, she thought she would wait until later to read the letter, but she recognized a familiar script and took it in her hand, touching the directions with her fingertips. "Ah, Charlotte, if we could go back to a gentler time," she mused out loud.

Elizabeth broke the seal and unfolded the paper to read the news from Charlotte Collins. Their relationship once was so close, but with Elizabeth's refusal of her cousin's proposal and Charlotte's eventual marriage to the ostentatious Mr. Collins, Elizabeth lost respect for Charlotte. Elizabeth knew Charlotte, never a romantic, chose Mr. Collins because she reasoned she possessed so few marriage offers his would be the best she could do. Elizabeth understood Charlotte's motives, but she hated to see her friend saddled with the supercilious Mr. Collins.

She leaned back in Darcy's chair. The finely worn leather gave Elizabeth comfort like no other piece of furniture in the house did. The chair held his form etched in the cushions, and Elizabeth often curled up in the chair to nap because she felt Darcy's form around her, holding her close to him. It was a silly idea, but she learned to hold on to silly ideas of late.

My dear Lizzy,

I hide away in my room writing this for I want neither Mr. Collins nor Lady Catherine to know I send this to you. Lady Catherine would remove my husband from his position if she finds out I share this, so I beg you to never tell from where you learned this information. Mr. Collins recently returned from Brigg. He was summoned there by a Miss Elizabeth Donnelly to perform a wedding between Miss Donnelly and her cousin, reportedly the son of a lord. Mr. Collins was anxious for such an honor, but he did not perform the ceremony. Miss Donnelly sent him away immediately when Mr. Collins recognized the groom to be your Mr. Darcy. Miss Donnelly introduced the cousin to Mr. Collins, but Mr. Darcy did not seem to recognize my husband.

Mr. Collins shared the knowledge with Lady Catherine, but she swore him to secrecy. That is why I implore you to keep knowledge of my involvement from others. Yet, I could not sleep if I kept this news from you. I love you, Lizzy, as I would my own sister. Your friend forever,

C. C.

Elizabeth's hand shook so badly she could barely read the words on the page, but she forced herself to reread the letter again to be sure she saw it correctly. She was unsure where Brigg was, but Elizabeth knew it to be near Hull, which made sense. She screamed for a maid, knowing she could not stand on her own.

"Yes, Mrs. Darcy." The maid appeared immediately.

"Send Miss Darcy and my family in to see me—now!" she demanded. "Find Colonel Fitzwilliam also."

The maid dropped a quick curtsy and then went off at a near run to check the various rooms for family members.

Jane and Mr. Bingley were the first to enter. Elizabeth's distraught appearance scared Jane, who first thought it to be a problem with the baby. She rushed to Elizabeth's side, and Bingley poured a glass of water. "Is it the child?" Jane gasped.

"No," Elizabeth began to stutter, "read . . . read the . . . read the letter." She shoved Charlotte's letter into Bingley's hand.

Immediately Colonel Fitzwilliam appeared in the doorway, followed closely by Georgiana. Darcy's sister rushed to Elizabeth's side.

By now Bingley perused the letter. His voice shook, but he exclaimed, "Capital, I knew Darcy lived!"

The colonel snatched the letter from Bingley's hand and started to read, but Georgiana asked him to read it out loud. He started; yet Elizabeth stopped him to ask Jane to close the study door first. "I want this news kept within this room."

Slowly and meticulously, the colonel started his recitation again. He cursed with the knowledge of Lady Catherine's involvement. "Thank you for keeping Anne out of this, Elizabeth," he offered.

"It is important to me to protect Charlotte. I do not care what happens to Mr. Collins, but Charlotte does not deserve Lady Catherine's censure."

"We must go after Fitzwilliam at once," Georgiana spoke up first.

The colonel agreed. "We will tell everyone Mr. Howard's inquiries finally paid off, and we heard where Darcy might be. We will not mention Mrs. Collins to anyone; does everyone concur?"

"Of course." Georgiana came around to look at the letter herself.

"I would like to go with you, Colonel," Bingley added. "Darcy is my best friend."

"I am going also," Georgiana stated.

Elizabeth started forward, but Jane caught her hand. "Elizabeth, you cannot think of going. You are too far with child to go. They must travel quickly, and you will just slow them down."

"But Jane," Elizabeth started, although she knew the truth of her eldest sister's words.

"We will bring my brother home." Georgiana encircled Elizabeth with her arms.

"Then waste no time," Elizabeth began to usher them toward the door. "I will order the coach. Please hurry, Edward; I am so frightened. If Fitzwilliam did not openly recognize Mr. Collins, that could mean he is in some kind of trouble."

"We will not come back without Darcy," Bingley added with an air of bravado.

Then the three were out the door and headed to their rooms, leaving Elizabeth with her steadfast sister Jane. "Elizabeth, have a seat."

"I cannot, Jane; Fitzwilliam could be home within a few days. I think I will go help Georgiana. There are things I want her to say to my husband. Why do you not go help Mr. Bingley? We may speak more once they are gone off to Brigg." Elizabeth held the door open. "Come, Jane; my prayers have been answered."

★ ★ ★

Darcy descended the staircase as quietly as he could. Of late, Miss Donnelly made a point of disappearing when he approached a room. Today, he wanted the opportunity to finally face her. The door to the study stood ajar, but Darcy recognized the two figures that occupied the room.

His first inclination told him to enter immediately, but his instinct told him to hold back. So, he stood near the open door and listened to their exchange.

"What happened to the cleric?" Mr. Lansing demanded as he paced back and forth.

Miss Donnelly looked frustrated. She unconsciously removed her gloves and then replaced them, pulling the kid covering on one finger at a time. "I sent the pretentious ass away."

"But why?" Darcy was surprised at the familiarity with which Lansing addressed his mistress.

"He knew Frederick's real identity," she confided at last.

Lansing stopped in front of Miss Donnelly and took up a dominant position. "That was a costly mistake."

"How was I to know his cousin was married to the man?" Miss Donnelly nearly whined.

Darcy listened carefully. Obviously, they spoke of him, but he possessed no memory of the clergyman he met several days ago nor did he know anything of a wife.

Miss Donnelly pressed down the seam along each finger of the right glove with the other hand. "The plan fell apart at that point."

"The plan fell apart when he threw you out of his bedroom," Lansing accused.

Miss Donnelly began to sob. "I made a mess of everything." She covered her face with her hands, indicating her remorse.

Lansing moved in closer and placed his arm leisurely around her shoulders. "There is no need for tears," he began and then cleared his throat before speaking again. "We may still fix this."

"But how?" Miss Donnelly buried her face into his shoulder for comfort.

Her behavior appalled Darcy. The man was the steward for the estate; he clearly overstepped his bounds, and Miss Donnelly accepted his attentions willingly. However, even though Darcy disapproved, he did nothing because such actions on the part of Miss Donnelly could easily be justified as grounds for terminating their engagement if she chose to make an issue of it. Although Darcy knew their relationship was a sham, he still had trouble delineating what was real and what was not.

"Miss Donnelly, you must by now realize my regard for you," Mr. Lansing tried to assure her. "We both know you had your heart set on marrying a fine gentleman, but the codicil your parents placed on the inheritance simply says you must marry. It does not stipulate to whom. If you will consider it, I would offer myself as an alternative."

Miss Donnelly raised her face to look squarely at Mr. Lansing. "Are you sure that will work?"

"We may have your solicitor review the document, but I read it. We could take over the estate together and run it as we should." Lansing took the woman's gloved hand in his.

"Would we then get the monetary settlement?" she asked unbelievingly.

"I am persuaded as such," Lansing told her. "So, will you accept my offer?"

"It seems I have no other choice; it would, therefore, be my honor," she whispered. Lansing took her in his arms, carefully making a point not to touch her skin on skin.

At this point, Darcy made his entrance, capturing their tender moment forever in their minds. "It seems you, Madam, chose to leave my affections behind." Darcy's voice boomed through the room.

Miss Donnelly looked aghast, but Mr. Lansing did not release his hold on her. The man found his voice first. "Miss Donnelly did nothing wrong. You must realize there was a mistake made on your behalf."

"A mistake?" Darcy accused. "A mistake, Sir, is a result of an accident—something unplanned—you and Miss Donnelly planned to deceive. Did you not? I heard you say as much a few moments ago."

"I never meant to hurt you." Miss Donnelly turned to Darcy, her tear-stained face showing some regret, but Darcy wondered whether it came from a result of the pain she caused him or from the fact her plan failed miserably.

"You lied to me." Darcy stepped closer to emphasize the point. "You said my name was Frederick Donnelly. What is it in reality?"

Lansing helped the lady to a seat before she answered. Her voice quivered with emotion. "Your name is Fitzwilliam Darcy."

Darcy demanded, "How do we know each other?"

"We met in London at the home of Mr. and Mrs. Hurst about a year ago," she explained. Lansing sat beside her and took Miss Donnelly's hand in his.

"I remember no one by the name of Hurst."

"I did not know who you were when we found you on the road—only after we brought you here. We spoke often at the party so I remembered you. That part makes sense—unfortunately, the rest does not. I need to marry to secure an inheritance. Your memory loss made it so easy to exaggerate the truth. Foolishly, I thought you would not deny me, even if your memory returned—you would owe me a debt." By now, the words were peppered with Miss Donnelly's sobs.

Darcy had her where he wanted her; Miss Donnelly openly admitted her guilt. "What else do you know of my real family?" Darcy's authoritative nature required Miss Donnelly respond truthfully. When he took that resolve, few could deny him.

"Actually, Sir, very little—we met only the one time. You are from somewhere in Derbyshire."

"And who was the clergyman?" Darcy cut in.

She looked around nervously. "I met Sir William Lucas," Miss Donnelly began.

"You mentioned him before," Darcy interrupted again.

Miss Donnelly swallowed hard. "Sir William Lucas comes from Hertfordshire; the clergyman Mr. Collins is Sir William's son by marriage. Mr. Collins claims you are married to his cousin."

"I find that fact hard to believe; even if I am not your cousin, obviously, I am of higher rank than that insipid man I met in your study the other day," Darcy reasoned. "How could I be married to someone in his family?"

"We cannot answer that question, Sir." Having been silent too long, Lansing joined the conversation.

"Cannot or will not answer?" Darcy insisted.

"Cannot," Lansing reaffirmed. "It was happenstance Mr. Collins ended up here. There is little else we can tell you."

"And—my accident—what of it?" Darcy took a dominant position in front of the mantelpiece.

"The coach was ransacked—your things scattered about the grounds. Miss Donnelly ordered us to save what we could, but most things of value were taken before we arrived," Lansing recited. "Your driver and postilion were dead, and you were left bleeding. Evidently, you were struck several times. Plus, you hit your head on a large rock." Darcy actually had a flash of memory of a blond gentleman snarling down from horseback at him. Unconsciously, he nodded with the words.

"Anything else?"

"Nothing of merit," Miss Donnelly interjected.

"Then where does that leave us in the situation you created here?" Darcy's anger returned.

Mr. Lansing would not be intimidated by the tone of Darcy's voice. "It seems prudent we help you to get on your way as soon as possible. We will arrange for the coach to take you into the village. You may stay at the inn until the next coach to London leaves day after tomorrow. Appropriate passage from there would be easily arranged."

"You plan to send me off to London without my knowing any more than what you have told me?" Darcy looked on in disbelief.

Lansing wanted to be rid of the stranger so he could advance his own plans with Miss Donnelly. "How else might we be of service to you, Sir? You can only find your way if you leave here. Perhaps someone in Derbyshire will recognize you."

"So I am just to roam around Derbyshire until someone recognizes me? That is not much of a plan, now is it, Sir?"

"We could contact Mr. Collins for more information or even Sir William Lucas," Miss Donnelly reasoned.

Darcy began to pace. "I suppose that is a start."

Miss Donnelly got up and moved to the desk. "It seems reasonable," she started, "to compensate you for the pain we caused you, Mr. Darcy."

"In other words, you wish me to not call the constable," Darcy said sarcastically.

"The constable will not solve your problem," Lansing added quickly. "Miss Donnelly saved your life, Sir; if not for her, you would be dead by now. Do not forget you owe her that much forgiveness."

Darcy chuckled lightly. "I shall permit Miss Donnelly to continue here at Darling Hall; however, my forgiveness is not likely to come."

"Mr. Darcy, I wronged you. I can only hope you will find your real family soon. You know your name and from where you come; your search cannot be that difficult. You are a well-known gentleman in London. This task cannot be as bothersome as you portray it to be." Miss Donnelly took control once more. "A Bow Street runner could bring you the information you seek within a day."

Lansing jumped at the chance. "It seems a hundred pounds is ample compensation to allow you to find your way home."

"I was thinking more like two hundred pounds," Darcy countered.

Lansing wanted to barter, but Miss Donnelly cut him off by readily agreeing to the two hundred pounds. Removing the payment from the safe, she added, "I will have Conrad pack your things; the coach will be ready to take you into the village in an hour." With those words, she dismissed Darcy. Miss Donnelly spent all the energy and time she would with her failed attempt at marriage. Mr. Lansing awaited her, and she wanted to move on. She went through what was expected of her in the form of regret, but the lady was not of the nature to dwell on her mistakes; she was a woman of action.

Handing Darcy the funds, she walked over to Lansing and took his arm while saying, "We have things to discuss, Sir." They left the room immediately.

Darcy stood in disbelief. "It figures," he said sarcastically. He looked at the money in his hand and then laughed out loud. "I guess I am to Derbyshire."

★ ★ ★

Colonel Fitzwilliam found rooms for himself, Bingley, and Georgiana at the inn in Brigg and then he secured directions to the estate owned by Miss Donnelly. Once they unpacked and settled in, the three of them would find out what Miss Donnelly knew of Darcy.

"I am so nervous," Georgiana told the two men. "I cannot imagine my brother staying away from Pemberley on purpose."

"Mrs. Collins's letter held elements of incredulity. Why would Darcy not respond to seeing Mr. Collins? It makes little sense," Bingley added.

They took tea in the inn as the stable harnessed fresh horses for their journey to Darling Hall. "My cousin cannot be in a good way. Darcy could not pledge himself to Miss Donnelly; Mr. Collins must be mistaken." Colonel Fitzwilliam shifted his weight uncomfortably.

Bingley stood. "I think I will check on the progress of the coach; I will return in a few minutes." He made his traveling partners a quick bow and left the inn.

"I am sure news of Darcy and this Donnelly woman does not sit well with Mr. Bingley," the colonel thought out loud. "With his wife being Elizabeth's sister, he must have trouble considering Darcy might abandon Elizabeth. Bingley would be forced to face Darcy as a matter of honor."

Georgiana gasped, "Edward, you cannot think as such about Fitzwilliam; he adores Elizabeth!"

"I agree, Georgiana, but something bizarre is happening here. If Darcy is healthy, why has he not returned home? Could he consider Elizabeth's connections to be a detriment after all?"

Georgiana began to sob. "Please do not say such things. How can you say you love Anne and think Fitzwilliam does not love Elizabeth? True love must exist in this world."

"I am sorry, Georgiana." Concerned his words upset his cousin, the colonel took her hand in his. "Of course, there must be a different explanation. There is too much chaos of late for any of us to think clearly. Darcy loves Elizabeth as I love Anne."

CHAPTER 13

*"It is always incomprehensible to a man that a woman should
ever refuse an offer of marriage. A man always imagines a woman
to be ready for anybody who asks her."*
Jane Austen, *Emma*, 1815

Darcy stepped from the Donnelly coach and looked around
the village. People bustled from one building to another,
mostly women holding onto hands of younger children—
through the very crowded street. He walked to the front of the
coach, and a stranger passed, spitting tobacco juice not a foot
from Darcy's polished boots. He scanned the half dozen
soldiers drilling beside the jail. Darcy lifted his head, his heart
pounding, and spoke to Conrad for probably the last time.
"Would you take my trunk to the inn, Conrad?"

"Yes, Sir." The man made Darcy a slight bow. "May I say,
Sir, you will be missed. It was an honor and a pleasure serving
you, Sir."

"I appreciate your tolerance, Conrad. If I may be of service
to you somehow, please feel free to contact my estate. According to Miss Donnelly, my name is Darcy, and I am from Derbyshire. If you tire of Darling Hall, I am sure I can find you
employment elsewhere." Darcy felt an obligation to the man
who nursed him back to health.

"Maybe I will consider your offer someday, Mr. Darcy, but,
at the moment, my family is here, and I must remain." Conrad
was apologetic, but thankful. He picked up the trunk and
headed toward the inn.

Darcy looked around the street again, hoping something might look familiar. Yet, a profound sense of loneliness crept into his veins. Since waking from his attack, the one face he felt he could trust belonged to a middle-aged man lugging his trunk toward the inn. Once Conrad returned to Darling Hall, Darcy would be entirely alone until he found someone he knew or who knew him.

He stepped off the wooden walkway to cross the cobble-stone street to the inn when he came face to face with Charles Bingley. The look of astonishment on the man's face took Darcy by surprise.

"I beg your pardon, Sir," Darcy quipped and started past Bingley.

Charles recovered and then faltered, "Darcy?"

Hearing his name called, Darcy spun back toward the man. "You know my name, Sir?"

"Of course, I know you. You are Fitzwilliam Darcy."

"I have never been more pleased to hear someone call my name." Darcy smiled and grabbed Bingley's hand to shake it. "May I inquire as to your name, Sir?"

Although elated to find Darcy in health, Bingley looked puzzled. "Come on, Darcy, you know me; we have been intimate friends for several years. Plus, we are brothers as we share family."

Darcy stepped back to look closely at Bingley, hoping a better examination would stimulate his memory, but nothing about the man seemed familiar, although the stranger was amiable enough. "I am sorry to say, Sir," Darcy stammered, "I cannot recall our acquaintance."

"My name is Charles Bingley, but why am I detaining you here on the street? Your sister and cousin are waiting for me at the inn; we came to bring you home."

"Home?" Darcy seemed confused with the word, but he allowed Bingley to lead him toward the inn and the uncertainty. Bingley ushered Darcy through the main doorway, where a few people were seated in the dining area. The dimly lit room offered little ambiance, but it was clean and warm. A well-dressed military officer and a young lady rose as Bingley approached. A look of mirth overspread both their faces.

"Look who I found," Bingley called in a cheerful voice.

The girl gasped and then rushed forward to encircle Darcy's waist with her arms and bury her tear-stained face into his chest. Instinctively, he clasped her to him. "Fitzwilliam," she sobbed, "we were so worried about you."

"It is fine—I am fine," Darcy whispered softly to her. Then the name *Georgiana* resurfaced. He used the word to make it stick and make it his own. "I am fine, Georgiana."

Hearing him call her name caused Georgiana to collapse against him. By now, Edward, too, wanted to embrace Darcy. He hugged him and slapped Darcy's back in a typical male form of bonding. "Darcy, the family has looked high and low for you. We thought you met with foul play." Edward stepped back to examine Darcy's face, trying to assess whether his cousin was hurt in some way.

Conrad took a position close by; he made Darcy a quick bow. Darcy's attention came to rest on the man. "Thank you, Conrad."

"I left the trunk in the care of the innkeeper, Sir. I will bid you farewell, Mr. Donnelly. Pardon me, Sir—I mean, Mr. Darcy. It is good to see you found someone waiting for you. Goodbye, Sir." Conrad offered up a near-toothless smile and then bowed out of the scene.

"Mr. Donnelly?" Edward questioned while directing Darcy to a chair. Bingley held out one for Georgiana, and they all settled in at the table in the back room to decipher what happened.

Just as Georgiana's name came to Darcy when he saw her, so did Edward's. At least, glimmers of memory returned—just as the doctor predicted. "Edward," Darcy stuttered, "I remember very little until today." His eyes darted from face to face. Finally, Darcy's eyes settled on his sister, and he reached out to caress her face with his palm. Georgiana turned her head slightly, kissing his hand. "I remember your face, my Dear, although in my memory you are much younger. How have you grown without my knowledge?"

"You always wanted Georgiana to remain a young girl."

"How is our father?" Darcy's expression showed concern. His memory came in bursts of energy, much like a candle flame fighting to stay alive against a light breeze.

"Our father? Our father, Fitzwilliam?" Georgiana's voice quivered. "Our father died six years ago." The tears welled in her eyes again; her brother's words scared Georgiana.

"Our father is dead?" Darcy's own voice shook as he looked to Edward and Bingley for confirmation. "It cannot be. I remember his weakness; my memory told me of such several days ago, but I know nothing of his passing." Darcy's hands shook as well, and he let his head fall onto Georgiana's shoulder.

"Perhaps," the colonel spoke softly, "we should start at the beginning. Obviously, there are things amiss of which we must speak." He ordered drinks for all of them. "Darcy, why do you not tell us what you know, and we will try to fill in the blanks."

Darcy did not know where to start; the details bounced about chaotically in his brain. Looking at Edward and Georgiana helped him make connections, but the need to complete the picture consumed him. "I woke up several weeks ago at Darling Hall, an estate owned by a Miss Elizabeth Donnelly. Miss Donnelly is a bizarre creature of which I shall speak more at a later time. Let us just say the lady tried to convince me I was her cousin Frederick, and we were to marry."

"Well, that explains Mr. Collins," Edward mumbled.

"Mr. Collins? The cleric?" Darcy wheeled around to question his cousin.

"Then you truly do not remember Mr. Collins?" Edward's voice held all his seriousness.

"I know of what Miss Donnelly told me." Darcy returned Edward's serious gaze.

Edward asked warily, "And that would be?"

"I am married to the man's cousin." Darcy found this idea amusing, but he saw the others did not share his mirth. Finally, he said, "Then, this is true? I am married?"

"Of course," Georgiana gasped. "Elizabeth carries your child, or she would be with us."

"My child?" Darcy still looked confused.

"Let us return to the infamous Miss Donnelly." Edward refocused Darcy's attention in an area less disturbing for him.

Darcy shook his head, trying to clear his thoughts. "Miss Donnelly claimed she found me on the road after an attack. I was wounded and in bad shape, but I remember nothing of such an attack."

"That confirms what Mr. Howard reported," Edward joined the conversation again. "Your coach was found on the road to Hull; you were on your way there to meet Hannah More."

Darcy shook his head again as if this information made sense. "Hannah More? She was an acquaintance of father's."

Edward let this pass for now. "Your coachman and postilion were dead. We brought their bodies home to Pemberley for burial. First the thieves and then the locals ransacked the coach."

"At least, Miss Donnelly told the truth there." Darcy's words held irony. "Much of what Miss Donnelly told me did not make sense; she invented a family—a father whose approval I lost and an older brother who earned the family estate by birth order. She wished to marry by her eight and twenty birthday for, I discovered, she is to inherit a substantial sum if she does."

Innocently, Georgiana reasoned, "Then she is a hideous creature?"

"Miss Donnelly is attractive enough," Darcy continued,

"but she has fits of anger, and she is obsessed with cleanliness. In fact, the lady refuses to remove her gloves for fear she might encounter dirt on any surface, be it furniture, fixtures, or human skin." Darcy shared a look of bewilderment with his loved ones. "As I said earlier, her stories began to crumble a little over a week ago. In her desperation, the lady initiated a tryst, which I refused." He heard Georgiana's quick intake of air. "I apologize, my Dear, I should choose my words more wisely. I am trying to reason out loud." Darcy reached out to take his sister's hand.

"I am well, Fitzwilliam," she offered. "I just did not expect such devious actions from a *lady*."

Darcy took up the story again. "I discovered only yesterday Miss Donnelly knew my identity all along—a fact for which I will never be able to forgive her."

Again, Georgiana's eyes grew large in surprise, and a mumbled imprecation escaped Edward's lips. Darcy continued, "It seems I met Miss Donnelly briefly in London last year at the home of the Hursts, whoever they are."

Edward and Georgiana turned automatically to Charles Bingley, and Darcy's eyes followed suit. "The Hursts—my sister Louisa is married to Mr. Hurst," Bingley began. "Miss Donnelly?" he questioned. "I remember her vaguely. It was shortly after we left Netherfield, and the Festive Season began in London. You seemed to notice her at first, but you abandoned the lady after introductions. Caroline was not too pleased to see your attentions go elsewhere."

"Caroline?" Darcy looked confused. "I thought you said *Elizabeth*, Sir."

"Accept my apologies, Darcy," Mr. Bingley stumbled through the words. "My sister Caroline and I once hoped she would be the object of your attentions, but we still ended as brothers. My dear Jane is your Elizabeth's sister."

"May I ask where Netherfield is?" Darcy tried to take in all they told him.

"Netherfield is my estate in Hertfordshire," Bingley explained. "Our wives are from there, Sir." Bingley felt awkward, as Darcy had not recognized him as he did Georgiana and Edward.

"Hertfordshire? That explains why references to that area played true in my memory. Miss Donnelly claimed Hertfordshire to be my home; little did she know I hold memories from there." Darcy looked pleased in making the connection. "Our wives come from an estate in that area?"

Darcy directed the question to Bingley; however, Edward made the response. "Longbourn is a simple estate but is nothing in comparison to Netherfield or Rosings or Pemberley. The Bennet family has five daughters, and Mr. Bennet has limited resources."

"What did my wife bring to the marriage?" Darcy seemed businesslike.

"You love Elizabeth," Georgiana tried to assure her brother.

"Then it was a prudent match for her." Darcy's words held a coldness no one expected.

"No," Georgiana demanded. "Elizabeth is not like that. Fitzwilliam, you must remember her; Elizabeth is your other half. You risked censure of our family because you fell in love with her. You were miserable until my sister finally accepted your proposal." Her words trailed off as she looked in her brother's face. Georgiana dropped her eyes, and tears streamed down her cheeks.

Darcy looked for affirmation from the two men. Having received it, he softened his tone for his sister's sake. "The doctor, Mr. Addison, suspects my memory to return. I did often dream of someone, but I never knew our connection. Mr. Addison says dreams and memories are related."

"It must be Elizabeth," Georgiana grasped at Darcy's hand. "Elizabeth is so strong; she has been running Pemberley in your absence."

"A woman running Pemberley?" Darcy laughed out loud.

"Elizabeth and I managed without a man to protect us." His sister's words cut short Darcy's amusement.

"I just witnessed a woman's ability to run an estate," he quipped.

"Elizabeth is not Miss Donnelly, and neither am I." Georgiana's anger grew quickly. "You taught us how to run the estate; it was your idea, Fitzwilliam. You said the times were changing, and we needed to help you save Pemberley."

"I suggest you guard your words, Georgiana." Darcy offered her a reprimand. "I realize this situation is unusual, and our relationship has changed, but I am still your guardian." His words held a veiled threat.

Georgiana forced her eyes closed to fight back the emotions coursing through her. "You are wrong, Brother," she whispered.

"If I am, I shall offer you my apologies." Darcy's words held inroads of his once-reserved nature.

"Yes, Fitzwilliam," she said automatically, once again assuming her position as Darcy's subordinate. "If you have no objections, I will retire to my room." She stood to take her leave. "I love you, Fitzwilliam," she said, uncharacteristically raising her eyes to challenge him when he, too, stood. "I am happy you are safe."

Darcy kissed her cheek. "I will see you at dinner."

Edward, Bingley, and Darcy spent another hour trying to help Darcy remember what seemed to be a lifetime of changes. Darcy knew the gist of what happened up to his father's death, but the last six years had blurry edges. He possessed no real memory of much of what they shared; he simply accepted what the men told him. Darcy recalled assuming responsibility for Georgiana, and his mother's death, but he had no memory of his relationship with Bingley or, more importantly, of the mysterious woman to whom he was married.

Both his cousin and Mr. Bingley spoke highly of Elizabeth Darcy, and, evidently, his sister had an admirable relationship with the woman. Yet, could she be the woman in his dreams? "What else should I know about my wife?" he asked his cousin.

"Elizabeth Bennet is a true match for you, Fitzwilliam. You met in Hertfordshire when you accompanied Mr. Bingley to his estate. By your own words, you insulted her at an assembly, and then spent the next nine months regretting your off-handed remark because Mrs. Darcy overheard you, and your words set her against you. When she refused your first proposal, you went into a tailspin of depression."

"What do you mean—refused my first proposal?" Darcy interrupted.

The colonel chuckled. "I found you in a drunken stupor. Mrs. Darcy would not accept your advances; that should say something of her character. Even for all your fortune and all her low connections, Elizabeth Bennet refused the offer of your hand. When she finally accepted you, Fitzwilliam, it was because you won her heart, not because she accepted your wealth."

Darcy took in the words in silence, not knowing what to think. "What is your estimation of the woman, Edward?"

"Mrs. Darcy is incomparable, Cousin. Georgiana is correct; she is the perfect fit for you. Elizabeth can tease you out of your reticence. Mrs. Darcy possesses the strength of character to do the right thing. She is witty and intelligent."

"Of course, I would agree," Bingley added. "Mrs. Darcy created a change in you I often saw in private moments. Although she and my Jane are as close as sisters may be, they differ in temperament. Mrs. Darcy speaks her mind, but she is not caustic or acrimonious. I witnessed her verbally battling with you on more than one occasion. You once told me those moments were when you realized you loved Mrs. Darcy. We married sisters on the same day in Meryton. We came to

Hertfordshire as close friends and became brothers in bonds of marriage."

"Then you both approve of my choice?" Darcy asked, still a bit unconvinced at the possibilities.

"We approve, as do my parents and the Penningtons," Edward added. "Only Lady Catherine disapproves."

"Lady Catherine," Darcy mused. Images of his mother's sister returned to his catalogue of recollections. "Her Ladyship always wanted me to marry my cousin Anne."

Edward told him with a smile. "That will be my pleasure."

"You and Anne?" Darcy asked. "When did that happen?"

"Just recently—after your marriage to Mrs. Darcy, our aunt consented, although she has displayed her discontent more than once. In fact, Lady Catherine knew of your whereabouts here, but she concealed it in hopes of running Mrs. Darcy from Pemberley." Edward's contempt showed.

This news was more than Darcy could handle. "Gentlemen," he stood, "I need time to think this through. I believe I will emulate my sister and retire for a few hours; this is exhausting."

"Of course, Darcy," Edward told him. "We will continue when you are ready."

Darcy bowed and made his exit. At the door, he turned back toward them. "I am sorry to have been such a worry to you." He spoke the words solemnly. Then he added, "What do I do if my memory of all this never returns?" With that said, he slipped through the open door.

Bingley and the colonel sank back into their seats in exasperation. "What will he do?" Bingley questioned.

"What will Elizabeth do is more the question," the colonel corrected.

Over dinner in the same private room, Darcy continued his quest for knowledge of his life. "If I understand you, Edward,

Mr. Howard has been a competent successor to Mr. Wickham as the estate's steward."

"Mr. Howard serves the family well," Georgiana added softly. "He was most helpful to Elizabeth and me in your absence, Fitzwilliam."

"What of George?" Darcy inquired as an afterthought.

Everyone else at the table froze, eating utensils suspended in midair, never completing their journey to the diner's mouth. Edward finally put down his fork and turned calmly to Darcy. "We assume you mean George Wickham."

"Of course, George Wickham—whom did you think I meant, Edward?" Darcy answered innocently, not taking in their looks of disbelief.

"Actually, the blackguard is back in Newcastle, I suppose," Edward began slowly. "In the past six years, George Wickham tried to blackmail you and to compromise your family name on several occasions," Edward confided.

"George Wickham was always impetuous," Darcy added, "but he was one of father's favorites."

"To the extent that your father often ignored you," Edward reminded him.

Darcy defended his father's actions. "George Wickham simply played to father's vanity."

"Then let me summarize the highlights for you, my cousin. Mr. Wickham turned down the living at Kympton for three thousand pounds." Edward nodded to Georgiana, and she silently agreed to his sharing her problems with George Wickham in front of Mr. Bingley. "When you refused him further funds, Mr. Wickham tried to convince our dearest charge he loved her in order to obtain control of her thirty thousand pounds." Darcy looked shocked and dismayed. "His lies were one of the reasons Mrs. Darcy initially refused your hand; most recently he seduced your wife's youngest sister in order to escape his debts. It cost you several thousand pounds to make an honest woman of Lydia Bennet and to save the reputations of Mrs. Darcy, Mrs. Bingley, and the other two sisters. That pretty much sums up the infamous George Wickham."

"Not quite," Georgiana looked directly at her brother.

"There is more?" He took her hand in his.

Georgiana swallowed hard before beginning. "Most recently, Mr. Wickham showed up at Pemberley with Mrs. Wickham."

"He did what?" the colonel fumed. "Why did you not tell me?"

"I am sorry, Edward. Things happened so quickly with the knowledge we might find Fitzwilliam that the thoughts of Mr. Wickham were far from my mind at the time."

"What happened?" he demanded.

"Lydia Wickham showed up unexpectedly and presented herself to Kitty. Kitty knew Elizabeth would be upset so she went to find her sister; Kitty did not know Mr. Wickham came with Lydia. I found him in Fitzwilliam's study; I attempted to face down my fears by confronting the man and demanding he leave Pemberley at once. He refused, and my resolve began to crumble, but Elizabeth appeared. She helped me to the side, and then she, too, asked Mr. Wickham to leave. She would not let Mr. Wickham insinuate himself back into the running of Pemberley. Mr. Wickham tried to laugh off Elizabeth's objections so she took out the gun Fitzwilliam bought her; it rested in the top drawer of the desk."

"I bought Elizabeth a gun?" Darcy seemed surprised, but also a bit amused.

Georgiana laughed. "One of her wedding presents—anyway, Mr. Wickham in desperation grabbed my arm. I foolishly screamed, and Elizabeth fired, grazing Mr. Wickham's shoulder. The bullet is still embedded in the wall beside the bookcase," she teased. "Then Mr. Harrison entered the room and physically removed Mr. Wickham from the estate."

"Thank God Harrison was there." Bingley sounded amazed.

"Actually, Elizabeth took control. Besides protecting me from Mr. Wickham, she made sure Mr. and Mrs. Wickham were sent back to Newcastle. Then, Mr. Harrison and I rode out to inspect the lands along with Mr. Howard, letting the tenants know even in Fitzwilliam's absence, the Darcy family would still take care of Pemberley. Elizabeth reasoned even though she and I tended to Fitzwilliam's duties, seeing a male, other than Mr. Howard—another landed gentleman—with us in completing our duties to the estate would paint the picture of stability to the tenants," Georgiana explained.

Darcy took in all this information with interest. Evidently, the woman he chose to be his wife possessed some tenaciousness. If what Edward said about George Wickham were true, then Elizabeth's protection of his sister's innocence spoke well of her. Plus, her intuition about the tenant's conventional need to have a male in charge proved an insightful maneuver. Yet, her low connections meant a loss of standing in the *ton*, and Darcy knew name and reputation meant more than common sense in a woman.

Another thought crossed his mind. "Who is this Mr. Harrison, and who is Kitty?"

"Kitty is one of our wives' sisters." Bingley was quiet to this point. "She stays at Pemberley to help with Mrs. Darcy's confinement."

"Mr. Harrison is a young man, very much like you once were," Edward pointed out, "who recently took over his father's estate of Hines Park in Dove Dale, close to my parents; he was a guest at Pemberley during the Festive Season." Edward thankfully omitted his knowledge of Harrison's interest in Georgiana Darcy. He also omitted Harrison's connection to the emancipation issues, Darcy's reason for going to Hull in the first place.

Darcy and Colonel Fitzwilliam sat up half the night with the colonel "reminding" Darcy of many details of family business, which could not be discussed with either Georgiana or Mr. Bingley present. Although he had no direct memory of the occurrences, Darcy, at least, now possessed knowledge of the events and the people involved.

"My biggest concern," Darcy added, "is what do I do about my marriage?"

"I do not understand," Colonel Fitzwilliam commented.

"My father once told me to marry well—to remember my family's name," Darcy reasoned. "Obviously, I failed him in that respect."

"Darcy, you cannot assume your marriage is not a sound one. You may have additional memory recovery once you are home at Pemberley with Elizabeth. I realize Mrs. Darcy was not part of society as you know it, but you never seemed so content as you did these last six months. Fitz, your parents wanted you to be happy; Mrs. Darcy brought out a different side of you." The colonel did not know what to say to his cousin. For Darcy to return to Pemberley to a woman he could not remember offered him a bizarre life, and Edward knew not how to counsel him.

"What if I cannot learn to love her again?" Darcy's words brought the situation home to both of them.

"Many men do not love their wives," Edward stated simply, "but they live comfortable lives. You learned to love Elizabeth once; why could you not do so again?"

"Of course, that is a possibility," Darcy reasoned. "I am only being overcautious." Darcy tried to convince himself of his future.

So it was when Fitzwilliam Darcy crawled into the coach bedecked with the Darcy livery the next morning to return to Pemberley and Derbyshire, he lived in two worlds: the world of which he had memories—those of Pemberley and his father's death, and the world his relatives described to him—but of which he held no recollection. Darcy seemed confident on the surface, a role he learned to play early in his life, but beneath the surface, he feared he would never remember the years missing at the moment. How would he function with all the holes in his instincts, his experiences, and his past?

"I wish we had time to send a message to Elizabeth before our arrival," Georgiana said softly. She did not know how they would explain to her beloved sister Fitzwilliam no longer held a memory of their time together.

"I cannot imagine the shock this will bring to Mrs. Darcy," Bingley added. "I have no way of explaining it all to myself as well as my dear Jane and her sister. How can Darcy and I no longer have a friendship? He is my closest friend."

Georgiana and Bingley sat side by side in the coach. They watched as both Darcy and the colonel snoozed with the rhythm of the journey. "Elizabeth will be devastated; she prayed for Fitzwilliam's return. What of their marriage? Of their baby?" Tears began to slip down her cheeks, and Georgiana turned away to hide her distress.

Bingley sheepishly handed her his handkerchief, and Georgiana offered him a smile of gratitude. "To whom do I turn for help with Netherfield? Do I stay at Pemberley when your brother knows me not? I do not know what my family and I should do. How may I leave—how may I get Mrs. Bingley to leave her sister at Pemberley with no resolution?" Bingley shifted uncomfortably in his seat.

Georgiana touched his arm lightly for reassurance. "How will Fitzwilliam greet Elizabeth? Truthfully, Mr. Bingley, I cannot predict my brother at this time. When I think about how he was when our father died—when all of the responsibility became his, I fear for the Pemberley I have enjoyed the last year." She looked around nervously and lowered her voice before finishing her thoughts. "Although Fitzwilliam always found time for me in those days, I do not want to return to that time. My brother took life too seriously then; I would miss what Elizabeth gives me." They rode in silence after that, lost in their thoughts of how Fitzwilliam Darcy would change life at Pemberley. Dread rode with them, as did empathy.

At a small, unfamiliar inn, they spent another night on the road. Caught in a cold, drenching rain, the travelers decided reluctantly to delay their return to Pemberley one more day. They might press on and stay with the Penningtons again, but the colonel reasoned that with Darcy's current condition, a limit must be maintained on how much he might be subjected to from those to whom his memories were combined.

Darcy tapped lightly on his sister's door. "Georgiana, may I come in?"

After a few brief but tense moments, she opened the door to him. Dropping her eyes in submission, she said, "Good evening, Fitzwilliam."

"I hoped we would have the opportunity to speak privately." His voice held a confidence he did not truly feel.

"Of course," she stammered. Stepping away from the door, she led her brother to a chair in the chamber.

Comfortably settled, Darcy turned his attention to his sister. "Everything has changed so quickly," he began. "I feared you were distressed about what happened."

"I am as well as can be expected under the circumstances." Georgiana's voice remained soft and noncommittal.

Darcy leaned forward to speak more informally. "Georgiana, you must know our relationship has not changed; you will always be my Dearest One." He called her his pet name. "I admit it is somewhat awkward—in my mind's eyes, you are but a child, barely two and ten, when, in reality, you are a young lady who should be anticipating her coming-out parties and the new Season in London."

Her tears began to flow as she spoke. "Fitzwilliam, once again I ruined everything," she nearly wailed.

Darcy moved quickly, kneeling in front of Georgiana and taking her hand. "Georgiana, you ruined nothing," he tried to assure her. "Everything will be as it was before."

"Oh, Fitzwilliam!" Her sobs rocked her body with grief.

"Please, Dearest One," he implored her. "Help me to understand your anxiousness."

"If it was not for me, you would never have gone to Hull, and you would be home at Pemberley with Elizabeth anticipating the birth of your first child." Georgiana's words came in bursts of emotions.

"Who says I shall not be anticipating the birth of my child?" Darcy tried to sound casual.

Georgiana's eyes searched his countenance. "Then you remember Elizabeth after all?"

Darcy guarded his words, not wishing to give his sister false hope. "I admit to experiencing difficulty in determining what I actually remember and what I have been told about my wife; I can only say I will do my best to make things pleasant and agreeable for all of us."

"Pleasant and agreeable?" she challenged. "It may be the last time I get the opportunity to say this, Brother, but I do not want to see you only pleasant and agreeable with Elizabeth. You were *pleasant* and *agreeable* from the time of our mother's death, through the passing of our father, and up until you met Elizabeth Bennet. Yet, you did not live; you never showed the passion you have for our ancestral home, for me, and for life. Please, Fitzwilliam, do not just pretend to be *pleasant* and *agreeable*."

Not accustomed to her asserting herself, Darcy leaned back away from Georgiana. "It appears my wife has a profound influence on you," he cautioned. "I am not sure whether I approve. Men do not prefer their women so spirited."

"Then you will find no preference for my sister," Georgiana asserted. "You were exposed to fine society, Fitzwilliam, your entire life. Why then did you wait until you were eight and twenty to take a wife? I saw women give deference to your every thought, but you never seriously considered any of them as marriageable material. You may need to ask yourself what it is Elizabeth has which the others did not. You fell in love with her once; allow yourself to do so again."

"As I said before, I will try, Georgiana." Darcy placated her disquietude with a condescending tone. "I will do what is best for you and for the estate."

"Do what is best for *you*, Fitzwilliam, and the rest will come naturally."

He patted her hand to calm his sister's anxiety. "Would it be too much to ask why you blame yourself for my accident?"

"When we attended Edward and Anne's engagement party, we met Captain Rutherford, who took an interest in Mr. Harrison."

"Mr. Harrison again?" Darcy questioned. "Exactly what is his connection to our family?"

"Your horse Cerberus is from his father's estate. Mr. Harrison sought your advice when he assumed the running of Hines Park." Georgiana shifted her eyes away from Darcy's, fearing he might recognize her regard for Chadwick Harrison in her countenance.

"Then why did the captain take an interest in Mr. Harrison? Harrison is not in debt to the man, is he?" Darcy's voice became louder.

"Mr. Harrison," Georgiana began, with some nervousness, "carries strong beliefs regarding the emancipation of the African slaves. The captain has an opposing viewpoint."

"Then why would I go to see Hannah More? I have not taken up the flag of the abolitionist?" Darcy found the idea amusing.

Georgiana did not know how to explain her feelings about

Mr. Harrison without upsetting Darcy further. "The captain noted our family held Mr. Harrison in some regard, and while we shared a dance set, the man questioned me extensively about Mr. Harrison. I foolishly told Mr. Harrison, and he approached you about the 'supposed' danger in which the captain placed our family. Miss More was to share some information regarding the captain with you."

Darcy quickly realized Georgiana omitted some pertinent details. "May I ask what else you have not told me about Mr. Harrison?"

Again, Georgiana lowered her eyes. Darcy noted a blush overspread her face. "Mr. Harrison has indicated a desire to get to know me better." She barely whispered the words.

"He did what?" Darcy demanded. Georgiana jumped at the sound of his anger. "I will not have it, Georgiana. You have not even been presented to society!"

Georgiana fought back the tears that formed in her eyes. "Elizabeth told Mr. Harrison you would not entertain such ideas until after my next birthday; she handled it as she thought you would want it to be done, Sir."

"Elizabeth again!" he fumed. "She takes on a great deal speaking for me in my absence."

"You asked her to do so, Fitzwilliam," Georgiana pleaded for his reason. "Her decisions do not come lightly; you will find my sister is very astute."

Darcy tried to calm his racing heart. "Before I will entertain any offers for your hand, Georgiana, you will be presented to Society as a proper lady—as is your due. I will not tolerate your being whisked off into a marriage to the first man who presents himself to you."

By now, Georgiana's own nerves frayed. Her fears of an arranged marriage to a man she could not affect resurfaced. "The first man who wished to whisk me off into a marriage was George Wickham. You thwarted that plan, Brother. Please do not assume Mr. Harrison is of the same material. He is amiable and shows great promise. Those were your own words come back to haunt you. As far as Society and the Season, how may I go to London? Elizabeth's confinement will come about the same time."

"That does not mean we should postpone your Coming Out," Darcy protested.

"It most certainly does," she countered. "You cannot desert your wife during her lying in!"

"Then we will consider a shortened season. You are my first responsibility, Georgiana. Our father charged me to take care of your future."

Georgiana looked at him in disbelief. She knew from the past she was not likely to change her brother's mind. Their relationship progressed so much this year. Darcy accepted her—valued her. How could she return to the submissive being she was in those years following her parents' passing? "My future is secure as long as I am with you and Elizabeth at Pemberley. Please do not send me away, Fitzwilliam. I have no desire to return to London. Everything I need to be happy is tied to my life at Pemberley." Georgiana's voice came out small.

"I would not be sending you away, Dearest One, if we present you to Society," Darcy reasoned. "We would both be doing our duty to our name—to our family."

"Name and family do not guarantee the merit of a person's life," she mumbled under her breath. Georgiana knew her chance of finding happiness with Mr. Harrison suddenly decreased with her brother's return to Pemberley. *How shall I survive without the chance of one day being Mr. Harrison's wife? What may I do to change Fitzwilliam's mind?* Georgiana offered her brother a faint smile of affirmation, but the chaos of her mind continued well after he departed. It robbed her of much of the sleep she needed to face the quagmire awaiting them at Pemberley.

CHAPTER 14

*"Surprises are foolish things. The pleasure is not enhanced,
and the inconvenience is often considerable."*
Jane Austen, *Emma*, 1815

When the coach pulled up in front of the house, Elizabeth, Kitty, Jane Bingley, and Anne de Bourgh awaited the travelers. Evidently, Elizabeth ordered the servants to relay the first sightings of the coach. The colonel alighted first and helped Georgiana to debark. Mr. Bingley followed her closely. There were a few brief seconds of absolute stillness before Darcy stepped from the livery. Elizabeth gasped and immediately rushed to him, encircling his waist with her arms while sobbing into the collar of his waistcoat. Burying her face into his chest, she mumbled, "Thank God—Fitzwilliam—thank God, you are all right."

Darcy knew instinctively who the woman who held him so closely must be, but from the coach's window, he realized this woman's countenance was not one he readily recognized, although subconsciously he knew her to be the one from his dreams. He nodded to the colonel to take the others into the house before he took Elizabeth forcibly by the arms and removed her grip on his being. "Mrs. Darcy," he stammered. "May we not go into the house? We are making quite a scene. I do not wish to be the talk of the servant quarters this evening." His voice held a coldness Elizabeth did not recognize.

"A scene?" Elizabeth questioned while looking around sheepishly.

"Yes, Madam," Darcy addressed her formally. "If you have no objection, I will freshen my clothes and then meet you in the study." Then he strode away from her toward the open door. Elizabeth stood bewitched by the abruptness of her husband's exit as a single teardrop slid down her face. Slowly and methodically, she, too, turned toward the house.

Georgiana came back to wait for Elizabeth once she noted how Darcy purposely left his wife in the carriageway. When Elizabeth reached the top step leading to the entrance, Georgiana rushed forward to take the woman, whom she felt knew her better than anyone, into her arms. Elizabeth swayed as the adrenaline rush left her, and Georgiana supported her until they seated themselves in the drawing room.

Miraculously, all the travelers, and even Kitty, disappeared into their chambers. "Fitzwilliam is not well, Elizabeth," Georgiana tried to explain. "He was attacked along the road and apparently is having some trouble remembering all the details of his life."

The girl's words dug deep into Elizabeth's subconscious. Her eyes enlarged as she softly responded, "Do you mean Fitzwilliam knows me not?"

Georgiana dropped her eyes. She instinctively moved closer to support Elizabeth's sagging body, and Elizabeth rested her head on the girl's shoulder. "My brother," she began quietly, "remembers little after our father's death. He no longer knows Mr. Bingley, your family, his life the last six years, or you. Edward and I tried to explain things, and Fitzwilliam knows what happened; yet, he possesses no actual recollection of the events."

The finality of her words hurt Elizabeth with an indescribable pain. *How could Darcy not remember her—they were like kindred souls crying out to each other in the night.* "It cannot be, Georgiana," Elizabeth whispered. "Fitzwilliam and I are mysteriously united by some association of the spirit—you have seen it, have you not? We only know each other."

Georgiana took Elizabeth's hand. "You will find each other again—of that fact, I have no doubt. You must be patient; Fitzwilliam six years ago was so frightened, believing he could not handle Pemberley and be my guardian. It was daunting—an experience he must now relive, along with the knowledge he now has you and your unborn child as additional responsibilities. This has to be exasperating for him, and I can honestly say he was not always the easiest person with whom to live in those days. We must remember the Fitzwilliam we loved of late is part of that scared young man of three and twenty."

Elizabeth gasped, "I do not know what to do, Georgiana."

"I am sure neither does Fitzwilliam," Georgiana reasoned.

"Tell me." Elizabeth searched Georgiana's countenance for the truth. "Tell me what you remember of him in those days." Elizabeth stifled her sobs. "I must know what to expect when I speak to him again."

"My brother has—had an idolized opinion of our parents. They married for love, but they were a product of their time. They taught my brother duty first—above all other things. You know of my parents' *duty* to our tenants. Fitzwilliam was brought up in opulence, and often he came off as proud and leaden, but we know he is a different man; he is a man who desperately needs to be loved. Do not stop loving my brother," Georgiana pleaded.

"I will always love your brother, Georgiana." Elizabeth's voice trembled from fear of what would happen next; yet, the unspoken truth led her to realize loving Darcy and living with him were two different things.

When Darcy reached the top of the staircase, he turned to the left toward his chambers. "Mr. Darcy, Sir," Henry caught his attention. "This way, Sir."

"Henry, I am pleased to see you." Henry served Fitzwilliam Darcy for many years, long before the passing of the elder Mr.

Darcy. Darcy followed the valet to what was once his father's chambers. Darcy stepped into the room, and memories of playing on the floor of this very room as a small child flooded his mind.

"My father's old room," he mumbled as he turned round and round in the center of the floor. On sensory overload, flashes of memories invaded his mind. Nearly dizzy from the swirling images, Darcy grabbed his head for balance.

Henry immediately rushed to support his master. "I am here, Mr. Darcy. Let me help you to a chair. We are so pleased to have you back at Pemberley; the staff and your family felt your absence considerably. I arranged a bath for you and clean attire, Sir."

"Thank you, Henry," Darcy nearly whispered. "I will rest here until you are ready for me."

"Yes, Sir." Henry made his bow and exited toward Darcy's dressing room.

"Henry," Darcy called.

The man paused at the door. "Yes, Mr. Darcy?"

"Am I to assume Mrs. Darcy has my mother's previous quarters?" Darcy did not know why he asked, but it seemed important somehow.

"Yes, Sir," Henry nodded, "through the sitting room, Sir."

Darcy nodded also and then leaned back in the chair, closing his eyes to think about his life at Pemberley and how everything had changed.

He sat, heart racing, trying to recapture his composure. Just stepping into this bedroom took Darcy's senses to another level. Images of his mother and his father surrounded him. The furnishings were different—more muted tones—more to Darcy's liking—but definitely his father's quarters. His father's dominating presence filled him as he sat there, trying to remember his life—remember anything. *Could he do this again? Could he become the Master of Pemberley?*

The elder Darcy warned his son repeatedly of those who would flatter him to become an intimate. Darcy learned his place in the world—an air of confidence and an aristocratic demeanor. He wanted desperately to replicate his father—a great man—a well-respected man. The elder Darcy came from a respectable, honorable, and ancient family. His mother Lady Anne came from a line of noble earls; she gave him his identity, his name of Fitzwilliam. But he lost all that—all that history—on the road to Hull. Now, he knew not what to do. *His responsibilities were so numerous. Could he be the man his father taught him to be? Darcy feared failure; he feared loss of respect—loss of face in society.*

Another fear crept into his memory. As he circled the room moments ago, an image of the woman who was his wife flashed across the reaches of his mind. She lay across his bed, muddy and covered in blood, and he cut her clothing from her body, cleaning and bandaging her wounds. Tears streamed down his face, and he offered the woman endearments. *How could he love this woman so much and now have no feelings for her? How could he learn to love her again?* His wife's connections went against *everything* his parents expected of him, but Darcy could not turn the woman away. She carried the heir to Pemberley, and duty required he have an heir.

Darcy spent nearly an hour in his study reviewing the estate books before Elizabeth found enough courage to approach him. The light tap on the door told Darcy the moment he anticipated since leaving Darling Hall arrived. "Come," he called automatically.

Elizabeth Darcy entered his study unsure of her reception. "Mrs. Darcy," he said, upon seeing her enter the room. He left the desk and came forward to meet her. Darcy led Elizabeth to a chair and took the adjoining one. Elizabeth searched his face for a semblance of her dear husband in the man seated across from her. Trying to get enough nerve to begin his conversation, Darcy cleared his throat twice and ran his fingers through his hair. "This is an awkward occurrence in which we find ourselves, Mrs. Darcy," he still spoke formally.

"It is indeed, Sir," Elizabeth tried to keep her voice even.

"I suppose I should offer you an explanation."

Elizabeth looked about nervously, not wishing to meet his eyes with hers. "There is no need, Sir; your sister volunteered an explanation of your homecoming."

Darcy looked at her shamefacedly. "I am sorry this brings you grief." He tried to look directly into her eyes to relay his truth, but the depth of the emotions he found there bothered him, and he looked away without knowing. "I want to assure you, I will treat you with all the respect due you as my wife. I will do my best to allow my regard for you to grow naturally. Of course, our child will receive the best of care as the heir to this estate."

"I understand your expectations, Sir, for our child," Elizabeth stammered, "but I do not understand your expectations for me as your wife. Am I expected to pretend not to love you?" Tears filled her eyes. "The prayer the devil answers."

"What? What did you say?"

"The prayer the devil answers," Elizabeth muttered. "It is a phrase I learned from you, Fitzwilliam."

"I know it well; my mother said it often." Darcy felt the agitation inherent in the moment, and he strode to the window to ease his discomfort.

"I prayed continuously for your return," Elizabeth lamented. "Little did I know my prayers would. . . ."

Darcy turned back to look at her. "I wish I could say something," he whispered, "to make this easier."

Elizabeth could hear no more; she bolted from the chair and fled the room without even a "by your leave." Darcy stood in amazement. How had he become involved with such a highly emotional woman? She knew not even how to have a civil conversation. Many couples in society held no regard for each other, but they managed households with civilities. It was not his fault the last couple of years no longer existed in his memory. He hoped to make the best of a bad situation; he tried to do his duty by the woman. He thought he was being very reasonable.

Darcy sent for his steward to address the estate books. His ability to run his estate must be proven for the world to accept him, an area often addressed by his father; Darcy wanted to establish his worth. Mr. Howard came laden with his copies of the estate books to his master's study. Howard was made aware of Mr. Darcy's health problems, and the steward knew not what to expect. Mr. Howard had served Pemberley since the death of the former steward, Mr. Wickham, George Wickham's father. Demanding, the elder Mr. Darcy spent much of his time reprimanding Mr. Howard. Early on, Fitzwilliam Darcy chose to imitate his father, but the younger Darcy learned his lessons and took a more cooperative turn in the estate's business. Pemberley flourished under the son's control. Howard wondered if the young master would have to learn those lessons again, and would he have to once again withstand Mr. Darcy's criticisms?

"Mr. Howard," Darcy began upon seeing the man, "thank you for coming so quickly."

Mr. Howard made Darcy a proper bow. "We are happy to see you well, Sir." Howard brought the estate books to Darcy's desk. "When we found your coach, we knew not what might have become of you, Sir."

"You found my coach?" Darcy looked surprised.

"Yes, Sir, Mrs. Darcy had a premonition of what had

happened, and then she received the letter from Miss More, indicating you failed to arrive in Hull. Distraught, Mrs. Darcy sent us immediately to retrace your route. I do believe if Mrs. Darcy was not with child, your wife would have led the search party herself."

"A premonition, you say?" Darcy tried to look amused but really felt agitation.

"Yes, Sir, Mrs. Darcy nearly swooned from her strong feelings regarding the matter." Mr. Howard opened the estate books to the current pages.

Darcy shifted in his seat, disturbed by his own ideas. "When exactly did this happen?"

Mr. Howard paused to recollect when they attended to Mrs. Darcy's misgivings. "You could not have been more than two days out, Sir. Mrs. Darcy suddenly took on a dreadful feeling and collapsed in this very room. Mrs. Reynolds and Miss Darcy attended to her. I am unaware of all the particulars, but the irony of the situation once we knew of your not achieving Hull did not escape the men in the search party."

Darcy sat back in the chair. He brought his fingers together in supposition, resting his chin as he meditated on what Mr. Howard shared about Elizabeth Darcy. *How could she know? Could she have arranged the attack? No, that was impossible. Elizabeth would not bring attention to herself if she were a culprit in his encounter. Then that meant they had an unusual connection—one not found in most marriages.* Darcy could not explain how confused the stories of Elizabeth made him. His brief observation of her told him his wife did not meet the standards of what his father drummed into Darcy. Yet, from all accounts, they had a loving—a trusting—relationship. Perplexity ruled his thoughts about the woman he married. How could they achieve some semblance of marital felicity?

Mr. Howard's voice brought Darcy's attention back to the books. "As you can observe, Sir, the recent changes instituted by you and your wife proved wise ones. The estate is on solid footing, and the promise of new crops opened markets we did not anticipate."

"Really?" Darcy seemed surprised.

"Of course, Sir," Mr. Howard beamed. "Your insights proved themselves, and Mrs. Darcy's attention to the needs of the tenants creates a feeling of solidarity among them. They band together to help each other. I, personally, have seen nothing to compare to what you achieved here, Sir."

Again, Darcy leaned back in the chair. "Would you explain how these changes affected the tenants? Give me specific examples."

"There is a general feeling of—of—how to explain this— of congeniality. When Mr. Lucas hurt his leg last week, Meyers, Littleton, and Sanderson came to help him finish the plowing and mended Lucas's fence wall. Your wife and sister make regular tenant calls; they listen to the women and praise the efforts of the men. They bring food and comfort to the families."

"From where does the food come?"

"Most of the food comes from the controlled kills," Mr. Howard added nonchalantly, forgetting Darcy had no memory of this recent change in how the estate handled nature's tendency to allow some species to be more abundant than others.

"Controlled kills?"

"Miss Darcy's idea, Sir. Forgive me—when I spoke, I forgot about your recent attack. Miss Darcy reasoned we could cut down on poachers if we controlled the number of deer ourselves. We thin the herd periodically and give the meat to the tenants. In return, they help with repairs upon the estate. We become our own state, taking care of our own. It is quite simple in concept, but the positive tendrils have spread among the cottagers."

"And this was my sister's idea? Are you sure, Mr. Howard?"

"Quite sure, Sir. Your family and I sat in this very room

when the plan came into fruition. Miss Darcy and your wife assumed much of the control of the estate while you were away. Your jointure on Mrs. Darcy proved prudent." Mr. Howard's praise of the two women continued for several minutes.

At dinner, Darcy planned to extend his congratulations to Elizabeth for her insights in regards to the estate, but his house-guests, anticipating the strain of his first evening at Pemberley, all begged off and took their meals in their rooms. Earlier in the day, Mr. Bingley came briefly to Darcy's study to inform him he and Mrs. Bingley would depart from Pemberley tomorrow. "You are welcome to stay, Sir. Mrs. Bingley, as Mrs. Darcy's sister, should not be deprived of her relations on my account."

Yet, Bingley insisted; the garbled relationships played havoc on Mrs. Bingley's kind nature, and he would remove her from Pemberley until Darcy could reestablish his position with his wife. Therefore, their absence from the dinner table did not surprise Darcy. Kitty Bennet, not used to confrontations, followed suit.

Edward insisted he and Anne had extensive wedding plans to discuss. Darcy did not believe him; he knew Anne did not want to witness the problems in Darcy's marriage. If Lady Catherine, according to Edward, thought Darcy might withdraw his attention from Elizabeth and take Anne as his wife, then difficulties would occur for his cousins.

Mr. Harrison, suspecting a change in the dynamics of the household, made an early exit and took a room at the Royal Crown in Lambton. He promised Georgiana to call tomorrow before leaving for Hines Park.

Finally, Darcy received word through her maid that his wife had a headache and would take a light meal in her room. As he sat down to dinner, Darcy found only his sister as company.

"It seems only you, Dearest One, seeks my company this evening." Georgiana recognized the hurt in Darcy's voice.

"With Elizabeth's condition, I am sure today created problems for her," his sister tried to reason with him.

"What can I do, Georgiana? I hear tales of my wife's resilience and her amiability, but I cannot justify my decision in regards to our father's directives."

"Fitzwilliam, I admit Elizabeth is not what you say you want and is not what our father on first glance would find appropriate, but I know she is what you need. Our father would approve of how happy you are with Elizabeth. No one who saw the two of you together would think otherwise." Georgiana laughed nervously. "Of course, no one except our formidable aunt."

Darcy looked surprised to see his sister speak out about their aunt. "Lady Catherine? Obviously, our aunt would disapprove of my marriage to Mrs. Darcy. Lady Catherine would approve of no one except Anne as my wife."

"Fitzwilliam, she did not just disapprove," Georgiana protested. "She tried to stop your marriage. Our aunt presented herself to Elizabeth before you proposed the second time. Lady Catherine's words demonstrated a lack of breeding, but Elizabeth refused to deny or confirm your relationship."

"Second time? I know I proposed to Elizabeth more than once, but why would she refuse me? It is, evidently, a prudent match for her."

"Elizabeth refused you at Easter time at Hunsford. Fitzwilliam, you were very disrespectful to her," Georgiana half teased. "I will explain more later, but Elizabeth found your proposal insulting at best; then you spent several months in misery. Elizabeth traveled to Derbyshire with her Aunt and Uncle Gardiner; you came home a day early to find her at Pemberley. By then, she had a better understanding of what an honorable man you are and was able to finally accept you."

"Do you not mean Mrs. Darcy saw Pemberley and realized what a wealthy man I am?" Darcy sarcastically added.

Again, Georgiana came to Elizabeth's defense. "Elizabeth is not like that, Fitzwilliam. She knew of your wealth in Hunsford and refused you. Elizabeth was misled by Mr. Wickham's lies about you. When she realized she—she misunderstood the situation, Elizabeth allowed herself to see the man you are."

"What else should I know about my wife?" Darcy asked suspiciously.

"I esteem her above anyone I ever met. Elizabeth took over the estate when you were missing; she is the most capable person I know beside you, Fitzwilliam. At her suggestion, I learned much about how to run an estate. Elizabeth could legally make all decisions regarding our ancestral home in your absence, but Mrs. Darcy would not allow that. Plus, Elizabeth reasoned a man who really esteemed me would accept my knowledge as an asset to our marriage."

Darcy mused, "She did, did she?"

"Do you doubt me, Brother?"

"Of course not, Georgiana."

"Elizabeth protected me from Mr. Wickham." Georgiana tossed in a reminder of her sister's loyalty. "Of course, I protected her earlier from Lady Catherine."

"You spoke disrespectfully to our aunt?" Darcy was not sure whether he was appalled or amused by the concept.

"Our aunt, Fitzwilliam, came here with the purpose of removing Elizabeth from the estate. Lady Catherine was unaware of the jointure placed on Elizabeth, but even if no such document existed, our aunt could have shown more solicitous feelings toward Elizabeth. Lady Catherine even insinuated your child belonged to someone else. I could not tolerate such expurgents in your house, Brother!" Georgiana's voice rose with indignation.

"Lady Catherine claimed what?"

"Fitzwilliam, our aunt knew where you were, but she kept the information from Elizabeth—from me. How could she?

How could she place her disapproval of your wife above your safe return home?"

"I do not know, Dearest One." Darcy reached out to caress her cheek; Georgiana turned her head to kiss his palm. "There is so much I do not know."

A light tap came at Elizabeth's bedchamber door, and she looked up to see Darcy standing in the doorway. For a moment, she wondered if he intended to take his husbandly rights, but he approached her not. She rose to address him. The translucent silky fabric of her nightdress revealed the lilt turn of Elizabeth's figure, only enhanced by the fullness of her breast and her abdomen. Her auburn curls cascaded over her shoulders, and Darcy's eyes found both the depth of her eyes and the enigmatic smile she wore very enticing. "Yes, Sir," she said softly.

"I came to inquire about your health. You were missed at dinner." He guarded his words, not wishing to amplify the strain obviously between them.

"It was only a headache." Elizabeth tried to smile at him. "It will pass. I am very tired. I slept very little while you were gone."

"You must think of yourself and our child first." Elizabeth's appearance shook his resolve to make amends and then leave. "Would you feel well enough to join me in the sitting room for a few minutes?" For some reason Darcy really did not want to leave her.

Elizabeth wanted to rush into his arms and kiss his face until the hurt went away. "May I beg off, Fitzwilliam? The child has been quite active today, and the need to reevaluate how we live our lives has taken its toll on me." Elizabeth looked at her bed, nervously wishing to be there with Darcy. "My sister and Mr. Bingley depart early tomorrow. I wish to give my dear Jane the comfort of seeing me refreshed and rested." She finally allowed her eyes to rest on her husband's countenance.

"Naturally, Madam." He gave Elizabeth a slight bow. "I will see you in the morning then." With those words, he left the room. Entering his own bedchamber, Darcy leaned back against the door and took several deep breaths. He rakishly ran his hand through his hair. "My wife has some appealing qualities," he smiled at his own jest, "some appealing qualities, indeed." He reached to remove his cravat and tossed it on the back of a chair.

CHAPTER 15

"How wonderful, how very wonderful the operations of time,
and the changes of the human mind."
Jane Austen, *Mansfield Park*, 1814

Early afternoon found Georgiana climbing the hill behind the house, taking in the warmth of the spring sun. The stress of finding her brother required a more demanding walk than usual for the delicate-natured Georgiana. She neared the glade separating the lake from the foothills and took a seat on a hollowed-out log. Raising her face to the sun, Georgiana closed her eyes and listened to the world.

From the hill overlooking Pemberley House, Chadwick Harrison espied her walking away from her home and immediately turned his mount from the road leading to the carriageway and instead circled the building to follow Georgiana to her destination. In reality, it was she he came to see; it was she to whom he must say his goodbyes.

Georgiana took her pleasure in the quiet of the glade and the unseasonable warmth of the day. Unaware of Mr. Harrison's presence, she gathered some wildflowers and sat twirling a long stalk as if conducting an orchestra, eyes closed and engrossed in her own world.

Harrison, captivated by the image of the sunlight reflecting off her golden locks, watched with longing. He wanted to take her in his embrace and kiss the nape of her neck. His eyes drank in her beauty, and it was with great difficulty he finally spoke her name. "Miss Darcy." His voice was husky with desire.

She turned calmly as if expecting him to find her here. "Mr. Harrison, this is a most pleasant surprise." Her eyes held a new light of recognition especially for him.

"It seems I lost my way to Pemberley." He gave her a smile of amusement. "But I managed to find you." His smile grew by the moment. "Maybe you might save a wayward soul."

"I am afraid, Sir, saving souls belongs in the realm of duties of Mr. Ashford. All I might offer you is the music." Georgiana dropped her eyes as he approached.

Harrison found her words intriguing. "The music, Miss Darcy?"

"Come, Mr. Harrison, and sit by me, and let me introduce you to the music." Georgiana looked him directly in the eyes and bid him do as she said.

Harrison, as if mesmerized by Georgiana's beauty, moved to the log and took a seat. "Give me your hand, Mr. Harrison, and close your eyes." Georgiana touched each of his eyelids with her fingertips. She heard the deep intake of breath he took, giving her the confidence to continue.

She spoke softly, nearly in his ear, and Harrison could feel the warmth of Georgiana's breath against his cheek. "Keep your eyes closed, Mr. Harrison, and listen to the music—the music is in the wind, in the rush of the reeds by the lake, and in the sun dancing off your face." She slipped her hand in his, and he tightened the grip. They sat as such for a few moments; then she said, "Do you hear the music, Mr. Harrison?"

A smile crept into the corners of his mouth. "Who would think it possible? A man can hear something where nothing is there. Do you hear the grasshopper singing, Miss Darcy? How about the wings of the birds beating out a rhythm overhead?"

Harrison sat still, enjoying the feeling of her hand in his and of her closeness—her warmth along his shoulder. His words brought Georgiana's attention to his face, at first thinking he teased, but realizing Harrison listened with all his being just as she did. She could not look away, memorizing the lines forming on his forehead and around his eyes.

"Do you hear the sandy swish of the leaves against each other at the top of the tree? Can you hear the rippling sound of the water as it drips from the hill to the waiting pool?" she whispered in his ear.

Harrison turned his head slowly, gradually opening his eyes and coming face to face with her at last. Only inches apart, he asked, "Georgiana, can you hear the beating of my heart?"

His use of her familiar name opened an intimacy denied to them in public. "I hear it, Chadwick."

"Georgiana," the word nearly stuck in his throat. Hypnotized by her closeness, he felt compelled to kiss her; she actually took his breath away. The delicate control he tried to show dissolved into the desire he felt. He lowered his lips to touch hers, and the firmness with which she responded surprised him. His arms encircled her as he deepened the kiss. When he reluctantly withdrew, Harrison's breath came in short bursts. Georgiana instinctively rested her head against his shoulder, breathing in the smell of his desire and mixing it with the essence of hers. "My dearest Georgiana," he whispered into her ear, "what does a wish sound like?"

He could hear the delight of her giggle as it started deep within her. She withdrew just far enough to see his eyes. "I do not know the music found in a wish, but I know the feel of it." She traced his lips with her fingertips.

Harrison kissed her fingertips lightly and then returned to her mouth for one last time before he would have to part from her. The memory of those kisses would sustain him for many months. "Georgiana," his voice played soft against her hair, "I must take my leave of your family today."

"I know, Mr. Harrison." Her voice muffled into his chest.

"Must it be *Mr. Harrison,* Georgiana?"

"Chadwick." She smiled at him.

Harrison nearly laughed out loud. "You never cease to amaze me, Georgiana."

"You will be missed, Sir." She sat up and began to straighten her dress, but she looked back to caress Harrison's jaw line.

Harrison looked deep into her eyes, and an imprecation escaped his lips. "I wish I never made a promise to your sister."

"My birthday is not until late August," she taunted.

Harrison gasped, "You know?"

"Of course I know."

"Then you will wait for me?" Harrison knew he overstepped the bounds of propriety, but with the changes in the assemblage at Pemberley, he did not expect to be invited often to the house, if at all. His chances of seeing Georgiana Darcy decreased with the return of her brother.

Georgiana looked away. "My brother plans to present me to Society this year."

"How? With Mrs. Darcy's lying in?"

"I made the same argument." The tears welled in Georgiana's eyes. "He says it is our duty—my duty to my family."

Harrison could see the distress play across her face. "Georgiana," his voice came out huskily, "I will do what you want me to do. You know my desire—my regard lies with you. Send word, and I will come for you at any time. I know I should not say these words to you, but I love you."

Georgiana blushed, but she did not look away. "I will not allow my brother to arrange a marriage for me. I will choose to whom I give my regard. I will wait for you, Chadwick." The resolve in her voice gave him some comfort. "I must return to the house; they will miss me soon." Looking about anxiously, she stood to take her leave.

Harrison walked to where his horse grazed nearby. "I will circle around the house and come out on the carriageway. I should be making my farewells by the time you arrive home." He prepared to mount, but Georgiana stood too close for him to want to leave her. "Miss Darcy, thank you for giving me the gift of music." He caressed her jaw line, and then he swung himself up into the saddle.

"I will wait," she said again with more determination, "for you, Mr. Harrison, I will wait."

Mr. Harrison's departure meant little to Fitzwilliam Darcy. He had no history with the man that he could recall, but Darcy did scrutinize the man's manners and especially the way he reacted to Georgiana. However, Darcy felt both Mr. Harrison and his sister showed no affection for one another, and the way this stay ended satisfied him.

Harrison could not have reached the end of Pemberley's lane when a servant announced the presence of Lady Marion Haverty. Darcy agreed to meet Lady Haverty in the drawing room. "Lady Haverty," Darcy made her a proper bow when he entered the room, "how nice to see you. What brings you to Pemberley?"

"Mr. Darcy, I came when I heard of your return." She took the chair to which he gestured. "The news of your safe return to your home spread quickly through the surrounding villages. As one of your mother's closest friends, I felt it my duty to come and seek assurances of your health."

"Of course, Lady Haverty." Darcy nodded his head. "Allow me to order some refreshments." He rang for a servant, asking for tea and something to eat to be brought immediately. "Ask my wife to join us," he added.

As soon as the words escaped his mouth, Darcy noted Lady Haverty's frown. "Have you met Mrs. Darcy?" he asked out of curiosity.

"I have not." Lady Haverty's disdain showed.

"I noted what appeared to be your disapproval." His statement held the inflection of a question.

Lady Haverty shifted her weight uncomfortably. Finally, she spoke, but the lady guarded her words. "Mr. Darcy, you are aware of my relationship with your mother and Lady Catherine. We were very close as children; your mother and I shared our First Season in Society. I was instrumental in introducing Lady Anne and your father. They were such a happy couple, but they chose from those of their own rank. I heard from several people you appear to be happy with your choice, but I cannot imagine either your mother or your father would approve of your bringing a person of such low connections to your ancestral home as the Mistress of Pemberley. Can you really say your wife deserves such a lofty station?"

"Mrs. Darcy has her sincere advocates, including my sister."

"Miss Darcy is an impressionable young lady, and you must admit she has little point of reference. Your mother's acquaintances all admire Mrs. Darcy for bettering her lot with such a sagacious match, but she cannot achieve such lofty aspirations. Mrs. Darcy will need to prove herself to your parents' colleagues; just because she is your wife does not guarantee her a place in our society, Mr. Darcy."

Lady Haverty's words ate away at Darcy's instinct. Part of what she said rang true. Elizabeth's connections could not match any of his acquaintances, and Darcy treasured the approval of those with whom he always associated. His pride would not accept their disapproval, and he wondered momentarily if there might be some way to extricate himself from the situation. Then, a stab of arrogance struck him; the fact anyone would disapprove of the woman *he chose* irritated Darcy beyond compare.

"I am grieved you feel as you do, Lady Haverty." Darcy handed her a cup of tea. "Yet, I disagree; my parents placed my happiness and that of my sister above social commitments and relationships."

As he said the words, Elizabeth stepped through the open

door. "You sent for me, Sir?" Elizabeth made a quick curtsy.

"Yes, Mrs. Darcy, I have someone I would like you to meet." His breeding allowed him to stand and lead Elizabeth to a seat next to him. Darcy planned to use this opportunity to observe Elizabeth under the close scrutiny of Lady Haverty. "This is Lady Haverty; her Ladyship was one of my mother's closest confidantes."

Elizabeth made a proper curtsy and accepted the seat Darcy offered. He had no idea Elizabeth heard much of his and Lady Haverty's conversation. The old Darcy would recognize Elizabeth's well-concealed amusement. Throughout the discourse, Elizabeth maintained a most properly attentive pose to Lady Haverty's protracted cordial interest. The nervous prattle of her Ladyship entertained Darcy, and his wife's astute comments and graciousness illuminated his opinion of Elizabeth. She wore a warm smile and dropped her eyes appropriately, and no one could criticize how Elizabeth's look conveyed an earnest pleasure in meeting someone from Darcy's past. By the time the encounter finished, Lady Haverty's resolve weakened, and she presented a promise they would meet again.

Before her Ladyship could take her leave, Elizabeth subdolously excused her own withdrawal. "I beg your leave, Lady Haverty. My sister Georgiana and I plan to call upon some of Pemberley's tenants this afternoon, and I must see to the charitable supplies we will take with us. Please spend some more time with my husband before you leave Pemberley. I find he is excellent company with his close intimates." Momentarily, Darcy wondered about her words. Could Elizabeth mean he treated others, including her, without civility? Elizabeth gave Darcy a warm smile, but he could not tell her true thoughts.

Once in the hallway, Elizabeth, literally, rubbed her cheeks. The smile she wore for Lady Haverty hurt Elizabeth's facial muscles, and Darcy's doubting of her worth hurt Elizabeth's self-esteem. She understood her husband had no direct memories of their relationship, but Elizabeth could not fathom how Darcy might be reevaluating whether he thought her worthy to be his wife. Darcy did not speak out against her; yet, he listened to Lady Haverty's expurgents and accepted them as possibilities. His betrayal brought tears to her eyes. Using the knuckles of her hands, Elizabeth flicked the tears away from her cheeks, took a deep breath, squared her shoulders, and headed off to find Georgiana. If her husband wanted an exemplary Mistress of Pemberley, then Elizabeth would deliver.

Darcy sat on Cerberus atop one of the hills overlooking Pemberley House. He rode out with Mr. Howard to survey some of the property. Below he could see the carriage carrying his wife and sister on their rounds to the tenants. The carriage, loaded with various supplies, snaked its way toward the houses beyond the far-reaching hedgerow.

"How often does my family visit the tenants?" Darcy asked out of amused curiosity.

"Mrs. Darcy and your sister visit at least twice weekly—generally, three times a week. Miss Darcy has a generous nature, Sir; she seems to see this as a part of her duty to the estate."

"Do you not see Mrs. Darcy as having as generous a nature as my sister?" Darcy's voice held a bit of irritation. He might not approve of much of Elizabeth's consanguinity, but she was still his wife, and he would not allow his steward to criticize her.

"I beg your pardon, Mr. Darcy," Mr. Howard cowered under Darcy's stare. "I chose my words poorly." He glanced nervously at the master. "Mrs. Darcy's value to the estate cannot be explained by how she fills the stomachs of the tenants, but how she fills their spirits—their hearts—their belief in your dream for this land."

"Excuse me, Mr. Howard; you spoke in a similar vein earlier."

"I really know not how to explain it, Mr. Darcy. When you chose to include Mrs. Darcy in the running of the estate, I admit to questioning your reason. Yet, Mrs. Darcy is exactly what this estate needs. The people believe in her; they adore her. The tenants might even riot against someone who opposes Mrs. Darcy." The man half laughed, trying to gauge his employer's true interest.

Darcy shifted impatiently in the saddle. It seemed his wife, despite her lack of "breeding," or possibly because of it, created a bridge of understanding among his residentiaries. He did not know what to make of the many reports he received regarding Elizabeth. Unsettled, he turned his mount toward the open fields. He rode hard, allowing the horse's heat to create a warmth—a feeling of release from the chaos of late. Darcy pulled up the reins, slowing Cerberus to a meandering trot. Mr. Howard caught him at last, and the men rode side by side. "Let us check Jefferson's place." Darcy motioned to the small cottage close to the stream.

As they dismounted, Mrs. Jefferson hustled out to greet them, a child of less than two on her hip. "Mr. Darcy, Sir," she spoke quickly, "we be thankin' the Lord to see ye safe. Ye honor us with yur presence at our home, Sir."

"Mrs. Jefferson," Darcy's voice held some caution, "would your husband be about?"

"He be in the fields, Sir." The woman wiped the child's dirty face with her apron. "Be there somethin' wrong, Mr. Darcy? Me man he be sorry for stirrin' up troubles for Mrs. Darcy, Sir." She rushed through the apology. "He be frightened by anythin' new— that be all it be, Sir. It be no respect for you, Sir."

Mr. Howard stepped forward. "Mr. Darcy came not to exact justice with your husband; we simply wish to check on Mr. Jefferson's progress." Darcy allowed his steward to address the woman's concerns for he knew not of what she spoke.

She looked relieved. "Mr. Jefferson be plowin' today, Sir."

Darcy nodded toward their horses, indicating he wished to leave. Mr. Howard instructed Mrs. Jefferson to tell her husband they would call again soon, and then he joined Darcy in the saddle. As they rode back toward the main house, Darcy asked, "Would you care to explain that conversation to me, Mr. Howard?"

His steward looked around nervously. "Mr. Jefferson spoke out against your plan for the four-crop rotation. I could not calm the fears; the men needed to hear from the voice of Pemberley. Mrs. Darcy brokered no discontent. She told Jefferson if he did not believe in the future of Pemberley—in your heir, Sir—and in your dream, he could leave, but he could never return. Mrs. Darcy would never welcome him here again, and his land would be divided among his neighbors."

Darcy laughed. "Mrs. Darcy possesses a strength of character—a perfection—so to speak." His estimation of the woman he married continued in transition. Darcy knew Elizabeth could never measure up to his family's standards, and, no matter what she did, he could never warrant his choice. Yet, by all accounts, his wife demonstrated superb qualities when it came to how she served as Pemberley's mistress. There was the slight possibility he could tolerate a life with her after all.

For five days, his cousin observed Darcy's interactions with Elizabeth, but Darcy treated her with all civility. Comparing the current treatment with his previous responses to his wife, one could easily observe the change in their relationship. Darcy had, for example, yet to call her by her familiar name; he always referred to Elizabeth as "Mrs. Darcy" or "Madam." Darcy reasoned calling her "Elizabeth" indicated a more intimate coupling than they possessed; he reserved her given name for when he developed a true allegiance to this woman.

Although Edward and Anne had noted Darcy withheld calling Elizabeth by her name, Elizabeth ached each time he addressed her, longing for the tenderness and the passion in his voice when he called her such. To hear him call her "Lizzy" would be select pleasure. Often she bit her bottom lip to keep from screaming out at the injustice of losing her husband's love just as they began their life together.

Darcy's cousins should have noted how easy Elizabeth made it for Darcy. Generally, she took two of her meals alone within her room, only appearing at the evening meal. During the day, Elizabeth tended to correspondence, her sewing, reading, and practicing her music. She had not continued helping with the running of Pemberley; her duties as the estate's mistress did not include making decisions affecting the financial soundness of the holdings. She limited her time to the running of the house and to her charity work. At first, Darcy wondered why she withdrew from the liberties he bequeathed to her, but with each day he celebrated her relinquishing what was rightfully his as the estate's master. Elizabeth did not force him to interact with her any more than necessary, and she did not demand what he once freely gave to her.

Darcy seemed content to live the quietness of his life; he would prove he could be the man his father was; he could do it all—alone and independent.

Assured of Darcy's success, Edward and Anne retreated to Rosings Park, leaving Darcy to fend for himself in this fledgling relationship. At their departure, Elizabeth stood beside him as his wife and made the necessary farewells. Darcy appreciated her efforts, but his feelings had not changed, and his memory had not returned.

To say Darcy held no memory of Elizabeth Bennet Darcy would be a mistruth. Although he could not think of her as a vital part of his life during his waking hours, each night she invaded his dreams. He saw her smile—her fine eyes—her petite body. She beckoned him to come to her, and Darcy took his delight in her embrace. Often, he awoke with a start, shaken by his thoughts about this woman. He often crawled out of the bed and sat before the dying embers of the fire feeling both the heat of his growing desire for her and his repugnance at having such thoughts. A gentleman would not think such lubricious thoughts about any woman, especially the woman he chose to be his wife. Did he have such base thoughts of this woman because she was below him? Did his dreams put Elizabeth in her proper place? However, no matter what his reason told him, Elizabeth was more than a memory; she waited for him in his dreams, and no matter what he did to prevent falling asleep, eventually his dreams won out, and Darcy lost himself in the desire found in her eyes and the passion of her touch.

Darcy stood at the window; he watched Elizabeth leave the garden and head away from the house. Her dog romped beside her, making excursions to the water's edge to chase the water-fowl and yapping at the small animals and rodents found in the underbrush. She carried a basket, and he watched as she lightly swung it as she walked. For a change, Elizabeth did not look down nor withdrawn; she walked with a purpose.

Surprised by her demeanor, he impulsively decided to follow her. It took him nearly a quarter hour to find her, having taken a wrong turn on the other side of the lake. When he did finally espy her, Elizabeth sat on the bank of the stream, which fed the lake. She casually tossed a stick to the dog to retrieve, tugging it from the animal's mouth and throwing it out further. A mirthful giggle escaped her, and Darcy found himself smiling at the image she presented.

Not realizing he was there, Elizabeth removed her bonnet and loosened the simple knot in which she wore her hair, allowing her auburn waves to cascade over her shoulders and down her back. Darcy found her innocent choice enticing. Elizabeth leaned back on her elbows, closed her eyes, and let the early spring breeze blow her hair about.

At first, Darcy held back, not wishing to disturb her, but finally he said, "May I join you?"

His presence obviously troubled Elizabeth, but Darcy tried to take no note of the shift in her deportment. "Certainly, Sir." She sat up and began to twist her hair in a close style.

"Why do you not leave it alone?" He gestured toward her efforts.

She asked tentatively, "Are you sure, Sir?"

He forced himself to smile at her as he sat next to her on the ground. "You have beautiful hair."

Unsure how to react to Darcy's soft expression, Elizabeth hesitated before shaking out her hair and letting it fall casually along her neck and shoulders.

"I have seen very little of you since my return to Pemberley," Darcy began after an awkward silence.

"I apologize if I offended you, Fitzwilliam." Her use of his name seemed natural; the way the word rolled off Elizabeth's tongue made Darcy feel as if she caressed him. "I thought it best to give you time to determine what you want of me."

"And I sought you out today to determine whether you wish to leave Pemberley—to establish yourself elsewhere."

Tears welled in her eyes, and he noted Elizabeth struggled to find her voice. "If it is your wish for me to do so." Elizabeth's voice trembled, and a tear cascaded down her cheek before she could brush it away.

"What is *your* wish, Madam?" Darcy tried to control the intonation in his words.

Elizabeth looked away, afraid to meet his eyes or to allow his words to undo her. "I am not sure I can learn to live without your love, Fitzwilliam, but if you have no objections, for some time, I considered Pemberley to be my home." She brought her eyes to rest on his countenance and to await his decision.

For a brief, fleeting moment, Darcy saw the same look in Elizabeth's eyes he saw in his dreams. "I would prefer to allow us a chance to create a home for our family; beyond that, I can offer you no promises. Obviously, though, we cannot find a balance in our lives if we avoid each other."

His words hurt Elizabeth deeply, but she tried to control the unevenness in her voice before speaking. "Do you suppose you could begin by calling me by my name? It hurts to be only Mrs. Darcy to you."

Darcy gave her half a smile and reached out to hook a strand of hair behind her ear. Elizabeth fought the urge to kiss the palm of his hand. In the past, she would not deny her impulsive nature and would enjoy the pleasure of his touch, but this was a Darcy she did not know. "You noted my reluctance to speak as such?"

Elizabeth allowed herself the simple pleasure of leaning her head into the touch of Darcy's hand before saying, "I am afraid, Sir, there is very little about you of which I take no note." She automatically gave him a teasing smile.

About that time, the dog returned from the water's edge, bounding up and sniffing at Darcy's legs. "May I?" He indicated the stick, and she nodded in affirmation. Darcy picked up the stick, teased the animal with it, and then tossed it out for the spaniel to retrieve.

"Go, Hero," she instructed the animal before it took off to capture the "prey."

Darcy's voice rose in inflection, "Hero?"

"From Shakespeare's *Much Ado about Nothing*," Elizabeth stammered. "During our courtship, we once exchanged the lines between Benedick and Beatrice. It seemed only appropriate," she bantered, and Darcy felt himself warm to her expression.

"Obviously, like its Greek name, the animal loves the water." He returned Elizabeth's teasing tone.

"As long as she does not find a Leander and choose to drown herself while chasing the waterfowl." Elizabeth tried to continue her light repartee with him; she remembered she originally won Darcy by engaging him. "Of course, you warned me as such when you talked Mr. Harvey into selling Hero."

He asked innocently, "I gave you Hero?"

"One of my wedding gifts." She offered Darcy a winsome smile.

"I understand from Georgiana I also gave you a gun. It seems I need to find more personal ways to celebrate our marriage." He looked at Elizabeth closely.

Elizabeth laughed spontaneously. "Actually, along with my horse, the gifts were of what I asked. I never wanted the jewels or the fancy gowns. Hero is a good companion on my walks. I wanted the horse to be able to ride out across the estate with you."

Darcy wanted to see what else she knew so he asked, "Do you believe Mr. Shakespeare chose Ariosto's *Orlando Furioso* as the basis for Hero's and Claudio's characters?"

"It seems to me Spenser's *The Faerie Queene* is more likely the source."

Darcy smiled with her response. "Delineating Claudio and Don Pedro could come from Bandello's *La Prima Parte de le Novelle*."

"I am afraid I am not familiar with that particular piece." Not wishing to demonstrate her lack of a formal education, Elizabeth dropped her eyes. Then she recovered her voice, afraid to let the moment pass. "*Nothing* and *noting*—so much convergence on these words. Shakespeare recognized and reveled in the possibilities."

"Noting—observing—understanding and misreporting." Darcy moved in a bit closer where he could see only Elizabeth's face as he spoke. "I noted her not, but I looked on her," (1.1.158) he quoted Benedick's line about Hero.

Elizabeth feigned innocence. "The sweetest lady that ever I looked on." (1.1.181)

"She is too low for a high praise, too brown for a fair praise, and too little for a great praise." (1.1.165) Darcy enjoyed the recitation.

Elizabeth, on the other hand, wondered about his choice of quotes. Could it mean Darcy thought her below him? "It is the perfect play to teach how some people trust what they see rather than what they believe in their hearts or know in their minds. I once foolishly judged you on visual proof—my tendency to see in others whatever character and experience I am predisposed to see." Elizabeth hoped her words struck a chord with Darcy.

"Neither Claudio nor Benedick really see Hero, do they? Are your words a warning to see beyond what others offer?"

"Society often leads one to think subjectivity of perception as acceptable, while, in reality, adhering to convention can distort a person's views." Elizabeth resisted the urge to caress Darcy's face as she spoke.

"I suppose there is some peril in noting incorrectly," he offered as he searched Elizabeth's face for some familiarity besides the images of her found in his dreams. "Are you well— I mean, with the child?" he finally asked. Slowly, he placed his hand on the swell of her abdomen.

"The changes are becoming more evident." Elizabeth rested her hand on top of Darcy's; the corners of her lips turned up briefly. If her Darcy made this gesture, it would be a very intimate one, but with this Darcy, there was an oddity. Uncomfortable with the intensity of his look, Elizabeth raised his fingertips to her mouth and kissed them lightly. "It will be several more months," she laughed lightly. "Can you wait that long?"

He sounded a bit petulant when he said, "I do not like to wait; patience is not one of my virtues."

"Well, it is one of mine," she giggled lightly. "I have many things to do before the arrival of our child." She held his hand in hers.

"I do also." He looked away. "There is something of which I would like to speak. I was thinking of taking Georgiana to London for an abbreviated season before your lying in. That would mean your being here alone." Darcy waited to see Elizabeth's reaction.

"Fitzwilliam," she gushed, "has Georgiana agreed to this?"

"My sister knows her duty to her family." Elizabeth watched the warmth he displayed a few moments ago retreat; Darcy now offered her a lecture on familial duty. "My sister and I understand each other. Georgiana will do what is expected of her. My sister's world is different from what others may surmise."

Without thinking about her response, Elizabeth said, "Disdain and scorn ride sparkling in her eyes, misprising what they look on." (3.1.51)

Darcy asked incredulously, "Then you believe my sister will refuse?"

Elizabeth blushed. "Georgiana will do her duty; however, as your wife, I hope you will not force her to do so."

"You may say such things; our match brought you the security you did not have before."

Immediately, Elizabeth was on her feet. "Please tell me you do not believe that is why I married you."

"I have been told otherwise." Darcy moved quickly to dominate over her stance.

"That is not what I asked."

"I have no waking memory of our relationship. I must base my opinions on what I know." He forced Elizabeth to turn and look at him. "I must give Georgiana a chance at securing a suitable match. I hoped as my wife you would support me on this matter."

"If the *suitable match* is a man my sister can also affect, I will be happy to support you." Elizabeth squared her shoulders to let him know she would not relent. "However, if Georgiana is not happy, I will be less inclined to see things your way, Sir." Elizabeth turned quickly and strode away, not bothering to fix her hair or to replace her bonnet. Hero darted past Darcy's legs, nearly knocking him off balance, scrambling after her mistress.

"No waking memories," he mumbled to her retreating form, "none, whatsoever." Despite feeling agitated because of the confrontation, Darcy smiled from looking at her. Elizabeth's auburn curls bounced as she walked away, and Darcy tried to suppress an urge to touch her hair and to revisit the feel of their entangled hands.

CHAPTER 16

*"A scheme of which every part promises delight
can never be successful;
and general disappointment is only warded off
by the defence of some little peculiar vexation."*
Jane Austen, *Pride and Prejudice*, 1813

"I have come to abduct you, my Husband." Elizabeth appeared before Darcy's desk. They maintained a level of civility the last two days, although strained by their heated discussion that fateful afternoon.

"I am quite busy, Mrs. Darcy." His voice held a sense of frustration.

Elizabeth folded her arms across her chest and gave him a look of like interception. "First, I know my spontaneity drives your need to control your universe crazy, Fitzwilliam, but you did express a desire to get to know me better. I wish to show you some of the things I value in our life together. Please come with me; the curricle awaits."

Darcy leaned back in the chair to examine this woman who was his wife. A smile betrayed his amusement when he looked at her. "You said *first*. Am I to assume you have more than one demand of me today?"

A laugh escaped her lips. "*Second*, you promised to call me *Elizabeth*."

"So I did, *Elizabeth*," he emphasized the last word. "Is this really necessary?" Darcy leaned forward and looked at the papers on his desk. "I have many things to address here." He picked up a stack of papers to highlight his point.

Elizabeth splayed her fingers and leaned down on his desk. "Fitzwilliam, our life together—the one in which we raise our child—should supersede any of these issues." She gestured to the papers. "These will wait for a few hours; people's feelings cannot be placed on hold. What is it to be, my Husband?"

Darcy knew she tossed down the gauntlet. Elizabeth asked him what he valued most: the estate or their marriage. Darcy's natural instinct told him to choose the estate; it was an area within his control—his wife was a different story. In the short time since his return to Pemberley, Darcy's emotional bond to Elizabeth Bennet Darcy ran the gamut of highs and lows. A smile began to creep into the corners of his mouth. He enjoyed how Elizabeth refused to back down when she believed strongly in something—how her eyes locked in on his and told him stories he never heard. "I will get my beaver and coat," he said at last.

A like smile erupted from Elizabeth as she said, "Thank you, Fitzwilliam." She rushed from the room before he could change his mind.

Outside, Darcy handed her into the curricle. Elizabeth adjusted a blanket across both of their laps before he took up the reins. "The weather in Derbyshire is more temperamental than it is in Hertfordshire; it changes as often as I change my mind." She tucked the blanket in on the far side of Darcy's lap, forcing her to lean across his body to do so. With her mouth only inches from his, Darcy fought the impulse to kiss her, but Elizabeth's presence sent a rush through him. "Is that better, my Love?" she asked as she again looked deeply into Darcy's eyes.

"I am well, Mrs.—I mean, Elizabeth."

"Good." She adjusted a blanket across her own lap. "I would not wish you to return to the troubles which beset you of late."

Turning her head to take in his profile, Elizabeth laced her arm through Darcy's as he picked up the reins. As he flicked them across the horse's hindquarters, she called, "Hero, come." The English Springer spaniel leapt into the vehicle and curled up immediately at Elizabeth's feet.

"The dog gives you great pleasure?" Darcy said with some finality.

"The man who gave it to me because he knew I never had a pet of my own gives me great pleasure." Again, Elizabeth's closeness sent a shiver through him. "Are you chilled, my Love?"

Her concern for him seemed genuine. "I am fine. I just did not expect such frankness." They sat looking deeply into each other's eyes.

"I would prefer if we could be truthful. We do not have time to play games. We are married and must establish a life together at Pemberley; yet, we must do so under absurd conditions. Many of the assumptions we previously put aside may resurface. We both once misconstrued the essence of each other; we have not the time to hide our feelings. We may not like many of our encounters, but we have no real choice, in my estimation."

"You are a very astute woman, Elizabeth." Darcy forced himself to look away, having become lost in her eyes. "Where would be our destination for the day?" He tried to sound casual.

"I have something I want to show you, which I hope will please you." Elizabeth snuggled in closer to him to feel his warmth. "I want to return to the glade behind the stream where we talked the other day."

"We return to the scene of the crime?"

Elizabeth dropped her eyes. "I am sorry we argued; I should guard my tone."

"But not your sentiments?"

"You know me. . . ." She stopped, and a nervous laugh escaped. "That is just it; you do not know me, do you? I have a tendency to speak before thinking. I would not say my objections changed, but I would change my approach. I should use a feather but instead use a hammer." Darcy chuckled with her metaphor. "Our disagreements are part of the legend of our courtship."

"I assume you refer to my first proposal?" Darcy's statement came out as a question.

"Ah, our infamous time at Hunsford. Do you remember that day?"

"My sister tells me I insulted you?" Again, the question returned.

"You were very *fluent* on your trials in overcoming my family connections. I took offense because you separated my dearest Jane and Mr. Bingley. Toss in the lies Mr. Wickham fed me, and we were nearly in a state of fisticuffs."

Darcy stopped the curricle. "You jest?"

"We agreed to be frank," she answered quickly. "I certainly considered striking you for a few brief seconds. I kept your letter where you defended yourself against my misplaced accusations. You are welcome to read it if it will help you recover some of that time."

"I will believe you for now." Then he flicked the reins again to see where the day would lead.

"Let us stop here," Elizabeth said softly at last, turning the blanket back. Darcy came around to help her from the curricle. He lifted her by the waist while she supported herself by placing her hands on his shoulders. When he placed Elizabeth on the ground in front of him, he hesitated in withdrawing his hands. Her hands now rested on his chest, and she moved in instinctively to be closer to him. "You are exceedingly handsome, my Husband," she said as she caressed Darcy's cheek.

"It pleases me you are trying to make my transition easier." Darcy found he once again became lost in her eyes. He held Elizabeth there next to him, unable to move. Darcy wanted to kiss her, to take his rights as her husband, but a part of his brain demanded he wait. No doubt Elizabeth would not refuse him; her eyes told him as much, but it was indubitable for him to do so without some affection for the woman. He could feel the tension between them growing so he did the gentlemanly thing: He took her hand and kissed the back of it lightly before hooking her arm in his.

"Is our destination close by?" he asked to try to distract his thoughts from kissing Elizabeth's lips and from caressing her body.

"Very close." She motioned toward the tree line. Elizabeth led him to a small glade behind the tree line created by the natural bed of the stream leading to the lake. "I hoped to find something more hidden, but when I saw this glade from the uppermost windows of Pemberley, I knew it was the one."

"The one?"

Elizabeth pushed back the low branches and stepped into the open. Darcy followed but stopped short. "Elizabeth," he gasped, "when—how?"

Before him stood a field of wildflowers. Many fledglings in their growth—but all of them with heads turned toward the sun. Darcy took a few steps forward, looking about him in disbelief. "The clearing—your mother's favorite at Huns-ford—you honored me when you shared it. After your first proposal and the letter, I wanted to bring something of you home with me." Elizabeth's voice was soft and inviting. "I thought I would never see you again; you left Rosings before I did. I returned to your mother's clearing and cut many of the flowers. I dried some for a sachet, but for many of them I took them for the seeds. I planned to plant them in the fall at Long-bourn, but then you returned to me so I brought them here.

"In November and December, I came here often, bringing the seeds with me. I scattered some every time there came a snow or a rain. I even elicited Mr. Howard's help. Some of the tenants helped plant the seeds; some even furnished seeds. With your disappearance, the field became a place of solace—a place where part of you could be here with me at Pemberley." Elizabeth tried to search Darcy's face to judge his reaction to what she told him. "I have a hedgerow of yellow rosebushes on the back side of the field because you gave me yellow roses when we married. It has a long way to go, but do you not think it to be beautiful?" Elizabeth waited impatiently, trying to steel her nerves. "Please say something, Fitzwilliam."

Darcy closed his eyes and drank in the emotions coursing through him. For a brief, fleeting moment he saw Elizabeth turning round and round in a field of wildflowers. *Her rich, mellow eyes sparkled and filled Darcy with happiness. He loved Elizabeth. The realization of admitting his feelings flashed through his being; no more would he say he loved her eyes or loved how she spoke her mind; no longer would he think of his feelings being only a strong attraction; he loved Elizabeth.* The memory clearly played across his mind. Darcy turned back to her; tears misted his eyes. He had trouble separating the memory of that moment from the real woman currently standing in front of him. He took Elizabeth in his arms. "You did all this for me?" He seemed surprised by the depth of her devotion to him.

"We could not return to Rosings with Lady Catherine's objections so I thought I would bring Rosings to us—to you. It is one of my favorite memories of our time there. Georgiana helped, too." She rushed through the words, afraid to let him respond. "She was always jealous you shared your mother's clearing with me. Now we can enjoy it together. Would it please your mother?" Elizabeth asked innocently.

Darcy pulled Elizabeth's head to his chest as he looked around at the early-blooming flowers. "It is a great gift you give me and Pemberley," he whispered in her ear. "It would astound my mother you would think of this. You say we can see the field from Pemberley?"

"From the baby's nursery it is quite obvious. I thought it would be a good story to share with our children." She wondered how Darcy would react to her reference to *children*, indicating she wanted a future with him. All he did, however, was stroke her head and kiss her forehead. They stood as such, her hands caressing the muscles of his back within his waistcoat and Darcy holding her tightly to him.

"Elizabeth," he began at last, "I need more time; I am not ready for all this." His words held the sorrow he knew she would feel when he released her.

Darcy heard her swallow hard, but when she raised her face to look at him, other than the tears welling in her eyes, no one would know Elizabeth felt anything besides joy. "Like the clearing, it is a beginning, my Husband. I will wait for your love to grow."

Darcy could understand how he aligned himself with Elizabeth Bennet. She possessed a fortitude he did not know could be found in a woman, especially one so petite and lively. "The air is cool today; let me get you back to the curricle before you become chilled." He coaxed her to walk with him.

Once Darcy placed Elizabeth in the curricle, he tended to her needs, giving her his blanket also. Again, he resisted his urge to kiss her, sure if he did, he would not want to stop until he possessed her. The woman of his dreams and the woman in the curricle could not be one and the same; he would not allow it to be so. "Where to now, Elizabeth?"

"I need to call on Mrs. Fleming if you do not mind, Sir." Elizabeth reached to secure the basket she planned to give the woman. "Her gout has her unable to get about this past week. I just wish to check on her, and then we may return to Pemberley."

"How many of the tenants do you know, Elizabeth?"

"Georgiana and I called on them all at least once; some are more readily accessible because of the roads. When we could not get through in a carriage, we sent some of the staff on horseback with supplies. Our efforts began during the Festive Season. We sectioned off the estate to better manage our time." Elizabeth seemed all businesslike when discussing the estate's cottagers.

"I appreciate your helping Georgiana to assume such duties."

"She has a very generous nature; when your sister marries, her husband will have to guard against her giving away everything he owns." Elizabeth laughed at the image of Georgiana handing over tapestries to the poor.

By now they were at the Fleming cottage, and Darcy again helped Elizabeth from the curricle. He carried the basket of supplies. When she knocked on the door, he heard cries of "Mrs. Darcy be here" as several children scrambled to answer the door. Having Darcy with her silenced the rabble, but as she stepped through the open door, Darcy noted how Elizabeth reached out to touch their heads or their faces and how she called each by name.

"Mrs. Fleming," she said softly as she advanced toward the bed, "I hope you are feeling better." Elizabeth sat on the edge of the bed without being asked. Darcy surreptitiously looked around the cottage; it was cleaner than most in which he had been. He placed the basket on the table.

"Mrs. Darcy, ye be honoring us by comin' to us today," Mrs. Fleming gushed, "and ye brought the Master with ye. How blessed we be in yur doin' so." The woman beamed at being so recognized.

"We brought some food for you and your grandchildren," Elizabeth gestured to the basket. "Is your son in the fields?"

"He be so, Mrs. Darcy. Me son works hard to raise the children and to take care of his old mum."

"You must be very proud of him. We will not keep you. I was concerned with your health." Elizabeth stood to take her leave.

Mrs. Fleming caught her hand. "The Master—he be takin' ye to Tissington for the well dressin' this year?"

"Mr. Darcy and I have not discussed it, Mrs. Fleming." Elizabeth shot a glance at Darcy. "We have several commitments including the marriage of Mr. Darcy's cousins to which we must attend." Elizabeth knew Darcy would not be comfortable at such a *pagan* gathering.

"Ye be lookin' like the maids in the fields last year. I be sayin' so me self at the Festive Season gatherin'."

"I thank you, Mrs. Fleming," Elizabeth smiled. "Mr. Darcy and I will do our best. Please take care of yourself. There are treats for the children for after dinner."

"Mr. Darcy, yur wife be a special one," Mrs. Fleming called out to him.

"So I have noted, Mrs. Fleming." Darcy extended his hand to Elizabeth. She slipped her arm through his and returned to the curricle.

"Tissington well dressing?" he asked once they were on their way again.

"Hannah told me about last year's mosaic when I was here last August. At the tenant celebration, Georgiana and I dressed as the two women in the mosaic dressed. Your sister wore the rich brown earth tones while I dressed in the green found in Derbyshire's rolling hills. I wanted to create a mood to assure the tenants Pemberley—the land—would always be there for them. Mrs. Fleming made the connection and told the others. Pretty soon Georgiana and I were part of the legend." Elizabeth shifted, uneasy about how Darcy would react to such out-and-out manipulation on her part.

However, as he did that December afternoon, Darcy found the retelling amusing. A temporary sensation of Elizabeth interacting with his tenants in one of the public rooms at Pemberley overcame his senses. He heard Mr. Howard's voice. *"These people are not sophisticated, Mr. Darcy; they live their hard lives based on their beliefs and their traditions. Old Mrs. Fleming over there swears the mosaic art at the Tissington well dressing this summer was your wife and your sister."* As he did that day in December, almost as if he relived the moment in his memory, he turned to Elizabeth and asked, "And from where, may I ask, did you learn such devious manipulations, Mrs. Darcy?" His smile portrayed an unspoken interest.

"Should I respond as I did before?" Elizabeth searched Darcy's countenance for how far to push the memory.

"Please do," Darcy said softly. By now they sat in the carriageway before the house.

Elizabeth forced herself to breathe. An emotional day, she knew not whether to allow herself to continue this trip down "memory lane" with Darcy. Finally she said enticingly, "From the master, my Love—from you."

Darcy felt himself lost to her. The passion grew quickly as he looked at her upturned face, and he again fought the urge to kiss her. His breath came in short bursts. "You gave me a great deal upon which to think, Elizabeth."

He reached out and touched her chin with his index finger. To a stranger, such a gesture might seem an insignificant one, but Elizabeth knew Darcy only did such to those he most closely affected. "I will see you at dinner," she taunted him by slowly parting her lips as if to kiss him. "Thank you, Fitzwilliam." A footman stepped forward to help Elizabeth from the vehicle. Darcy watched as she started to climb the steps to Pemberley. "Come, Hero," she called without looking around. The dog jumped about for her attention, while Elizabeth bent to pat its head. "How is my good dog?" she laughed. "We had a full day, did we not? A very full day." She stood again and looked back briefly at Darcy before entering the house.

Darcy let out the breath he did not realize he held. A smile turned up the corners of his mouth as he, too, climbed the steps to Pemberley. "A very full day," he mumbled. "She has no idea how full my day was." With that, he allowed himself an audible chuckle before handing his coat and beaver to the waiting servant.

The days progressed as such. Darcy continued to fight his recent recognition of the merits of Elizabeth Bennet Darcy. She certainly had a way with other people; he would give her that. His staff, his tenants, and his sister all offered Elizabeth their respect; the people in Lambton spoke highly of her amiability and her compassion. Other than Darcy himself, and, evidently, Lady Catherine, Elizabeth won over everyone. Edward and Anne thought her to be a good choice for Darcy; in an uncharacteristically lengthy letter, Lord and Lady Pennington sang Elizabeth's praises.

Yet, Darcy saw in the accounts what a deficit the estate took when he brought Elizabeth to Pemberley as his wife. Financially, she brought nothing of which to speak to his holdings, and although she spent very little from the generous pin money Darcy provided her, the estate lost value with the marriage. Elizabeth's thousand pounds from Mr. Bennet did not ease the pecuniary differences.

Elizabeth's manners impressed those below her—those with country manners of their own, but members of the *ton* would eat her alive for their dinner. Once they smelled her fear, members of the *ton* would attack Elizabeth's manners, her bearing, and her connections. The mob mentality would overcome her, and Darcy would be unable to help. Elizabeth's inability to succeed in London would reflect on his family and his sister's chances of an appropriate match. The more he thought about it, the more he realized he must bring Georgiana to London this Season while Elizabeth would have to remain behind. He could keep his wife in Derbyshire where London's finest could not evaluate her, and the new Mrs. Darcy could not tarnish Georgiana's chances.

However disagreeable Darcy found these circumstances surrounding his wife, he could not withdraw his eyes from her when she entered a room, and he began to concoct situations about which he had to speak to Elizabeth. Every day he rushed down to breakfast to be there when she entered the room; he took pleasure in preparing a plate for her. Darcy sought her out throughout the house, and he often found his thoughts drifted to Elizabeth. Maybe having her at Pemberley without interruptions would not be such a bad thing, at least for him. Possibly, he could function in both worlds: in London's social scene and as a country gentleman. Darcy saw no real reason it could not happen. He could have Elizabeth at Pemberley and live a life of a respected landowner in London. The thoughts of such an arrangement pleased him. He would spend several months a year at his London home, and then he would return to Pemberley. A smile of pure pleasure crept across his face, and Darcy leaned back in his chair to savor the moment. He would go to London on Monday to arrange for Georgiana's abbreviated season; afterwards, he would return to Pemberley and resume his husbandly rights with his wife. Elizabeth would not refuse him; she conveyed her receptiveness quite clearly, and Darcy would make her his again.

On the Saturday before his departure for London, finding Elizabeth dressed to go out took Darcy by surprise when she entered the breakfast room. His eyes shot up to meet hers when she entered the room. "Good morning, Elizabeth," he spoke her name softly, giving it a special emphasis.

"Good morning, my Husband." She offered him a bright smile. "I hope you slept well, Sir." Politeness hid her question.

Darcy walked to the sideboard to refill his plate. "I did, Madam." Darcy, too, found himself smiling. "May I fix you some tea?"

"May I have some chocolate?" Elizabeth half teased. "I seem to have developed a taste for it these last few months."

"Certainly, Elizabeth." Darcy brought her the cup.

"The heir to Pemberley is restless today." Elizabeth gently stroked her ever-increasing abdomen.

Being alone with her in the breakfast room, Darcy felt compelled to kneel next to her chair. "Are you pleased with the child?" He examined Elizabeth's countenance, searching for the answer to a question he did not know how to ask. "I mean—are you . . . ?" Darcy broke off, not wanting to know if having his child meant something to her.

Elizabeth took Darcy's hand and placed it over the quickening movement. Her smile curled upward when the child's shifting moved against Darcy's hand, and tears welled in his eyes. "I told you before our child loves your touch." Her voice softly caressed Darcy's ear as she leaned closer to him.

His hand moved gently, and he could not resist the pull Elizabeth had on him. He let his other hand stroke her ankle at the hem of her skirt, and he heard Elizabeth let out a little gasp. "You did not answer my question, Elizabeth." Darcy's voice took on a husky tone.

Elizabeth caressed the side of his face; she forced herself not to even blink, afraid the least change would break the spell between them. "I anticipate your happiness when the child arrives; it will please me to see you holding your heir." Elizabeth slid her hand into his. Darcy's other hand continued to stroke her ankle, and slowly he moved his thumb up her calf.

"How can we make this work?" His words came out jagged and breathy. "I feel I am cheating you out of happiness. You want something from me I may never be able to give you."

"I know you are the same man with whom I fell in love." Elizabeth craved Darcy's touch. "The question is whether you can love me again, my Husband. I must admit this is the most difficult thing I ever did, and I do not know whether I am strong enough to take your answer when you finally decide."

Their gaze locked, and neither of them could move—the desire thick between them. How long they would stay as such one cannot know, but soon voices penetrated their thoughts, forcing Darcy to withdraw once again. Elizabeth shifted uncomfortably as Kitty and Georgiana entered the room. They bubbled with excitement. Darcy looked up from the sidebar, to where he pretended to examine the selections, to note his sister's appearance. He sheepishly remembered his earlier surprise at seeing Elizabeth dressed to go out for the day. Wanting to know where Elizabeth might be going and understanding she and his sister would be going together, Darcy asked casually, "Do you intend to go out today, Georgiana?"

Georgiana shot a quick glance at Elizabeth, wondering how to answer her brother. Noting his sister's discomfort, Elizabeth answered for her. "We decided to make an appearance at the Tissington Well Dressing Festival after all, Fitzwilliam." Elizabeth's voice held a special caution in telling her husband about their plans. She assumed he would disapprove, and she did not want to lose the ground she made in earning his attention once again.

"Surely, you are not in truth!" Darcy whirled around to confront his wife.

"No, Sir, that is our plan. Mr. Ashford is to bless the well; he asked Kitty to accompany him. I cannot allow my sister to attend alone. I chose to represent the estate while securing my sister's reputation. I am sorry you disapprove, Fitzwilliam, but I will not likely change my mind." Elizabeth's heart sank. She knew her husband would withdraw from her; he would see her as functioning as the Mistress of Pemberley only in the basest form.

Darcy guarded his words, but his tone betrayed his feelings. "These people are not sophisticated, Elizabeth. Well dressing ceremonies are based in deep-rooted heathenish superstitions." He literally puffed up with disdain.

Elizabeth allowed her eyes to lock with his—only this time instead of desire, it was a test of will. "I realize these people live hard lives based on their beliefs and their traditions. I realize this celebration, although lacking in worldliness, is important to them. I believe it is important to support our Pemberley family—to understand them better." Elizabeth did not allow her eyes to falter even though she did not feel confident in this confrontation with Darcy.

Georgiana and Kitty sat immobilized, afraid even to breathe. They prayed Elizabeth would prevail, for both girls looked forward to the outing; therefore, their composures lapsed when Darcy said, "What if I forbid it?" The stare became an intense battleground between Darcy and Elizabeth.

The moments crawled by before she answered him. "I pray, my Husband, you do not choose to do so for we are at odds on this issue. I know you have the legal right to control my use of the coach, but please do not exercise that right, Fitzwilliam. We have more important issues between us than a peasant celebration."

Her words said, Elizabeth waited, holding her breath, trying to reason how she would react if Darcy went through with his threat. Finally, he threw the napkin on the table and stormed from the room.

The tension lessened, but did not totally dissipate. "Ladies," Elizabeth's voice trembled, "please be ready to leave as soon as you eat. We are to pick up Mr. Ashford at the parsonage within the hour." Elizabeth, having lost her appetite, returned to her chambers. Legs shaking, she collapsed into a nearby chair. "Please, Fitzwilliam," she whispered before breaking into tears.

CHAPTER 17

*"If any one faculty of our nature may be called more wonderful
than the rest, I do think it is memory."*
Jane Austen, *Mansfield Park*, 1814

The carriage stopped briefly in front of the parsonage; Mr.
Ashford exited the house immediately. Joining the ladies in the
coach, Ashford made his polite greetings to all three before
turning his attentions to Kitty Bennet.

"Have you attended such a festival before, Mr. Ashford?"
Kitty asked quietly.

His smile flooded the coach. "Once when I was a child, my
mother's brother took my older brother and me to one in the
eastern parts of the county."

"I did not realize you had an older brother." Elizabeth's
head turned quickly at his words.

"It is true, Mrs. Darcy. My brother Rowland was two years
my senior." Ashford looked out the coach's window. "He resided
with my father in Brighton, but he passed three years ago."

Even Georgiana seemed surprised by this disclosure. "I
am ashamed, Mr. Ashford, I never thought to inquire about
your family prior to today. It grieves me I could have been
so shallow."

"Do not fret, Miss Darcy." Ashford swallowed hard. "I speak
very little of my family; my father would prefer I chose law as
my profession, but I love the church and my calling. Your
brother is aware of my situation; I assumed the rest of the
family was also."

"As you are part of the Pemberley family now, Mr. Ashford," Georgiana warned, "we will all be into your business to the point you will drive us away."

Mr. Ashford smiled at her assertion. "I could not find myself in better company, Miss Darcy." No one said anything for a few, brief moments, all a bit uncomfortable with the personal disclosure.

Elizabeth took it upon herself to change the discourse by retelling Mr. Ashford and Kitty about how she and Georgiana used the well dressing mosaic from last year in the tenant celebration.

"Well, that explains some of the rumors about your being the 'Mother of the Land,' Mrs. Darcy." The group fell into a comfortable conversation.

The journey took less than an hour, and as the carriage pulled into the Tissington village center, a crush of people rushed forward, waiting for the riders of such an expensive coach to step down. Those in the coach shifted their seats and straightened their clothing before disembarking. The coach's door swung open, and Elizabeth moved to step down, expecting a footman to assist her.

Instead, her hand slid into Darcy's. He stood in all his glory waiting for her; Elizabeth's eyes welled with tears as she mouthed the words "thank you" when he helped her to the ground. Then he turned back to aid first Georgiana and then Kitty, both of whom did not control their composure as well as did Elizabeth.

While her husband helped their sisters, Elizabeth's eyes searched the area. She smiled seeing Cerberus hitched to a nearby post. Darcy turned back to her, offering Elizabeth his arm before they started to make their way through the crowd. Murmurs of "the Darcys are here," "the master Darcy," and "Mrs. Darcy has come" flitted through the crowd as they made their way toward the village pump. Elizabeth acknowledged those from Pemberley and held the astonished gaze of others with her watery green eyes.

Darcy walked slowly and a bit majestically, his jaw line set in a tight grin and his eyes straight ahead. He and Elizabeth took center stage in front of the crowd gathering for Mr. Ashford's blessing. The people parted to make way for them and then closed ranks behind the couple. Georgiana and Kitty flanked them on either side. Darcy noted some of the smaller landowners in attendance, but no one of his standing stood about.

Ashford stepped forward, and the crowd grew quiet, waiting for his words. His clear, resonant voice echoed across the square as he delivered the blessing of the water before joining the Darcy party once again. The crowd started to break apart; some brought picnic meals while others bought goods from hawkers on the village streets.

Ashford asked Kitty to walk with him at least once around the square. Darcy agreed but cautioned them to not tarry for he did not intend to stay long. As they walked away together, several of the tenants came to address the Darcys. Mrs. Fleming led the way. "Oh, Mrs. Darcy," she literally cried joyful tears, "ye be makin' me family so proud to be knowin' ye and the Master. None of them high fluentin' other lords care enough to be showin' them faces here. We be blessed to be knowin' ye." She made a quick bow and left the Darcys feeling a sense of pride.

Georgiana stepped to the side to look at the floral wares an old lady offered. Darcy seized the moment to address Elizabeth. "I must apologize, Mrs. Darcy," he whispered so only Elizabeth could hear. "Your intuition proved correct; our appearance here won us much loyalty."

"Thank you for changing your mind, Fitzwilliam." Her eyes danced with pleasure. "I was never happier to see anyone; I feared you to be angry with me."

"You should know by now, Elizabeth, my anger comes quickly, but reason always rules my head." Darcy leaned in closer where he could smell her lavender rushing over him.

"I am truly pleased, Fitzwilliam." She gifted Darcy with a huge smile. "Now, if I can find out what rules your heart, then my life may be complete once again." She dropped her eyes, not able to look at him when he responded. She hooked her arm through Darcy's. "May we walk before returning home?" He cupped her hand with his free hand as they made their way among the revelers.

Georgiana joined them as they stepped into a village shop out of the weather. Elizabeth wandered over to a display of silk gloves, and Darcy came up behind her. "My heart is learning a new language," he whispered seductively to her.

Elizabeth did not turn her head to look at him, but instinctively she leaned back to feel Darcy's closeness. She could detect the shallowness of his breathing. She felt his thumb caress her back above her waistline. "Do you like the gloves, Mrs. Darcy?" he said a bit louder so anyone who might be looking at them would not question his nearness to her. "May I buy them for you, Elizabeth?"

"I need no gifts to make me happy, Mr. Darcy." Elizabeth turned to face him, the two standing closer than propriety allowed.

"It would please me to give them to you." Darcy's voice was shallow with breathiness.

"Your happiness is important to me." She looked at him seriously. "I would love to have them." Elizabeth handed him the gloves, and Darcy reluctantly stepped away from her.

Georgiana caught Elizabeth's arm. She whispered, "I was so surprised to see my brother today."

Elizabeth let out a deep sigh. "My husband surprised me, too."

"He stands closer." Georgiana blushed as she said it.

"I should not say this to you as an unmarried woman, but I decided your brother and I share a *passion*, and I would use that to bring him back to me. I will do some of the things which won him before. I have no choice; I cannot live without Fitzwilliam."

"Do you plot my downfall?" Darcy's voice made both women jump.

"Women always plot the downfall of men," Elizabeth teased. "You are at our whim," she said as she interlaced their arms again. Darcy consciously smiled at his wife.

As they reached the door to leave the shop, Chadwick Harrison stepped through the opening. Elizabeth heard Georgiana gasp. Trying to cover so Darcy would not become agitated, Elizabeth greeted their friend. "Mr. Harrison, what a pleasant surprise."

He offered the Darcys a polite bow. "Mr. and Mrs. Darcy," the words tumbled from his mouth, "Mr. Ashford told me you were in the village; I felt I must pay my respects."

"Please join us, Mr. Harrison," Elizabeth offered before Darcy became aware of the change in the makeup of their little group. Harrison knew he would have no chance of speaking to Georgiana alone, but he was happy to be in her presence and thankful to Elizabeth Darcy for "covering" for him. He missed Georgiana Darcy desperately, and Harrison savored every moment with her.

On the other side of the village, Mr. Ashford bought Kitty a seed cake at a local bakery. They found a private wooden bench and sat down to share the warm cake. "Katherine," Ashford spoke her name softly, "I am so happy to be here with you."

"And I, you." Kitty fed him a bite of the cake, and Ashford allowed his lips to touch her fingers seductively.

"Katherine—Miss Bennet," Ashford stammered, "you know my feelings for you. You would make me the happiest man in the world if you would agree to be my wife."

Kitty froze; she knew Mr. Ashford would eventually ask her to marry him, but she did not expect him to do so today. "Mr. Ashford," she, too, began to stutter. Ashford's eyes searched her countenance, praying he did not anticipate her response incorrectly. "I would be pleased to be known as Mrs. Ashford." She finally got the words out.

"Miss Bennet." Ashford's happiness burst forth. "My life is now complete. You bring me such joy." He wanted to embrace her, but instead he took her hand in his. Ashford reached in his pocket, removed a ring from it, and placed the ring on her finger. "The ring belonged to my paternal grandmother." The emotions choked him. "She wanted me to give it to my wife."

Kitty looked down to see a diamond-and-emerald-encrusted setting. It was nothing compared to the sapphire and diamond ring Mr. Darcy gave Elizabeth, but it was still a respectable offering, almost gaudy in some ways.

"It is magnificent, Sir," she gushed, while admiring the stones in the light.

"You are magnificent," Ashford whispered close to her ear, and Kitty turned to caress his face. At just that time, Kitty heard Elizabeth clear her throat in warning.

Kitty jumped to her feet, leaving Mr. Ashford to look embarrassed for being caught in an intimate moment. "Oh, Lizzy," Kitty grabbed her sister in a happy embrace, "look." Kitty displayed her hand so all could see; she wiggled like a new puppy. "Is it not beautiful?"

Elizabeth began to laugh. "I assume you gave Mr. Ashford an affirmative response?"

Ashford recovered from his disconcertion. "Your sister agreed to make me the happiest of men, Mrs. Darcy," Ashford's exuberance flowed forth.

"I must say I hoped for this fine day, Mr. Ashford; we are so happy for you."

"Of course, I still need to write to Mr. Bennet for his consent," Ashford reasoned.

"My father should be no obstacle," Elizabeth told him. "He expects his daughters to know their hearts."

Kitty added impetuously, "Our father already gave Mr. Darcy permission to act in his stead."

All eyes turned to Darcy; he never thought he would act as the head of Elizabeth's family—to make decisions for the Bennets. Kitty's presence at Pemberley shifted that role for him, and Darcy did not want to acknowledge that responsibility and that connection to his family. Kitty lived in his household, but Darcy wanted to separate his feelings for Elizabeth from his responsibility to his family name. He only recently delineated how he could have both in his memory and his future; now Kitty's engagement to Clayton Ashford, a man who depended on Darcy for a living, blurred those lines. "It would still be prudent of Mr. Ashford to seek Mr. Bennet's blessing," Darcy finally responded to their inquiring eyes.

If Ashford married Kitty Bennet, the entire community would realize his wife's connections. He did not anticipate these concerns, and an uneasy feeling crept through his system. His wife's sister would marry Darcy's cleric, and everyone in Derbyshire, as well as much of London, would know of his new relations. This development necessitated his moving up his plans for Georgiana's future. Hopefully, his sister would find a suitable match during her first Season; then he could insist on a long engagement, keeping Georgiana at Pemberley with him until he was ready for her to become the mistress of her own estate. A great deal depended on a successful first season.

"Fitzwilliam," Elizabeth's voice brought his thoughts back to the moment, "before you go to London, may we celebrate Kitty's engagement at Pemberley this evening—just something informal, among the family."

"Certainly, Mrs. Darcy," he spoke formally again, "whatever you wish." Elizabeth's words of sharing Pemberley with her family brought Darcy's objections to his questionable marriage to Elizabeth Bennet to the forefront. Only this morning Darcy wondered if he could make his marriage to Elizabeth work; now he wondered if he should not pursue a way to extricate himself, his sister, and his family's name from a connection to his Hertfordshire relations.

"Elizabeth, may we stay for the unveiling of the mosaic before we return to Pemberley?" Georgiana asked. She wanted to delay their departure in hopes of speaking privately to Mr. Harrison. She had to let Harrison know somehow her brother's plans for her first season.

"That would be interesting to see. Should we all walk that way?" Elizabeth's excitement bubbled as she turned to Darcy to take his arm. Everyone fell in step, but only Darcy and Elizabeth held arms. They would all set an example of perfect propriety among their Derbyshire neighbors.

"Are any of your tenants in attendance, Sir?" Georgiana asked shyly as Harrison moved naturally to a place beside her at the back of the party.

"A few—but most attend similar celebrations closer to my estate. I came in hopes you might be here; it seems I have trouble staying away from the beauty of Pemberley, Miss Darcy."

"You have not found the beauty of Pemberley today, Sir," she blushed lightly.

Harrison chuckled. "The music of my heart tells me otherwise, Miss Darcy." Harrison watched as Georgiana diverted her eyes from his. "I promise not to say more of music." He stepped briefly toward her, touching Georgiana's back for only a few seconds.

A shiver went down her spine, followed by the warmth of Harrison's touch. "Mr. Harrison," Georgiana said, taking her chance, "my brother goes to London on Monday to make arrangements for my presentation. I will spend much of my time there soon; do you ever venture into London?" She knew she should not speak so boldly, but Georgiana had to let him know her dreams still rested in him.

"Usually, I do not prefer London's society, Miss Darcy, but I may choose to give it another chance this season." Harrison smiled broadly with the thought of spending time at the theatre or at museums with Georgiana Darcy. He knew she would make the most mundane venture into society an event to remember. If Georgiana Darcy were to live with him in London as his wife, perhaps he might reconsider Mr. Wilberforce's suggestion he seek a Parliamentary position.

"Did I say something amusing, Mr. Harrison?"

"Forgive me, Miss Darcy, I was woolgathering." Harrison continued to find his thoughts of Georgiana very desirable.

By now, the Darcy party came to the cloth-covered mosaic. The crowd prevailed upon Mr. Ashford to help with the unveiling. The tenants from Pemberley pressed forward; after the Festive Season celebration, they wondered if the mosaic would once more portray the Darcys or whether it was a pure coincidence. When Ashford helped to lift the cloth covering the well dressing mosaic, a hushed murmur ran through the assembled throng. Immortalized in seeds, nuts, small stones, and other natural materials stood a nearly four-foot picture of an auburn-haired woman standing in an open field. She wore a yellow muslin dress, and the woman lifted a dark-haired child in the air, as if offering it to the light of the new day. The woman's face could not be seen in the mosaic as she faced away from the viewer, but the eyes of all the Pemberley tenants came to rest on the countenance of Elizabeth Darcy. There she stood, over four months with child—with Mr. Darcy's child, the heir to Pemberley.

Elizabeth knew the expectations of all who looked so intently at her and Mr. Darcy. So much rested on her delivery of a healthy heir for the estate. "What do you think, Fitzwilliam?" she asked softly.

"Do not let the superstitions of a bunch of good Protestants dictate your life, Mrs. Darcy," he cautioned.

Kitty touched her sister's shoulder. "Look at the bottom righthand corner," she whispered in Elizabeth's ear.

Elizabeth's eyes left the central image of the woman and looked to where Kitty indicated. A blond-haired woman stood in a wedding dress before a small chapel; dark seeds showed the shadows of five children exiting the back of the church. Elizabeth stifled her desire to laugh out loud. "Georgiana," she exchanged a nearly inaudible message with Darcy's sister.

Georgiana followed Elizabeth's eyes to where she looked. An amused smile crossed the fair-haired Georgiana Darcy's face, and as if brushing away a strand of hair from her forehead, she wiggled her five fingers and mouthed the word "five" to Elizabeth before allowing her eyes to drift to Chadwick Harrison's face and to gauge his delight in the picture's rendering.

The ever-practical gentleman, Darcy cleared his throat, indicating his desire to leave for Pemberley. With her eyes, Elizabeth encouraged him to extend an invitation to Mr. Harrison to join them for dinner and the evening. Darcy followed her suggestion, and Harrison readily agreed, stealing every moment he could with Georgiana. Returning to his estate, Darcy chose to ride back on Cerberus rather than accept Harrison's offer of sharing his carriage. Although the strain of being with his wife subsided a bit each day, Darcy still needed the freedom of a hard ride on his favorite mount to clear his head. By the time he arrived at the main house, Darcy had meticulous plans for his life, his sister's life, and his child's life. He planned it all.

The company that evening was all anyone could hope it to be. Clayton Ashford continually expressed his gratitude to the

Darcys for the opportunity of being chosen for his position. He made promises to Elizabeth to cherish and provide for her sister and to protect Kitty from all harm.

"You will have your hands full with Kitty," Elizabeth told him, "but she will make you a fine wife. She possesses a loving nature and a good heart. Kitty will be a gift of fresh air in your life. Treat her as a gift and not an obligation, and you will know her love, Mr. Ashford."

"Those are very wise words, Mrs. Darcy." When no one was close, he added, "Your husband has made great progress. I pray each day Mr. Darcy finds *his way home*."

"It is my prayer too, Mr. Ashford. I am afraid I am very selfish; I would like *my* Fitzwilliam back immediately. I miss him in my life, but I will try to be satisfied with what God gives me."

"I do not think even God could fault you for wanting your husband's love as you once knew it. God will bring him back to you; I told your sister that long before Mr. Darcy was found, and nothing has changed my beliefs."

"Thank you, Mr. Ashford. I did not believe I needed to hear those words, but I was miserably wrong." Elizabeth's eyes misted with tears before she forced her grief to retreat; she put on a smile as Darcy approached.

"Mrs. Darcy, are you ready to go in to dinner?" He offered Elizabeth his arm.

Elizabeth took his proffered arm and allowed Darcy to lead her to the head of his table.

The conversation dwelt on estate business, the sermon Ashford would deliver tomorrow, the finished nursery, Georgiana's music, and Harrison's new horses. By silent consensus, no one discussed the images in the mosaic. After dinner, Georgiana played, and Elizabeth sang. Her voice flooded Darcy with memories of hearing her before. Tokens of remembrances flickered before his eyes, bright and dull—throughout each of her three songs.

When Elizabeth returned to sit by Darcy, his memories caused his composure to falter. "Are you well, Fitzwilliam?" Elizabeth whispered when the music began again.

"You sang for me before?" he asked under his breath.

"You used to say my singing at Sir William Lucas's party was when you first noticed my eyes. I sang for you many times, my Love." Elizabeth slipped her hand in his, and Darcy lifted it to his lips and caressed it gently.

"I had a few brief images of you at a pianoforte," his voice came out raspy.

Elizabeth caressed his jaw line, not sure how to respond to Darcy's disclosure. His words held her dreams, but she did not wish him to suffer emotionally from it. "Was it painful?"

"Not really." Darcy shifted his weight a bit before adding, "It was just a bit unexpected."

"I would not want you to experience any pain." Elizabeth's concern grew by the moment.

"I am well, I assure you," he repeated his assessment. "Your concern is certainly admirable, but I am glad to have any memory return."

The evening brought Darcy another restless night. Briefly, he dreamed of Georgiana and Elizabeth and their tenants in one of the public rooms at Pemberley. Mr. Harrison was there, too. He kept thinking Elizabeth was the most beautiful woman he ever saw, and he could not be happier knowing she was his at last.

Then he was transported back to before they were married. He saw what he assumed must be her home in Hertfordshire. He recognized only Mr. and Mrs. Bingley and Kitty in the dream, but he felt no stress. Instinctively, Darcy knew he prepared to ask her father for Mr. Bennet's consent.

After dinner, Mr. Bennet made his usual retreat to his library, and Darcy followed. "Mr. Darcy." Seeing this guest in his library surprised

Mr. Bennet. "May I help you find something to read or would you care for a glass of port?"

"Thank you, Mr. Bennet," Darcy cleared his voice, "but I would like to speak to you on a matter of importance."

"Of course, Mr. Darcy, please have a seat. What may I do for you? It would give me pleasure to be of service to you."

"Mr. Bennet." Darcy paused, wondering how to tell Elizabeth's father of his love. "I asked your daughter Elizabeth to be my wife, and she accepted my proposal. I come here tonight to ask your permission for our union."

Mr. Bennet sat bolt upright in his chair and gripped the handles tightly. The color drained from his face, and he was momentarily speechless. "Mr. Darcy, are you sure? This is not some joke the family is playing, is it?" Mr. Bennet seemed to be looking for an explanation.

"Mr. Bennet, I realize you are unaware of my relationship with Miss Elizabeth. We have been more secretive than my friend Mr. Bingley. Our natures are not so open, but, I assure you, Elizabeth and I are deeply in love; she agreed to be my wife." Darcy's voice sounded calmer than his body felt.

Her father got up and walked to the window before he spoke again. "Mr. Darcy, I do not wish to offend you, but Elizabeth is my favorite of all my children. Her nature will not be dictated to; Elizabeth has a spirit I would not wish to see her caged by your society's rules and regulations."

"Mr. Bennet, I am well aware of your daughter's spirit; she humbled me. I learned about myself thanks to her. I realize I offended Elizabeth at the Meryton Assembly, and from that you drew your opinion of me." All this frankness made Mr. Bennet uncomfortable, but it also made him see Darcy in a different light. "When I saw Elizabeth care for Miss Bennet at Netherfield, I realized she was the type of person I would want to be a friend to my own sister Georgiana. We spent time together at Hunsford and most recently at my estate in Derbyshire. I did not fall in love with Elizabeth overnight; even when I thought we would never be together, my love for her stood the test. I adore Elizabeth."

"Mr. Darcy, I understand your affection for my daughter, but you must understand as her father I want to be sure she is protected. You can provide for Elizabeth, no doubt, but I would prefer to speak to my daughter before I give my final consent. If Elizabeth loves you as you say, my consent will be yours immediately and willingly."

Darcy thanked the man and said he would send Elizabeth to him shortly. "When you satisfy your inclinations, we can meet again regarding Elizabeth's settlement, but please know I already decided to create a jointure for Elizabeth as part of the marriage articles; even without an heir, Pemberley will be hers."

"Mr. Darcy, your being able to provide for Elizabeth is not my concern. Elizabeth will choose with her heart. If you own her heart, you are an incomparable man indeed."

He woke with a start. Shaken, Darcy threw back the counterpane and stood beside the bed. Elizabeth's hold on him increased the past week; defining what he felt about her troubled him. She invaded his thoughts during the day and during the night. Walking to the mantel, he ran his hand through his hair.

Darcy knew what he wanted to do; he wanted to go to his wife and lie beside her, to feel the regular beating of her heart as he took her in his arms. "Why not?" He said the words out loud. "She is my wife. I have rights, do I not?"

Unsure whether he could do what he thought, Darcy walked to the table and poured himself a brandy, which he gulped down, wiping his mouth with the back of his hand. Pouring another, Darcy downed it nearly as quickly as the first. On the third drink, he sat in the high-backed chair holding the glass to his lips and visualizing his sleeping wife's face before him.

The three quick drinks steadied his nerves somewhat, but Darcy visibly shook when he found himself outside of Elizabeth's bedchamber. His hand slowly turned the handle. In the dwindling candlelight, he saw Elizabeth lay across the bed, a book beside her and a pillow crushed in her embrace.

As if mesmerized, Darcy found himself beside her bed, drinking in her image. How innocently beautiful she looked lying there, her auburn curls draped across the pillow. Darcy debated briefly whether to leave her there alone and return to his own room. It was late; he should not disturb her, but he could not resist Elizabeth's allure.

Elizabeth felt herself being lifted by the closeness of her husband. "Is this a dream?" she murmured softly while snuggling into his chest.

"It is no dream." Darcy caressed her cheek with his lips. "You are chilled, and I would not want you to catch a cold." He placed her back on the pillows and brought the coverlet up to bring her warmth. Leaning over her, Darcy began to tuck in the counterpane until Elizabeth's arms snaked around his neck, pulling him toward her. "Elizabeth," he whispered with desire.

"In my dreams you always kiss me." Her words increased Darcy's need for her.

His breath came hot against Elizabeth's cheek. "I do not know why I came."

"I do not care why you came," she said, allowing her lips to brush against his, "as long as you are here."

Darcy's lips captured hers at last, and Elizabeth moaned with the pressure of his mouth on hers. In a breathy moment, Darcy pulled back as if to withdraw. "Please do not leave," Elizabeth nearly begged.

Hesitation came while Darcy argued with himself on the question of should he stay or not, but then he looked back at the passion present in Elizabeth's eyes, and he was lost to her. He removed his nightshirt and slid his long frame under the bedclothes, taking Elizabeth into his arms. "Help me to love you again," he pleaded.

"You are mine, Fitzwilliam Darcy," Elizabeth teased as she rubbed her hands across his chest and whispered in his ear. She kissed him deeply, promising her devotion.

Darcy allowed himself to take pleasure in touching her soft skin. "Elizabeth, I do not want to promise you something I cannot give; yet, there is no place else I want to be right now." He began to kiss along her shoulder line and neck.

"Then there is no place else you should be." Elizabeth pulled herself closer to him while kissing behind his ear. "Stay with me tonight."

"Should I not be more of a gentleman? After all, you are with child." He searched her eyes for an answer.

"Mr. Spencer says we may continue our relationship until my lying in." She moved in close to him again, afraid Darcy would withdraw.

"I am afraid," he said quietly, as if saying the words cost him something dearly. "I do not know how to please you; I have no memory of us." He caressed her face with the back of his hand.

"Then let us discover each other together." Elizabeth brushed his lips with hers. "I will give you a hint, my Husband," she teased. "I love it when you call me Lizzy."

"Come to me, Lizzy." Darcy's voice came thick with desire. He pulled her hips toward him and captured her mouth with his.

CHAPTER 18

"Why not seize pleasure at once?
How often is happiness destroyed by preparation, foolish preparation!"
Jane Austen, *Emma*, 1815

If Elizabeth thought their night of passion would make their relationship come easier, she was sadly mistaken. Darcy withdrew into himself and avoided her through much of the day. She sulked about the house, at her wit's end as to what to do next. During the night Darcy was responsive and tender and loving—just as Elizabeth remembered him to be, but the daylight brought her a different man. He seemed repulsed by her and indifferent to Elizabeth's offers of civility.

Darcy planned to leave for London the next day, and Elizabeth did not wish him to be gone on such "strained" terms. Try as she may, she would let him leave without addressing the issue. She yearned for someone to advise her how to handle the situation, but there was no one to whom to turn. Neither Georgiana nor Kitty should even know what to expect in the marriage bedroom, nor how to advise her on how to handle her husband's dual nature. She would give anything to be able to talk to Jane or her Aunt Gardiner; they would understand and not judge her for such a personal subject. There was nothing to do but to use her instincts and pray those instincts were in tune to Darcy.

Earlier, Elizabeth encouraged Mr. Harrison to wait until Monday morning to return to Hines Park. "No gentleman should travel on the Sabbath," she reasoned, "even if your estate is only a few hours away."

"Must you encourage my sister's relationship with Mr. Harrison?" Darcy asked her sharply as he passed Elizabeth in the front foyer.

Elizabeth, already irritated by his foul mood, did not guard her words. "Your sister prefers Mr. Harrison's company. There was a time, Mr. Darcy, you would want Georgiana to be happy; now it seems you want her simply to obey. My opinion of Mr. Harrison was never one of his inappropriateness for Georgiana, it only was with the timing of his entreaty. That opinion changed when Mr. Harrison protected Georgiana from George Wickham and the day he came here to help me with this estate while you were off kissing the gloved hand of Elizabeth Donnelly at Darling Hall."

"If Mr. Harrison's connections had not put my sister's life in danger, I would not have gone to Hull in the first place," he snapped.

"You cannot possibly be thinking of putting the blame for that ill-fated trip and your attack on Mr. Harrison," Elizabeth hissed. She moved in closer to challenge Darcy. Trying to control the volume of her voice so as not to alert the whole household of their dispute, she continued, "It was Captain Rutherford whom we feared. Mr. Harrison shows nothing but the highest respect for Georgiana. He has a fine estate, worth six thousand pounds a year; he cares for Georgiana, and she has feelings for him. How is this such a bad arrangement for *our* sister?"

"It just goes to show how little you know about fine society." Darcy's words affected Elizabeth, but she did not move. His face was inches from hers. "Country society is not what I would choose for Georgiana. She will inhabit a world different from what you know."

"I see we are back to my poor connections," Elizabeth retorted, never once giving him forgiveness for his lack of civility. "Do you want me gone, too, Fitzwilliam?" she demanded.

"Of course not," he began but then stopped short. They stood staring at each other. Darcy made grown men retreat with that stare, but Elizabeth refused to budge. Finally, he turned and walked away from her, retreating to his study and slamming the door along the way.

Hours later, Elizabeth came to him; Darcy sat behind his desk, his work left unfinished. Elizabeth's light tap on the door brought him some relief. He held remorse for arguing with her earlier. "May I come in?" Elizabeth asked quietly, remaining at the door until she could assess his mood.

Darcy stood to greet her. "Please do."

"Fitzwilliam, I am sorry for my foul temper earlier; it was unconscionable of me to speak to you thusly." Elizabeth had practiced what she wanted to say to him. She would not apologize for her opinions, but she would offer regrets for her tone.

"I, too, was out of line." To prove he forgave her, Darcy embraced her, pulling her to him so Elizabeth's head rested on his chest. "I should be more considerate of your condition; I understand many women are temperamental when they are with child." He stroked her head gently as he spoke.

Elizabeth paused, trying to decide whether she heard him correctly. She loosened his grip on her and walked several steps away before turning to Darcy and saying, "You cannot possibly think my opinion of your sister's position has anything to do with my condition? Do not think I am just being emotional; my opinions have nothing to do with the child I carry."

"Elizabeth," he stammered, "I chose my words poorly. Please, I do not wish to leave tomorrow with our being at odds."

Elizabeth's countenance softened as she returned to Darcy's arms.

"Sweet, Elizabeth, we should not argue," he whispered, feeling the closeness of her body to his.

Elizabeth could not speak; being in Darcy's arms was where she wanted to be, and she began to evaluate how much she was willing to give into him just to have this closeness continue.

"It is true Mr. Harrison could be a viable candidate for Georgiana," Darcy said softly, "yet, I strongly believe a more suitable man exists, and I will find my sister such a match." Darcy's confidence played through his voice. "I seek your support with my sister, Elizabeth. You earned Georgiana's trust, and I expect you to help me convince her otherwise."

Again, her husband's words affected her being, and impulsively, Elizabeth stiffened in his embrace. "Fitzwilliam, I do not think I can speak out against Mr. Harrison. Because I have Georgiana's trust, I cannot betray her. If your sister affects another, then I will support her choice, but I will not try to convince her to go against her heart."

"As my wife, you must do what I ask of you!" His voice rose in volume as he strode away from her.

Elizabeth's face flushed. "Do not take the love, honor, and *obey* vow too seriously, Mr. Darcy. I am not of the nature to be reprimanded and expected to *behave*. My father tried for years, much to his chagrin, but I prefer sugar to vinegar in my dealings."

"God, how did I become so ensnared?" Darcy threw up his hands in a lament.

A flash of anger sparked in her eyes. "Last night you seemed happy to be *so ensnared!*" Elizabeth nearly shouted.

"Please control your voice, Elizabeth," Darcy seethed with fury.

"Of course, Mr. Darcy," she spoke through gritted teeth. "Heaven forbid we show any emotion. Do you know, Fitzwilliam, you used to kiss me in front of the servants?"

"Maybe in Hertfordshire such lax impropriety is acceptable," he quipped, "but I will maintain a standard at Pemberley."

Elizabeth demanded sarcastically, "Please instruct me, Mr. Darcy—I am all ears. Make me an able student!"

Darcy moved in close so his words would not be misunderstood. "From what I experienced last night. . . ." He stopped short, stifling his words.

Emotion misted her eyes, and Elizabeth's lip trembled, but her voice held no fear of Darcy's presence. "Of what do you accuse me, Sir?"

"Nothing—I spoke out of place." Darcy moved past her to return to his desk.

"Fitzwilliam, I cannot believe you think so poorly of me." Tears streamed down her face.

"I never said anything," he began. "I was surprised—that is all." She demanded, "Surprised! About what?"

"I assumed you might be. . . ." Again, Darcy could not say the words, but to Elizabeth's dismay he, obviously, thought them.

Her voice shook, but Elizabeth spoke vehemently. "Sir, you seem to imply my low connections make me a pure wanton. What I know of the marriage bedroom, I learned from you. How dare you imply otherwise! It is my shame I love you enough to abandon my mother's warnings. However, you will not have to worry about my shortcomings again; my bedroom door is closed to you, Sir." Elizabeth turned on her heels and exited the room.

At dinner, Elizabeth pretended a headache and excused herself from the meal. She could not face Darcy and his censure. What seemed a renewal of their relationship during the night now loomed like a wall through which there was no access. Her tears flowed constantly, and the pain of her loss hurt throughout her being. Darcy sent word to Elizabeth through Hannah he wished her to join them, but Elizabeth sent back her regrets. He tried to shrug off her refusal in front of the others in the household, but her reaction to his words earlier created a gulf between them.

Why did he react to their night together as such? He did not object during the throes of desire. His wife knew exactly what flamed his passion, and when Elizabeth touched him, Darcy's willpower crumbled; yet, he could not in the light of day justify how their passion went beyond the laws of propriety, and how he allowed himself to be placed in such a position. Darcy could not imagine any gentleman taking such pleasures in his wife—maybe in his mistress, but never in his wife. A wife was to be treated gently and with respect. The contradiction, however, was Darcy wanted Elizabeth; he wanted her more than he could admit even to himself, but his desires mortified him. If he were to take her again, Darcy would treat Elizabeth with more respect—the respect she deserved as his wife and the Mistress of Pemberley.

Elizabeth paced back and forth in her room. Where had everything gone so wrong? She and Darcy faced every trial and found each other despite their earlier misconstructions; then her world imploded. Darcy lost his memories—their memories—and now he judged her, judged their devotion to each other by standards she had not considered to be in effect. When he came to her, she reacted to him the way she always had—not society and not propriety—only this conflagration, which connected them. The solace of Darcy's embrace seemed so right, but now Elizabeth in a paroxysm of guilt regretted their intimacies. It was as if Darcy considered their time together a flagrant breach of propriety. How could she unlearn how to love him? How could she control her vulnerability to Darcy?

It was late Sunday evening when Darcy knocked on Elizabeth's door. She would know it to be him because only he had access from their shared sitting room to her bedroom. He wondered whether she would admit him after their earlier argument. When he heard her call out, "Come," he took a deep breath before turning the door's handle. Darcy stood outlined by the door's frame, not sure what he should do next. Elizabeth sat in the window seat, refusing to even look at him.

"I came to see if your headache subsided," he stumbled through the words.

The coldness in her voice could not be hidden. "We both know, Fitzwilliam, a headache was not why I refused to come to the table." Still, she spoke to her own reflection in the window rather than to Darcy.

"I am sorry to hear it," he said softly as he stepped further into the room. "I did not wish you to be ill, but I would prefer your temporary discomfort to a more permanent riff between us. I should have tempered my words earlier." By now, he stood at the foot of her bed.

"Tempering your words means nothing unless you changed your sentiment, too."

Darcy pleaded, "Elizabeth, please look at me."

Slowly, she turned her head, but Darcy saw only contempt in her eyes. "Do you have other commands for me to follow, Sir?" Her voice dripped with sarcasm.

"It was not an order," he whispered. With a bit more effort he said, "I plan to leave for London early tomorrow. I hoped we could resolve this before I left."

Needing to move, Elizabeth got up from her seat and started past him. "Tell me what you want me to say, Fitzwilliam, and I will say the words, and you may be on your merry way. It is getting late, and I have a busy day tomorrow *pretending* to be the Mistress of Pemberley."

Darcy could not follow her line of thinking. "You are the Mistress of Pemberley," he said flatly.

"I am your wife," Elizabeth turned on him, "but without your respect and your love, I have no real identity. I am no better than your property—no better than your steward or your tenants or your valet. I perform my job as the Mistress of

Pemberley, but I will *not* perform my job as chattel—as the woman with whom you take your pleasures but to whom you give no respect."

Darcy reached for her, but Elizabeth shied away from him. "God, Elizabeth, I did not mean what I said. I am confused—my emotions are out of control; I cannot leave tomorrow knowing I caused you such pain." His voice held his regret.

"Go, Mr. Darcy." Her icy words had not softened. "I will manage the estate in your absence, just as I promised on our wedding night. Do not ask more of me; I do not think I can promise you anything beyond that. You hurt me as only you can do. I will not speak of this again except to tell you I am sorry to be such a disappointment to you."

"Elizabeth," he started, before a flip of her hand told him she was not finished.

"Why was what we experienced in the privacy of our bedroom for society to decide? Why is anything close to real intimacy to you a break in propriety? If I could take it all back, I would; I would take it and put it on the shelf, not to be disturbed again. For me, Fitzwilliam, being with you is like no other place I have ever been—we are great together. I thought with me you would not have to work so hard at being happy. Love cannot be planned like a society event—it happens. It is spontaneous." Elizabeth's voice rose as she began to pace once more. "Fitzwilliam, do you understand? Life happens despite all your best planning."

Darcy turned away, not wishing to see the torment he caused her. "Elizabeth, things are different, but we said we did not want it to be different."

"It is a logical catenation," she said listlessly, defeated by the quagmire in which they found themselves. "At one time we were the greatest plan you ever made. Now, you feel embarrassed by me." During this speech she crossed to the door leading to their sitting room and held it open for him.

"Nothing can hurt me as much as your reaction to what we once shared. Good night, Mr. Darcy."

He stood, mesmerized by her beauty, needing to touch her and wanting nothing more than to take Elizabeth to her bed and enjoy the sensation of loving her freely, but instead Darcy straightened his shoulders and strode from the room.

When Elizabeth arose on Monday morning, she knew Darcy left Pemberley for London. Part of her felt relief at not having to face him again; yet, she yearned for Darcy—for the love she once had. She stepped into the sitting room to find the breakfast tray for which she had asked Hannah.

On the tray, a letter written in the fine scrawl with which she was now familiar lay. Elizabeth touched the letters "E. D.," tracing them with her fingertips. Should she open it right away? If it was a request from Darcy for her to leave Pemberley, Elizabeth did not want to read the words. However, maybe he considered her words as he had long ago at Hunsford. Elizabeth could not believe their love could not survive; yet, Darcy's behavior of late told her he preferred a different lifestyle from what they once knew.

Elizabeth sat the note to the side; she could not read it and then conduct her duties as Darcy's wife. No matter what it said, she would wait. She would visit tenants with Georgiana; she would help plan the opening of the village school, along with advertising for a schoolmistress. Whatever Darcy had to say to her, Elizabeth's fragile emotional state could do without.

Therefore, late morning found her making her way to bid farewell to Mr. Harrison. She found him alone in the drawing room and joined him in front of the fireplace. "Mr. Harrison, you will be sorely missed, Sir."

Realizing Elizabeth's delicate situation, Harrison offered her a compliment. "Your generosity in accepting me into your home, Mrs. Darcy, speaks well of you."

Elizabeth half chuckled. "You are wise beyond your years, Mr. Harrison."

"I am truly sorry Mr. Darcy's homecoming created so much distress for you." His voice and words comforted Elizabeth, but still tears misted her eyes.

"My husband," she began with a slight catch in her throat, "believes he is doing what is best for his family."

"Needless to say, I do not favor Mr. Darcy's new resolve."

Elizabeth wanted Harrison to know she could not help him in his pursuit of her sister. "I wish I could speak to Mr. Darcy, but I fear he no longer seeks my opinions."

"Then it is much to his loss, Mrs. Darcy."

"Mr. Harrison," Elizabeth hesitated before asking, "would you tell me about your trips to the Americas? I would like to know about your voyages."

Harrison searched Elizabeth's face to know the truth of her question. "I have made three trips, Mrs. Darcy, since the age of two and ten," he began. For the next hour, he told Elizabeth about the conditions one might find onboard ship and the settlements found in the American states. Harrison did not know why Elizabeth showed an interest in this topic, but as a woman he respected, Harrison would not deny her his insights.

"That is very interesting, Mr. Harrison." She seemed deep in thought.

Harrison picked up on her serious nature. Finally, he said, "If I had a friend who felt the need to leave England, I certainly hope he would consult with me before going. I have many connections which would serve him well."

Elizabeth lowered her eyes. "Your friends are privileged to know you, Sir."

"I am afraid it is time for me to take my leave, Mrs. Darcy. With your permission I shall bid adieu to Miss Darcy before I go." Harrison stood and made Elizabeth a bow.

"My sister will be sad to hear of your leaving; she will be in the music room." Elizabeth no longer objected to Harrison; she trusted him to make Georgiana happy. "Tell Miss Darcy I await her for our tenant visits. Please have a safe journey, Mr. Harrison." She gave him an appropriate curtsy before he left to find Georgiana.

★ ★ ★

A letter from Darcy arrived on the fifth day of his journey. This time Elizabeth opened it; she had no choice. Georgiana and Kitty watched her take it from the tray the butler held out to her.

23 March

Mrs. Darcy,

My time in London has been well spent. Arrangements for my sister's presentation into society are underway. I made it known she and I will be in London, and early invitations arrived. Among these early acquaintances are Lord Dorchester and his son Henry. I am very impressed with Henry Dorchester; he has an impeccable lineage and is a pleasant young man. I most enjoy speaking to him about Napoleon's exploits; he and I share that interest.

Staying with the Dorchesters is their cousin Miss Cecelia McFarland. She is an articulate woman of refined opinions; society would judge Miss McFarland to be an accomplished woman. Miss McFarland's parents left her a substantial dowry; she will make some gentleman an excellent wife.

Elizabeth broke off from reading the letter. So her husband prepared to carry out his plans; he would take Georgiana to London and leave Elizabeth at Pemberley to oversee his estate and wait for her lying in. Darcy promised an abbreviated season for Georgiana, but now there, would he abandon her for someone else more to his liking— maybe even this Miss McFarland? Obviously, Darcy esteemed the woman; otherwise, why would he mention her. Once she delivered a healthy heir, would Darcy send Elizabeth off to some other place, or worse, would he disengage himself completely? Would he take their child and apply for divorce? Her earlier worries resurfaced.

These thoughts sent Elizabeth into the deepest depression. What would she do if Darcy no longer allowed her to remain at Pemberley? Each day she felt their baby move within her, and Elizabeth wanted this baby. Yet, legally Darcy could take the child and leave her with nothing. Tears filled Elizabeth's eyes again; it seemed all she did lately was cry. The fact she had any tears left surprised her.

Mrs. Darcy, I will return to Pemberley in less than a week. I hope this letter finds you in health, and you considered my wishes.

Your husband,
F. D.

Elizabeth handed Georgiana the letter to read. Georgiana rolled her eyes upon reading the part about Henry Dorchester, but she shook her head in disbelief that her brother would mention another woman in a letter to his wife. How could he not see what he did to Elizabeth? Georgiana could no longer imagine Pemberley without Elizabeth. The house had been a shrine to her parents; now, with Elizabeth, Georgiana felt the past but lived for the future. She prayed Fitzwilliam would not foolishly destroy the happiness she now knew. "Well, it seems my brother has been quite busy," Georgiana said cautiously as she handed the letter back to Elizabeth.

"Quite busy," Elizabeth nearly snapped. She stood quickly and turned to leave the room, but before she did, she crumpled the letter and threw it in the fireplace.

"Miss Bennet," Ashford said as he approached her in the garden.

"Mr. Ashford," she answered softly. "I wondered if I might see you today."

He laughed lightly. "As if I could stay away from you, my dearest Katherine."

Kitty let out a full laugh. "You cannot stay away from me, Mr. Ashford?"

"I fear I cannot; you stole my heart, dear lady." Ashford took her hand in his, and Kitty gave him her version of an enigmatic smile. "I heard from your father, Miss Bennet. He gave his consent; if you are still of a mind to be my wife, I would be the happiest of men."

Ashford searched Kitty's face, looking for the reassurance he desperately needed from her. "Clayton, as you already know, I anticipate being your wife; that fact has not changed." She caressed his jaw line.

"I love you, Katherine." Ashford turned his head to kiss her palm.

Kitty giggled. "I do not know what I have done to earn your regard, Sir."

"You did nothing, my Dearest; you simply have to smile at me or glance my way or enter a room, and I am lost to you."

Kitty blushed from the intensity of his declaration. "Clayton," she began before breaking off, but that was enough. He could see the desire in her eyes, and without forethought he leaned forward to kiss her lips tenderly.

When he withdrew, his next words showed how such an innocent act affected him. "May we set a date for our wedding?" he gasped.

Kitty laughed lightly; she thoroughly enjoyed the power she had over this complicated man. "I do not think I could consider a date until after my sister's lying in. I would want Elizabeth there, for if not for her, we would never have met."

"Six months," he whispered the words, unsure of whether that was Kitty's wish.

"Six months," she laughed, "the first of September. Does the first Monday in September meet your approval, Sir?"

"Tomorrow would be more to my liking," he teased, "or even this afternoon."

Kitty reminded him, "We have no license."

"I know the local vicar," Ashford continued his jest. "I believe I could arrange it if only I could convince you to change your mind."

"The first Monday in September," Kitty repeated her assertion.

"A person should not wish his life away, but I wish the autumn approached rather than the spring." Ashford stood and offered her his hand. "May we take a walk together, Miss Bennet?"

Ashford's smile told Kitty how happy he felt. "I would enjoy a walk; may we continue our plans for our day?" Kitty wrapped her arm through his.

"As long as you agree to smile at me as you are doing now, I will be satisfied. The first Monday in September is not so long, is it?"

"Not so long before our dreams will be complete," she giggled again.

Darcy sat at the desk in his London townhouse. For days he expected a response to the letter he left for Elizabeth, but nothing came, and he did not know what to do next to resolve their conflict. He acted foolishly and hurt Elizabeth. Despite his belief the resurgence of his qualms regarding Elizabeth's connections could be justified, a part of him enjoyed the freedom she brought to his life.

Elizabeth offered no pretense; she dealt with the estate in an honest manner. The tenants doted on her, and the Derbyshire community offered a different type of loyalty—one based on respect rather than need. She was affectionate, and the way she teased him created a growing passion in Darcy he could no longer explain. His sister developed a loving relationship with his wife, and in many ways, Georgiana grew into a confident young woman under Elizabeth's tutelage. Elizabeth Darcy challenged him intellectually, refused to be dominated by him, and performed her duties as the Mistress of Pemberley in an honorable manner; plus, her desires brought a flush to his being.

In the letter Darcy told her of his wishes. He wished he had not hurt her; he wished for Elizabeth's forgiveness; he wished she would let him learn to love her again. More importantly, Darcy wished for her to never leave him. In the letter, he allowed his growing vulnerability to Elizabeth to be laid open. Now, she refused him a response; he asked her specifically to send him word of her exculpation, but Elizabeth's wrath must be beyond quelling. Now, what must he do? It was a severe blow to his confidence.

Darcy knew when he returned to Pemberley, he would find Elizabeth doing her duty as his wife. She would smile when her duties required her to do so. She would say what was expected. She would give him an heir for the estate, but could Elizabeth love him again? He wanted her affection, not her obligation. How had it come to this? One moment he regretted aligning himself with Elizabeth Bennet; her Hertfordshire relations added nothing to his family; however, Darcy found when he thought of taking Elizabeth to his bed, a sensation of completeness washed over him. What could he do? He was a man caught between two worlds—two things he desired—two dreams.

★ ★ ★

As promised, within the week, Darcy returned to Pemberley. His plans for Georgiana's presentation complete, he half expected the household to be abuzz with excitement. Instead, he found Elizabeth contrite, Georgiana depressed, and Kitty a bit jealous of all the fuss being made. "I wish I could go to London," Kitty told Georgiana one day as they sat in the music room.

"Oh, Kitty," Georgiana nearly moaned, "you have no idea how much more you possess right here in Derbyshire. You won the affections of a man who loves you honestly and honorably. Mr. Ashford chose you because you complete him, not because you come with a purse to increase his wealth. You are assured of Mr. Ashford's affections while I am to go to the highest bidder. Be careful of what you wish; it is not always something you want."

"I am sorry, Georgiana," Kitty offered her apology. "I thought only of the parties and the balls and the fine dresses. I was not thinking about your future. Of course, I would prefer Mr. Ashford's attentions to the uncertainty you face."

CHAPTER 19

*"The memory is sometimes so retentive, so serviceable,
so obedient; at others, so bewildered and so weak; and at others again,
so tyrannic, so beyond control!"*
Jane Austen, *Mansfield Park*, 1814

Darcy had been home for two days, and he had yet to have a private conversation with Elizabeth. She offered civilities, but no signs of the return of her regard for him. Every once in awhile, he would note what he thought to be a flicker of desire in her eyes when she looked at him, but then Elizabeth would purposely look away. When she looked at him again, an empty vessel sat before him—devoid of feelings.

He caught her in the upstairs hallway. "Will you not speak to me, Elizabeth?"

"What do you wish me to say, Fitzwilliam? I am still willing to be the student." She forced herself to look him directly in his eyes as the sarcasm dripped from her lips.

Anger sprang to his bearing, but he squashed his urge to deliver a retort. "You ask of what I wish from you." Darcy tried to control the evenness in his voice, not wanting to betray his need for a positive response from her. "I told you of my wishes previously if you care to address any of them."

"Your wishes change so often, Fitzwilliam; I am not sure which ones you mean." Her hurt could not be hidden. "Would you care to enlighten me?"

"No," he shook his head in disbelief, "I will ask nothing more of you than what you are willing to give." With that, Darcy walked away.

Elizabeth wanted desperately to call him back—to throw her arms around Darcy's neck and to kiss him until he thought of nothing but loving her. Could she continue on like this? She did not want to be just Darcy's wife in name only. She loved Darcy against her will.

Darcy, too, felt the sting of their exchange. Clearly what was happening to them was his fault, and he experienced guilt at causing Elizabeth such distress. She offered him overtures of love, and he irresponsibly threw them away with a show of familial pride. He tried to be the perfect gentleman, the man his father expected him to show the world, but Elizabeth created a sense of abandon in him, a sense which she now withdrew with a dose of sarcasm; frustration ruled his day. It troubled him deeply that this frustration had no impact on his perfidious desire to find Elizabeth, take her in his arms, and kiss her until she thought of nothing but loving him. Could he continue on like this? Darcy did not want her to be his wife in name only. He loved her against his reason and against his character.

At dinner, he returned to his favorite topics of late: the accomplished Miss McFarland and the incomparable Henry Dorchester. Both Elizabeth and Georgiana sat with lowered eyes and with unresponsive thoughts. Mr. Ashford, who was asked to dine with the Darcys, noted the effect Darcy's speech had on Mrs. Darcy and Georgiana, and he tried unsuccessfully to redirect Darcy's interest. He even resorted to discussing military history, a subject Ashford abhorred, but Darcy loved.

"Miss McFarland knows all the right people, Georgiana. She will be an asset to your presentation."

"Yes, Fitzwilliam," Georgiana barely whispered.

"The lady is quite lovely; this is her second season. If I understand it correctly, Miss McFarland turned down several offers last season. The Dorchesters took possession of Lord Suterland's place for the spring. Lady Suterland is quite ill, and his Lordship let the house to the Dorchesters."

Georgiana's voice held her dismay. "They will be close to Kensington Place then?"

"Very close—I expect we will see Miss McFarland and the Dorchesters often." Darcy sat back in his chair, pleased he made such a connection for his sister's first season; a smile of satisfaction played across his face.

His revelry was short in duration, as Elizabeth violently shoved her chair back from the table as she stood to leave. "Beware, Fitzwilliam," she snapped, "illusions are dangerous as they have no flaws." She took a step away from the table, her hand still on the back of the chair. With the anger pent up in her since before Darcy left for London, Elizabeth forcefully slammed the chair again, sending it tumbling over with a banging sound and sending an ornate spindle from the leg sliding across the room. She gathered her skirts and ran from the room.

Kitty excused herself to attend to Elizabeth, and Georgiana followed closely behind the two. Darcy sat suspended with the impropriety of the scene. "I apologize for my wife's manners, Mr. Ashford. She has been very emotional since the conception of our child." Darcy forced himself to steady his countenance as he addressed the clergyman.

Ashford cleared his throat before he spoke. "Mr. Darcy, may I speak as a ministerial adviser?" Darcy nodded briefly. "I know very little of the female constitution, but you may want to temper your praise of Miss McFarland in your wife's presence."

Darcy reasoned out loud. "I meant nothing by it, Mr. Ashford. I simply spoke of the connection for my sister's sake."

"You may be speaking of your sister's connection, but Mrs. Darcy, obviously, heard something different. Women, I suspect, would not like to compare themselves to a woman of high connections, accomplishments, and beauty. Mrs. Darcy could be hearing your praise of another woman from a different perspective." Ashford tried not to say any more. Criticizing his benefactor could be a mistake.

"I take note of your advice," Darcy said casually. "I will guard my words next time."

Ashford said nothing else. Not only was Fitzwilliam Darcy Ashford's benefactor, he would be Ashford's brother through marriage. Sometimes the wealthy wrapped themselves in their petty concerns and missed the everyday happiness within their grasps. Ashford hoped to be wiser in his dealings with Kitty Bennet.

Elizabeth did not return downstairs that evening. Darcy sat in their sitting room until late, hoping she would "accidentally" find him there. Hannah told him her mistress cried herself to sleep. He did not like being the cause of Elizabeth's pain once again. It seemed he caused her constant grief with his presence in her life. He wondered how they could continue in this manner. The simplest answer was to go on—pretending to be polite and obliging—and hoping for a chance at a revival of Elizabeth's old feelings. He supposed he should avoid her as much as possible considering his company made her life more difficult.

Before he retired for the night, Darcy opened the door to her bedchamber to peer in on her. Elizabeth lay on her side, her back to him. She did not move, and Darcy assumed she slept. "I am truly sorry, Elizabeth," he whispered to the reclining figure. If he could have seen her face, he would have seen a tear sliding down her cheek and Elizabeth biting her lower lip to keep from calling out his name.

In the morning after breakfast, Elizabeth set off along the pathways behind the house. Taking her time, she made the climb toward the hunting lodge she and Darcy shared before he left for Hull—before her life changed—before she lost Darcy's love.

Having finally achieved her destination, she entered the lodge and sat in front of the cold fireplace. She wrapped her arms around herself to fight off the chill of the room and the depth of her despair. Elizabeth did not know why she came here today; the place held memories of the joy of being with Darcy when he loved her unconditionally. She wondered what he meant about being sorry. Was he sorry he hurt her or sorry he married her? As much as she did want not to do so, she could not stop loving her husband.

After a nearly sleepless night, Darcy joined Mr. Howard and several other Pemberley workers as they took some of the excess game on the estate. The plan to thin the deer herd and the rabbits and use the meat turned out to be a good one so far. This was their third hunt. Today, the hunters would drive the deer to an enclosed glade on the back part of the estate and then kill a portion of the animals before allowing the rest to escape. Darcy did not plan to hunt; instead, he would observe the effectiveness of the idea while sitting atop Cerberus on an overlooking hill.

The men moved the deer toward the prescribed glade as he rode hard to the crest of the hill. To the left sat his father's favorite hunting lodge on the estate. Pulling up on Cerberus's reins, he circled the animal at the summit of an outcropping. He stared down at the lodge, thinking about his father taking him there—teaching him to hunt—the smell of his father's favorite tobacco flooding his senses. Darcy closed his eyes to relish the image, but instead, visions of Elizabeth awashed him, passionately entangled upon a bearskin rug, feeding each other from a picnic basket, smelling her lavender rushing over him. The image was so vivid, Darcy actually moaned from desire. "Elizabeth," he whispered her name.

Slowly, he opened his eyes to bring life back into focus, but the image of the woman for whom he felt desire remained before him. She stepped from the door of the lodge and walked casually across the lawn, looking out as if waiting for him to come to her. "Elizabeth," he said the name a bit louder, captured by the dream.

Then his mind registered what really happened. The herd ran right toward where she stood; the hunters would not see his wife clearly. The cross fire rang out, and almost in slow motion he saw her look of horror and heard Elizabeth's cry before she fell. Several deer jumped her body, rocking her back and forth as the hoofs struck her.

"Elizabeth!" he screamed as he forced Cerberus down the incline toward where she lay in a clump. When he finally got to her, blood gushed from a wound in her leg. Darcy rolled her over on her back and pulled his cravat from around his neck, wrapping the cloth tightly around the gushing wound in her leg and then tearing the ribbon from her dress hem to secure it.

He neither spoke anything to her when he dismounted nor when he bandaged her leg. Now, Darcy began to caress Elizabeth's face and to try to get a response from her as the hunters approached. "Mr. Howard, keep the men back," he demanded, not willing to have Elizabeth exposed to the eyes of strangers. Howard halted his horse and forced the others away from the scene.

"Mr. Howard, come here," Darcy's voice commanded. "Help me support Mrs. Darcy onto my horse. Then I want you to ride for Mr. Spencer."

"Of course." Howard swallowed hard when he saw all the blood.

Darcy scooped Elizabeth into his arms, and with Howard's

help settled her in his lap on Cerberus's back. She lay limp against him. The blood soaked the bandage he placed on her leg. Darcy turned toward the house. Within minutes he galloped into the carriageway. Footmen scrambled to help with the horse and with Elizabeth's body. Darcy raced toward the house's main doorway, carrying Elizabeth close to his chest.

"My God, not again," Georgiana gasped as he burst through the doorway with the limp body of Elizabeth Darcy slumped against him.

"Mrs. Reynolds!" he yelled. "Hannah!"

Darcy raced toward Elizabeth's room, Georgiana barely a step ahead of him. Reaching her bed, he laid Elizabeth back on the pillows; then lifting the skirt of her dress, he pulled another strip of material to use as part of her dressing. Jerking off his jacket, he threw it on the back of a chair. "Where is Mrs. Reynolds?" he shouted, pressing his hand against the wound to slow the bleeding.

"Here, Mr. Darcy." Mrs. Reynolds appeared beside the bed and began to remove the blood-soaked cravat to clean the wound. She applied a folded bandage. "Hold this, Mr. Darcy." He did as the housekeeper said. "What happened?" Mrs. Reynolds asked.

"She stepped out of the hunting lodge just as the men drove the deer toward her for the hunt. I could not get to her to stop it." With concern, he looked up at his wife. "How bad is it?" he pleaded.

"We must wait for Mr. Spencer to know for sure," Mrs. Reynolds hissed, as both Georgiana and Kitty stood huddled by the door in a tearful embrace.

Darcy took the hint. "Georgiana—Kitty, we need more bandages, and one of you must meet Mr. Spencer as soon as he gets here." Darcy's voice did not hold his usual reticence, but enough of his bearing remained for both girls to hustle out of the room to do his bidding.

Mrs. Reynolds took to cleaning the wound once again, and Darcy set about checking for other injuries. "Elizabeth seems to have some bruises and cuts, but I see no other open wounds or anything which is broken." He addressed his housekeeper as Hannah rushed in with additional bandages.

"What about the baby?" Hannah asked the question both Mrs. Reynolds and Darcy avoided. "It will kill Mrs. Darcy if she loses the child now. Each day, the mistress sits in the nursery and rocks while she sings softly to the baby. She rubs her stomach and talks to the child. I heard Mrs. Darcy tell the child about what she sees out the nursery's window." By now, Hannah's tears flowed freely.

Darcy swallowed back the hurt he felt; he did not know Elizabeth cared so about their child. He dropped to his knees beside the bed and began to pray, an earnest prayer for Elizabeth's safety and the life of their child.

"The blood flow slows," Mrs. Reynolds said as she removed the latest bandage. "Hannah, I think I hear the men in the front foyer. Go see if it be Mr. Spencer at last."

Hannah hurried from the room as Mr. Spencer entered. Seeing the bloody rags on the floor, the doctor expected a major wound, but closer inspection told him otherwise. "I will need to remove the bullet. Mr. Darcy, I need for you to hold down your wife's arms and keep her from moving. Mrs. Reynolds and Hannah, I need the same from you for Mrs. Darcy's legs."

"The Mistress has not moved since the Master carried her in here," Mrs. Reynolds shared her observation.

"Mrs. Darcy will move when I begin to cut the wound to remove the bullet," Spencer assured them. "The mind cannot block out such pain completely."

Spencer cleaned his tools and placed them where he could reach them. He positioned Darcy and the two ladies where he needed them. Spencer was correct; the moment he began to cut close to the wound, Elizabeth began to fight them. Darcy laid his body across her to keep her from moving. "Help me, Fitzwilliam, please," she cried, trying to push him away.

"I am helping, Elizabeth. Mr. Spencer must remove the bullet." Darcy fought for a breath as she struggled against him.

"The baby!" she shrieked.

"A few more minutes," Mr. Spencer encouraged them to hold Elizabeth still.

Darcy whispered close to her ear. "Please, Elizabeth."

"Let me die, Fitzwilliam, let me die," she moaned.

"No, Elizabeth," he gasped.

"Let me die," she yelled before collapsing back against the pillows.

"I have it," the doctor said at last, and her "wardens" released their grips on her. "Hannah, clean the wound and dress it. Mr. Darcy, if you will step outside, I will check your wife for other wounds and for the baby."

"I will be in the sitting room, Mr. Spencer." Darcy looked about, feeling rather useless at the moment.

"Mrs. Reynolds, let us get Mrs. Darcy clean clothes as we check her wounds." He set the older woman in action.

Darcy stepped into the hallway and closed the door behind him. Georgiana rushed to his arms and even Kitty snuggled into his shoulder. "Elizabeth will be all right," he assured them.

"The baby?" Kitty sobbed.

"I am not sure. The herd trampled her once Elizabeth was shot." The images flashing in front of his eyes told Darcy Elizabeth could be in danger. He closed his eyes and stroked each girl's head to offer her comfort. "I saw her—but at first I thought it a dream," Darcy stammered. "I saw her—saw Elizabeth and me in our father's lodge," he told Georgiana.

"You took Elizabeth there right before you went to Hull; you said you wanted a private evening with your wife after all the company we had at Pemberley during the Festive Season," Georgiana retold the tale.

"What did you mean by *not again*?"

"You and Elizabeth fought about the tenant celebration." Georgiana dropped her eyes and lowered her voice. "She ran out; later Hero returned to the house without her. You found Elizabeth on the backside of Briton Gorge. You took care of her yourself; you would let no one else in. Elizabeth protected the child when she fell. Your carrying her through the door reminded me of before."

"I see," Darcy said, and he did see as images of Elizabeth's fragile body lying across his bed mixed with the vision of holding her for the doctor a few minutes earlier. "Why do you two not wait in your sitting room, Georgiana? I will come to you when I have information from the doctor."

"Yes, Mr. Darcy," Kitty said as she led Georgiana away.

Nearly a half hour later, Mr. Spencer joined Darcy in the sitting room. "Mrs. Darcy is lucky once again, Sir. I am ordering her to bed for a week, but I see no problems for her or for your child. Again, she protected the baby from harm; you married a phenomenal woman, Sir."

"Thank you, Mr. Spencer." Darcy knew not how to respond to the doctor's accolades.

"I gave Mrs. Darcy a weak dose of laudanum. It will ease her pain; she may not take too much, however, because of the child."

Darcy looked concerned. "I understand, Sir."

"May I ask why Mrs. Darcy begged to die?" The doctor took Darcy by surprise with his directness.

"We have been at odds of late," Darcy confessed. "Other than that, I know not Mrs. Darcy's reason."

"I ask because your wife's mental state is as important as her physical recovery," Spencer tried to explain his reasoning to Darcy.

"I will see to it, Mr. Spencer," Darcy assured the man. "I will let nothing happen to Mrs. Darcy."

"That is all I ask, Mr. Darcy. I will come to check on your wife tomorrow."

Like Mr. Spencer, Darcy wondered why Elizabeth cried out to die. Did she hate him so much she no longer wanted to live—to live with him—to share his life—to bear his children? Did Elizabeth purposely put herself in harm's way? Mr. Spencer said she protected the child so that did not appear a possibility. Yet, why did she go to the lodge? Did she plan to meet someone there? Was she really looking for someone to come to her?

Could there be another man in Elizabeth's life? Would she find solace in someone else's arms? Mr. Howard? A tradesman? Mr. Harrison? Could that be the reason Elizabeth changed her mind about the man? They were closer in age than he and Elizabeth. She spoke of how much he meant to her when Darcy was missing; Elizabeth even portrayed Harrison to Darcy's tenants as a man in charge of Pemberley. Could she do so in the guise of presenting him with Georgiana? Darcy's thoughts ran rampant. Just as he allowed himself to care for Elizabeth, could he lose her to another man? Her request to die haunted him.

Elizabeth lay in the bed recovering from her wound and other injuries. The laudanum helped her to sleep, something she had not done fully since Darcy left for Hull, but it did not keep her from dreaming of him. He carried her lovingly to the safety of her bed; Darcy whispered endearments to her; he prayed for her recovery. Elizabeth enjoyed dreams of his coming to her—of her happiness.

For two days Kitty, Georgiana, Hannah, and Mrs. Reynolds took turns sitting with her. Mr. Spencer reported to Darcy each day regarding Elizabeth's progress, but he could not force himself to return to Elizabeth's room. Late in the evening as Hannah slept close to tend her mistress, Darcy stood at the door watching his sleeping wife. He wanted her; he did not think he could survive Elizabeth's leaving him. For a reason he could not explain, Elizabeth fit his plan for Pemberley and for his life.

Mrs. Reynolds found him leaning against the doorframe. "Why do you not go to your wife, Master Fitzwilliam?" she whispered as she came up behind him.

Darcy spun around, ashamed at being caught watching Elizabeth. "I have other things to address," he snapped as he started past his housekeeper.

"Master Fitzwilliam." Her words stopped Darcy short. The woman helped raise him, especially after Darcy's mother became so ill. "What troubles you?"

Her words of concern nearly undid his resolve, but finally he answered, "I have no troubles, Mrs. Reynolds."

"Then explain to me, Mr. Darcy, how a man who once was so devoted to his wife he would risk his own life to save her could now not go to that same woman when she needs him?" Mrs. Reynolds looked him directly in the eye.

"I need not explain myself to you, Mrs. Reynolds." Darcy gave her a look, which would scare most, but she knew that look really meant Darcy hid his feelings.

"Master Fitzwilliam," she began slowly, "Mrs. Darcy is the best thing to happen to you. You were profoundly sad; you were lost until that woman came into your life. You have been given a great gift—a love to last the ages. Go to your wife, Mr. Darcy."

"Do not tell me how to conduct my personal life, Mrs. Reynolds." Darcy continued his resistance.

"Mr. Darcy, I was never ashamed to be a close member of your staff until now." She reprimanded him in the tone she used on him in his youth.

"Mrs. Reynolds, you overstep your bounds," he warned.

The housekeeper shook her head in disbelief. "So do you, Mr. Darcy." Her voice held the sadness he felt. Mrs. Reynolds entered Elizabeth's room and closed the door to Darcy's presence.

He returned to his room and tried to rest. Could Mrs. Reynolds be right? Had he allowed his growing vulnerability to Elizabeth to turn into insane jealousy? Where did his loyalties lie? He was a *Darcy*—his ancestral name meant something in England. *Fitzwilliam*, his mother's name, came from a long line of nobility; it gave him a conscious awareness of his own social position.

He wanted to be able to turn to Elizabeth; he wanted to be rid of the sorrow he felt at losing both his parents; he wanted to make his parents proud; he wanted to make the right decisions for Georgiana. Darcy had Pemberley; he had respect; he had wealth, but he did not have contentment.

Brought up in opulence, he learned superiority at his father's knee; had he not been warned repeatedly of those who would flatter him to become an intimate? When he remembered his interactions with Elizabeth, Darcy saw himself as proud and leaden. Elizabeth accused him of not only arrogance but of conceit and disdain for others.

He often, of late, wondered how he would feel if someone spoke to Georgiana as he spoke to his wife. Even if he and Georgiana had no more than what Elizabeth had to offer, Darcy knew he would call the dastard out, and a duel would ensue. His place in the world was unthreatened until there was Elizabeth; now he had become more pensive and introspective—his life a quandary—he wanted to once more try to make Elizabeth a part of his life. He wanted to show her he changed, but first, he would need what his sister said; he would have to find value in himself; he would alter how he spoke to people and how he thought of people and how he treated people. If he could do so without *glory*, but because it was the right action, then maybe he could someday present himself to Elizabeth again.

Unable to sleep, he made his way once more to Elizabeth's room. "I will stay, Hannah," he told her maid. "Come back in the morning."

"Yes, Sir." Hannah made a quick curtsy. "It has been several hours since Mrs. Darcy had any medication for the pain. She may need it soon."

"Thank you, Hannah." Darcy took the seat next to Elizabeth's bed. Without thinking about it, he took his wife's hand, subconsciously massaging her palm and wrist with his fingertips.

Within a few minutes, Elizabeth's eyelids fluttered open to find Darcy beside her. "Fitzwilliam," her voice came out soft and breathy.

He moved to the edge of her bed, never releasing her hand. "May I get something for you?" he said while moving the hair away from her face.

Elizabeth smiled briefly. "No, I have everything I need at the moment." She moved her hand to catch his with hers.

They remained as such, eyes locked onto each other. "Hannah says you are due for medication. May I prepare a dose of laudanum for you?"

Her eyes searched Darcy's features. "I would prefer not to take any more medication. I worry about it hurting our child."

"That is very brave of you." Darcy caressed her face.

Elizabeth tentatively asked, "Would you stay with me, my Husband?"

"If you so desire." Darcy moved closer. "How does your leg feel?"

"It burns, and it feels so heavy." Elizabeth struggled to compose her words. "I may not be able to sleep without the laudanum, but I want to try."

"I hate laudanum. I understand. It makes me see things which do not exist. We may talk or just sit together, but I will not leave you tonight."

His words made Elizabeth shiver with anticipation. "Thank you, Fitzwilliam. I missed just being with you." With his help, Elizabeth moved up in the bed where she could address him. "I am sorry I have been such a bother to you."

"I worried about you, but I would not term you to be a bother. If you are able, may we talk about something of our lives? I have images of some things which confuse me." Darcy's voice contained a tenderness Elizabeth had not heard for some time.

"Certainly, Fitzwilliam, of what would you wish to speak?"

"Would you tell me about us? I mean, from the beginning—I need to know how we came to be."

She swallowed hard, thinking where and how to begin; then Elizabeth tightened her hold on his hand. "We first met when you came to Netherfield Park with Mr. Bingley. At an assembly you criticized me as being *only tolerable*," Elizabeth began. Nearly two hours later, exhausted, she told him of his leaving for Hull.

During this, Darcy seemed captivated by their interactions and how they came to a better understanding. Elizabeth told him what she knew of his transformation after his first proposal at Hunsford. Some anecdotes made him laugh; others shocked him. "We make a science of misconstruing each other," Darcy offered.

"At times, it seems so," Elizabeth chuckled lightly, "but once we came together, I like to think we completed one another. You once told Jane I was your other half."

Moved by her words, Darcy leaned forward to kiss Elizabeth lightly, but quickly he deepened the kiss, and Elizabeth pulled him to her. "I did not come here for this." Darcy's lips were only inches from hers. "Plus, you should rest."

"Would you lie with me? The pain increases, and I doubt I can sustain my deference to the medications alone." Elizabeth stroked his jaw line.

"If it will help you." Darcy repositioned Elizabeth in the bed, and then he slid in beside her. "May I hold you?"

Elizabeth nodded and then moved her head to rest on Darcy's shoulder. "I love your hair when you have it down," he whispered to her as he twisted a curl around his finger. Darcy felt Elizabeth stiffen with pain. "I do not want to see you suffer." He stroked her arm.

"Just hold me tight—do not let me go." Darcy pulled Elizabeth to him, wrapping his arms closely around her and allowing Elizabeth's warmth to radiate through him. Elizabeth laced her fingers into his hair and felt the fine lawn of his nightshirt along her arm. She kissed his neck under his chin line. "I like the way you distract me," she murmured.

"Mr. Spencer told me to address both your mental and your physical recovery," Darcy's voice came out breathy.

Elizabeth's eyes sparkled as her voice was laced with desire. "Tell Mr. Spencer I could overdose on this type of medicine; I would never deny I need all this I can get."

"Tonight you concentrate on getting well." Darcy ran his hand down Elizabeth's back and over her hips. "We do not need to resolve everything in one night. I want this to be a beginning for us." Darcy lifted her chin and brushed his lips over hers. "May we try, Elizabeth?"

"Fitzwilliam, your *medicine* is a powerful force of which I can never get enough," Elizabeth teased. She traced his mouth with her fingertips. "I will do anything for more of this—more of you in my life."

Darcy kissed her tenderly and then pulled Elizabeth's head once again to his chest. "Rest, my Lizzy," he laughed lightly.

She laughed, too. "You should know better than to call me *Lizzy*."

"I forgot." Darcy feigned innocence.

She warned him in a mocking manner, "Do not pretend memory loss with me, Mr. Darcy."

"Never, Mrs. Darcy," he chuckled. "Rest, be well for us. If you can, get some sleep. I will be here next to you." With that, he pulled her to him once more, and Elizabeth allowed herself to be lulled into a state of complete happiness.

CHAPTER 20

"If I loved you less, I might be able to talk about it more."
Jane Austen, *Emma*, 1815

———◦◦◦◦———

For the next three days, Darcy repeated his actions. He left Elizabeth's bed early in the morning, rising to address the running of his estate. He came to her in early afternoon to check on her progress, spending time helping her with her bath before Hannah addressed his wife's toilette. Late in the evening, he returned to her room; they sat together; he read to Elizabeth, or she told him more specifics about their life. Darcy touched her intimately, but he did not resume his husbandly privileges. He would wait; he reasoned they rushed the relationship before, and that was why they fought.

Elizabeth loved being in his arms, but he showed no renewal of their once passionate relationship. She offered him a pleasant smile when he came to her room, but the fact he showed no interest in a renewal of their enjoyments troubled her. A promise for their future stayed in her thoughts, but occasionally Elizabeth wondered whether he wanted a civil relationship, one, which would allow them to survive their marriage, but not be a resumption of their love.

He must know she would not object to his advances; she could barely contain her desires when he moved in close to her. He was confused, and so was she. Darcy did not remember much of their life together, but they did maintain a connection—an unexplainable attraction. Elizabeth sometimes wondered about the lack of sanity in her life. Her husband's brooding nature and tendency to withdraw frustrated her. Yet, she knew beneath the façade Darcy displayed to the world lay the man most suited for her.

One afternoon Georgiana joined Elizabeth in her chambers. "I am pleased to see you recovering," Georgiana offered as she took the seat to which Elizabeth indicated.

"My spirits are of a higher order." Elizabeth's desire to leave her bed and resume her duties became evident.

Georgiana only half listened; she had not come to her sister's chambers simply for company. "May we speak?" she said at last.

"Of course, Georgiana."

The young girl fidgeted in her chair. "Fitzwilliam indicates we will leave for London next week."

"I hoped my husband might change his mind," Elizabeth thought out loud.

Georgiana's eyes misted over. "Your sentiments mimic mine."

"Fitzwilliam feels a strong sense of duty." Elizabeth took Georgiana's hand.

The girl finally looked in her sister's eyes. "I never desired a presentation in society. When I was younger, I prayed my brother would simply choose a husband for me and eliminate the need for my society debut. Now, I know I will disappoint him; I will disgrace the Darcy name."

"Georgiana, simply be yourself; your beauty and goodness will serve you well in London." Elizabeth tried to reassure her.

Wistfully, Georgiana said, "I wish my brother would allow me free choice."

"It is not likely. Once your brother chooses a course, he is single-minded in his execution," Elizabeth cautioned.

"I cannot believe we will leave you in Derbyshire," Georgiana nearly moaned. "I might be able to handle this if you were with me."

"You will be off to fine society." Elizabeth had her own concerns with the situation. Without thinking about what she said, she added, "I wonder if I was not with child whether I would be allowed to accompany you to London."

Georgiana snapped out of her own misery. "Elizabeth, you cannot think as such!"

"Georgiana, I am a realist. Although I see inroads into Fitzwilliam's affections for me, some parts of my being begs for his assurances. The 'different' Fitzwilliam is hard for me to gauge. One moment he is the man to whom I gave my love, and the next he is a man I never met. Could he still be ashamed of me?"

Georgiana did not know how to answer. She wanted to believe her brother to be true to Elizabeth, but she knew how determined he once was to prove to the world he deserved to be Master of Pemberley, and the Fitzwilliam Darcy who inhabited that narrow world he created for himself often did things which hurt others. Not wishing to address Elizabeth's concerns, Georgiana changed the subject. "I wish Fitzwilliam would allow Mr. Harrison to make his intentions known. I fear he decided Henry Dorchester to be an ideal husband choice."

Elizabeth bit her lower lip. "Who is not to say Henry Dorchester is not agreeable? Your brother's estimation of the man is likely to be an accurate one."

"Accurate, yes—passionate, no," Georgiana gave her.

Elizabeth questioned, "It sounds as if you wish me to intercede for you?"

"I would never ask you to do so, but I would gladly accept your modulation in this situation," Georgiana said softly.

"I am not sure Fitzwilliam will accept my meddling in what he clearly sees to be in the realm of his responsibilities." Elizabeth watched as Georgiana's countenance faded. "Yet, I will do my best to convince him otherwise."

"Mrs. Darcy," Darcy said as he entered her room an hour or so later, "I came to rescue you." He took a teasing tone.

Elizabeth loved when he challenged her. "Am I in danger, Sir?" Her eyes sparkled with the attention.

"I thought you might enjoy an outing. I asked the stables to bring around the curricle." He came to stand at the end of her bed.

"Oh, Fitzwilliam," she gasped, "that is a delightful idea."

"Then I will send Hannah to you, and I will come back to help you negotiate the stairs." Darcy made her a quick bow and left.

A half hour later, he returned to Elizabeth's chambers. "Are you ready, Mrs. Darcy?" he asked as he entered the room.

"I am, Sir." Elizabeth bubbled with excitement.

Her enthusiasm was contagious, and Darcy could not resist her smile. "You look beautiful today," he said softly.

"Thank you, my Husband," she murmured lightly, "but how you could think a woman of my girth to possess beauty is beyond me." Elizabeth lightly patted her increasing abdomen.

Darcy crossed the room to where she gingerly stood; he cupped Elizabeth's face in his palm. "How could I not think you to be beautiful?" Darcy whispered in her ear before kissing Elizabeth's cheek. "You carry my child."

Elizabeth closed her eyes during his caress, and now she opened them to see the passion-darkened eyes of her husband. She turned her head to kiss Darcy's palm. "I look forward to presenting you with your child. I could not wait to tell you on New Year's Eve although I feared we took on too much too soon, but Georgiana told us God gives us no more than we can endure." Elizabeth's voice was breathy.

"Then the news brought you happiness?" Darcy's statements often came out as questions.

She half teased, "To be the mother of your children, Mr. Darcy, is my honor."

"You will stay at Pemberley?" Darcy needed Elizabeth's pledges.

"I will stay as long as you wish me here." Elizabeth did not know whether Darcy considered her leaving Pemberley or not; she wanted to believe he never wished her away from their home.

Darcy watched the change in Elizabeth's countenance, and he wondered if she considered leaving him. What had he seen in her eyes? Was it fear? Of what could Elizabeth be afraid? Did she fear he would reject her? Did Elizabeth fear she would displease him? Or, worse yet, did she have a secret she did not want him to know? She covered her doubts quickly by forcing herself to look at him intently.

"Do you wish to walk on your own?" Darcy asked at last.

"May I have your arm for support, Sir?"

"I would enjoy that."

Elizabeth found maneuvering the steps after lying abed for several days to be difficult, but she gritted her teeth and held Darcy's arm tightly as she moved. "Shall I carry you?" Darcy asked quietly, close to her ear.

"Although your offer is most tempting, it is best if I do this on my own." Elizabeth leaned on Darcy, and he caught her around the waist to stabilize her descent. At the bottom of the steps, Elizabeth released the breath she held. "Thank you, Fitz-william," she said quickly before squaring her shoulders to walk to the curricle.

"Are you sure I may not carry you?" Darcy's concern showed.

"There is truly nothing more that I would like," Elizabeth smiled at him shyly, "but it is important for the staff to know I am well, and the future of Pemberley is safe. We both realize how I manage will be common knowledge to the entire staff before I make it to the carriage. Your carrying me tells them I am too weak to be your wife and the mother of your children. I will not allow them to see any weakness on my part."

Darcy seemed pleased. "You speak well, Mrs. Darcy." He realized how much this "mysterious" woman understood her duties as his wife and as the mistress of his estate. They were married less than five months ago, but Elizabeth assimilated into his "society" quite well. Darcy smiled at her. "Then feel free to lean on me as much as you so choose, Madam."

"With pleasure, Mr. Darcy."

When they reached the curricle, Darcy lifted her to the seat and covered her legs with a light blanket before crawling in beside her. "Where to, Mrs. Darcy?"

"As long as I am with you, my Love, I will be most satisfied." Elizabeth laced her arm through his.

Darcy looked at her for a long time before flicking the reins of the carriage. They rode down Pemberley Lane; eventually, Darcy asked, "Should we go into Lambton?"

"I would be happy just to see parts of Pemberley with you," she offered. "Show me some of your favorite spots."

Darcy nodded briefly and returned his attention to maneuvering the horses. As they passed the different cottages, tenants waved from the fields or laundry lines, and children scampered after them. "The tenants seem pleased to see you," Darcy noted as they passed.

"They are pleased to see us," Elizabeth corrected. "What we do affects how they feel about their future. I never realized how many responsibilities you had until you were missing. Keeping Pemberley strong is a daunting task, one I gladly abdicate back to you." Elizabeth looked out over the landscape as she spoke. "Pemberley is so much more than a fine piece of land and a magnificent house. It is the lifeblood of this community—this county. If Pemberley bleeds, so does the rest of Derbyshire."

Her words moved Darcy, as nothing else he could remember. At that moment he pulled up the horse; turning to Elizabeth, he scooped her up in his arms and kissed her passionately, quickly deepening the kiss as she responded to this spontaneous show of affection. When he pulled away, Darcy could barely breathe. "I apologize," he stammered.

"Apologize?" Elizabeth queried. "For kissing your wife on a private road you own while seated in a curricle, which you also own?" she teased.

Darcy's lips turned up in the beginnings of a smile. "I noted you kindly delineated the fact I do not own you, my Wife."

"You possess me, Fitzwilliam, because I freely give myself to you." Elizabeth shifted a bit; she wondered whether Darcy wanted to control her—whether he thought of her more in the terms of his property.

Reluctantly, Darcy released her and picked up the reins once more. "I have a special place to show you." He maneuvered the curricle along a narrow pathway until they emerged upon an overhang, which looked down on the house. He lifted Elizabeth from the carriage and held her close to him as he pointed out places easily seen from this vantage point.

Darcy allowed Elizabeth to lean back against him as he encircled her with his arms. "Fitzwilliam, it is beyond words," she gasped. "I love Pemberley as I love you."

"Do you love me, Elizabeth, or do you love another man, a person I do not know?"

Elizabeth turned to face him head on. "Fitzwilliam, I love both men. Of course, I love the man who won my heart by never giving up on us, but I also love the man I see before me now because it explains the journey you took to get to where we began. How could I not love what you were if I love you?"

Darcy knew not how to answer her. For the second time that day, Elizabeth surprised him with her depth of emotions and her insights. "Do you mean what you say, Elizabeth?" He searched her face for the truth of his wife's words.

"You know my heart, Fitzwilliam," she replied. "You know it rests in you. You *will be happy* at Pemberley, my Husband."

Darcy crushed her to him, pulling Elizabeth's head to his chest. He held her there, wondering how they could make it together but feeling the dream could live in his wife. She, obviously, knew how to manipulate the image his tenants saw of Pemberley; she held a vision for the land, very much like the one he had. The woman befuddled him and fascinated him. The prejudices he felt earlier regarding Elizabeth Bennet now appeared wholly undeserved. When he thought about it, she improved upon acquaintance—neither her mind nor her manners were in a state of improvement, but that from knowing her better her disposition was better understood.

Upon the return to Pemberley, Elizabeth moved closer to Darcy in the curricle, resting her hand on his arm. "Do you still leave for London on Monday?" she asked softly.

"It is my intention." Darcy stiffened and spoke formally.

"Could we not postpone Georgiana's presentation until I may go to London with you?" Elizabeth knew his answer, but she felt compelled to ask.

Darcy hated this moment; part of him wanted to agree—to stay here at Pemberley and learn more about Elizabeth. Then a more dominant need to prove himself resurfaced. "I fear, Mrs. Darcy, I must complete my responsibilities to my sister as planned."

Dreading his response, Elizabeth added, "Georgiana would prefer to wait also."

"If I know my sister, Georgiana would prefer to never be presented, but she must. She is a Darcy, and meeting her responsibility to her family name must take precedence over her discomfort in public." Darcy stole a glance at Elizabeth.

For Elizabeth, this was a moment of truth. "Then could I still not go with you?"

"In your condition, I fear the demands of London's Season would be too daunting." Darcy guarded his words, but the damage was done.

Elizabeth released her hold on his arm and shifted her weight away from Darcy. "I see," she hesitated but did not stifle her thoughts. "I am an embarrassment to you." Tears began to stream down her cheeks, but she swallowed her sobs.

Darcy's honor would not let him deny he had these thoughts before. He refused to turn and look at Elizabeth, and each second he delayed his assurance reopened the gulf between them. "Elizabeth, I do not wish to hurt you." The words seemed to stick in his mouth.

"Fitzwilliam, I would turn myself inside out for you, but no matter what I do I will never be good enough." Elizabeth's lip began to quiver. "Please take me home," she urged him.

Darcy sucked in his breath; all the progress they made evaporated in a few seconds. "What may I say or do to alleviate your worries?" he asked sincerely.

Elizabeth jerked her head around to look at him. "I am not in the habit of having to instruct my husband on how to show me his love and respect; he knew those things instinctively. You were right earlier, Sir, the Fitzwilliam Darcy I love no longer exists. I expect any day you will ask me to leave Pemberley." By now, all her sense of reason abandoned her, and only Elizabeth's fear of being found wanting by Darcy remained. "That is it, is it not, Mr. Darcy? That is what gentlemen in fine society do—they send the wife they no longer want off to live in another of their properties while they reap the benefits of the attention of other women. Is that to be my fate? Shall you send me away, Fitzwilliam?"

"Elizabeth, I would never. . . ." he began, but her anger interrupted him.

"It is the worst kind of extravagance, Fitzwilliam," her voice rose in volume, "the way you waste your chances for happiness. If you wish me gone, then say so." Then another thought struck her, but this time Elizabeth forced her words away; she would not consider the possibility of his divorcing her.

They reached Pemberley, and Elizabeth allowed the footman to help her from the carriage; she did not look back at Darcy as she limped up the steps to the house. Kitty met her in the front hall, and she and Mr. Ashford helped Elizabeth back to her room.

Darcy watched her escape from him, remaining behind the reins of the carriage for several minutes. By the time he reached the main door, he saw Elizabeth turn toward her rooms. He regretted the fight and wanted to go to her to "fix" things, but he knew not what to say to his wife. Everything she just said was true except he never considered sending Elizabeth away. He had at one time thought of hiding her away at Pemberley, but Darcy abandoned that thought long ago. Why could he not simply love the woman who was his wife? He hated the obligations of the *ton,* but his father expected—actually demanded—Darcy give Georgiana a proper start in life. He could not in all conscience abandon his father's final wishes so instead he abandoned the woman he needed.

For the next two days, Darcy barely saw Elizabeth. She and Georgiana resumed their tenant visits, but Elizabeth feigned weariness when it came time to join the family for meals. The breach between them now loomed larger than ever, and Darcy spent hours in his study trying to figure a way to resolve the issues. He would wait until his return from London—when she began her lying in—and then prove to this woman, whom he could not forget, he was willing to resume their love and their life. Darcy would serve Georgiana's needs, and then he would return to Pemberley and to Elizabeth and to his child.

On Saturday, Colonel Fitzwilliam appeared unannounced on Darcy's doorstep. "Edward," Darcy called, "what brings you this way?"

"On my way to Brighton by way of London—I have new orders." Edward stripped off his hat and coat. "May I spend the evening, Fitz?"

"Of course," Darcy said, "you need no invitation."

Later, they sequestered themselves in Darcy's study. "How goes the marriage plans?" Darcy asked.

"Lady Catherine is most displeased, but Anne makes great progress; I escorted her to Bath to escape Rosings in my absence. Recently, I suggested our aunt might consider a European tour after the wedding." Edward poured himself a glass of brandy.

Darcy laughed. "I am surprised you are so astute in your handling of our formidable aunt."

"Actually, Fitz, it was your idea." Edward saluted Darcy with his glass.

Darcy seemed confused. "My idea?"

"After Lady Catherine's invectives at my parents' anniversary celebration, you suggested I remove her from Rosings when Anne and I marry."

"Who was the target for Lady Catherine's barbs that particular evening?"

"You, Elizabeth, and even I suffered from her Ladyship's censure that evening. She took no prisoners, and her disdain was caustic."

"I wish I could remember such little details," Darcy mused. "It might make my time with my wife easier."

Edward asked tentatively, "Then the two of you still struggle?"

"We share exquisite moments, and then we fight over things I cannot control."

Edward poured himself another drink. "Have you rediscovered Mrs. Darcy's charms?" he asked with a shrewd smile.

Darcy's mind drifted to hold Elizabeth close and to relive the effect she had on him. "It is not just my wife's beauty, it is also how quickly she charms whomever she meets, how astute she is at the running of Pemberley, and how she changed Georgiana for the better. I could add to that list with little effort."

"It sounds as if you are falling in love all over again, Cousin. Mrs. Darcy's charms are many. If I was not so besotted with Anne, I might have considered her myself, although her lack of fortune would be an issue for me. However, when I noted your interest and how easily she brought a smile to your face, I knew Elizabeth Bennet could love none but you."

"Our contention of late lies in my taking Georgiana to London. Elizabeth assumes I leave her behind because I am embarrassed by her."

Edward stared at his cousin for a long time before he spoke. "Is there any truth to Mrs. Darcy's assertions, Fitz?"

Darcy sat deep in thought. "Unfortunately, her perceptive insights do not just rest in the running of this estate. I began by abhorring her connections, and I even considered hiding Elizabeth away at Pemberley, away from the *ton*, but I long since discarded that idea. If my wife knew my real concern about taking her to London, she might even be flattered."

Edward chuckled, "And that would be?"

"I find when Mrs. Darcy is around, I think of nothing but her, and I am afraid if a gentleman gave her too much attention I might demand justice at dawn. Is that not bizarre? She is nearly five months with my child, and it is all I can do not to continually take her passionately in my arms." The alcohol allowed Darcy to relax, and he, naturally, shared his thoughts with his cousin; he and Edward were more like brothers. "I feel a duty to take Georgiana to London—a duty to my esteemed father. Once that deed is done, I will come home to Pemberley and to Elizabeth."

"Why do you not declare your returned affections for Mrs. Darcy? From what I know of your wife, that is all she desires from you."

"I thought as much, too, but before I went to London to arrange for Georgiana's presentation, I left a letter for my wife telling her of my dreams for our future together. I requested a response from her, but Elizabeth never replied whether she wishes the same future. I hate to say that part of me questions whether Elizabeth changed her mind about us. I do not go to her because I am unsure of my reception. Until I am positive Elizabeth still loves me, I cannot take my pleasure in her. I refuse her obligation—I want her love."

"It sounds as if your turmoil continues, Fitz. I am sorry to hear it, but must our Georgiana go to London this season?"

"Elizabeth and my sister asked the same thing. Georgiana would, I fear, accept Mr. Harrison if I do not expose her to other young suitors."

"Is Mr. Harrison a bad choice for our ward?"

"My wife sang Mr. Harrison's praises to the point I thought she might prefer his attentions to mine," Darcy confided.

"Then why do you insist on Georgiana going to London? If she affects Mr. Harrison, and he returns her regard, how can you ignore her wishes?"

"My parents dreamed of presenting their daughter as they dreamed of my becoming the master of this estate. My mother purchased jewels for Georgiana to wear. Father, for the purpose of her presentation, purchased her carriage. My sister's education and training were designed for London to recognize her worth. It was one of my father's last charges to me before he died. I cannot ignore his desires for his daughter."

"What are Georgiana's prospects?" Edward conceded to Darcy's need for familial responsibility. Both men were brought up to believe in duty to family first.

"Lord Dorchester took the Suterlands' house. Dorchester's

son Henry would make a fine prospect. Being at the Suter-lands' house will make him accessible."

Anxious to share the latest gossip, Edward laughed. "Did you hear why Suterland was not coming to London this season?"

"According to Lord Dorchester, Lady Suterland is ill," Darcy assured him.

"Is that what he calls it?" Edward shook his head in disbelief.

Darcy seemed amused. "Would you care to explain?"

"Lady Suterland caught his Lordship with Lord Midland's wife. Lady Midland is with child, but to whom the child belongs is the question. Lady Suterland took young Mr. Worthing as a lover. Worthing's estate is in trouble, and he has been romancing several of the wealthier members of court to finance his gambling habit. Some say Lady Suterland may be with child also. Again, parenthood is in question."

Darcy walked across the room to pour himself another brandy and to look out the window of his estate. "Few people know how tenuous relationships within a marriage can be," he said.

Elizabeth, who just returned to the estate from her tenant visits, stood outside the study door. She intended to greet Colonel Fitzwilliam, but her husband's words required she tarry in the shadows of the hallway. Could he be speaking of their marriage?

As if Edward could hear her thoughts, he asked, "Are we back to your relationship with Elizabeth?"

Darcy shook his head in the negative, but he offered no verbal response. He crossed back to his desk, taking the drink with him. "Entangled webs," he laughed lightly. "Men take mistresses, looking for pleasures to quench their desires." Darcy shook his head in disbelief. "I should think a man in such a position should send his wife away, legally claiming the child as his own. A small manor house would serve her well, more than she deserves under the circumstances. After the child is born, any gentleman in such a position should seek a divorce."

Elizabeth's worst fears grew with her husband's words. Darcy planned to terminate their relationship; he would claim their child and send her away once the child was born. Her heart stood still, and she ached with a pain unlike any other. She could hear no more and hurried away to find solace in her rooms.

"You are very harsh in your estimation, Fitz," Edward gave him.

"A man should not take his marriage vows so lightly." Darcy looked uncomfortable. "Even if he does not marry for love, a gentleman should treat his wife with more respect."

Edward grinned shamefacedly. "And if he is lucky enough to marry for love?"

"The man is blessed if he can take his pleasures in a woman who returns his desires with those of her own." Darcy again got a silly smile on his face as he remembered Elizabeth touching him with a heat he could not describe.

"I must wait a few more months to have such knowledge," Edward said as he got up to leave, "but I do so look forward to it."

Darcy followed his cousin from the room. "A blessing is worth the wait, Edward—worth the wait."

Elizabeth forced herself to pretend ignorance regarding her husband's plans for their marriage. The realization of the loss of Darcy's regard devastated her, but she would not let the rest of the household see her hurt. Until Darcy ordered her to leave, Elizabeth would maintain her role as the Mistress of Pemberley. She determined Darcy would wait until the birth of their child before demanding her parting. As she had not officially greeted Colonel Fitzwilliam, Elizabeth sought him out, finding him in the music room with Georgiana, who quickly excused herself to join Kitty on a walk with Mr. Ashford.

"Come, Colonel," Elizabeth said with a false happiness instilled in her words, "it has been a long time since you turned the pages for me as I play."

"Since Hunsford." The colonel moved to sit by her on the bench.

"Will Mozart be acceptable, Sir?" Elizabeth smiled at him, trying to seem calm.

Edward spread the music in front of her. "Your company is preferable to the Mozart, Mrs. Darcy."

Elizabeth laughed nervously. "That is wise, Sir, considering my fingers do not do Mozart justice."

"You always claimed a lack of accomplishment, but you greatly undervalued your talents, Elizabeth." Edward reached over to turn the page for her.

Uncharacteristically, Elizabeth spoke softly and without confidence. "I would give anything to go back to Hunsford and know what I know now."

Edward looked at her, surprised by the sudden shift in her mood. "Would you have accepted my cousin then?" Edward mused.

Elizabeth suddenly stopped playing and turned to him with tear-filled eyes. "I would marry Fitzwilliam immediately, then my time with my Husband would have been longer. . . ." Her voice trailed off.

Edward spoke cautiously, "Would you truly risk it all again knowing what you know now?"

"I would," she whispered.

"Then you still love him despite what comes between you?" Edward wanted to assess the situation.

Elizabeth bit her lower lip, trying to hold back the tears. "Most ardently," she gasped.

Edward asked at last, "Yet, you understand my cousin's wishes?"

Elizabeth looked away, unable to respond with the hurt building inside her. "I am well aware of Mr. Darcy's plans for our future." She dabbed her eyes with a delicate lace handkerchief.

"Then may I ask, Elizabeth, why you did not respond to your husband? Does he not deserve to know how you feel?"

"Oh, Edward, I cannot," she wailed. "I want *my* Fitzwilliam back."

"*Your* Fitzwilliam may never return. Can you not accept what this man—this Fitzwilliam wishes? Darcy is very serious about what he expects from you. The man was born serious." Edward tried unsuccessfully to lighten the mood. "He was left with too much responsibility at too young of an age—raising Georgiana at such a delicate time in her life played heavy on your husband. His responsibilities are great for such a young man, and Darcy is a bit selfish in his dealings with others. He never had to take second place."

Edward meant to give Elizabeth comfort—to tell her Darcy was determined to make their marriage work, but the woman's emotions heard a different story. Elizabeth heard Darcy's cousin and friend say her husband was determined to have things his way, and she must succumb to Darcy's wants. Women in England had no legal rights; she lived at her husband's whim. Without him, she had nothing; ironically, with Darcy, Elizabeth would still have nothing.

CHAPTER 21

"The truth is, that in London it is always a sickly season.
Nobody is healthy in London, nobody can be."
Jane Austen, *Emma*, 1815

On Monday morning, Darcy and Georgiana prepared to board his chaise and four to leave for London. The colonel departed on Sunday, having to report to his commanding officer by late afternoon on Monday. "I will miss you, Elizabeth." Georgiana hugged her sister for the third time. "You will write to me often?"

"We will keep the post busy, my Sweet One." Elizabeth caressed Georgiana's face and kissed the girl's cheek lightly.

Darcy stood by the coach's door, waiting patiently for his sister to say her goodbyes. He wanted Elizabeth to caress his face—to embrace him; yet, she withheld her attentions to him.

"I will tell you all about my *endeavors*," Georgiana said nervously.

"Kitty and I will live vicariously through your letters so leave out no details." Elizabeth offered Georgiana her best smile. "Now, you must go; your brother waits patiently."

Elizabeth allowed her eyes to drift to where Darcy stood; his serious gaze encompassed her, making her shiver uncomfortably. She stepped past Georgiana, who now hugged Kitty, to speak to her husband. "Be safe, Sir," she said softly.

"I will keep you informed of Georgiana's triumphs," Darcy offered, although these were not the words he wanted to say to his wife at this time.

357

"Between the two of you, I will feel as if I am there with you." Elizabeth meant her words to have a double meaning and serve as a cut.

Darcy winched, and she took some pleasure in knowing he felt the pain of her words. He steadied his voice before saying, "Please take care of yourself and our child."

"I will protect the heir to Pemberley, Sir; you may be assured of that fact." Elizabeth looked away; the realization of his concern for her lay in her ability to deliver a healthy child.

"We will return before your lying in," Darcy told her, trying to assure Elizabeth he had no plans to abandon her.

Yet, Elizabeth thought about what would happen to her after delivering the child. Instinctively, she rested her hand on her abdomen. "I love this child, Fitzwilliam," she mumbled, not sure what she wanted him to know.

"We must leave," he said at last, knowing he could not walk away from Elizabeth if he delayed any longer. Darcy took Elizabeth's hand and brought it to his lips, kissing the back of it and then pulling it to his face to feel her skin against his.

Elizabeth watched as he closed his eyes to savor the moment, and her body betrayed her vulnerability to Darcy because she impulsively moved in closer to him. "Fitzwilliam," the word sounded like a plea.

Darcy's eyes flew open at the sound of desire in her voice. This was the stuff of which his dreams were made. The connection between them existed on a higher level, and he would come back to Elizabeth and love her forever. "Soon," he whispered, "I will return soon." He reached out and touched her face, tracing her lips with his fingers, and then he turned, climbed in the coach, and took his leave without ever looking back.

Elizabeth fell into a pattern: taking breakfast alone, making visits to tenants, addressing estate business, dining with Kitty and Mr. Ashford, and crying herself to sleep each evening.

Some days she broke the "program" by addressing a letter to Darcy or Georgiana. To his sister, Elizabeth sent news of the tenants, the birth of several new children in Lambton, her plans for the conservatory, the changing weather, new music she learned, and anecdotes about catching Kitty and Mr. Ashford sharing loving embraces. To Darcy, Elizabeth sent information regarding estate business. She did not wish to purposely hurt Darcy, but she could not let the feeling of "dread" escape into her letters to him.

15 April

Elizabeth,

Once again, my brother and I attended an exhibition at the art museum. I cannot say I enjoyed the offerings. My tastes tend to prefer landscapes to scenes of barely clad females being subjugated to domineering males, but the artist received critical acclaim and the stamp of approval from leading members of society, many of whom paid high prices for the privilege of hanging the artwork on their walls.

As usual, the Dorchesters and Miss McFarland joined us for the dinner at Lord Collingsworth's house, following the museum show. It is a fine house, but it could use Kitty's eye for color and attention to details. The rooms lacked a sense of cohesiveness even to my untrained eye.

Neither my brother nor I belong at these functions. I abhor conversing and dancing with strangers; I never find an appropriate thing to say although I practice ideas before going to each of the events. I read the newspaper daily trying to glean topics, which might be conversation starters, but I stumble and stutter too much to be a success in that area. Fitzwilliam converses easily, but he dreads being around strangers as much as I. I believe that is why he seeks out the Dorchesters—for the familiarity they provide. Otherwise, I see no reason why he would tolerate them.

I withheld my opinion of these companions until I had time to be around them more, but I share them with you, my darling sister, for I am sure you will find them amusing and will be proud of how astute I have become, even if I cannot hold an intelligent conversation.

Henry Dorchester is very much his father's son so a description of the elder will often apply to his offspring. They are both elegantly dressed at all times, possess impeccable manners, and are perfectly foppish, deep-in-the-pocket dandies. Henry Dorchester is a favorite of the doting mothers seeking matches for their daughters, and as far as I am concerned, those mothers and daughters are welcome to him. The man is self-indulgent and could love no one except himself. I pray Fitzwilliam will tire of the man's company and allow me to look elsewhere for a match.

Miss McFarland, as part of the Dorchester family, has similar qualities. In your sister's humble opinion, the woman is a pure example of educated shallowness. A pampered, wasteful life is a mark of her social foible. Miss McFarland constantly wears a plastered-on smile, and although she has a lovely face and is a veritable perfectionist on the dance floor, Miss McFarland is too ambitious and cares for no one but herself. Reportedly, last season she turned down two different marquises.

I do not like the attention the lady delivers to either Fitzwilliam or me; it is very reminiscent of Caroline Bingley. I do not trust the woman, and I often note my brother's glazed-over look, also very reminiscent of his conversations with Miss Bingley when Mr. Bingley and his sisters used to visit Pemberley.

I will send you more of my most astute insights soon, Elizabeth. Unfortunately, I must close for now; I wish to get this in the next post.

> Your loving sister,
> Georgiana Darcy

Elizabeth read the letter carefully, especially the part about Cecelia McFarland. A jealous rage went through her. If the woman reminded Georgiana of Caroline Bingley, Elizabeth worried whether Miss McFarland might be her replacement at Pemberley. Obviously, Miss McFarland would make a better mate for her husband than Elizabeth, but she could never imagine why the man she loved would even consider such a woman.

Her husband's letter offered a more sterile version of the events and had less emphasis on the company they kept and more emphasis on his sister's apparent growing apprehension. Elizabeth answered them both politely but with little enthusiasm. Her life was a façade. She wrote polite letters to a husband who planned to divorce her and take her child and to a girl she cherished as her family but who would soon be forbidden to see her. The irony of it was not lost on Elizabeth.

★ ★ ★

Georgiana anxiously opened the letter from Elizabeth. The letters from her brother's wife soothed Georgiana's homesickness, and the girl reread them religiously. She and her brother had been in London nearly three weeks, and all she wanted was to return to Pemberley.

20 April

My dearest sister,

Your letters continue to delight Kitty and me. Your "astute" observations open a window on London society, and I admit to no longer desiring to being among the social elite.

Fitzwilliam's letters give us the schedule you keep, but yours provide the depth of self-possession I do often imagine. With what all you describe, I am surprised you have not encountered the Prince Regent at every turn.

I am afraid, my lovely sister, I have sad news to share this time. A violent late-night thunderstorm rattled across the county two nights ago, and a lightning strike found its way to the small barn. Smoke and fire spread quickly, flames licking the roof as Mr. Howard, the stable staff, and many of the household staff fought valiantly to save the structure.

I feared we would lose it all—the horses and the barns—but Mr. Howard would not allow that to happen. The man risked everything, Georgiana, rushing into the burning building to release the horses from their stalls. The water brigade labored long and hard before they contained the blaze. Of course, the rain helped to squelch the fire more quickly than if it were from another source. Please tell Fitzwilliam his Cerberus is safe, and no men were seriously injured.

The only loss that evening was my sweet Penelope. I feel her loss greatly as she was a wedding gift from my husband. He chose her for her gentleness and her spirit, and I miss the trust she had in me. We did not lose Penelope directly to the fire, but to the excitement and fright she felt before Mr. Howard could reach her. She bolted, according to Mr. Howard, and one flaying hoof wedged into the gate. Spooked by the flames, my Penelope thrashed, trying to free her leg, and shattered it. A grieving Mr. Howard put Penelope down.

A cold sickness seeps into my being when I think of the end of Penelope's life, but please tell Fitzwilliam not to rush to replace her. I know his generous nature, but it will be some time before I ride again, and maybe by then, I will be more inclined to accept her replacement.

I leave you with this sad news. Give Fitzwilliam my regard.

Your sister,
E. D.

When her brother returned from his club, Georgiana shared Elizabeth's letter. She watched his reaction closely. "Elizabeth handles the estate well, Fitzwilliam," Georgiana said cautiously.

"She does," he added, but did not quit reading the letter. "I should have been there," he whispered.

"What, Fitzwilliam?" Georgiana called, although she heard him plainly.

"Nothing, Georgiana." He turned back to her. "I am sure Mr. Howard sent his report." A feeling of jealousy rose in Darcy again. His wife's praise of his steward did not set well with him. He pictured Elizabeth desolate at the loss of her horse, and Mr. Howard comforting her before putting the horse down. The image rocked his being. It also bothered Darcy the horse was one of his wedding gifts to his wife, and now it was gone.

Darcy sat at the desk in his study wondering about this decision to come to London and to leave Elizabeth at Pemberley. Each night he dreamed of her—of how she touched him—of how she kissed him. Each night he dreamed of her with the tenants and with the staff at Pemberley; Elizabeth made his house a home. Darcy had been in London for several weeks, and he had yet to see a woman half as pretty as his Elizabeth. A fleeting smile played across his lips. Soon—soon he would go home to her.

* * *

Elizabeth opened the letter from her Aunt Gardiner expecting news about her nieces and nephews. She had an image of Darcy holding Cassandra Gardiner at Christmastime and how she rejoiced in knowing she would give him his own child soon. Elizabeth ached from the memory, feeling deprived of her great love.

21 April

My dearest Lizzy,
Your uncle and I hope this letter finds you in health and

anticipating your lying in. If you so wish, I will come to Pemberley to be with you at that time. My child, we are so worried about your condition. Your uncle and I know of the stress in which you find yourself, and we are grieved we can do nothing to alter your situation.

My husband demanded I write to you this evening although I, truthfully, question whether the information I share will not cause you more alarm. Mr. Gardiner and I attended the theatre earlier this evening, and much to our chagrin, we found Mr. Darcy and his sister in attendance. Miss Darcy acknowledged us from their box, but, of course, Mr. Darcy did not. We understood from your father the result of your husband's recent attack and were not offended by this oversight.

What did infuriate your uncle was the conduct of Mr. Darcy during the performance. Lord Dorchester and his son, as well as a fashionably dressed lady who we were later to find out to be Miss Cecelia McFarland, accompanied Mr. Darcy. We watched in horror as the young woman often reached out to touch Mr. Darcy's arm, and he repeatedly leaned toward her as they exchanged comments on the performance.

Mr. Gardiner sought them out during the interlude and demanded Mr. Darcy speak to him privately. Although Mr. Darcy did not recognize Mr. Gardiner, Miss Darcy discreetly explained the connection, and he and your uncle stepped outside to discuss the events which transpired. I stayed with Miss Darcy and the Dorchester party, trying to make small talk.

When Mr. Gardiner and your husband returned before the start of the next act, they were both clearly agitated. My dear husband refuses to give me the content of the exchange, saying such language should not be shared with ladies, but both men obviously spoke their minds. Mr. Gardiner demanded Mr. Darcy consider what he did to you, my dear, by his conduct. Mr. Gardiner believes Mr. Darcy's lack of decorum to be a product of the ton. He told your husband as such. I do not know what Mr. Darcy's *response was, but I am sure indignation played into it.*

My dearest Lizzy, I wish I was not so compelled to tell you of this incident; I would prefer to shield you from it forever, but as a married woman, you must face these possibilities from Mr. Darcy.

Your loving aunt,
M.G.

As the weeks passed and Elizabeth continued to hear news of Darcy's keeping company with Miss McFarland, she became more convinced her earlier fears of his disengagement a reality. She resolved she would not "allow" Darcy to take their child from her. Men had legal rights to their children, but Elizabeth would find a way.

As an educated woman, she could take a position as a governess; she would feign being a widow and escape. However, Elizabeth realized that would mean she would have to leave everything and everyone she knew. Darcy would spare no expense at tracking her so she must be thorough in her plan.

If Darcy planned to send Elizabeth away, she had no choice. She could not return to Longbourn; her mother would never forgive Elizabeth's shame, and although Jane would offer her a home, Elizabeth could not live at Netherfield each day and not think of Darcy. That is where their "history" began; it would be too painful to endure. Leaving it all behind would be her only choice. She would never contact any of her loved ones again for they could not withstand the pressure Darcy's stature could place on them.

Over the past month, Elizabeth played this scenario through her mind many times. Darcy's obsession with social status told her she would be found wanting. Her husband took his sister to London because he expected Georgiana to live in a world foreign to the one in which Elizabeth was raised. Expectations for Georgiana were high; her thirty thousand pounds would make Miss Darcy desirable. Elizabeth knew what she expected as acceptable in country society would be regarded with the greatest disapprobation by the *ton*. Her manners were once attractive to Darcy, but the novelty wore off, and her husband now judged her by different standards. *I cannot forget the follies and vices of others so soon as I ought . . . My good opinion once lost is lost forever.* His words ricocheted through Elizabeth, and she shivered instinctively.

Although Elizabeth had few choices, she would not be separated from both the man she loved and the child she carried. She could not lose both of them. Where could she go? It would have to be a place Darcy would not find her. Elizabeth considered Scotland or Ireland, but those were too accessible. Of late her dreams were of India, where many English women traveled to find European husbands, or she could find passage to America, a more uncivilized society, but one in which she and her child could easily disappear.

In that vein, Elizabeth penned a letter to Mr. Harrison. It was another act of impropriety, but her gut feeling told her Harrison would answer her questions and not betray her confidences. As a woman, she could not seek this information without raising eyebrows; Elizabeth had to trust someone, and Chadwick Harrison became her choice.

The letter she received from him clarified some of her concerns. If the child were born onboard ship, its nationality would, generally, depend upon whose waters in which the ship was found. If in British waters, the child was a British citizen. Her "fight" to keep her child could be better portrayed if the child was born in foreign waters. Elizabeth could not believe she even considered such a possibility, but desperation now controlled her every thought.

★ ★ ★

The confrontation with Elizabeth's uncle irritated Darcy at

first. In fact, initially he thought it typical of Elizabeth's reported low connections; yet, upon further reflection he realized although Mr. Gardiner's accusations were ill founded and formed on mistaken premises, Darcy's behavior at the time merited a severe reproof. He could not think on his behavior without abhorrence. Elizabeth did not deserve such reflected censure. His friends must think her so poor in manners he wished to be elsewhere—away from her—and that was far from the truth. Darcy wanted to be with Elizabeth, not with Cecelia McFarland and her inane chatter about social events. How did he manage to get into this situation?

As bits of his memory returned, Darcy recalled his life with his parents and realized how selfish he had been. His parents taught him the "right" thing to do, but they left him to practice and interact in pride and conceit. Although his parents had a reputation as benevolent and amiable, they actually taught him to care for none but his family circle and to think poorly of those with less stature. Elizabeth demanded he become a man worthy of pleasing a woman such as his wife. Others deferred to his preferences simply because of his social position, but not Elizabeth. She loved him not for his fortune or his position. Now, Darcy taught those same elevated principles to his younger sister. Would it not be better for Georgiana to learn about what to value in life from his Elizabeth?

★ ★ ★

Georgiana Darcy entered the ball on her brother's arm. She took a deep breath, hating the next few hours before they began. Smiling and making conversation with strangers never got any easier, no matter how often she was exposed to fine society. If she could just go home to Pemberley, she would be happy.

When the first set came, Henry Dorchester appeared before her to lead Georgiana to the dance floor. Georgiana looked around at the glittering chandeliers and the orchestra as it echoed through the ballroom. She watched debutantes tittering behind their fans, thinking of nothing but securing a wealthy husband while she would prefer being in the carriage with Elizabeth and administering to Pemberley's poor. She found satisfaction and self-respect there; here she was another tittering debutante.

Henry Dorchester bowed prettily; he, in Georgiana's estimation, was a brainless Beau Brummell, more concerned with the cut of his coat and the tie of his cravat than of anything else. The half hour of the dance set seemed interminable. The conversation dwelt too long on the fabric he chose at his tailor's that day and how he commissioned an entire wardrobe. As the set ended, he returned Georgiana to Darcy's side and hurried off to speak with a viscount who owed Dorchester money.

"What do you think of Henry Dorchester?" Darcy whispered his question as he leaned in to speak only to his sister.

"Truthfully, Fitzwilliam," she said cautiously, not sure how her brother would react to her honest appraisal of Henry Dorchester, "I do not think of him at all; thinking of Henry Dorchester would be a waste of my precious time. I would prefer to be more gainfully employed."

Darcy smiled at her. "I detect a note of loathsomeness in your tone."

"I am sorry to disappoint you, Brother; I know my actions are not what you expect from me. I want to please you, but I do not know how unless I deflate my consequence. I know not whether I can tolerate such a droll and less-than-amusing man."

"Do you not think he could pen a sonnet to your beauty?" Darcy teased.

Georgiana giggled lightly, "Only if he paid someone to do the writing."

Darcy arched an eyebrow in response and tapped his sister

on the chin with his index finger, a private sign of his affection for her. "Maybe standing up with me would be more to your liking?" he asked lightly.

Georgiana gifted him with a smile of delight. "I thought you would never ask, Sir."

Dancing with Darcy allowed Georgiana to relax, knowing she would not be judged during the process. They chattered on throughout the dance, speaking of Pemberley and of family and of Elizabeth. "Do you miss your sister?" Darcy asked on one of the passes.

"No more than you," she answered perceptively.

Darcy's grin overspread his face. "Pemberley has its attractions," he smiled a teasing wickedness. "We will finish the time we have here, and then we will return to our home."

"I look forward to it." Georgiana smiled brightly.

Going down the line on Darcy's arm, Georgiana's eyes surveyed the room. Out of the shadows stepped a familiar figure, and she felt her heart skip a beat. He motioned with his eyes to the balcony, and she nodded slightly in acquiescence. A blush overspread her body, and Georgiana suddenly felt warmth spread through each of her limbs. Darcy, thankfully, dropped into his usual silence and did not take note of the changes in his sister. When the set concluded, Georgiana excused herself, saying she needed some fresh air, and headed toward the main entrance. She wanted her brother to think she exited the way they came into the hall, but once out of his sightlines, she circled inconspicuously until she slipped through the barely opened door to the small balcony.

"Miss Darcy," she heard his voice before she could make out his features.

"Mr. Harrison," she gasped, unable to control her excitement. They made quick bows to one another before she boldly stepped forward to face him head on. "You were missed, Sir," she whispered.

"As were you, Miss Darcy." His voice suddenly became hoarse.

"I did not expect to see you in London," she whispered again, thinking her voice betrayed her delight at seeing him.

"I am being courted by some members of Parliament," he told her quickly, "to accept a seat recently vacated in the House of Commons."

She asked hopefully, "Then you will be in London for some time?"

Harrison's countenance fell, and Georgiana saw how her words bothered him. "My time in London is short—only a few days, but I could not let it pass without seeing you, Miss Darcy."

"Say my name," she said suddenly and moved closer still.

Harrison caressed her jaw line, letting his thumb massage her temple. "Georgiana," he whispered, earnestly filled with desire.

"Chadwick." Georgiana snaked her arms around his neck as he pulled her closer to him.

"You are the most unpredictable woman I ever saw," he gasped.

"Do I shock you?" She buried her face into his chest, not believing her boldness.

Harrison lifted her chin and looked deeply into Georgiana's eyes. "I am a man deeply in need of your assurances; if I am shocked, it is of the most pleasant kind." He bent to kiss her lips, willing Georgiana to respond to him.

The kiss built in intensity. His tongue parted her lips and searched the inside of her mouth. At first, she held back her passion, but then Georgiana followed suit, allowing herself to taste his lips and mouth fully.

Breathing heavily, they parted reluctantly, and Georgiana stepped away from him to settle her composure. "I must return before my brother misses me," she said at last.

Harrison moved up behind her. "Like at Matlock, the set before we go into dinner is mine, Georgiana." He laced his fingers through hers.

Georgiana rested her head upon his shoulder to feel his closeness once more. "I will be waiting for you." Her heart fluttered with excitement as she touched his face briefly and then slipped back through the door to the ballroom.

Harrison waited ten minutes before he, too, returned to the room, partly because he wanted to make sure no signs of impropriety followed her and partly because it took nearly that long for him to recover from his need to hold Georgiana Darcy in his arms.

Returning to the room, Georgiana danced with several other partners and once more with Henry Dorchester, thankful it would be the last time she would have to tolerate his attentions this evening. Throughout the set, she searched for Chadwick Harrison's face, nearly believing she dreamed him up, and he was not really here in this same arena as she. Distractedly, she mumbled her responses to Dorchester's silly observations. At last, the dance ended, and she found herself by Darcy's side once again.

Nervously, she waited Harrison's approach, finally feeling his presence before he actually stood behind her. "Miss Darcy," his voice recovered its resonant qualities, "if you are not otherwise engaged, may I request the honor of the next dance?"

Georgiana shot a quick glance at her brother, who betrayed nothing in his countenance, before answering him. "Mr. Harrison," she feigned surprise, "I was unaware you were in London, Sir."

"I only arrived this afternoon," he bowed to Darcy, and then he extended his hand to Georgiana.

She smiled brightly at him and accepted his arm as he led her to the dance floor. For thirty minutes he would be able to drink in her beauty and goodness; heaven enveloped him. Georgiana felt very much the same; for the next half hour her life would be perfect.

Darcy watched his sister carefully. Suddenly, Georgiana's usually sedate presence was alive and animated. Chadwick Harrison's effect on her was pronounced, and although he should be upset about the turn of events, Darcy took pleasure in seeing her happy for a change. Maybe Elizabeth's estimation of the increasing regard between the two of them should be reevaluated. Other than the political climate surrounding Harrison, did he really have objections regarding the man?

The dance began, and they were silent for the first few minutes, engrossed in the pleasure each gave to the other. Finally, Harrison broke the revelry. "Miss Darcy, although I relish each moment of being in your presence, some form of speech seems necessary, or your brother will assume I offend you."

"We would not wish him to think such a thought." Georgiana gave him a smile.

Harrison returned her look of delight. "Then you welcome my return?" he asked when they crossed each other and caught hands in the form.

"I would think my earlier impropriety should answer that question quite clearly, Sir." Georgiana dropped her eyes and blushed lightly.

"I told you I need assurances, Miss Darcy." He squeezed her hand as they progressed down the line.

"I would never wish you to feel unwelcome, Sir," Georgiana actually leaned in toward him as they crossed once more.

They separated again, each facing a partner from another couple. When reunited, Harrison asked, "When do you return to Pemberley?"

"My sister's lying in should begin soon; my brother promised to go home before then," she confided.

Harrison seemed surprised, "Really?"

Georgiana did not like the implication in his voice. "My brother is anxious to see his wife again," she emphasized the words.

"Miss Darcy," Harrison tried to calm her sudden change in attitude, "I meant nothing by my words." There was a pause before he continued. "I was in London only a few hours, and I heard the rumors about Mr. Darcy and Miss McFarland." Harrison felt Georgiana stiffen with his words.

"Fitzwilliam loves his wife," she said with more determination.

"I am pleased to hear it," Harrison responded, still concerned with her ire. "Mrs. Darcy, I believe, thinks otherwise."

Georgiana turned to him. "My sister believes what?"

Harrison lowered his voice as they came together again. "Mrs. Darcy believes your brother intends to send her away after the child is born."

Georgiana gasped, "She cannot!"

"Mrs. Darcy confided as such," he said, embarrassed at having said so much.

Georgiana asked at last, "Should I tell my brother?"

"As long as he returns to Mrs. Darcy's side soon, all should be well," Harrison added quietly. Eventually, he suggested, "Maybe Mr. Darcy should avoid Miss McFarland's company, however. Rumors may reach even Derbyshire."

Georgiana nodded but did not respond. Instinctively, she sought her brother's presence in the crowd, but winched when she saw Miss McFarland taking his arm and heading toward the dining room.

The rest of the dance set was quiet, mostly small talk, and for some time, Georgiana was engrossed in thoughts of her brother; yet, the connection between her and Harrison could not be denied. Their eyes could not leave the other.

When they went into dinner, Harrison purposely escorted Georgiana to the far end of the table, not wanting her too close to her brother and the Dorchester party. "I noted you stood up twice with Lord Dorchester's son," Harrison tried to sound nonchalant.

"I did," she giggled. "Do you object, Sir?"

"Miss Darcy, there is little about you to which I object, but it seems at dances you continually try my patience."

"That sounds a bit provocative, Mr. Harrison." Georgiana smiled up at him brightly.

"I do intend to claim one more dance set if you are willing?" he asked, sounding unsure again.

"Mr. Harrison, you know my answer without asking." This time she dropped her eyes, as well as her voice.

"May I also ask you to ride out with me tomorrow?" Harrison would waste no time in claiming Georgiana as his own, at least for the day. "I was thinking a cream ice from Gunter's in Berkeley Square."

"My brother will not be pleased, but I will risk his wrath. Now tell me about the political seat of which you spoke earlier." Georgiana lost herself and the time in Harrison's eyes and his smile.

At the other end of the table, Darcy kept close tabs on his sister's fascination with Chadwick Harrison. Georgiana, obviously, enthralled the men, and Darcy suspected even if a member of royalty presented himself to her, his sister would refuse everyone except Mr. Harrison. Darcy wondered if he should not just take her home and accept the inevitable.

He was so in tune with his sister that for a few minutes, he was unaware of Miss McFarland's flirtatious movements toward him. When he felt her hand slide into his, at first he was flattered—she was a beautiful woman, but immediately disgust shot through him. Darcy was disgusted with himself for encouraging this superficial woman and disgusted she would delude herself into thinking he to be as shallow as she. Looking around the table, he noted several people turned their eyes from him, not wishing to see another member of the *ton* succumb to temptation.

Definitively, Darcy took Miss McFarland's hand and placed it back into her lap.

"Do I offend you, Sir?" Miss McFarland asked softly, barely at a whisper.

Darcy surveyed the table again, wondering how many were taking note of his actions. "Miss McFarland, I appreciate your family's friendship, but if I led you to think I wish something more, I must apologize." Darcy's voice held a steady determination.

"It is I who should apologize then," she said with assurance, knowing Darcy found her attractive. "I understood you were unhappy in your current situation; I wished to give you options for the Mistress of Pemberley."

Darcy lowered his voice, but his anger could not be hidden. "Miss McFarland, I take umbrage at your suggestion; Mrs. Darcy owns my respect and my love. I *have* a mistress for my estate; I do not need a different one for my bed."

"Then I will take my leave, Sir." She stood quickly and left in a huff before Darcy could even make her a proper bow.

He flushed with the notice given to Miss McFarland's exit, but he recovered and turned to the viscount seated to his left and made small talk through the rest of the meal. He would prefer to leave the gathering, but he allowed Georgiana another dance set with Mr. Harrison before they bid their hosts adieu.

CHAPTER 22

"If one scheme of happiness fails, human nature turns to another."
Jane Austen, *Mansfield Park*, 1814

In the carriage returning to Kensington Place, Darcy laughed lightly at seeing Georgiana happy at last. "Mr. Harrison still favors you, my dear," Darcy mused.

"I was surprised to see him at the ball tonight." Georgiana tried not to betray her satisfaction with her brother's assertion.

"I am sure he knew of your presence at the ball. Even you could not convince me that was a coincidence." Darcy watched her squirm under his close inspection.

"Mr. Harrison has been asked to assume a seat in Parliament in the House of Commons." Georgiana wanted Darcy to know Harrison was a viable match. "If elected, he would spend part of his time regularly in London."

Darcy grinned at Georgiana's sudden blush. "Then Mr. Harrison is still a favorite?"

Again, she avoided his question with a redirect of her own. "I noticed an early exit by Miss McFarland," she said cautiously.

"We had a disagreement." Darcy looked out the carriage window into the night.

Georgiana mustered her courage. "I am not sorry to see it happen. Miss McFarland's attentions to you have become common knowledge. I would not wish Elizabeth to hear such rumors."

Darcy turned back to look at her in surprise. "Are you telling me I am a source of gossip?"

Georgiana blushed at having this conversation with her elder brother. "I would not wish to offend you, Fitzwilliam, but even Mr. Harrison heard the rumors, and he only arrived in London today. Miss McFarland let it be known she intended to replace Elizabeth in your life."

A curse escaped his lips before he could stifle it. "How did I let this happen?"

"People in the *ton* often look the other way when indiscretions occur. My concern is for Elizabeth," Georgiana added at last.

A look of bewilderment flooded Darcy's face. "I will not let my actions harm my wife; Elizabeth will never forgive me."

"Then what do we do, Fitzwilliam?" Georgiana asked softly.

Darcy returned to looking at the night. "My first inclination is to immediately return home, but that would allow the gossip to continue. We will remain in London for another three to four weeks. During that time we will offer civilities to the Dorchesters and Miss McFarland, but they will no longer be *favorites*. At each opportunity, we will explain how Elizabeth is not only my wife, but she owns my heart as well."

Georgiana asked tentatively, "Do you mean it, Fitzwilliam?"

"I tried to counter Elizabeth's hold on me, but I cannot. At Darling Hall, I dreamed of her constantly even though I had no memory of Elizabeth at the time. I cannot disengage my wife's presence from my being, and I will not allow my foolish mistakes to tarnish her reputation. Then I will pray some part of my wife still wants me in her life." He paused as if trying to make a decision. "You have her confidence, Georgiana; could Elizabeth still love me?"

Georgiana could not mistake the pain in Darcy's voice. "Elizabeth loves none but you, but whether you can earn her forgiveness, I cannot say."

★ ★ ★

Elizabeth walked the halls of Pemberley; it was days since she had even been out of the house—her turmoil so great she literally ached from the pain of it. She loved Darcy with every fiber of her being, and she could not convince herself he did not still love her. If she were not with child, Elizabeth might try to entice him back to her; after all, they possessed a mutual passion; but how could a woman whose stomach protruded out so far she could no longer see her own feet seduce a man as attractive as her husband? In London, beautiful, well-mannered, refined women surrounded him. How could she compete? The truth was she could not; Elizabeth had *nothing* to offer him.

She sat at Darcy's desk, recording figures in the estate's ledger. Her heart found no pleasure in the effort; Elizabeth simply went through the motions of completing her duties as Pemberley's mistress. By her calculations, Darcy would remain in London for another month. Whatever she was going to do, she would have to do it soon. The closer to her lying in, the less likely she could travel.

Being resourceful, she wrote several newsy letters for Darcy and for Georgiana. She would pay one of the villagers to post one every few days, creating the illusion she was still at Pemberley. Another concern was what to do about Kitty. Elizabeth could not simply leave Kitty at Pemberley to face Darcy's wrath. Mr. Ashford could provide immediate relief. He would gladly marry Kitty before their September planned nuptials; that was a fact; however, Mr. Ashford's living depended on Darcy. That could be a problem; she would not wish Mr. Ashford to suffer because of her cowardice. Kitty and Clayton Ashford deserved a fresh start in life; Elizabeth did not want them to live like her dear friend Charlotte and Mr. Collins, groveling for any kindness Darcy may send their way.

Originally, she wanted to leave all of Darcy's wealth behind when she left Pemberley—all the gifts he gave her, including his mother's jewelry. Instead, she decided to take enough money for Kitty and Mr. Ashford to survive Darcy's anger or to move on to another position. She would use her pin money for her own expenses. Darcy would assume she took it all for herself; he would not look at Ashford's household. Elizabeth did not marry him for his wealth, and she would not steal from him now.

She hated this deception; it went against everything by which she defined herself. Plotting against the man she loved seemed so out of character for her; Elizabeth could not imagine it, but here she was anticipating the loss of Darcy's love and how she would survive afterwards.

One of the footmen brought in a letter for her inspection; addressed to Darcy, initially Elizabeth placed it on the tray on his desk, not knowing whether she should open it or not. It lay there, calling to her, demanding her attention, but she instinctively knew it was not something she wished to see. At first she walked away from the desk, but then returned to stand in front of the furniture; and, like the Forbidden Fruit, the letter sought her. Eventually, reasoning Darcy would not return to Pemberley for several weeks, her duty defined her actions, and Elizabeth broke the seal on the message. Tentatively, with hands shaking, she unfolded the paper, and a lock of hair slipped out; Elizabeth recoiled from the strand, her mouth going dry and her eyes misting over with tears.

24 April

My darling Fitzwilliam,

I must return to our family estate before we planned, and I knew not how to reach you except through this post. I assume you are preparing to return to your estate as we discussed last night; I pray, my Beloved, you will forgive my impropriety. I anticipate your return to Pemberley, and I wait impatiently until I have the opportunity to join you there. My dearest, I long to be once more in your arms; my love rests in you.

I take my leave from you, but I will not bid you farewell.

Yours forever,
Cecelia

Elizabeth sank to her knees, no longer able to breathe—she lost him! She tried to ascertain her husband's thoughts, but now everything was clear: Darcy chose someone else. She lost everything she valued in life; the day Darcy left for Hull, Elizabeth's existence ceased to be. She knew the pleasure of his love for a few brief moments, a few brief months, but now she knew only bitterness and rejection. Her love for Darcy not only cost her her life at Pemberley, it also cost Elizabeth her life at Longbourn. She had nothing left. Sobs consumed her, and she lay crumpled on the floor in a discouraged heap.

Kitty found her there, exhausted from the effort of just breathing. "Elizabeth!" she cried, rushing forward to help her older sister. "Lizzy? Are you are right?" She cradled Elizabeth's head in her lap.

Still consumed by her grief, Elizabeth lay limp in Kitty's arms, cherishing this moment of tenderness as possibly being one of the last ones she would receive from her family.

"Lizzy, please," Kitty nearly begged. "Let me help you." Kitty supported her sister as she helped Elizabeth to a nearby settee. "Shall I send for Mr. Spencer?"

Elizabeth shook her head in the negative, but she could not verbalize her thoughts. She rested her head on Kitty's shoulder while Kitty whispered endearments and stroked Elizabeth's hair.

Eventually, Elizabeth wiped her eyes and straightened her shoulders. Softly, but with determination she said, "Kitty, would you please read the letter on Mr. Darcy's desk? Then we have something to discuss."

Unsure of her sister's intent, Kitty crossed to the desk to read the words which destroyed her sister's life. "Lizzy, this cannot be true!" Her words filled with disbelief as she came back to sit with Elizabeth.

"My husband expressed a desire to his cousin the colonel to be rid of me. I overheard his words clearly. Georgiana writes of his spending time with Miss McFarland and the Dorchester party. Aunt Gardiner saw him with her at the theatre. Even you heard Mr. Darcy praise Miss McFarland at dinner. Our connections cannot compete with that lady's lineage."

Kitty reasoned, "Mr. Darcy loves you, Lizzy; he told me so himself."

"That was before my husband left for Hull. He has no memory of us; Fitzwilliam and I no longer exist," Elizabeth bemoaned her fate.

"What will you do?" Kitty wondered.

Elizabeth got up and walked slowly to the window. She did not want to look at her sister; fearing Kitty could read the deception on her face, Elizabeth spoke to her own reflection in the glass. "I cannot let Mr. Darcy send me away; I must leave on my own terms—be my own person. Fitzwilliam should be generous, and I will survive." Elizabeth fidgeted with the knowledge of her manipulation of the words. "The problem is when I should depart Pemberley. One of the issues is your and Mr. Ashford's relationship; I cannot leave you here to face Mr. Darcy's rage, and I cannot allow Mr. Ashford to suffer on my behalf."

Kitty's eyes misted over; she wondered whether Clayton Ashford would withdraw his offer of marriage if Mr. Darcy refused Ashford's living because of Kitty's relationship to Elizabeth. "I never thought of such turmoil," Kitty nearly whined.

Elizabeth turned toward her younger sister. "Well, luckily, I did." Elizabeth crossed back toward the settee. "Come, Kitty, we need to talk." They settled in together. "This is what I propose. We will tell the staff you were called home to help take care of our mother. I will send you home to Longbourn tomorrow accompanied by a household servant. If we leave together, Mrs. Reynolds and Hannah will suspect something, especially considering my condition, and so we must travel separately. Once you are there, I need for you to let Jane know of my arrival. Our mother will not be happy if Mr. Darcy abandons me; I will not be welcomed to our home."

"Our mother could not be so stringent," Kitty gulped the words.

Elizabeth said without emotion, "I will be a shamed woman; our mother will be displeased. Anyway, I will follow you in a few days. I think it best if I maintain my usual schedule of tenant calls and other obligations; it will paint a picture of contentment." Elizabeth dropped her eyes, knowing she had no intention of going to Hertfordshire. "Does this seem reasonable?"

"It is as reasonable as a state of chaos might be," Kitty whispered softly.

"Now, will you ask Mr. Ashford to attend me? I wish to speak to him privately."

"Yes, Lizzy." Kitty dejectedly left the room.

After a few brief minutes, Mr. Ashford appeared at the door of the study. "Mrs. Darcy," he said as he bowed briefly, "you wished to speak to me?"

"Yes, Mr. Ashford." Elizabeth looked up to make eye contact. "Please come join me. I have some issues with which I must speak to you."

Ashford, aware of Elizabeth's formality and Kitty Bennet's distraught look, knew not what happened, but the composition suddenly changed. He came to sit gingerly on the edge of the settee's cushion.

Elizabeth looked him directly in the eyes, needing for Ashford to see her as determined. "Mr. Ashford, I wish to speak to you on a matter of importance, and I hope you will excuse the impropriety of my frankness in doing so."

"Mrs. Darcy, I respect your thoughts and would find no offense in your manners."

Elizabeth took a deep breath. "Do you love my sister?" she asked suddenly.

"Most ardently." He looked away uncomfortably.

"I am pleased to hear it, Sir." Elizabeth added a smile to her countenance, and Ashford let out his breath, feeling Elizabeth tested him. "Now, I must ask you to make a decision which will change your life."

Ashford looked bewildered. "I do not understand, Mrs. Darcy."

"Bear with me, Mr. Ashford; these are not words easy for me to say." Elizabeth's eyes misted over.

"Mrs. Darcy, I will do anything to help you; you must just tell me your desire."

Elizabeth swallowed hard. "It is my belief, Sir, that my marriage to Mr. Darcy is over, and I will be asked to leave Pemberley. My concern now is for you and my sister. Obviously, you are placed in a precarious situation. If I must leave Pemberley, Kitty cannot remain here; Mr. Darcy will never tolerate that. I am sending her back to Longbourn tomorrow."

Ashford looked around, not sure how to respond. "Are you positive this is Mr. Darcy's wish?"

"My husband through his actions and his words expressed his wishes," Elizabeth confided. "What you must decide, Sir, is what you will do. I will not ask you for your answer at this moment—it is not a decision you can take lightly. If you choose to marry Kitty, you must decide whether to stay here and risk Mr. Darcy's censure; I know not how he will react. I assume my husband will be fair as is always his nature, but Mr. Darcy's anger may be an issue, as well as if he chooses to take another wife. The new Mrs. Darcy may resent my sister living under Mr. Darcy's care. Your other choice is to seek another living."

"Neither choice would be mine. I cannot fathom your distress, Mrs. Darcy." Ashford's comforting tone nearly undid Elizabeth's resolve.

"Mr. Ashford, if you marry Kitty, I will give you five hundred pounds. It is not much, but it will help you survive your choice. With economy, you can live comfortably while you seek another position, or you may use it to live quietly while you wait for the hubbub revolving my disengagement to die down."

"Mrs. Darcy, you are generous to a fault, but you need not do this," Ashford protested.

Elizabeth reached out and patted his hand. "Mr. Ashford, your goodness is such a blessing," Elizabeth said quietly, "but I cannot allow my sister's chance at happiness to be destroyed by my situation. If I had more, I would give it to you to secure Kitty's love for you."

"Then you think Miss Bennet loves me, too?" Ashford asked in disbelief. He always knew Kitty held him in affection, but never really thought she loved him, even though she professed it often enough.

"My sister's heart belongs to you, Sir; however, Kitty is afraid of her commitment to you. She has few good examples of the pleasure of marriage which to emulate. My parents married impulsively, and theirs is not a loving one. Mr. Wickham neglects our youngest sister Lydia. Now, Mr. Darcy and I are doomed. Other than my eldest sister Jane and Mr. Bingley, Kitty has no models of success. She fears you will tire of her soon so she keeps her emotions in check."

"How can Miss Bennet so doubt my regard?" Ashford baffled.

"My dear, Mr. Ashford," Elizabeth laughed lightly, "you will find the Bennet sisters are experts at misconstruing the men they love. I once thought myself an expert in judging others, but my relationship with Mr. Darcy proved my prejudices were many."

Ashford questioned, "Is it possible, Mrs. Darcy, you misconstrue your husband's motives again?"

Elizabeth paused briefly, looking off into space. "My dream
would be to find this is a nightmare, and I would wake in my
husband's arms; but I fear those dreams cannot come true."

"Mrs. Darcy, what should I do?" Ashford's tone held his sorrow.

"Go find my sister and make your plans. Love and cherish
Kitty, and you will prove all my dreams are not pure frustra-
tion." Elizabeth grasped his hand. "Now, off with you. Find
Kitty—she will be gone tomorrow."

"Yes, Mrs. Darcy." Ashford stood reluctantly. "I am forever
your servant." With that, he bowed and made his exit.

Ashford found Kitty in the music room. She buried her face in
her hands, and sobs rocked her shoulders. Ashford rushed
forward and knelt in front of her. "Miss Bennet," he spoke
softly, "please look at me."

"I cannot," she nearly wailed.

He pleaded, "Please, Kitty, we must talk now."

Kitty stifled her tears and tried to raise her eyes to meet his.
"I am sorry to be such a trouble to you, Sir," she finally
managed to say.

"You did nothing wrong," he tried to assure her. "We just
must decide what will be our next action." Ashford stood up
and walked over to the pianoforte, mindlessly stroking some of
the keys.

Kitty watched him walk away; her heart dropped, realizing
how much she came to depend on his regard, and the thoughts
of how she would miss Clayton Ashford in her life nearly
brought her to tears again. But, she would not let what was
happening in her own life hurt the man she learned to love.
Finally, Kitty stood and squared her shoulders. "Mr. Ashford,"
she said the words with resolve, "I release you from our
engagement, Sir."

Ashford spun around, not expecting Kitty's reaction to their situation. "You do what?" he exclaimed.

Kitty tried to steady her voice; she raised her chin to look into his eyes. "I release you from your promise of marriage." Her voice broke despite her efforts.

"No!" Ashford rushed forward. "I will not have it; you promised to marry me," he nearly pleaded.

Trying to control her emotions, Kitty looked away as he took her by the shoulders. "Your marrying me will cost you dearly." Her voice came out small.

"Katherine, look at me," he demanded of her. "Do you not love me?"

Kitty could deny herself no longer. "Yes, I love you, Clayton; that is why I must let you go. Mr. Darcy will not tolerate your marrying me; you owe your living to him." Kitty tried to pull away, but Clayton Ashford would have none of it.

"Mr. Darcy does not own me, Katherine; I have my own ideas and my own abilities to provide for you as my wife. You cannot refuse me; I cannot live without you. You scare me when you say such things; my heart cannot take the possibility I may have to spend my life without you." By now, Ashford's arms encircled her.

"What will we do?" Kitty buried her face into his shoulder.

Feeling relief at her giving in, he whispered into Kitty's ear, "First, you will give me your assurance you will still be my wife."

Impulsively, Kitty kissed along his chin line, punctuating her words with a staccato of kisses. "Clayton Ashford . . . I will . . . marry you . . . and share . . . your life."

"I may need for you to remind me of your regard from time to time," Ashford teased as he lifted her chin to look into Kitty's eyes.

"Any time, my Love," she smiled at him.

"Then let us together decide what we must do," he said as he led Kitty to adjoining chairs.

"Elizabeth will not let Mr. Darcy drive her away in shame; she plans to leave on her own terms," Kitty confided.

"Your sister is a proud woman." Ashford showed his respect. "Miss Bennet, could Mrs. Darcy be mistaken?"

"Oh, no," Kitty blushed, "I saw the letter."

Ashford demanded, "What letter?"

"Lizzy received letters from both Miss Darcy and our Aunt Gardiner indicating Mr. Darcy spends much of his time with a lady of the *ton*. Elizabeth overheard Mr. Darcy tell Colonel Fitzwilliam he would send my sister away. Today an intimate letter came for Mr. Darcy from the same lady seen with him in London. The lady even included a lock of her hair; how could my sister mistake that? Mr. Darcy does poorly by Elizabeth."

"I find it hard to believe Mr. Darcy could love anyone but your sister. The look in his eyes when she announced their child spoke volumes of his love." Ashford reached for Kitty's hand; speaking of love and children created a powerful need in him to feel her closeness.

"These great men are only concerned with their heirs," Kitty added as she tightened her hold on Ashford's hand.

"Never doubt my love for you." Ashford brought her hand to his lips to kiss it tenderly.

"Nor mine for you," Kitty returned his regard.

"When will you leave Pemberley?" he asked, dreading her answer.

"Elizabeth must leave soon—before Mr. Darcy's return. Her condition limits how much time she has before her lying in. I will return to Longbourn tomorrow. My sister will continue her duties for a few days before she follows me; Elizabeth plans to stay with Mr. and Mrs. Bingley at Netherfield."

"Then I will seek another living; I will come for you as soon as I can secure another position. Will you wait for me, my Dearest?" Ashford was on his knees in front of her once again.

Kitty leaned forward to brush his lips with hers; she heard his quick intake of air. "I will wait; I love you, Clayton."

Against the rules of conduct, Ashford captured Kitty's lips with his. She would be gone tomorrow, and he could chastise himself then.

The next day Kitty left for Longbourn. Elizabeth diverted her eyes when Kitty impulsively slipped her arms around Mr. Ashford's waist and kissed him lightly before stepping into the Darcy carriage.

"Give our parents my love," Elizabeth said loud enough for the servants to hear.

"I will miss you, Lizzy." Kitty sniffled and dabbed her eyes with a handkerchief. "Take care of yourself and the child." Kitty looked worried.

"I will do my best," Elizabeth returned as she stepped away from the coach.

Mr. Ashford gave Kitty a proper bow. "Miss Bennet," he said as he, too, stepped away to allow the coachman free rein, and the coach to slowly pull away.

Elizabeth asked Mr. Ashford in for tea, but he declined, begging off with an excuse of calling on some parishioners. Elizabeth knew the man needed time to assimilate to the changes in his life. With Kitty's departure, he had to look for another position, and today seemed a good day to start that search.

For the next several days, Elizabeth maintained her regular schedule; she called on several of her favorite tenants. She traveled into Lambton on the premise she needed to have a few new day dresses made. While in the village, she paid one of the street urchins five schillings to mail the letters she wrote. She instructed the child to mail one each day for the next four days. She provided him the additional funds for the posting fees. That matter resolved, Elizabeth returned to Pemberley.

Discreetly, she chose clothing and personal items, placing them where she could reach them easily. She planned to leave Lady Anne's jewelry and the other expensive gifts Darcy gave her. She hated most of all to leave Hero, finally deciding to take the dog with her.

The newspapers provided her two options for her escape. Now, with her time at Pemberley limited, she chose a ship leaving midweek in the first part of the month for the Americas. She would leave out of Bristol. Elizabeth hated taking money from Darcy's household funds for her trip, but she had no choice. With no fortune of her own, she would depend on her husband one last time.

Likely, she would give birth aboard ship, an idea that petrified her. With no one she knew to help her, she would be at the mercy of strangers. Mr. Harrison gave her the names of several dependable captains and vessels from which to choose. The ship leaving out of Bristol would take her to Virginia. Elizabeth had the names of people to contact upon her arrival in the States. She expected to take a position as a schoolteacher, being given a small house, a place where she could raise her child in private. It was a gamble, but she had no other options. If she stayed in England, she would be a shamed woman, and Darcy would have her child; she had no legal rights.

Everything was in place; now all she had to do was play the role of the concerned daughter, pretending to rush to Hertfordshire to care for a parent. Tomorrow, she would leave Pemberley.

After retiring to her room, Elizabeth penned a letter to Darcy, explaining her actions. She had not been in his study since the day Miss McFarland's letter arrived. In fact, the letter still lay on the desk, along with the lock of hair. She forbid any of the servants to touch the study—to disturb the evidence she would leave for his eyes—a way to disclose his deceit. Part of her prayed he would feel sorrow at his loss; part of her wanted Darcy to allow her to start over.

30 April

My dearest Fitzwilliam,

By the time you read this, I will be gone from Pemberley and no longer a part of your life. I leave you, my Love, so you may find true happiness with someone of your own kind. I shall love you for the rest of my life, and I thank you for giving me some of the most complete days I ever knew.

I leave behind all the gifts, which rightly belong to whomever you choose to be your wife. I take only a few personal gifts by which to remember you and to remember the love we once knew.

Please do not try to find me. I purposely deceived even my own family for they think I am on my way to Longbourn. Fitzwilliam, I beg you to get on with your life. I will never request more of you than that. The love I once offered you came from knowing the man you were when we came together; knowledge of your wealth and status was never part of the formula.

Tell Georgiana I cherish the love and respect she freely gave me. Having her as a part of my life was a blessing I could never repay.

Upon reflection, my qualms over never being able to replace your mother as the true Mistress of Pemberley played out. You once told me our love would be freer, more open—more hopeful than the loves our parents knew. If only your words could be true, but I failed as your wife, and now I release you from your promise to me. Be happy, my Love. This will be the last time I will claim the privilege of calling myself

Your loving wife,
Elizabeth Darcy

Elizabeth closed the letter, using the Darcy seal in the hot wax. She left the message on the mantel in their joint sitting room. Others would not find it there, but Darcy would discover it; he regularly stood in front of the fireplace enjoying the heat of the flame; he would see it there.

After a restless night, Elizabeth boarded the small coach, having feigned news of her mother's worsening health. Mrs. Reynolds clearly did not want her to leave, but Elizabeth, who packed most economically, assured both Mrs. Reynolds and Hannah she would be gone no longer than necessary, which was a back-door lie, but a believable one. Taking Hero made the deception more plausible, and by midmorning Elizabeth was on her way.

Her condition required her to spend the night at an inn. The next morning she told the coachman she received news her mother was taken to Bath for its medicinal waters, and she instructed the coach to take her there.

Arriving in Bath, Elizabeth disembarked at a moderately priced inn. Assuring Darcy's staff she would not need them any longer because her father's coach would serve her needs, she sent Darcy's men home. Reluctantly, they obeyed. Finally, she was alone with no one to which to turn.

CHAPTER 23

"If the first calculation is wrong, we make a second better:
we find comfort somewhere."
Jane Austen, *Mansfield Park*, 1814

Darcy kept hours at his club, having put into action his plan to reestablish Elizabeth's reputation as his wife. He drummed up conversations, turning each discourse to a description of his "amazing" Elizabeth. A few of his closer acquaintances made comments, which indicated they thought his inclination to be elsewhere. Darcy hated the fact his headstrong nature created such a Gordian knot. He wished for nothing more than to be at Pemberley with Elizabeth, but until he could check the rumors surrounding him, he would remain in London.

Mr. Harrison called upon Georgiana as he promised. She greeted him with delight; despite how it might look to others, she rode out with him. They drove through Hyde Park, and then he took her to Gunter's for the cream ice. Young men risked life and limb waiting on the various carriages peppering the east side of Berkeley Square.

As was proper, Mr. Harrison stopped the curricle and climbed out. Unmarried couples could not sit together in a carriage and talk, but a young man could stand beside the carriage and speak to his ladylove without raising too many eyebrows. A waiter scurried over, and Mr. Harrison turned on his charms, ordering each of them a flavored cream ice and a strong English tea. The waiter disappeared behind another carriage, adroitly darting between the harnesses.

"Miss Darcy, may I speak of your loveliness today?" Harrison smiled up at her.

Georgiana returned his happiness. "It seems, Mr. Harrison, whether I agree or decline, you already made your thoughts known."

He laughed lightly. "So, I did, fair maiden," he teased. "Was that not a most advantageous move on my part?"

"You are fortunate, Sir, I possess the disposition to forgive your teasing nature," Georgiana added.

Harrison overexaggerated his bow to her as he said, "A goddess of beauty and a forgiving disposition—I am blessed among men."

"Do not forget it, Sir." Georgiana gave him a pretend pout.

"Never, fair lady." Harrison's eyes came to rest upon her, and he lowered his voice so others could not hear. "You, Miss Darcy, are my imagination—my dreams—come to life." His voice was husky with desire.

Georgiana blushed, but for once, she did not look away. She drank in his face, caressing each line with her eyes. "Mr. Harrison, I should reprimand you for your boldness," she started.

"Yet, you will not," he said, in assurance.

"I will not—never to you," she whispered, unable to remove her eyes from his countenance.

"Georgiana." The use of her familiar name was an intimate gesture. "I made a promise to your sister Mrs. Darcy, but I now feel that promise to be void."

Georgiana for a few seconds was lost to the sound of his voice, and Harrison's words did not register at first. "A promise to Elizabeth?" she asked.

Mr. Harrison blushed slightly. "You are aware I promised Mrs. Darcy I would not declare myself to you until your next birthday, but if you are to receive offers in London, I must let you know my dreams lie in your hands."

"Mr. Harrison," Georgiana stumbled over the words, "I cannot go against my sister's wishes; Elizabeth would not ask this of you unless she feared for my future somehow. I trust Elizabeth's instincts. However, I will promise you this—I will accept no others until my next birthday."

"Even if your brother insists?" Harrison's face showed the pain he felt at those words.

"Fitzwilliam will not force me into an unwelcome marriage," Georgiana tried to assure him.

The waiter returned at that moment, carrying a tray with teacups. They took the offering, amused by the novelty of sharing the tea publicly. When they finished, Mr. Harrison joined Georgiana in the curricle once more and began to maneuver the horses through the crowded street. As they cleared the worst of the clamor, Mr. Harrison leaned toward her. "Georgiana, if Mrs. Darcy was not around, would you feel differently?"

"Why would Elizabeth not be around?" Georgiana looked confused.

Harrison paused, not wishing to betray Elizabeth's confidences, but needing to claim Georgiana's affections. "Mrs. Darcy will not, I think, wait for your brother to send her away."

Georgiana took in his words in all seriousness. "My brother stays in London only to squelch the rumors; otherwise, we would be returning to Pemberley."

"I am pleased to hear it. Mrs. Darcy has my deep respect."

Georgiana taunted, "Even if my sister keeps us apart?"

"I can tolerate much if I am allowed the opportunity to present myself to you properly." Harrison brought the carriage to a halt in front of Kensington Place.

Georgiana smiled largely at him. "You will be granted the opportunity, Sir."

Harrison handed her down from the carriage, allowing himself the pleasure of letting his fingers rest on her waist a few seconds longer than propriety required. "I will be patient, Miss Darcy."

Henry Dorchester appeared at Kensington Place after dinner. Neither Darcy nor Georgiana expected his call. "Dorchester?" Darcy offered his hand in greeting, but Dorchester returned only a polite bow.

Immaculately dressed, as usual, Henry Dorchester glided to the seat offered by Darcy. Georgiana sat quietly in a corner, attending to her embroidery. Dorchester took out his handkerchief to wipe the glass of port Darcy handed him while Darcy sucked in his breath in contempt. "Dorchester, this is an unexpected pleasure." He seated himself across from the man.

The visitor looked about the room, allowing his eyes to come to rest on Georgiana. "Maybe, Mr. Darcy, we should speak without an audience."

"I have no secrets from my sister, Dorchester." Darcy's voice indicated how unhappy this conversation made him.

"Very well then," Dorchester began, "some of what I have to say involves Miss Darcy as well."

Darcy offered the man no encouragement; the expression on his face showed no emotions. Finally, Dorchester cleared his throat. "Mr. Darcy, my mission is a delicate one, and it pains me to come here this evening." Darcy did not respond; his expression did not change, but if Dorchester knew him better, he would recognize the danger in angering him. When Darcy offered no comment, Dorchester took the freedom of taking the conversation to the next level. "My family takes offense, Sir, with your actions toward my cousin Cecelia. You played poorly by her."

"I take offense, *Sir,* your family thought I might be so debased as to defile my marriage vows. My wife, *Sir,* owns my heart now and forever." Darcy fought the urge to physically remove the man from his house.

Dorchester flushed, not expecting Darcy to respond as such. "I see; you do not intend to even apologize to my cousin for your actions?"

"I do not see I have anything of which to apologize, but if I offended Miss McFarland, I will plead ignorance of my offense."

"That is not the same as an apology, Mr. Darcy."

Darcy now displayed an amused smile upon his face. "It is the best I can do under the circumstances."

"And what of Miss Darcy's shameful actions today?" Dorchester's voice rose in inflection. Georgiana's head shot up; she did not want Darcy to know about her afternoon with Mr. Harrison. "You cannot expect me to offer your sister my regard if she carries on so in public." Dorchester puffed up with disdain.

"My sister is a fine lady." Darcy seethed with anger.

"Then you gave your permission for her accompanying a gentleman in public?" Dorchester accused.

Darcy shot his sister a quick glance, and he saw Dorchester's truths playing on her face. Instinctively, Darcy knew with whom Georgiana spent her time. "Mr. Harrison is a dear family friend; I trust him implicitly with my sister."

Dorchester did not expect Darcy to give his permission to Georgiana. As her guardian, Darcy must approve of her outing. "I still cannot consider such an alliance under the circumstances, especially if your friendship lies with the likes of Chadwick Harrison."

Darcy accepted all the censure he would tolerate. Criticism of his actions was one thing; he deserved it, but Georgiana did not. "Then I suppose this conversation is at an end." Darcy stood to show Dorchester to the door. "Your disdain is noted, Sir, but I am not of the habit of being told to whom I may offer my friendship. Mr. Harrison always treats my family with respect, and I return it gratefully." By now, Darcy held the door open for Dorchester.

"Well!" Dorchester huffed, as he quickly exited the room and the house.

Darcy growled, "Insufferable poppycock!"

"I am sorry, Fitzwilliam," Georgiana sobbed.

He crossed the room, taking her hand and pulling his sister to her feet. Darcy encircled her with his arms, clutching her to his chest. "We will have no more words of apology, Georgiana," he whispered.

Georgiana moaned, "I should have never gone without a chaperone."

"Did you do anything of which you should be ashamed?"

She gasped, "No, Fitzwilliam—never!"

"Then it is done; I cannot criticize you for I did so much worse." Darcy buried his face in her hair.

"Elizabeth will be ecstatic to have you home." Georgiana kissed the side of his cheek.

"Will she?" Darcy's voice held his worry.

"I have not changed my opinion," she assured her brother. "You and Elizabeth have a great love; you simply must find each other again."

"I pray you are correct, my Dearest One." He kissed her hand. "Now, come sit with me and honestly tell me about your day."

From the time the Darcys severed their connection with the Dorchesters, a week passed. Darcy and Georgiana continued to attend art displays, concerts, and the theatre. They enjoyed the company of several of Darcy's friends from his university days. He claimed an allegiance of those he knew for many years. He abandoned the "show" much of the *ton* regularly displayed. He secured his position in society, but Darcy shunned the frivolity found by the Dorchesters and others of lesser consequence.

Shamefaced, Darcy made a trip to the Gardiner home in Cheapside. Surprisingly, they greeted him with all civilities. While there, he spoke to Elizabeth's aunt and uncle about his undying love for their niece. He tried to explain to them his confusion after his return from Hull, and they related his transformation to the one he took before. Darcy assured them he would return to Elizabeth and Pemberley soon. The Gardiners knew him to be a man of his word and realized how much it cost such a proud man to confess his weaknesses. He left them with an invitation to Pemberley before Elizabeth's lying in.

During the week, both he and Georgiana received letters from Elizabeth. They were simple, loaded with news of the estate. He hoped for words of affection from her, but Elizabeth offered very little in her correspondence. Darcy did not blame her; he treated her badly. He offered his wife moments of tenderness, and then he turned on her and boldly judged his Elizabeth by standards he no longer considered important. If he could earn her forgiveness, Darcy would cherish her forever.

Colonel Fitzwilliam came to Kensington Place, hoping to spend the night before traveling on to Bath. "Darcy, it is good to see you," Edward laughed lightly upon seeing Darcy's drawn expression.

"You are to Bath?" Darcy asked as he poured his cousin a drink.

"Anne awaits my arrival; then we will return to Rosings." Edward gladly took the drink. "You seem less than pleased to be here, Darcy," Edward noted out loud.

"My return to Pemberley cannot come soon enough." Darcy held the glass to his lips but did not drink.

Edward knew Darcy's nature better than anyone. "Has not your time been well spent?"

"This was a foolish consideration; Georgiana fared well, but she still prefers the attentions of Mr. Harrison to all others." Darcy's countenance softened when he spoke of his sister. "And I am of the belief she should experience love; I will not force my sister into an arranged marriage."

Edward asked, "Is Mr. Harrison not a legitimate suitor?"

"Mr. Harrison's value increases each time I take his worth. I am not ready to part with Georgiana, but I can accept it when she makes her choice." Darcy seemed more at ease with his recipience.

"And what of your wife?" Edward cautiously approached the subject.

"Elizabeth's regard may be lost forever. I was quite foolish; in my rush to create a world of opportunities for my sister, I neglected my wife."

Edward took note of his cousin's self-censure. "Then the rumors my parents share are true?"

Darcy's head snapped up in shock. "What rumors, pray tell!"

"My father writes you replaced Mrs. Darcy with Miss McFarland." Edward leaned forward in his seat as if sharing a secret.

Darcy moaned and buried his face in his hands. "What have I done to my wife? I tried to replace my feelings for Elizabeth with the approval of fine society. Miss McFarland assumed I would return her regard, but I cannot get the image of Mrs. Darcy out of my mind. She is perfect for Pemberley."

"Elizabeth is perfect for you," Edward added quickly.

Darcy laughed lightly. "So, I am finding out."

"Then what will you do, Cousin?" Edward seemed serious.

"I plan to stay in London for at least a fortnight. I must check the spread of rumors, which might hurt Mrs. Darcy. If I leave now, busy tongues could destroy Elizabeth's reputation. She does not deserve such censure." Darcy laid out his plan.

"It is appropriate to protect your wife, Fitz," Edward added quickly. "Have you considered letting Mrs. Darcy know you plan to return home to her?"

Darcy's remorse returned. "I know not what to say to her."

"Tell her of your regard—tell her of your dreams for the two of you. Let Mrs. Darcy know the pledge of your love. I fear, Fitz, if my parents heard the rumors so has Elizabeth."

"How do I tell her of my chagrin?"

"Speak from your heart; Elizabeth will believe you."

Darcy nodded, accepting his cousin's advice. "Will you take a letter to Pemberley for me before you go to Bath?"

"It would be my pleasure, Fitz," Edward added with a sigh of relief.

Late in the evening, Darcy sat at the desk in his sitting room. Several wadded papers lay on the floor, not having made it into the lips of the flame of the fireplace. Darcy knew not what to say to his wife.

7 May

My dearest Elizabeth,

I sit at this desk surrounded by the finest things money may buy, but I have nothing of value around me for you, my dearest, loveliest Elizabeth, are not with me, and I wish more than anything I could see you now. I am embarrassed by my loneliness, for I should be complete; yet, a void exists which only your love can fill.

If you forgive me for my foolishness, I will be the happiest of men for my love for you is as strong as ever. I love how I can spend the day with you and still want more of your time. I love the raise of an eyebrow or an enigmatic smile when I say something challenging. I love the smell of lavender as it clings to my clothes long after I leave your embrace.

Georgiana and I return to Pemberley in a fortnight. Please send me word that you, my Dearest, will think kindly of me until I come home to you. I am yours as always, my Lizzy.

F.D.

Darcy sealed the letter, hoping it would change the course of his relationship with Elizabeth. His cousin's words echoed in his head as he crawled into bed and welcomed dreams of Elizabeth to his sleep. "Do not let your past dictate who you are. Instead, let it be the foundation, cousin, of whom you will become. Be Fitzwilliam Darcy, Master of Pemberley."

★ ★ ★

Colonel Fitzwilliam rode his mount into the carriageway at Pemberley. He half expected either Elizabeth or Kitty to greet him, but other than Darcy's servants, no one appeared. He supposed the ladies to be making tenant visits or to be in Lambton. Upon entering the house, the colonel found only Mrs. Reynolds in attendance.

"Colonel, Sir," she fussed about, hurrying servants to their stations, "Mr. Darcy and Miss Georgiana are still in London."

The colonel handed her his coat and hat. "I am aware of that, Mrs. Reynolds. I stayed at Kensington Place on my way here." Looking around casually, he asked, "Where are Mrs. Darcy and Miss Bennet?"

He headed toward the drawing room, expecting someone there to receive him. Mrs. Reynolds's words stopped his progress. "Neither Mrs. Darcy nor Miss Bennet are at Pemberley, Sir."

The colonel turned quickly, unsure he heard her correctly. "What do you mean *neither* is here?"

Mrs. Reynolds fidgeted with her apron, smoothing it down. "Mrs. Bennet reportedly took ill; Miss Bennet was called home nearly a fortnight ago. A week later, Mrs. Darcy followed her sister."

"Mrs. Darcy has been gone for over a week, and no one cared to inform Mr. Darcy?" His voice was incredulous.

"Mrs. Darcy posted a letter to Master Fitzwilliam the day she left. I assumed she informed him of her whereabouts." Mrs. Reynolds was uncomfortable; her suspicions seemed more accurate than before. "Colonel Fitzwilliam," she stammered, "there is something else not quite right."

"Tell me now, Mrs. Reynolds," the colonel urged.

The housekeeper lowered her voice and stepped in closer to maintain secrecy. "The day before Mrs. Darcy sent her sister to Longbourn, she locked the master's study and gave orders no one should enter the room until Master Fitzwilliam returned home. Mrs. Darcy loved to sit in the master's chair when he was away at Hull and even when he was in London, and then suddenly Mrs. Darcy refused to go into the room or let anyone else enter. Something is not right, Colonel."

"I agree, Mrs. Reynolds; get me the key immediately," he demanded.

The housekeeper dropped him a quick curtsy and disappeared. The colonel let out an expletive as he paced the hallway. When Mrs. Reynolds returned with the room key, he entered the study, closing the door behind him, not allowing anyone else access. It took him only seconds to find the incriminating letter; Elizabeth left it lying open on Darcy's desk. Edward read it and cursed again. *Why would Miss McFarland send such a letter? Even if it were true, the note was an act of impropriety, one a lady of the* ton *would not write. Poor Elizabeth! She must be devastated.* The letter obviously had the reaction Miss McFarland wanted. Edward knew he had to contact his cousin; Darcy must go to Longbourn. The colonel was smart enough to make sure he had all the details before he contacted Darcy. First, he checked the house; Elizabeth left much of the things she accumulated since marrying Darcy. From what Edward could tell, she took nothing with her, which had not once belonged to her. Then he rode into Lambton to speak to Mr. Ashford. The man would know where Miss Bennet could be found.

"Miss Bennet has not written for several days," Mr. Ashford confided. "She arrived at Longbourn in a timely manner; they were awaiting Mrs. Darcy's arrival at Mr. Bingley's estate."

"If Mrs. Bennet is ill, why would Mrs. Darcy travel to Netherfield?" Edward questioned.

Mr. Ashford looked away uncomfortably. "You must know by now, Colonel, Mrs. Darcy left for personal reasons. She sent

Miss Bennet away because Mr. Darcy would not approve of her being here." Ashford cleared his throat before going on. "I drafted a letter to Mr. Darcy requesting a release from my living. I love Miss Bennet, and I *will not* abandon her." The last words were the closest thing the clergyman could offer in the form of a condemnation for his benefactor.

"Do not do anything hastily, Mr. Ashford; perhaps a solution is still at hand," the colonel cautioned. "I must contact Mr. Darcy."

Edward returned to the house. He drafted a letter to Darcy, enclosing the damaging letter from Miss McFarland, before sending one of the Pemberley staff riding for London. He sent another letter to Anne in Bath, telling her his arrival would be delayed for a few days. He offered her no explanation except Darcy needed him at Pemberley.

★ ★ ★

When his man delivered the letter from his cousin, Darcy's heart sank, knowing something must be amiss. He rushed to his study; with trembling hands, he broke the seal.

9 May

Darcy,

I will make this as short as possible for I know when you receive it you will want to be on the road immediately. Neither Mrs. Darcy nor Miss Bennet is at Pemberley. The enclosed letter will explain their departure. I confirmed with Mr. Ashford Miss Bennet is at Longbourn. Elizabeth left on 30 April for Netherfield. Mrs. Bennet will not welcome your wife in disgrace. Hurry, Darcy, you must go to Elizabeth before the riff is too wide to bring you two together again.

E. F.

Darcy nearly ripped apart the other page. A curse escaped his lips as he read the letter Miss McFarland sent to Pemberley. "She knew I was not there," he said to himself. "Poor Elizabeth! How will I make her forgive me?" He rushed from the room, handing Georgiana the letters as he passed her in the hall. Darcy ordered his carriage and sent Henry scrambling to pack his bags. Within the hour, he was on the road to Hertfordshire.

★ ★ ★

When he called at Netherfield, Mr. Bingley, although surprised to see him, welcomed Darcy with all civility. "Darcy," Bingley offered the familiar greeting, "it is pleasant to have you here."

"Mr. Bingley." Darcy gave him a proper bow. "I am sorry to come to Netherfield unannounced; I wish to speak to Mrs. Darcy."

Bingley looked at his old friend in astonishment. "I am afraid, Sir, that is impossible; your wife is not here."

"Is Mrs. Darcy with her parents? I understood Mrs. Bennet refused Elizabeth because of a misunderstanding. That is why I came here; the reason for Mrs. Darcy to come to Hertfordshire does not exist." Darcy's confusion was obvious.

"Mrs. Darcy has not arrived; we expected her earlier in the week, but my Jane received a post yesterday saying your wife was delayed at Pemberley." Bingley became anxious.

Darcy's own agitation consumed him. "I assure you, Mr. Bingley, Mrs. Darcy is not at our home; Colonel Fitzwilliam is there."

"Let me get you a drink, Darcy." Bingley indicated a nearby chair. "I will ask Mrs. Bingley to join us, and I will send my carriage to Longbourn for Kitty."

Darcy accepted the seat to which Bingley indicated. "Thank you, Mr. Bingley; it seems I owe you much."

Bingley acknowledged Darcy's comments with a nod of the head before exiting to find Jane Bingley. Darcy sat back in the chair and closed his eyes. Stepping into Netherfield brought him multiple images of Elizabeth; just turning his head, he could see her standing in a doorway or on the top of a staircase or walking in the garden. It made him want her even more than before, and he feared he let their love slip through his fingers.

"Mrs. Bingley." He stood in acknowledgment when Jane entered.

"Mr. Darcy." She dropped a curtsy and then gestured toward the chair once more. As she seated herself across from him, she added, "Mr. Bingley tells me you thought Lizzy to be here."

"Colonel Fitzwilliam is at Pemberley. Mrs. Reynolds says Mrs. Darcy left the estate nine days ago." Darcy filled her in with what he knew.

"My sister wrote she was delayed at the estate. What can this mean, Mr. Darcy?" Jane wrung her hands.

"Mrs. Bingley, I wish I knew."

"Do you know why Lizzy left, Mr. Darcy?" Accusations were evident.

"Mrs. Bingley, I admit to allowing myself to appear to change my affections for your sister, but it is all a misunderstanding. I kept company with people whom I thought would advance my sister's position in society; little did I know I would become the victim of some sick game, which, unfortunately, hurt Elizabeth. Yet, I swear to you, Mrs. Bingley, there is no truth to what your sister believes."

"I pray you speak the truth, Mr. Darcy."

"You know me well enough, Mrs. Bingley, to know I abhor every form of deception; I speak the truth when I say I want your sister in my life." Darcy tried to convince her.

Jane offered a reprimand. "You do not deserve Lizzy, Mr. Darcy."

Darcy dropped his eyes; he paused with the realization of the truth of Jane Bingley's words. "You are right, Mrs. Bingley, but I want her, and I want for nothing."

"I am pleased to hear it. Then let us find Elizabeth as soon as possible."

Kitty Bennet had little to add to what they already knew. She expected Elizabeth to follow within the week. Hearing how carefully Elizabeth planned their departure told Darcy finding his wife would be more difficult than he first expected.

"Mr. Darcy." Kitty faced him. "You once told me kissing Lizzy was like coming home. Then how could you hurt her so badly?"

"I thoroughly deserve your censure, Miss Bennet, but please help me find Elizabeth," Darcy pleaded with her.

"Elizabeth not only knew of that scandalous letter from Miss McFarland, she had letters from your own sister describing your constant company with the lady and a description of your confrontation with our uncle at the theatre." Darcy flinched with the knowledge his actions created this chaos. "Add to that Lizzy's hearing your conversation with the good colonel about your desire to send my sister away after her delivering your heir."

"I never said any such thing!" he protested, but then Darcy realized what Elizabeth must have heard. "I supposedly had this conversation with my cousin?"

"That is what Lizzy disclosed to me."

"I swear the conversation had nothing to do with your sister. It dealt with Lord Suterland's affair with Lady Midland." Darcy now understood everything. "Mrs. Darcy was deceived, and she deceived herself. I must find her, Miss Bennet, before Elizabeth does something foolish."

CHAPTER 24

*"Nothing is more deceitful than the appearance of humility.
It is often only carelessness of opinion, and sometimes an indirect
boast."*
Jane Austen, *Mansfield Park*, 1814

Darcy reluctantly spent the night at Netherfield Park, but civilities did not come easy to him. He retired to the guest room early, still haunted by thoughts of Elizabeth in this house. He departed for Pemberley at the crack of dawn. By the time he arrived at his estate, Elizabeth had been gone for nearly a fortnight. How could he find her after such a long time? Where could he begin to look?

"Darcy, I am glad you are here. I found out Mrs. Darcy told the coachman her mother went to Bath for the medicinal waters. He left her there." Edward greeted his cousin with the news.

"Could she still be there? It has been eleven days. Elizabeth must have planned her disappearance for some time." Darcy paced the room.

Edward looked frustrated. "I know not who else to ask."

"As early as possible, I will be off to Bath," Darcy thought out loud. "At least, it is a beginning."

"Hannah reports Mrs. Darcy took few personal belongings. From what I know, it appears Elizabeth took none of Lady Anne's jewelry or other gifts."

Darcy set his jaw line. "Elizabeth never wanted the jewels. It is not in her nature. Edward, I think I will see if I can find any clues in Elizabeth's rooms; I will join you after for dinner."

Edward was right; few things were missing from his wife's room. Frustrated, he forced himself into their shared sitting room. Walking to the mantel, he rested his head on his arm while drinking in heat of the dying embers. "Elizabeth," he whispered her name. "Why did you do this?" Looking up at last, he saw the corner of the letter, his initials clearly in the familiar flourish of his wife's script. Darcy grabbed the letter and took it over to the light to read.

His wife's words rushed through him. Elizabeth loved him enough to leave him because she thought him unhappy with her. She also feared his wrath. What had he done to her that Elizabeth would so fear and distrust him? What kind of husband was he to her? Darcy thought of their child—a child he would never know—never hold. Evidently, from what Kitty told him, Elizabeth thought he meant to send her away after the child was born. Contempt filled his heart as he wandered aimlessly to the nursery designed for their child. Walking to the window, in the dying light of the day, he could clearly see the field of wildflowers Elizabeth started especially to give him pleasure. Fully in bloom, the blossoms danced as the breeze rustled the growing stems. Tears misted his eyes as he grieved for what he lost. Somehow he must find her before she disappeared from his life forever.

A late post arrived from Georgiana, and Darcy for a few minutes considered not opening it. The posts brought him nothing but pain of late, and he knew he had no news, which Georgiana would want to receive in return.

11 May

Fitzwilliam,

I hope this letter finds you and my sister reunited, but I fear the worst. After reading the letters you left in my hands as you rushed to Netherfield, I remembered a conversation I had with Mr.

Harrison about Elizabeth. She confided some of her fears to him.
Our conversation included no specifics, but I suspected he knew
more of her departure than he disclosed at the time.

Knowing I could not contact Mr. Harrison myself, I took the
carriage to see Mr. Gardiner. I could think of no one else I could
trust with this information, which would not bring disgrace upon
Elizabeth. Mr. Gardiner sent a dispatch to Mr. Harrison begging
for his help.

Mr. Harrison's return post says Elizabeth plans to take
passage to America. He gave her the names of reliable captains and
vessels sailing out of both Bristol and Liverpool. Find her,
Fitzwilliam, before we lose her.

G. D.

Darcy nearly sank to his knees in defeat. "What if Elizabeth took passage already?" he asked as he turned to Edward, who sat reading Georgiana's letter. "She is alone; how will she survive the birth of our child?"

"Mrs. Darcy will not risk losing the child, Fitzwilliam," Edward assured him. "At least, we know Elizabeth is going to Bristol; otherwise, she would not go to Bath."

"Maybe she wants us to believe her in Bristol; Elizabeth could take a public conveyance to Liverpool," Darcy reasoned. "My wife went to a lot of trouble to disappear completely."

"Then what do you propose we do, Fitz?"

However, before Darcy could answer, a maid announced Mr. Bingley's arrival.

"Darcy." Bingley greeted him with a quick bow before turning to the colonel. "Colonel Fitzwilliam, I am pleased to see you."

"Welcome, Mr. Bingley," Edward stammered.

"I am sorry, Darcy," Bingley returned his attention to his old friend, "to come unannounced, but Mrs. Bingley insisted I follow you to Pemberley to help find Mrs. Darcy. Jane worries for her sister's safety and demands my participation in her recovery."

Darcy actually looked relieved. "We welcome your help, Bingley." Darcy forced himself to return to the familiarity of his former friend's name, hoping to resume Mr. Bingley's devotion.

"Have a seat. Let me order you some refreshments, and then we can map out a plan to recover my wife." Darcy knew Bingley to be a man he could trust.

They decided Bingley would travel to Liverpool; he would check the bill of lading for ships leaving for the Americas. Bingley would pay special attention to single women taking passage. Elizabeth had Hero with her; they knew not whether she planned to take the dog aboard ship, but it would be a clue. Colonel Fitzwilliam would do the same thing in Bristol. Darcy would go to Bath to see if Elizabeth waited there before departing to the seaport.

★ ★ ★

Elizabeth hated sitting around at the inn she chose, but she had little choice. She could not be seen out and about in Bath. She had been there five days; by now, it was likely Darcy knew of her leaving Pemberley. She knew not whether he would follow her. Part of her wished her husband would come for her—to love her once again. Yet, another part of Elizabeth hoped he would let her go in peace.

★ ★ ★

Another week passed, and although Elizabeth often looked over her shoulder expecting Darcy to appear around every corner, she saw no news in the society pages of his arrival in Bath. If she could go undetected for another week, she could travel to Bristol and leave England, her homeland, forever.

The inn she chose was a small economical one on a less-traveled road; she paid for the room in advance, and the inn-

410

keeper showed deference for Elizabeth's wishes. She and Hero walked along the back streets each day. Knowing England would soon be behind her, Elizabeth relished the little pleasures she observed, etching the memories on her mind. Her condition allowed her a certain amount of anonymity. The citizens of the area accepted her as a married woman of some consequence and allowed Elizabeth the freedom to move among them as she always did with strangers. Within days of her arrival in Bath, the locals greeted Elizabeth and sought her out for conversation. She could almost picture herself living here among these people if she did not fear Darcy would find her.

$$\star \star \star$$

Darcy had been in Bath for three days, but he found no trace of Elizabeth. Systematically, he checked each inn in hopes she had been there or, better yet, was still there. However, all his inquires were for naught. No one knew of an Elizabeth Darcy nor was there a married woman with child. He spent time among those taking the waters, searching the crowd for Elizabeth's face. Knowing his wife's propensity for long walks, Darcy searched the parks, but he discovered no signs of her.

Finally, inquiries among the public cab drivers gave him a lead. For a fee, one of the drivers remembered taking a lady who fit Elizabeth's description to a secluded inn on the outskirts of Bath. Darcy, sitting in the comfort of his carriage, prayed his wife might still be there.

The area reminded Darcy of Lambton or Meryton, and he realized he should have looked here first; Elizabeth would not choose a high-level inn, one costing a premium. It was not in her nature. These were simple shopkeepers, the type of people who would appreciate Elizabeth's true worth.

So, it did not totally surprise Darcy to see her walking along one of the side streets, Hero nipping at her heels. He tapped on the roof of the carriage, indicating he wanted the driver to stop. Disembarking, he began to follow her at some distance, fascinated at how shopkeepers stepped to the street to speak to Elizabeth and engage her in simple conversation. She was the type of person anyone would want to meet and to know.

Nearly upon her, Darcy paused with the pleasure of watching his wife work her magic on complete strangers. Hero must have caught his scent for the dog scurried away from Elizabeth and rushed to greet Darcy. The animal jumped up on his leg, and Darcy reached out automatically to pat its head, but he never took his eyes off of his wife's retreating form.

Elizabeth realized Hero lagged behind, and she turned to call the animal to her. When her eyes took in Darcy's form, she froze, swallowing hard. For a fleeting moment, she considered running, but the futility of such an action, especially in her condition, brought a light chuckle to her being.

"I assume, Mrs. Darcy," Darcy's voice played softly through the air, "you find something amusing about our situation."

"Do you not think it would amuse the members of the *ton* to know the great Fitzwilliam Darcy had to search out his wife among the shopkeepers of Bath?" Elizabeth refused his intimidating stance.

Darcy stepped closer to her, holding Elizabeth's eyes locked with his. "If it may ease your mind, Mrs. Darcy, your husband cares not for what amuses the *ton*." He took Elizabeth's hand and placed it on his arm. "It seems we need to talk, Elizabeth. Would you care to show me where you are staying?"

She did not know how to judge her husband's demeanor; he could be performing for those who watched their interactions from shop windows and street corners. Of course, it did not matter. She was his wife, his property; she had no legal rights so she accepted his arm and led him back toward the inn. "Come, Hero," she called as they took steps toward their future.

At the inn she introduced Darcy to the innkeeper as her

husband. The proprietor was surprised his roomer came from such an obviously privileged family. "Your wife quickly became a favorite among the locals," the innkeeper told Darcy as a form of respect.

"My wife is an amazing woman," Darcy spoke evenly. "Now, if you will excuse us."

"Certainly, Mr. Darcy," the man bowed deeply.

Darcy followed Elizabeth up the narrow steps to the room she let. When he closed the door behind them, Elizabeth expected him to attack her verbally, or even physically, for her deceit. She turned to face him, waiting for the other shoe to drop.

Darcy looked at her, turmoil playing across his face. "Elizabeth," he said so softly she could barely hear him.

"Yes, Fitzwilliam." She turned a cold stare on him. "You have something you wish to say to me?" She knew he won; she would have to return to Pemberley with him. Once she delivered his child, she would be out of his life, but she would not let him see how much the loss of his love would affect her.

Darcy saw her defiance, and although he wanted to lambaste her for what she tried to do to him, he could not fight the impulse to take her into his arms. In a second he was across the room and encircling her in a tight embrace. "Please forgive me," he whispered into her ear as he pulled Elizabeth next to him. His closeness soothed her anxiety for a moment. "Forgive me, Elizabeth," he whispered again. "I never meant to hurt you."

Darcy's closeness nearly undid her resolve; she hungered for his touch for so long Elizabeth clung to him without thinking. Eventually, though, reality crept in to her desire for him, and Elizabeth pushed away and walked toward the fireplace. "For what am I to offer absolution, Fitzwilliam?"

He looked at her in benign amusement. "I am a foolish man, Mrs. Darcy." For some reason, Darcy thought he should be offering more penance, but the manner in which Elizabeth spoke told him she was as confused as he.

"How foolish, Mr. Darcy?" she offered him a bit of a challenge in her voice.

He gave her a start of a smile. "Unfortunately, very foolish, Madam."

"Foolish enough to criticize your wife's family connections?" Elizabeth placed her hands on her hips and tried to look angry.

Darcy took a step toward her. "Guilty as charged."

"Foolish enough to consider your wife a complete wanton?" Her angry look began to fade.

"May I claim temporary insanity?" Once more he stepped toward her, a look of desire in his eyes.

"Foolish enough to leave your wife at Pemberley and to go off to London?" Her voice held more contempt than before.

"Guilty again." Darcy reached out and grabbed her hand. Elizabeth resisted, but he held strong.

"Foolish enough to consider sending your wife away and taking up with another woman?" Tears stung the corners of Elizabeth's eyes, and her lip trembled, but she refused to back down from him.

"I am afraid on those counts I must plead not guilty," he said evenly. "Just foolishness again."

Elizabeth reacted with disappointment for she thought he lied to her. She turned away from him. "Do you expect me to believe you?"

Darcy knew he must convince her immediately before the mood changed. "Elizabeth, you know me better than I even know myself sometimes, and you above all people know I abhor deceit of any kind; I do not lie to you. You heard Edward and me discussing Lord Suterland and Lady Midland's affair. I never thought of sending you away. As far as my relationships in London, I foolishly aligned myself with people I thought would aid my sister's presentation, but I never offered Miss

McFarland any regard. In fact when she approached me, I told the lady you own my heart."

Darcy saw her face soften some. "Then why did she send that letter?"

"That part, I cannot answer, but as soon as I realized her intentions, I severed all connections with the woman and her cousins." He reached out and lightly stroked her jaw line with his fingertips. "I love only you, Elizabeth; please believe me."

Elizabeth's lip quivered again. "I am afraid," she said at last.

"How afraid?" He smiled as he saw her close her eyes to his touch.

"Very afraid," Elizabeth gasped at the intimacy Darcy offered.

"Afraid enough to pretend to be attending to your sick mother while hiding out here?" Darcy began to tease her.

"Guilty," she smiled.

"Afraid enough to try to go to America to escape your husband's foolish nature?" He pulled her closer.

Elizabeth actually blushed this time. "Guilty again."

"Afraid enough to take five hundred pounds from the household accounts?" Darcy cupped her face in his hands.

"An early wedding present for my sister and Mr. Ashford." Elizabeth indicated her receptivity with a tilt of her head, moving close enough to feel his breath on her cheek. Darcy could stand it no longer; he captured her mouth with his.

"I will offer you absolution if you can see your way to forgive me," Darcy whispered to her again. "We are both far from perfect, but Edward says you are perfect for me."

"What do you say, Mr. Darcy?" Elizabeth brushed his lips with hers.

"I say, my Love, we lost some common memories, but we still share common places in our hearts. You promised I would be happy at Pemberley; you did not mean without you there, too. How can I be happy without you, Lizzy?" Darcy pulled her closer to him. "I admit there are elements of the ridiculous about you, my Love." He kissed her deeply. "However, I found my romance does not need a thing but you." Darcy laid her across the bed.

"Yet, Mr. Darcy, you do not seem inclined to act upon it." Elizabeth's teasing struck a cord.

"I suppose as your husband I should punish you for trying to leave me." Darcy's hand ran up the length of her body.

Elizabeth remained still, trying not to react to him. "Do you think, Mr. Darcy," her voice becoming breathy, "I might consider finding myself in a bed with you to be a punishment? If so, please exercise your husbandly rights anytime you wish."

Darcy kissed her tenderly, letting his lips linger next to hers. "Am I to assume, my Wife, I am forgiven?"

"I do not know, Fitzwilliam; *forgive* is a mighty powerful word. May I wait until I see how severe my punishment might be for trying to deceive you? If the punishment turns out to be as exquisite as I recall, I may have to consider disobeying you more often."

Darcy laughed. "You have no idea how much I missed you." His hands began to search the curves of her body. "And you, Mrs. Darcy, promised before God to love, honor, and *obey* me."

Elizabeth instinctively slid her arms around his neck and pulled Darcy to her; she kissed him deeply. They both found their breathing shallow, and a heat flushed her cheeks. As she spoke again, Darcy scattered light kisses about her face. "My connections have not improved," Elizabeth said after swallowing hard, "and when it comes to you, Mr. Darcy, I am afraid my wanton tendencies are out of control."

By now, Darcy was lost to loving her. "I am counting on it, Lizzy."

"Ah, that is not fair." She slid her hands under his waistcoat to caress the muscles of his back. "You know I cannot resist you when you call me Lizzy."

Darcy's smile totally encompassed her. "I am counting on

that fact, too, Lizzy." The kisses came faster and with more passion than either of them could remember.

An hour later, spent in each other's arms, Darcy stroked her cheek with the back of his hand. "Elizabeth, you are never to try to leave me again." He used his best Master of Pemberley voice.

"Give me one good reason to stay, Fitzwilliam." She kissed his chin line.

"I can give you a thousand reasons not to stay, but stay anyway." Darcy pulled her to him again, feeling the warmth of her body against his. "Stay because I love you most ardently."

Elizabeth leaned over him, her mouth resting above his. "Maybe, Fitzwilliam, I should stay because I love you most ardently."

"Those would be two excellent reasons to stay." The kisses demanded their undivided attention for another half hour.

"Lizzy," Darcy said at last, "I used to think I was special—privileged—but I am only wealthy. I am actually an ordinary person—but you make me special. You make me into a man of consequence—a man of value. I never want to be ordinary again. Do not ever think about leaving me. I shall not tolerate it, my Love."

"Love, honor, and *obey*," Elizabeth murmured as she kissed him again.

Elizabeth moved her things out of the inn, bidding farewell to all her new acquaintances. Darcy looked pleased, and Elizabeth could not take her eyes off his countenance. *His* coach took them back to *his* inn where they had a leisurely meal in *their* room. "I must send word to Bingley and to Edward you are found," he said casually, reaching out to caress her hand.

"You were quite thorough in your search, Sir." She challenged him the way he liked for her to do.

"I had a worthy opponent." Darcy's fingertips caressed her palm. "Perhaps you could inform your sister of your return to

Pemberley and your expectation of her return also. I prefer not to replace Mr. Ashford if possible."

"And what of Georgiana? Will she return to Pemberley soon?" Elizabeth bit her lower lip, not sure what Darcy would think about Georgiana leaving London.

"My sister wishes to return to our home. Once Mr. Harrison appeared at Lord and Lady Elliott's ball, my plans for her to find a *suitable* match changed. She is quite bold where that gentleman is concerned."

"Do you think Mr. Harrison encourages her boldness?" Elizabeth asked softly.

"I think Georgiana is as much in love with Mr. Harrison as I am with you, Mrs. Darcy." He lifted her hand and kissed it, softly brushing his lips across her knuckles.

Nearly unable to think of anything but her husband, Elizabeth stammered, "Then we will no longer object to Mr. Harrison's attentions toward Georgiana?"

"My objection to Mr. Harrison lies in his cooperation with you, my Love, in trying to make your escape." Darcy held her eyes with his. "Yet, if he makes Georgiana happy, I will accept him willingly in my home. Mr. Harrison is being courted for a position in the House of Commons. My sister would be moving in a powerful circle as Mr. Harrison's wife. My parents would be pleased with that fact."

Elizabeth's eyes flashed with the humor of it all, and Darcy braced himself for her next cut. "Then there was no need for your going to London, no need for all the stress of the past few months, and no need for my risking everything. Your sister's great love simply walked through our front door and presented himself as a man of honor. The irony cannot escape even your notice, Fitzwilliam."

Darcy offered her another of his devastating smiles. "It seems so, my dearest Elizabeth. Some day I may shamefacedly proclaim I taught the man everything he knows."

"Something to tell our grandchildren?" she laughed lightly.

"I will tell our grandchildren to be themselves—to listen to their hearts, while respecting their parents. I will also tell them childhood ends soon enough, and they will have the rest of their lives to try to forget it."

"Darcy philosophy again—you are very profound, my Husband." Elizabeth moved from her chair to sit on Darcy's lap.

He pulled her to him, needing to hold her once again. "The advantage of a university education." Darcy traced a line of kisses along her shoulder.

"You are a devastatingly handsome man, Fitzwilliam Darcy." Elizabeth grasped the back of his neck to keep his mouth near hers. "And I am blessed among women you chose me as your wife." Elizabeth kissed him deeply again, trying to convey her passion for him.

When he eased away from the intensity of her kisses, Darcy breathed deeply, trying to control his desires. "We cannot allow Bingley and Edward to search fruitlessly for something I hold in my grasp at this moment; however, I have needed you in my arms for so long, I wonder whether another hour could make a difference."

Elizabeth trailed her fingers along the line where his hair met the back of his shirt. "I do not see where an hour would make a difference to Mr. Bingley or the colonel, but to us, I believe we have put our lives on hold for too long."

When Elizabeth awoke, Darcy sat at the desk in the room penning one of his letters. She allowed herself the pleasure of watching him undetected for several minutes. *Lord knows I love this man,* she thought. "Will you not come back to bed, my Husband?" Her voice was husky with desire.

Draping his arm over the back, Darcy turned slowly in the chair. "Again, Mrs. Darcy?" He looked amused while drinking in the beauty of his Elizabeth. With her wrapped in the bedclothes and her auburn curls draped over the pillow, Darcy fought the urge to take her once more. "Should I not finish my letters, my Wife?"

"If you must, Sir, but I am a very impatient woman." Elizabeth offered him a pretend pout.

"Within moments, Mrs. Darcy." He looked at her lovingly before returning to his pen and paper. Elizabeth rolled over to cuddle with his pillow, breathing in deeply the essence of him left on the cushion.

Shortly, he returned to the bed. "May I join you, Madam?" Darcy gathered her hair in one hand and then bent to kiss the nape of Elizabeth's neck. Discarding his robe, he slid back under the counterpane with her. "I will remind you, my Love, some things are worth the wait." He took Elizabeth in his arms to reclaim her mouth.

Awakening late in the morning, Darcy ordered breakfast for their room. Finishing her toilette herself, Elizabeth dressed simply for the day. "Do we not return to Pemberley today?" Elizabeth asked when Darcy did not indicate she should pack her belongings.

Placing jam on his toast, Darcy dropped his eyes from hers when he said, "I thought we might stay in Bath for a few days. Anne is already here, and I am sure Edward will rush to her side now I no longer need his services in your pursuit. Would you not enjoy a few days alone?"

Elizabeth did not answer right away. "I brought nothing with me to merit being seen in Bath's society." Darcy hid something, and she knew not what it might be.

He gave her half a smile. "That will give me a good excuse to take you shopping, my Love."

Stalling before saying anything, Elizabeth poured them both some more tea. "Fitzwilliam, I would love a few days of just the two of us for I can never get enough of you, but you, my Love, are not adept at deception. What else should I know?"

Darcy placed the teacup back on the saucer; he did not want to tell Elizabeth about the McFarland rumors. "Elizabeth, you are right; I keep something from you because I want no more pain on your pretty face, but you should be aware of how my foolishness cost you."

Elizabeth stiffened with his words, dreading what her husband would say. Darcy cleared his throat before continuing. "Miss McFarland let many people know the same lies she placed in her letter. Rumors are rampant; the Matlocks told Edward. We will be under the eyeglass for some time. My absence from London will be noted." He left the rest unsaid.

Elizabeth's eyes misted over with tears. "Upon what are these rumors based, Fitzwilliam?" Her voice was barely audible.

Darcy moved immediately to kneel at her side. "Elizabeth, there was nothing between Miss McFarland and me; she and her cousins repeatedly accompanied Georgiana and me to different events, but I never purposely gave her any encouragement. At the Elliott ball, the lady at dinner slipped her hand into mine."

He heard Elizabeth begin to sob, and, desperately, Darcy caught her hand in his. He would not allow them to slip apart again. "Elizabeth, please, you must listen to me. I emphatically removed my hand from hers immediately. I told Miss McFarland I love you. She stormed from the room, much to the obvious amusement of many of our tablemates. After this incident, I wanted to come home to you immediately, but Georgiana heard the rumors from Mr. Harrison that evening. I never considered how tongues might wag. When Georgiana made me aware of what was being said, she and I agreed we would remain in London and publicly shun the Dorchesters. I made a point of singing your praises at each opportunity, as has Georgiana."

Elizabeth finally raised her chin and turned to look at him. Darcy's eyes held the truth she needed from him. "Then those in Bath," she said slowly, "need to see Mr. and Mrs. Darcy in love; you left London because I wanted a holiday before my lying in."

Darcy allowed the breath he held to escape with an audible sigh. "You are magnificent, Elizabeth." He leaned in to kiss her tenderly, cupping her chin line in his palm.

"I believe I am ready to spend your money, Sir." Elizabeth gave him a quick kiss before standing. "I hope your pockets are deep, Mr. Darcy. It will be my revenge on you for placing us in such a precarious position. I cannot resist your appeal so exacting my vindication must come in a more flamboyant way."

Darcy laughed at her directness. "I am your obedient servant, Mrs. Darcy." He made her a proper bow.

Without warning, Elizabeth rushed into his arms, nearly knocking Darcy over with the impact. "I love you, Fitz-william." She buried her face into the lapel of his coat. "I love you more than life."

"Elizabeth, I will spend the rest of my life taking away any doubts you have of me. We will raise our children to know love." He held her to him for several long, exquisite moments. Finally, he said, "If we do not leave, Mrs. Darcy, you will need no new clothes at all."

"Enough, Mr. Darcy—we must reestablish your wife's reputation as the Mistress of Pemberley, but first some form of penance on your part is necessary," she teased as she led him toward the bed.

CHAPTER 25

"What is right to be done cannot be done too soon."
Jane Austen, *Emma*, 1815

Darcy bought Elizabeth several expensive dresses as well as jewelry, along with a satin-lined pelisse. They walked through Royal Victoria Park, visited the Roman Baths, strolled along the Royal Crescent, and explored Sydney Gardens. They laughed; they cuddled, often pushing the lines of propriety. When Edward finally arrived in Bath, they joined Edward and Anne for dinner in a very public setting. To everyone Darcy introduced to Elizabeth, they told the same story: Darcy left Georgiana in London to bring his wife to Bath for a surprise holiday before the arrival of their child. Georgiana would return to Pemberley as soon as Darcy could properly escort her there.

After four days of constantly smiling for the public, Elizabeth asked, "May we not return to Pemberley soon, Fitzwilliam?"

He took her hand in his. "I was thinking the day after tomorrow, if that is acceptable to you, my Dear."

"It cannot be soon enough for me." Elizabeth leaned in to feel his closeness, and Darcy laced his arm around her waist.

Constantly needing Elizabeth's assurances, Darcy asked, "Then you are satisfied at Pemberley?"

"Wherever you are, my Love, is my home, but how could I not love Pemberley. It is a part of you; Pemberley runs through your veins, and now with this child, it runs through mine."

Although in a very public forum at the time, Elizabeth's words were nearly Darcy's undoing. He cupped his free hand over hers and pulled Elizabeth closer. "I love you, my Wife, with all my heart; when you are not with me, I cannot get you off of mind. I love you most ardently."

In the carriage ride home, Darcy finally got enough nerve to ask something that had bothered him for some time. "Elizabeth, when I left for London the first time, I left a letter of apology with Hannah. I told you of my wishes for our happiness—our life together. I waited for a response from you, but one never came. Did you stop loving me during that time?" Obvious pain showed on his face.

"Fitzwilliam." She motioned for him to move to the seat bench next to her. When he complied, Elizabeth turned so she could look at him directly; they had a connection where their eyes told the true story. "When I saw the letter that morning, I could not face the possibility you planned to send me away from Pemberley. I never opened the letter; it is in my drawer in my dressing room."

"You never read it?" A bit of relief overspread his face. "I thought for the past two months you did not want me in your life."

Elizabeth laughed lightly. "I thought the same thing, but for different reasons. We always misconstrue each other. Do you suppose, Mr. Darcy, either of us will ever be secure in the knowledge of the other's regard?"

"I certainly hope so, my lovely Wife; the pain I felt when I needed your comfort is not something I would wish to live with forever." Darcy kissed her cheek lightly.

Elizabeth turned and snuggled into his shoulder. "I would wish more of this in my life—simply more of this."

★ ★ ★

Their return to Pemberley seemed so natural; it was where

they both belonged. They walked the grounds; they shared their passions; they rode out in the warm sunshine; they picnicked in the field of wildflowers. Life for Darcy could not seem more complete than it did in those days. He knew he should not leave Georgiana alone in London, but for the life of him, all he could think about was being with Elizabeth. He reasoned his sister could still attend some of the concerts with Mrs. Annesley, and his lack of presence would keep callers from making offers to her. Georgiana, he persuaded himself, would welcome not having the social obligations, and for him, he never felt such contentment.

One day, he rode out with Mr. Howard to inspect the crops, but because of his renewal of husbandly privileges with Elizabeth, he spent the whole time daydreaming of taking her to his bed. She was over seven months with child, but Darcy felt like a lovesick newlywed.

When he entered their bedchamber that evening, he expected to find Elizabeth there, but an empty room disappointed him. When she did not appear right away, he sought her out in the upper rooms. A flickering candlelight led him to the nursery. There she sat in the chair next to the child's crib, softly singing a lullaby. Darcy remembered an image of Elizabeth singing at a pianoforte, and the clarity of her voice mesmerized him as it did now.

He waited in the shadows until she finished. "Our child will be blessed, Elizabeth, to be lulled to sleep with such melodies." Darcy's voice took his wife by surprise, but she turned to him with a smile on her face.

"I should chastise you, Sir, for eavesdropping. This is my time with our child." Elizabeth's smile told Darcy her reprimand was in jest.

"I missed you, Mrs. Darcy; it seems I cannot make it through the day without your embrace." Darcy stepped into the room and offered Elizabeth his hand.

She stood and moved willingly into Darcy's arms. "Kiss me," he whispered into Elizabeth's ear.

Before she could answer, Darcy's body backed her up against the windowsill as he covered Elizabeth's mouth with his. She threw her arms around Darcy's neck and returned his kiss. The passion coursed through both of them. Elizabeth relaxed against his powerful body; it felt so good to be in Darcy's arms after all the months of uncertainty. Pressing her back against the window frame, his tongue parted her lips and passionately sought out the willingness she offered. All his thoughts dwelt in the delight of having Elizabeth in his arms and feeling her desire grow with his. Darcy's hand slid down Elizabeth's arm and then moved up to cup her breast as she arched into his touch, her own hands caressing his muscular back.

When Darcy finally broke the kiss, his chest rose and fell, rapidly breathing, as he stared deep into Elizabeth's passion-filled eyes. "How have I survived eight and twenty years without loving you? Now, I want you, my Lizzy, with me every second of every day."

Elizabeth murmured, "It is part of my plan, Fitzwilliam."

"What plan would that be, fair lady?" He kissed along her neck.

Elizabeth slid her hands up under his shirt. "My purposeful plan to possess you body and soul."

Darcy moaned with her touch. "You are bewitching, my Love, and your plan is complete."

★ ★ ★

Georgiana Darcy enjoyed London since her brother left her to her own devices. Fitzwilliam rushed away to find Elizabeth; it pleased Georgiana her brother finally realized how important Elizabeth was in his life. It pleased her more Fitzwilliam delayed his return to London because he wanted to be with Elizabeth.

When she met Darcy's friends in the park or at the concert, she explained how he and Elizabeth went to Bath with their cousins to serve as chaperones for the engaged couple and to share a holiday before Elizabeth's lying in. It pleased Georgiana to innocently add a comment about how now Darcy was home with his wife, he did not want to leave her alone at Pemberley. She would finish with how they decided for an abbreviated season, and Georgiana would return home soon.

She knew some people believed her; some took a wait-and-see attitude, and some preferred the gossip to the truth; yet, Georgiana cared not. Unlike her brother, Georgiana Darcy never cared for what others thought. She preferred a simple life full of music and helping others.

Darcy would return to London mid-June to take her back to Pemberley. They would call at Longbourn to secure Kitty as help for Elizabeth and the child. Darcy's letter indicated he did not wish to be long from his wife's side. Georgiana had a fortnight left to be home again.

★ ★ ★

Darcy and Elizabeth walked leisurely in the garden, enjoying the early summer warmth. Elizabeth leaned on him, allowing his muscular frame to support her weight. Her head rested on Darcy's shoulder when they sat together on a stone bench. "The sun feels wonderful after the overcast skies of the last few days," Darcy said absent-mindedly.

"I suppose," Elizabeth responded.

Darcy, recognizing his wife's propensity for being outside in all elements, turned to her immediately. "Do you feel poorly, my Love?"

Elizabeth shifted uncomfortably on the bench. "I cannot speak of feeling more than a bit uncomfortable. If I were not with child," she said with a blush to her cheeks, "I would suspect my courses were upon me." Something she would never discuss with her sisters, Elizabeth now explained to Darcy. The irony of how her life changed played across her mind.

Darcy asked in all concern, "Should we return to the house?"

"Would you mind if I chose to return to my chambers? I feel so tired today."

Darcy stood and offered Elizabeth his hand. "Come, Mrs. Darcy, I will not have you overextending yourself on my account."

Elizabeth stood, but a pain surged through her, and she could no longer ignore the situation. "Fitzwilliam," she gasped and clutched desperately at his arm.

Instinctively, Darcy scooped her into his arms. "I have you, my Love," a bit of panic laced through his voice. He took long strides as he approached the side entrance to the estate. He ordered one of the footmen to bring Mr. Spencer immediately. Upon entering the house, Darcy yelled for Mrs. Reynolds's help, carrying his wife toward her bedchamber.

"I am sorry, Fitzwilliam," Elizabeth sobbed, her head buried into the side of his neck.

Her words brought the fear he felt to the forefront. Could she lose the baby, or, even worse, could he lose her? "Mr. Spencer is on his way, Lizzy; I will protect you; I will let nothing happen to you." His words seemed useless under the circumstances for Darcy could do little to change what might happen.

As he laid her back against the pillows of her bed, the fear in Elizabeth's eyes shot through him. He never saw her this way—this was the same woman who never backed down from him—from Mr. Wickham—and even from Lady Catherine; now Elizabeth looked like a frightened fawn. He felt so inadequate, unable to help her.

Mrs. Reynolds rushed into the room. "I am here, Mrs. Darcy," she said as she literally pushed Darcy to the side.

Elizabeth thought out loud. "It is too early."

Mrs. Reynolds began to loosen the lacing on Elizabeth's

dress and corset. "Let us take some pressure off your body," the woman said thoughtfully. "I suppose I cannot convince you to wait outside, can I, Master Fitzwilliam?" She gave him a look of disapproval.

"I will not leave Elizabeth." His eyes searched his wife's face for some sign of her well-being.

"Then help me get your wife into one of her dressing gowns," Mrs. Reynolds demanded as Hannah rushed through the door with the gown.

Darcy lifted Elizabeth as the women administered to her needs. He kissed her softly and whispered endearments as the world around them bustled about furiously.

Noting how ashen white his face was, Elizabeth managed a slight smile. "I will be fine, Fitzwilliam." Her words were meant to convince both of them. Another pain gripped her, and Darcy pulled her to him until she relaxed once again. In his mind he began to calculate how far she was from her expected delivery—not quite six weeks told him Elizabeth could easily lose their baby.

As he had before his accident, Darcy took a close look at Elizabeth. Her personality filled a room, and he often forgot how small—very fragile—Elizabeth actually was. It never occurred to him Elizabeth's carrying his child could be dangerous for her. Darcy did not want to lose her; he would forego having an heir rather than to lose the joy he felt the last few weeks.

As each sharp pain increased Elizabeth's discomfort, Darcy watched helplessly as tears filled her brilliant eyes. "Look at me, Elizabeth," he commanded as he took her hands in his. "I will help you through this." His words soothed her anxiety, and despite her exhaustion, Elizabeth reached out to caress his jaw line.

Finally, Mr. Spencer rushed into the room, obviously flushed from his ride to Pemberley. He thought about sending everyone from the room, but the trio gathered in Mrs. Darcy's bedchamber quickly let him know they would not budge.

"Mrs. Darcy," Mr. Spencer said as he began to examine her, "we will take care of you. It is early, but not unmanageable." He wanted to give her some sort of surety.

Neither Darcy nor Hannah nor Mrs. Reynolds wanted to ask the obvious question so Elizabeth finally found her voice. "Will I lose this child?" Elizabeth's voice broke in fear. Tears trailed down Hannah's face, and Darcy looked away, unable to see the turmoil on his wife's face.

"I am hoping to postpone that possibility." Mr. Spencer reacted to the fear emanating from everyone in the room.

"How do we do that?" It was Darcy's voice, but the resonance was dulled by confusion and remorse.

"Listen carefully, all of you," Mr. Spencer demanded their attention. "I am going to propose something a bit controversial, but, believe me, I observed this to work before."

Darcy left Elizabeth's side. "Well, tell us, man."

"Mrs. Darcy has not shown she is in full labor. In fact, I suspect we can stop her pains and delay her delivery. If we do, Mrs. Darcy, you are on complete bed rest from this day until you deliver your child." He turned to give Elizabeth his orders.

"Anything, Mr. Spencer," Elizabeth wiped her tears away.

Darcy nearly pleaded, "What do we do, Mr. Spencer?"

"You, Mr. Darcy, are going to find your smoothest brandy because we are going to get your wife drunk." Mr. Spencer looked pleased with himself.

This ridiculous idea struck Elizabeth as funny, and she actually laughed out loud. Darcy looked stunned, but he managed to say, "Are you sure?"

Mr. Spencer turned his eyes on Darcy. Convincing him would convince everyone. "Please understand; Mrs. Darcy's current pains are not a sign she is ready to deliver this child, but if we do not stop them, she will soon be in full childbirth. My proposal is to let the alcohol relax Mrs. Darcy and her pains. If we can stop these pains now, we can delay her delivery. Whether we can postpone Mrs. Darcy's ultimate delivery for six weeks is unlikely, but each day we do gives your wife and your child a better chance."

Darcy noted Mr. Spencer did not say "a chance of survival," but they all knew what the man insinuated.

"Hannah, go get the brandy out of my study." Darcy gave the order without taking his eyes from Mr. Spencer's face. Finally, he turned and went to sit on the edge of Elizabeth's bed. Taking her hand in his, Darcy tried to tease her, "Well, Mrs. Darcy, it appears I will learn all your deepest secrets this evening; I promise to ply you with my finest brandy. Are you game?"

"You will not leave me?" she asked innocently, her fear in full view.

"The chance to see you with your guard down? How could I resist such charms?" Darcy tried to sound light, but he worried whether Mr. Spencer's idea had a chance.

Hannah rushed back into the room carrying the decanter and two glasses. Darcy took the decanter and poured a generous drink for Elizabeth and a much smaller one for himself. With a slight ironic smile, he handed her the glass. "A toast to my loveliest Elizabeth," he said, clinking his glass to hers. "You are the mirror of my dreams." Darcy placed the glass to his lips and took a sip, but with a nod of his head, he encouraged Elizabeth to take a large swallow.

Elizabeth's eyes teared up immediately, and she coughed repeatedly as the brandy left a burning sensation in her throat. When she could manage to speak again, she stammered, "You . . . you drink . . . you drink this willingly?"

"Men like to prove how powerful we are." Darcy held an amused look on his face. "Yet, it is you women who possess all the power. You consume us." He sipped again, and Elizabeth followed suit with another large gulp. This time she only had to clear her throat a few times.

Mr. Spencer hustled the women from the room. "We will be outside, Mr. Darcy."

Darcy barely turned his head as they left. His attention remained on Elizabeth. He would keep her calm; he would help her save their child. They sat together for some time, neither speaking but Darcy constantly gauging his wife's condition. Finally he teased, "Do I know you, Madam?"

Elizabeth took a more moderate sip of the alcohol; it already took its effect on her. She was at that "giggling" stage of intoxication where everything was funny. She gave him a semi-seductive smile. "Oh, yes, Sir, you know me intimately."

"Intimately?" he asked slyly. "How intimately?" He topped off her glass, and Elizabeth sloshed some of it on the cuff of his shirt.

"That depends on you, Mr. Darcy." Her words began to slur, and Darcy noted it had been some time since Elizabeth winced with pain.

"Intimate enough for this?" He allowed his fingers to trace across her shoulder and along the neckline of her gown. Elizabeth openly gasped, and Darcy held his glass to her for another sip of brandy, and then he kissed the last few drops from her lips.

"Intimate enough for this," she laughed lightly as she moved Darcy's hand down her body, letting it come to rest on her abdomen.

"Our child," he whispered.

"Loves your touch," Elizabeth finished his line.

He continued to entice her with words of love and sips of brandy for the next three-quarters hour. While his wife became pleasantly drunk, Darcy carefully noted how her pains totally disappeared.

By the time Mr. Spencer and Darcy's staff returned to Elizabeth's room, she was fully inebriated. They found Elizabeth singing and laughing at the top of her lungs. She sat propped against a stack of pillows, arms flailing about like an orchestra conductor.

Darcy stretched out across the foot of the bed, smiling contentedly, watching her.

"Sing with me, Fitzwilliam," she called and then started singing a bawdy number. "There was a fine lady who rode a white horse; she came to London, of course, of course; with rings on her fingers and bells on her toes; she has treasures wherever she goes."

Darcy laughed at her and stood where he could speak to the physician. "I wonder where she learned that one. At least my wife is a happy drunk," he remarked to no one in particular.

"Mrs. Darcy will have a headache like she has never known before." Mrs. Reynolds found it all amusing.

Mr. Spencer asked him privately, "Any more pains, Mr. Darcy?"

"None for nearly an hour." Darcy turned to answer the physician.

"Perfect." Mr. Spencer looked relieved. "Mrs. Darcy may have just saved her life and that of your child."

Darcy breathed at last. "Mr. Spencer, how may I thank you?"

"Help me keep Mrs. Darcy in bed for a few more weeks. I want her to bring joy back to Pemberley. It has been too solemn too long."

Darcy looked back at the giggling Elizabeth. "It certainly is not solemn in here this evening."

Mr. Spencer joined in the laughter. "Mrs. Darcy does know how to light up a room."

When Elizabeth finally awoke the next morning, she moaned with disgust. "Oh, my head," she muttered, trying to sit up in bed.

Darcy leaned down to kiss her cheek. "You, my Dear, were delightful last night."

"How long will I feel this way?" Darcy's look of amusement irritated Elizabeth.

"A few hours," he smiled as he helped her reposition herself in the bed.

Elizabeth looked around to see the blanket lying across the back of the chair. "Have you been here all night?"

"I told you I would not leave you," he reasoned. Darcy poured her some coffee. "Do you suppose you could eat something?" he asked casually.

"Maybe some toast," Elizabeth added. "Dry toast." Darcy brought her some from the serving tray.

"Now, Mrs. Darcy," he teased, "I want to know where you learned a certain song."

Darcy became her constant companion. Elizabeth delighted being with him although being confined to her quarters nearly drove her crazy. Eventually, Darcy began to carry her from room to room. At least, with moving her to where he could watch her, Darcy was able to stay abreast of estate business. Elizabeth read or did her needlework.

"One week closer," Elizabeth said as he placed her in her bed.

Darcy kissed her lips gently. "One week closer—soon, my Love, our child will be with us."

Elizabeth pulled him back to her, quickly deepening the kiss she offered. "Fitzwilliam," she breathed heavily, "I love you more than I can ever express."

Darcy had to touch her. He quickly discarded his cravat, coat, and waistcoat. "May I lie with you tonight, Lizzy? I want to hold you in my arms."

"I wish to be no place else," she said softly as Darcy finished stripping off his clothing. Finally, he settled her in his arms; her head nestled into the indentation of his shoulder. They kissed repeatedly. Darcy never felt such intense happiness.

★ ★ ★

Sitting back in the coach, Georgiana wondered what would happen when her brother found out what she planned. Darcy would be furious with her actions; he might never forgive her. At a minimum, her brother would likely force her into a speedy marriage, but Georgiana cared not for her loss of reputation. Mr. Harrison's life was on the line, and she must warn him of the dangers.

Darcy would question why she did not just send word to Mr. Harrison, an act of impropriety, but one of less severity than the one in which she currently participated. However, Georgiana could be nowhere else if Chadwick Harrison was in the kind of danger she expected. Georgiana knew Mr. Harrison would never back down, and if she did not warn him, he could die in the confrontation. She would be with him when the trouble came; she could be no place other than with the man she loved.

★ ★ ★

Mr. Gardiner's visit to Kensington Place came unexpectedly on Friday afternoon. Georgiana planned a leisurely evening alone; she sent Mrs. Annesley on a visit to the woman's favorite nephew, and she wanted nothing more than the comfort of her own company. When Mr. Thacker announced Mr. Gardiner's presence, Georgiana felt a bit annoyed, but she hid her concern from Elizabeth's uncle.

"Miss Darcy." Mr. Gardiner made his bow. "I hoped to find Mr. Darcy at home."

"My brother is not here today." It was the story upon which she and Darcy agreed. "He is addressing some personal business. May I be of service to you, Sir?"

Mr. Gardiner seemed agitated. "I have some distressing news of which Mr. Darcy should be made aware." He paced the length of the room.

"I could reach Fitzwilliam if necessary." Georgiana tried to sound nonchalant.

His decision made, Mr. Gardiner broke down and told her his secret. "It is imperative Mr. Darcy is made aware of what I share with you."

"I understand, Mr. Gardiner," Georgiana assured him.

"I have an associate who brings me news from time to time. He tells me a large contingent of anti-abolitionists plan to oppose Mr. Harrison's election as a PM. They will address the gentleman at the borough assembly. I suspect Mr. Harrison should be made aware of the situation. He could be in some danger if things escalate." Mr. Gardiner continued to pace.

Georgiana tried to steel her nerves. Mr. Harrison meant as much to her as did Fitzwilliam and Elizabeth. Her heart continued to beat, but Georgiana could barely breathe as fear gripped her throat. "Mr. Gardiner," she said at last, "my brother and I thank you for your devotion to our family. I will address your concerns to Fitzwilliam immediately."

Mr. Gardiner retrieved his hat from the table. "Again, Miss Darcy, I beg your forgiveness in disturbing your privacy today."

Although Georgiana already planned what she would do, she managed to say, "Think nothing of it, Mr. Gardiner; we are family." She showed him to the door, and then turned back to the butler. "Mr. Thacker, have the men prepare my coach." Then she rushed off to her chambers to prepare her bags. Georgiana would be off to Dove Dale in a matter of hours.

CHAPTER 26

"Next to being married,
a girl likes to be crossed in love a little now and then."
Jane Austen, *Pride and Prejudice*, 1813

On Saturday a post came from Georgiana, and Darcy carried it to Elizabeth's room to share with his wife. He and Elizabeth clicked off another week of waiting for the birth of their child. Darcy barely left her sight; he made the resolution that Elizabeth and this child were more important than anything else, for without them, he was nothing. "I have a post from Georgiana," he said as he entered his wife's bedchamber.

As Darcy settled into the chair beside Elizabeth's bed, she asked, "When will you go to London to bring Georgiana and Kitty back to Pemberley?"

"I considered sending Mr. Howard in my stead." He shared his thoughts to see how Elizabeth would react.

"Fitzwilliam, I will be well." Elizabeth looked on a bit amused. "I will remain in this bed if it means a healthy delivery for our child."

"Elizabeth, I cannot leave you," Darcy argued. "I have been out of your life too long. I should have been here when Mr. Jefferson brought up tenant rights, when Mr. Wickham came uninvited, and when the stable caught on fire. I failed you as a husband, and, no matter what, I will not fail you now. I will be with you when this child is born."

"Fitzwilliam, I never considered you as a failure as a husband." Elizabeth rolled onto her side so she could address him directly. "You allowed me to be a strong, independent woman. In a time when women have no voice, you allowed me to not only speak, but to sing. Life is not merely a haphazard series of events; our life is an exquisite plan, a perfect tapestry. Can you not see that, my Love?"

"Elizabeth," he choked with emotions, "I must see this through, or I will never be able to forgive myself." Darcy moved to sit on the edge of her bed. "If something would happen," he began but could not finish his thoughts.

Elizabeth opened herself to Darcy, and he snuggled into the crest of his wife's arms, resting his head on her now-ample chest. "We will be strong; it is our destiny to be together." Elizabeth lightly kissed the side of Darcy's face. "Have faith in your dreams, my Love—have faith in our destiny. Making the most of every moment is the single most important lesson of my life."

"Do you have faith in us, Lizzy? Can our dreams come true?" Darcy caressed the side of her face. "In less than a year, we have lived a lifetime. I lost so many of our memories; I cannot lose this memory, too." Darcy returned his attention to his wife's neckline.

Elizabeth could not answer him; all she could do was hold him. The realization of how much her husband lost made her ashamed of the fact she planned to deprive him of the gift of their child. Had she been successful, Darcy's natural tendency for self-censure would have left him devastated. It amazed her how little she learned about misjudging him. Back at Hunsford, when he first proposed, Elizabeth judged him to be vain and prideful. Later, she discovered Darcy to be honorable—to be the best man of her acquaintance. So, how had she thought Darcy would not treat her honorably? He lost part of his memory, but he did not lose the man he always was. Elizabeth wondered if she would ever deserve him.

They spent a couple of hours settling doubts which plagued both of them. Although they did not share a "marriage" bed, intimacy prevailed—both emotionally and physically. Elizabeth and Darcy pledged their devotion to one another. Darcy resolved to make a better life for his wife; Elizabeth resolved to recognize her husband's true worth.

When Darcy returned to his sister's letter, satisfaction could be seen on his face.

28 June

Fitzwilliam,

I must apologize for my actions for I fear when you discover what I chose to do, you may consider me not worthy of your love and devotion. I must thank you, my Brother, for demonstrating to me true love is worth all the riches in the world. As you noted, my affection for Mr. Harrison increases, and, of late, I learned Mr. Harrison is the one person who will complete me.

Through Mr. Gardiner, I discovered Mr. Harrison is to be censured by those who object to his future political position. I cannot turn my back on this man now that he faces his greatest obstacle. I must do what I can to protect him; Mr. Harrison owns my heart.

I promise you, my Brother, this is not an easy decision because I know my former actions were foolish schoolgirl illusions, but my devotion to Mr. Harrison cannot be denied. I go to Hines Park because Mr. Harrison needs someone on his side; I choose to be that person.

Your loving sister,
Georgiana

Darcy's hand shook when he read the letter and a curse escaped his lips. "What craziness is this?"

"Of what do you speak, my Love?" Elizabeth reacted to his agitation.

"Read it yourself." He handed her the letter as he strode to the nearby window.

Elizabeth looked at Darcy worriedly. "Will you go after her?"

"My sister is with Mr. Harrison by now; she knew she would be at Hines Park before I received this missive." Darcy did not turn around, and Elizabeth wondered if he now regretted not going after his sister instead of staying with her. She wondered whether this, too, might come between them.

"We must trust Georgiana; she will not allow something to happen of an inappropriate nature," Elizabeth began to reason out loud. "If your sister went to Hines Park, she must truly believe Mr. Harrison needs her. The worst, which could happen, is the man asks for her hand two months earlier than we anticipated. Mr. Harrison loves Georgiana, and he is an honorable man."

Darcy turned to look back at his wife. "Believe it or not, I accepted the inevitability of my sister's regard for Mr. Harrison some time ago. I cannot say I approve of her decision, but it is Georgiana's decision. I just wish she did not risk her reputation once again."

"Do you regret not going to London?" Elizabeth bit her bottom lip, assuming Darcy would blame her for what now happened to Georgiana.

Darcy, seeing her distress, returned to her side. "Elizabeth, you are my life. I helped raise Georgiana; I taught her our parents' values. Even if I were in London or Georgiana were here, she would find a way to be with Mr. Harrison. He is her destiny as you are mine."

"Do you truly believe what you profess, Fitzwilliam?" Elizabeth lightly touched his arm.

Darcy kept his serious look, but he softened his tone. "I am concerned with what drove my sister to such a decision, and I wish she was more specific as to why censure of Mr. Harrison was a new issue."

Elizabeth interrupted. "Did you not say Mr. Harrison was to accept an appointment as a Parliamentary Minister? That must be her reference to Harrison's *future political position*."

"At the moment my qualms with Georgiana's decision lie in the question in what Mr. Harrison is involved. I cannot believe Georgiana would risk everything for a romantic tryst; it is not in her character no matter how much her affection for the man increased." Darcy shook his head in disbelief.

Elizabeth took his hand in hers. "Of course, Georgiana would never disgrace the family name by committing an indiscretion."

"Then why did she make the trip to Hines Park?" Darcy could not clear his thinking.

"Fitzwilliam, I think you should go to Dove Dale," Elizabeth said with determination.

"Elizabeth, I just said I would not leave you," Darcy assured her. Looking at her, at last, it dawned on Darcy Elizabeth feared he blamed her. "Elizabeth, I cannot control my sister; if she is safe, I have no other wish."

"I still think you should consider going to find Georgiana. Mr. Harrison's estate is only a few hours away; you could ride Cerberus, and then we could be satisfied of Georgiana's intent. If you go and return in the same day, I am sure I could muster the energy to entertain myself in your absence." Elizabeth tried to act as if she, too, had not considered how precarious her own position might be. She shifted her concern to Georgiana's well-being.

"It is too late to ride today." Darcy began to consider the possibility.

"At dawn." Elizabeth stroked his chin as he looked away, deep in thought.

"Are you sure, my Elizabeth?" Darcy argued with himself over to whom he owed his allegiance.

"Fitzwilliam, I insist. Georgiana is my sister, too; I wish no harm to come to her. You must go, my Love." Elizabeth pushed herself up in the bed. "I would blame myself forever if she came to harm."

Darcy moved quickly to take Elizabeth in his arms. "Thank you, my Love." He caressed her cheek as he clutched her head to his chest.

Unfortunately, the dawn postponed Darcy's leaving as it brought a torrent of rain and wind. Sheets of precipitation blanketed the windowpanes, blurring the view, and the wind rushed down chimney flues. Branches and saplings bent with the force. Darcy paced from room to room, waiting for the storm to lessen, but it raged on for hours. When the end could be safely determined, the clearing of the skies brought additional agitation. Darcy, like a caged animal, needed to act.

"It is too dangerous, Fitzwilliam," Elizabeth reasoned. "Although on Cerberus you would not have the problems of a carriage ride, many roads must be covered in water or washed away completely. I will not have you risk your own life. This child needs you. I am distressed about Georgiana, but the thoughts of losing you are unacceptable."

"I know you speak the truth, but I am so worried about Georgiana. I feel there is something not right with all this." Darcy looked out the window again, hoping the conditions miraculously changed.

"I am sure the weather keeps my sister from us." Elizabeth anxiously watched his silhouette.

"I pray you are right." Darcy wanted to will his sister to safety. He said no more, but Elizabeth knew Darcy would not stop until it was clear for him to go to find Georgiana. Elizabeth had another reason for not wanting Darcy to leave—the discomfort she felt the night she nearly delivered the baby returned.

★ ★ ★

When the attack came, Chadwick Harrison did not expect it. The warning told of a public outcry at the borough's assemblage, but none came, and Harrison assumed the entail to be wrong. He should have recognized the subtle changes as his carriage approached his estate house, but Harrison was daydreaming of Georgiana Darcy, an event that occurred several times a day—actually, all day, most days. Going up the main steps, Harrison reacted too late to stop his attackers when they came. Before he could reach the door, Captain Rutherford appeared on its threshold; beside him, Rutherford's companion, a grimy-looking slug of a man, stood, a bloody sword in his hand.

"You are late," the man looked on gleefully.

Harrison froze momentarily, but as a flash of intent crossed the man's face, Harrison caught an empty pot, using it as a shield to deflect the blade. He turned to make his escape, but Rutherford's men surrounded him, grabbing his arms and pinning him back against the door. Harrison struggled, trying to assess the situation, but more men forced him to finally succumb.

Rutherford motioned for the men to take him inside, and before he could calculate the danger in which he found himself, they chained Harrison to a supporting post in a back sitting room. Rutherford held back until Harrison was secured; then he strode forward. Scowling scornfully, he said, "Did you think we forgot about you, Harrison?"

"I am unforgettable, am I not, Captain?" Harrison tried to look as if everything were normal.

The captain found nothing amusing, and Harrison's words infuriated him more. A backhand blow rocked Harrison's sensibilities, as well as split his lip.

Harrison licked the blood away. "What is wrong, Rutherford," he continued his teasing tone, "no sense of humor?"

Rutherford's lips suddenly curled. He snarled, "I will be laughing soon, Harrison. When you are dead, I will be consumed with laughter." The captain walked away, taking up a position in front of the windows.

Harrison spoke calmly, "Do you not realize, Captain, even if you manage to kill me, it will not stop the belief in freedom for all God's children?"

"I will manage to kill you, Mr. Harrison." Rutherford poured himself a drink. "It will be an elegantly slow death. You will be our example."

"I am insignificant. No one will care about my fate." Harrison hoped to buy time until he could figure out his escape. "May I ask about my household staff?"

"A few unfortunates chose to fight on your behalf and have met a suitable fate for their loyalty. The others are locked in the kitchen larder or one of the other storage areas. They will not be harmed." Rutherford sat in a nearby chair.

Harrison dropped his eyes. The blood on the mercenary's sword was one of his staff members. "Do not hurt them; I will do what you wish."

"Whether we hurt them or not, you *will do* what we wish." Rutherford's voice lowered, as if he spoke evil. The captain nodded imperceptively, and the slimy man's fist locked onto Harrison's jaw.

The beatings continued for what seemed like hours. Harrison's face was bruised and bleeding, and more than once his mouth filled with blood. A cat-and-nine-tails took flesh from his back, but nothing changed. Rutherford made no demands; the captain simply enjoyed the process of killing a man.

The dawn brought Harrison a bit of a reprieve. A powerful storm tore through the area, and Rutherford's men bemoaned how the wind and rain delayed their plans to kill Harrison and all his staff. Harrison heard them, but he reached a point where he no longer cared for his own life, only his staff members mattered. He hung from the post; his arms stretched above him. At first, he stood; now, he truly clung, waiting for death to come.

* * *

Georgiana Darcy's coach rumbled across the poorly maintained roads leading to Hines Park. The storm forced her to delay her journey to warn Chadwick Harrison, and now she anxiously looked out the coach's window at the approaching twilight. The coach moved slowly as it finally entered the gate leading to Hines Park. Georgiana wondered why no one was at the gatehouse to greet her, but her anxiety overrode her reason, and she had the driver press on.

When the house was in view, the carriage lurched to a stop. Suddenly a clatter of horses' hooves on the cobblestones and the angry shouts of men greeted them. A door flew open, and a masked intruder stood without, a gun drawn directly on her. Georgiana instinctively shrunk back into the shadows of the coach but the man grabbed her wrist, forcing her from the coach, literally pulling her down the steps before she could get her footing. She heard the door to the coach slam closed with a sinister thud.

"Come with me," the man sneered. Despite her genteel upbringing, Georgiana fought him desperately, digging her nails into his arm. Pulling her up the steps, the man physically threw Georgiana onto the floor of the nearest drawing room.

Before she could look around to assess her situation, she heard Captain Rutherford's voice and saw the polished tips of his boots. "Miss Darcy," his voice was sweetly ominous, and Georgiana intuitively shivered, "so nice of you to join us."

Georgiana forced herself to a seated position while straightening her clothing. "Captain Rutherford," she barely whispered.

"No traveling companion, Miss Darcy? My, you are a surprising young lady. I always suspected you to be all sugar and no substance. Maybe some spice and vinegar run through your veins after all?" Rutherford reached down to offer Georgiana his hand, and in that moment, she knew him to be the embodiment of evil. "Do not worry, Miss Darcy, I will not let them hurt you."

Georgiana reluctantly accepted his hand. "Where is Mr. Harrison?" she demanded as she stood.

"Oh, my darling Miss Darcy." Rutherford moved in closer to her. "You do not want to align yourself with such trash. The man is hardly worth your attention." His breath on her cheek caused her to shiver.

"That may be," she said with some determination, "but I still wish to see Mr. Harrison."

"Very well." Rutherford's sneer spread into a wicked smile. "Follow me."

Rutherford turned on his heels and strode away from her. A woman of lesser stature would have trouble keeping up with him, but Georgiana was used to following Darcy around. Rutherford was no challenge for her. The number of armed guards in the hallway bothered Georgiana, and she feared for Mr. Harrison's life. Finally, they entered a back sitting room.

Georgiana's eyes fell on the man she loved. She started to rush toward him, but Rutherford's hand gripped her arm. "You have a visitor, Mr. Harrison," the captain said sarcastically.

Harrison lay in a clump on the floor. Rutherford released him from the hanging position only moments ago. Harrison knew others were in the room, but his body ached from the pain, and he could not respond. Georgiana gasped. Harrison's badly beaten body lay twisted and barely conscious at her feet. Rutherford kicked at him with the toe of his boot, and Harrison rolled to his back, exposing a bloody face, swollen badly from the many blows he sustained.

"Say something to the gentleman, my dear," the captain taunted both of them.

Georgiana swallowed hard, trying to force evenness into her voice; yet, when she opened her mouth, no sounds escaped.

"What? Are you becoming shy once again? Then let me assist you." Rutherford held tight to Georgiana's wrist, smiling at her in a dark way. He pulled her closer to the bloody heap which was Mr. Harrison. Impulsively, she reached out for the man on the floor. "I see you prefer Harrison to me even today," Rutherford whispered in her ear as he forced Georgiana close to him. Caressing her face, he brushed his lips against her cheek, "But I will make you change your mind."

Georgiana finally found her voice. "You do not frighten me, Sir."

"I shall change your mind about that, too, but first I will give you some time with your lover." Rutherford twisted Georgiana's arm, forcing her to her knees in front of Harrison's body. Then he violently released her, strode through the door, and locked it behind him.

Georgiana momentarily followed him with her eyes; then she turned her attention to Chadwick Harrison. Nearly unconscious, but still alive, despite his wounds, Harrison lay limp. Immediately, she cradled his head in her lap. Using her handkerchief, Georgiana wiped the blood from his face. A pitcher of tepid water stood on a sidebar. She rushed to it, pouring some in a bowl and rushing back to him.

"Please, God," she whispered as she touched the damp cloth to his mouth. "Chadwick, I am here." She cleaned his face with the water and the handkerchief. Her touch had been part of Harrison's daily dream, and he wondered if Georgiana could be real. His head lolled forward, trying to focus on the reality of the woman. "Please," she begged, willing him back to her.

Harrison's eyes fluttered open; Georgiana's face hovered over his. If he died this moment, happiness would flow through his veins. "Are you real?" he managed to say through swollen lips.

"I am real, and I am here with you." Tears misted Georgiana's eyes. Frantically, she began to tear strips from her petticoat to bind his worst wounds. Georgiana felt each wound to be worse than the last. "Chadwick, stay with me. Please fight to stay with me," she whispered in his ear.

"I am here," he managed to say at last. Much more, he could not put into action, but Harrison gave in to her desire for his recovery. If Georgiana Darcy willed it, Chadwick Harrison would respond.

For the next thirty minutes, Georgiana nursed him. She placed drops of water in Mr. Harrison's mouth; she kissed him gently, afraid to hurt him more. Little did she know, to Harrison each kiss held ambrosia of the gods, but there was also a sadness that Georgiana would see him die. "Why are you here?" he said at last.

"I came because you were in trouble." Georgiana kept her voice low in case Rutherford listened.

"You should not be here; the captain plans to kill me." Harrison's voice held regret.

She spoke with determination, "I will not let that happen."

Rutherford finally reappeared. Coming into the room, the captain's eyes immediately alighted on Georgiana; she sat on the floor, Harrison's head cradled in her lap. "Ah, Miss Darcy." His lips curled in mockery. "I should have told you, you are wasting your time with Mr. Harrison; you cannot change his fate, but I suppose you can offer him some comfort before he meets his Maker." Neither Georgiana nor Harrison moved a muscle. "I am afraid you will need to come with me now, my dear." Sarcasm laced his tone.

"I would prefer to stay with Mr. Harrison." The strength of Georgiana's voice surprised them all.

Rutherford stepped forward, forcing her to look up sharply. "I am afraid you misunderstand me, Miss Darcy; the choice is not yours to make." He coldly took hold of Georgiana's wrist and forced her to her feet, leaving Harrison grabbing at the air as he tried to protect her. "I promised myself I would enjoy taking you from this scum," Rutherford declared loudly. He pulled Georgiana to him and forcibly kissed her lips. Georgiana fought with all her might, twisting and turning to get away from him, but Rutherford held her tightly. When he finally released the death grip with which he held Georgiana, he laughed derisively. "If all I take is you, Miss Darcy, I shall be satisfied."

He started to kiss her again, but this time Georgiana was ready. Very unladylike, she covered Rutherford's face with spit and then offered him a look of defiance. During all this, Harrison struggled to help her. Rutherford's hand reacted quickly, and Georgiana's head snapped to the right as he backhanded her along her cheekbone. He used his sleeve to wipe his face while Georgiana grabbed the side of her face with her one free hand. She wanted to cry, but she bit her bottom lip rather than do so. She would not let Rutherford see her defeat.

"Bastard!" Harrison tried to force himself upward, but a rifle butt to the stomach knocked him flat once again. He laid gasping for air and spitting blood as Rutherford dragged Georgiana from the room.

★ ★ ★

Darcy paced the room, trying to decide what to do about finding Georgiana. During the past hour, Elizabeth made a decision of her own. When the "discomfort" returned, she knew exactly with what she was dealing. Intuitively, she realized she could not postpone the birth of her child much longer. She was a little over three weeks from her delivery, but no longer did she worry for her safety. Her concerns now were twofold: delivering safely Darcy's heir and keeping her impending childbirth from her husband until he left to find Georgiana.

Elizabeth wanted Darcy with her, but if Georgiana was in trouble, Darcy would never forgive himself for not being there. It would eventually come between them so she forced herself to breathe through each of the pains while keeping her eye on the clock, mentally recording their frequency.

As the hours passed, and the rain slowed further, Darcy became more and more determined to ride for Hines Park. "The water must be subsiding," he reasoned. "I can take a lantern if it turns too dark."

A pain rocked Elizabeth's sensibilities, and she paused before she could answer her husband. "Although I fear for your safety, you, my Husband, must do what you think best for your sister; I will understand."

"Will you really, Elizabeth?" He caressed her jaw line.

"Most emphatically," she responded.

Darcy leaned forward to kiss her lips tenderly. When he withdrew, he said, "I must go; I feel something is terribly wrong."

"I know, my Love." She kissed him deeply this time. Her lips lingered over Darcy's. "Please remember I love you desperately. This child and I need you; be safe."

"I can be nothing else, my Love." Darcy touched her stomach lightly before he stood. "I will be back early tomorrow morning." With that, he left the room to prepare to leave for Hines Park.

When Colonel Fitzwilliam rode into the carriageway at Pemberley, he knew not whether his cousin returned to London. Bursting through the door, he screamed, "Darcy! Darcy, are you here?"

"The Master is upstairs with Mrs. Darcy," Mrs. Reynolds answered as she entered the foyer at a hurry.

"Darcy!" the colonel yelled again as he started up the staircase.

Darcy leaned over the railing at the top of the staircase. Sounding a bit annoyed, he responded, "I am here, Edward."

"Thank God," Edward stammered, now out of breath.

Darcy came down the stairs to meet his cousin. "What is the matter?"

Edward nearly panted, but he managed to say, "I got a letter ... in Bath ... from Hannah More ... She knew not that ... we found you ... So, she wrote to me ... Rutherford plans an attack ... on Mr. Harrison."

"Harrison?" Darcy's voice went cold. "When? When will Rutherford attack Harrison?" He grabbed Edward's shoulder to demand an answer.

"I suspect we may be ... too late even now." Edward looked more frightened.

Darcy sprang into action. "Come, Edward," he pulled his cousin to the door. "Georgiana left London. She went to Hines Park."

"My God!" Edward gasped, "I will get the horses."

Edward sprinted toward the stables while Darcy quickly took his leave from Elizabeth before taking his sword and gun from the study. All he told her was Edward found out about Georgiana, and they two would go retrieve his sister. It was a game they played. Darcy knew he hid the truth from her to protect Elizabeth, and she pretended to be none the wiser. However, Elizabeth knew Edward would know nothing of Georgiana's trip to Dove Dale unless he had been in London; yet, she and Darcy left Edward with Anne in Bath.

CHAPTER 27

"General benevolence, but not general friendship,
made a man what he ought to be."
Jane Austen, *Emma*, 1815

Once Darcy left, Elizabeth waited nearly twenty minutes before she rang for Hannah. "May I get you something, Mrs. Darcy?" Hannah asked as she entered her Mistress's bedchamber.

"Hannah, I need to see Mrs. Reynolds immediately." Elizabeth tried to keep her voice even, but fragments of fear flickered through her eyes. "And please send word to both Mr. Spencer and the midwife; I will need their services."

"Mrs. Darcy," Hannah shrieked, "should I send someone to catch Mr. Darcy?"

"No," Elizabeth's voice allowed no other choice. "I waited until Mr. Darcy was gone before I said anything. He must see to Miss Darcy; do you understand me, Hannah?"

"Yes, Mrs. Darcy." Hannah dropped a curtsy before she rushed from the room.

Within a minute, Mrs. Reynolds appeared in the room. "It is time, Mrs. Darcy?" The woman waited not for an answer before she began to prepare Elizabeth for the delivery. "I sent word to Mr. Spencer and the midwife. How far apart are the pains?"

"Less than a quarter hour." Elizabeth suddenly felt very alone. No one from her family was there, and Elizabeth clutched at Mrs. Reynolds's hand. "You will stay with me, Mrs. Reynolds?"

"I will not leave you, Mrs. Darcy," the woman assured her. "We have a long evening ahead of us. Now, let us get you as comfortable as possible." The housekeeper fluffed the pillows.

The midwife guaranteed the child would not be there until at least morning. Elizabeth's pains were still erratic, and her water had not broken. The intensity of each pain told the experienced woman Elizabeth's childbirth to be real, but it was still several hours away. To Elizabeth, each pain increased her fear. She wanted Darcy to go to Georgiana, but she needed him with her now. She needed him for the birth of their child.

★ ★ ★

The colonel ordered Mr. Howard and two of Darcy's best huntsmen to accompany them. All Darcy could think about was finding his sister, but Edward knew there was real danger at Hines Park. Riding hard, they made good time in reaching the outer lands of Harrison's estate. Edward forced them to stop before they got too close to the estate house.

"I suspect the captain has less than a dozen men, but they will be well armed." Edward spoke softly to demand their attention. "Mr. Darcy and I will check the house. Mr. Howard, I want you and your men to secure the stable and other out buildings. Make sure they have no way to escape."

Luckily, both Darcy and Edward had been to Hines Park previously, but as they snuck into a side entrance both men realized how many places such a house could hold where intruders could hide. Yet, they bypassed rooms unlikely to be occupied by the son of landed gentry.

They decided to work their way from the back to the front of the house, checking each room quickly but thoroughly. Both men knew something was amiss because no servants moved through the house. They did not speak to one another; Darcy and Edward knew what needed to be done without words. Moving quietly and swiftly, they slid from shadow to shadow, flattening themselves against the wall, ever vigilant. Coming upon a locked drawing room, Edward put a finger to his lips, wordlessly ordering Darcy to be ready for anything.

Edward, already on the move, jiggled the lock with his knife until it gave way, and the door slid open. The colonel's footsteps showed his years of military training; he moved cautiously but with determination. Edward motioned he would open the door and enter first; he wanted Darcy to cover the entrance. Darcy nodded in an affirmation of understanding. It took only seconds for both men to secure the door behind them and assess the near emptiness of the room, but a soft moan told them they were not alone. Allowing their eyes to adjust to the darkness, Darcy first discovered the man crawling along the floor. "Harrison," he whispered as he rushed forward to help him. The colonel continued to monitor the door.

"Darcy?" Harrison could barely speak, but with Darcy's help he managed to stand. "Your sister," he said as he stood gingerly.

Darcy hissed, "Where is Georgiana?"

"Rutherford . . . has her." Harrison steadied himself. "He plans . . . to take pleasure . . . in her. I believe . . . he took . . . Miss Darcy upstairs." Harrison managed to right himself completely.

"I will kill him," Darcy threatened. "Help me find Georgiana." His voice nearly pleaded.

"Follow me." Harrison motioned to them, leading the way through another room with a panel in the back, which ascended a narrow, twisting stairway coming into an unused guest room on the second story. It was in the part of the house Harrison earmarked for renovation.

"Let Darcy and me handle the intruders; you are in no shape to fight off anyone," Edward ordered.

Harrison had other thoughts, but he spoke them not. If they encountered any of Rutherford's men, Harrison would let Darcy and the colonel do the fighting. He would save his energy for Rutherford.

Meanwhile, Mr. Howard and his men discovered the Darcy livery on the coach housed in the stables; it was the coach purchased for Georgiana Darcy by old Mr. Darcy so they were ready for trouble when they entered through the servant entrance; a minor assault occurred, but even though they were outnumbered, Darcy's men were sober, and Rutherford's men spent nearly eight and forty hours enjoying Mr. Harrison's stock of wine and ale. The alcohol numbed their reactions, and Mr. Howard had the drop on the five intruders before they realized what happened.

Mr. Howard released the servants, putting the intruders in the cold storage larder. The estate staff assured Mr. Howard no one would escape. "We will see to it, Sir," said the butler as the butler shoved the last of the interlopers into the hole and secured the door.

When they reached the suite of bedrooms, it was easy for Darcy, Edward, and Harrison to determine in which room Rutherford held Georgiana. Again, Edward took control of their positioning for the assault. They held back as the guards stepped into the light.

"The captain be wastin' his time with the girl," one of the rougher-looking men shared. "That be not what we come here for."

One of his buddies pointed out their plans. "We be torchin' the place soon enough."

A third lit one of Harrison's cigars and laughed lightly. "No one be lettin' them savages free once we burn this one out."

When the men turned to step back against the wall, Edward moved quickly. A dagger lodged in the first man's back, purposely twisted by the colonel as he withdrew it to use on the second man. Darcy took the third, using a silken cord from a set of draperies to strangle the man, whose body twisted and turned, gyrating as Darcy kept tightening his hold until the man finally went limp.

As Edward wrestled with his third man, Darcy moved quickly to help his cousin, literally shoving the cigar the man dropped earlier into his open mouth, causing the uninvited guest to choke and cough as the colonel finished him off.

They knew Rutherford must be aware of their presence by now so any chance of surprise was gone. Kicking at the door latch, the colonel dove out of the way as Rutherford unloaded his pistol into the door. Regrouping, Edward and Darcy continued to work in tandem, forcing the door open by both hitting it at the same time. Again, the captain fired while Darcy and Edward launched themselves into the bedchamber, rolling to avoid Rutherford's attack.

Both men came up quickly, but then they froze, everyone posed in place in a terrible tableau. Georgiana stood shivering in a ripped dress, blood dripping from the corner of her mouth, and Rutherford's gun cocked next to her head. Caution prevailed for several minutes as each person locked eyes on the other.

"Mr. Darcy," Rutherford laughed lightly in amazement, "you are a hard man to kill." With another gun in his free hand, the captain motioned for Colonel Fitzwilliam to move closer to Darcy. "And you brought the colonel—how delightful!"

Georgiana's frightened eyes fell upon her brother; Darcy tried to silently tell her he would protect her.

"Easy, Rutherford," Edward said softly as he slowly moved closer to Darcy. "You do not really want to hurt Miss Darcy." Edward held his hands where Captain Rutherford could see them.

"Over there," the captain motioned for both Edward and Darcy to move toward the far corner of the room. Then he grabbed Georgiana around the neck, keeping the cocked gun to her temple, and began to back away from them, pulling Georgiana toward the open door. "Follow me, and I will kill her," he hissed.

Rutherford inched through the doorway, holding Georgiana tightly to him; thinking only of freedom, he nearly scrambled to get out of the way. Harrison knew whatever else he did with the rest of his life, the next minute would determine his real worth. No matter what it cost him, he would ensure Georgiana Darcy need never fear the likes of Captain Rutherford again. Moving like a cat, Harrison sprang to his feet. He grabbed the silken cord Darcy dropped earlier and wrapped it around Rutherford's throat, dragging him away from Georgiana. With what energy he had left, he held the captain as his captor.

Darcy sprang forward, pulling Georgiana clear of the fray while Edward charged Rutherford, knocking the captain and Harrison down. Rutherford leapt up from the floor first and turned to run, but it was Harrison, not Edward, who reacted. He scrambled to his feet and lunged for the man, pulling his stiletto from his boot as he moved. The blade winked in the light as Harrison moved in what felt like slow motion to him, but, in reality, was a sleek adeptness. Rutherford turned just as Harrison made contact, and the blade disappeared into the center of Rutherford's chest, sending them both collapsing to the floor. Exhausted, Harrison lay on top of Rutherford's body, the captain's blood seeping out on both of them.

Edward finally got to them, rolling Harrison off the captain, who now lay perfectly still. Harrison's chest rose and fell as he tried to control his breathing. With the silence, Darcy stepped to the hallway, Georgiana's face buried into his chest. He removed his jacket and placed it around her to cover her torn dress. Edward moved off to find Mr. Howard.

"It is over," Darcy whispered in Georgiana's ear as he loosened her hold on him.

Georgiana could not ask the question, afraid to even turn her head. "Is he?"

"Miss Darcy." Harrison's voice was breathy from all he had been through, but he forced himself to a seated position.

Georgiana peeked at him around her brother's shoulder, and immediately she was kneeling by Harrison's side, holding his head to her chest, tears streaming down her face. "You are alive," she kept repeating as she stroked the side of his head. "Thank God, you are alive." Harrison held her, bliss written across his beaten face.

Darcy allowed her a moment before he brought Georgiana back into his embrace. "Come, my Sweet One, let us get you and Mr. Harrison some medical help." He led her to one of the bedchambers further down the hall. "Stay here, Georgiana, while I see to Mr. Harrison." Darcy's voice held compassion.

In the hallway, Harrison forced himself from the floor just as Darcy returned to help him; Edward, followed by Mr. Howard, also returned. "The rest of Rutherford's men are locked in the cold storage larder."

"The men and I will remove these bodies to outside, Mr. Darcy."

"Thank you, Mr. Howard," Darcy responded automatically while helping Harrison to stand completely. "Hell is empty. All the Devils are here."[4] Darcy looked around in dismay at the melee their fight left in the hallway. "Edward, Mr. Harrison and Georgiana both need medical help."

"On the way, Darcy." Edward took Harrison's other arm as he helped brace the man's exhausted body.

"Miss Darcy?" Harrison managed to say.

Darcy offered, "My sister is fine."

"Thank God." Harrison nearly collapsed in the effort of the words, adrenaline fully drained from his body.

"Once I attend to her, I will allow Georgiana to come see you." Darcy accepted the changes coming in Georgiana's life.

"Thank you, Mr. Darcy." Harrison heard the resolve in the man's voice, realizing how hard it must be for the proud Fitzwilliam Darcy to find his sister in such a compromising situation. "You must realize my intentions toward Miss Darcy are honorable."

Edward laughed. "Well, I certainly hope so, Mr. Harrison, considering Miss Darcy's two guardians now, literally, carry you to your bed. If your intentions are not honorable, we could easily let you die with the riffraff who now litter your hallway."

Edward's poor attempt at humor seemed comforting to them all—as if a sense of normalcy would return after such a horrendous night. "I suppose words of gratitude may never re-pay my thanks," Harrison added as he collapsed onto the bed.

Georgiana insisted on going to see Mr. Harrison, even though her entering his bedchamber was another act of impropriety. Darcy insisted a house servant also be in the room. When she sat on the edge of his bed and took his hand, Chadwick Harrison's eyes fluttered open to see Georgiana's shining eyes filled with happiness. "Miss Darcy," he said, trying to smile through the bruises and the swelling, "you should not be here."

"Then you wish me to leave, Mr. Harrison?" Georgiana pretended to rise to her feet.

Harrison tightened his grip on her hand. "You know your power over me, Miss Darcy," he said softly so no one else could hear. "I wish you never to leave me again."

"Mr. Harrison." Georgiana teased a strand of hair from his face. "You are very bold, Sir, and very assured of yourself."

"I assumed, Miss Darcy, considering you risked your life to save mine, I might feel some assurance." Harrison's eyes drank in her beauty. "Though it grieves me you suffered because of me."

Georgiana lightly touched the bruise on the side of her cheek, and then she reached out to tenderly touch his face. Harrison turned his head to kiss her palm. "As long as you are safe, I can withstand this little bruise," she whispered softly.

At that moment, Darcy stepped through the door, clearing his throat as a way to let them know the visit was ended. "Come, Georgiana," he encouraged her with his tone, "Mr. Harrison needs his rest."

"Good night, Miss Darcy." Harrison's eyes followed her exit.

She turned to make him a proper curtsy, gifting him with an enigmatic smile. "Until tomorrow, Mr. Harrison."

Darcy and Edward sat up late in one of the downstairs drawing rooms. "We must contact the Constable, Darcy," Edward reaffirmed his earlier assertion. "We have a stack of bodies outside."

"How do we explain Georgiana's presence without a chaperone?" Darcy's concern lay in protecting his sister's reputation.

"From what I understand from Harrison and his staff, he appeared earlier yesterday at a borough's assemblage," Edward laid out his plan. "Mr. Harrison is slated to take a position in the House of Commons."

"I know all this, Edward," Darcy seemed irritated. "How does this affect Georgiana's presence here?"

"We will tell the Constable Mr. Harrison and Georgiana are engaged. He presented himself to her in London, and she accepted. She was on her way here so they could make the announcement official. As her guardians, we, too, were en route. You were elsewhere because of Elizabeth's lying in, and I was with my betrothed. Mr. Harrison's engagement would make him a more viable candidate as a married man. The storm delayed all of our efforts to get here. That is why Georgiana arrived before us and why Captain Rutherford was able to capture her and Mr. Harrison." Edward looked on, pleased with his ingenuity.

"Will Mr. Harrison agree to this story?"

Edward knew Darcy did not want to lose his sister. "The man loves Georgiana; he would swear on a stack of Bibles in order to save your sister's reputation."

"My life changed so much in less than a year. The Fitzwilliam Darcy I thought I was no longer exists. Now, I must lose my sister, too." Darcy grasped for the last vestiges of his former life.

"Lucky for you, Fitz, Harrison admires you as much as he does Georgiana. You may still influence your sister's life if you so choose." Edward found his words amusing. "In reality, Darcy, you should be pleased with how well Georgiana turned out. She is as refined as any lady of the *ton*, but Georgiana possesses a substance—she is not only beautiful; Georgiana is resourceful and brave. She will make Mr. Harrison a fine wife; he will be successful because Georgiana will lead him to it—subtly, but it will be your influence on her. Your parents would want nothing more *for her* or *from you*. You fulfilled their charge to you; now, it is time for you to get on with your own life. Fulfill your own dreams, Fitz."

"Do you believe so, Edward?" Darcy looked about a bit unsure.

"Elizabeth will make you happy at last." Edward stood and stretched. "Now, let us get some rest."

"I return to Pemberley tomorrow morning. Would you bring Georgiana home in her coach?"

"Of course, but I suppose I will need to bring Mr. Harrison, too, or else she is likely to refuse our leaving." Edward could not help but see the humor in the situation.

"Bring the man to Pemberley," Darcy nearly growled. "I am not sure I can stand any more independent women in my life."

Darcy took a large swig of brandy before he stood to go upstairs to one of the guest rooms.

"Good night, Fitz," Edward mocked Darcy's retreating form.

Darcy rode Cerberus hard, finally reaching the outskirts of Pemberley's lands, pushing the animal and himself to reach the house. Mr. Howard awakened him in the predawn hours with news from Pemberley that Mrs. Darcy was to deliver their child. "Come on, Boy," he urged the horse even harder, "Elizabeth needs me."

He bounded up the stairs, sending servants scrambling out of the way. Forcing the door open to her bedchambers, Darcy nearly knocked over Mrs. Reynolds with the force of his entrance. "Master Fitzwilliam, you should not be here." Mrs. Reynolds tried to shoo him from the room.

"Elizabeth is my life, Mrs. Reynolds. Where should I be?"

The housekeeper started to tell him he should be downstairs like a proper gentleman would be, but Elizabeth's voice interrupted her thoughts. "Fitzwilliam," Elizabeth called urgently.

Darcy moved quickly to her side. "I am here, Elizabeth." He moved an auburn curl from her face as he kissed her forehead.

"If you are going to be here, Master Fitzwilliam," Mrs. Reynolds ordered, "help us get Mrs. Darcy up; she must walk."

Darcy seemed confused. "Walk?"

"Yes, Mr. Darcy," Mrs. Reynolds insisted, "she must walk; it will speed up the process."

They walked the corridor for nearly an hour before helping Elizabeth to the bed. Darcy disappeared long enough to freshen his clothes and then returned to his wife's room. Each pain brought Darcy anguish; he feared Elizabeth would not survive. Yet, miraculously, she weathered the labor bravely, often biting her lower lip rather than crying out. Tears streamed down her face, but she fought her cries so as not to worry him more. Finally, Darcy realized she disguised the pain for his sake. Leaning forward, he whispered in her ear. "Elizabeth, please do not be brave for my comfort; I am here to help you; you do not need to protect me."

"The Master of Pemberley." She offered him half a smile.

"The Master and the Mistress of Pemberley," he corrected her. "Together we are invincible."

When the pain came again, she cried out, and Darcy held her tighter. "Elizabeth, listen to me. Look in my eyes; take my strength and use it with your own. We can do this together." She nodded, too exhausted to do anything else.

"You are about ready, Mrs. Darcy," the midwife told her. "When the next pain comes, you must quit riding it through. I need for you to begin to push."

The painless intermission ended too soon, and Darcy could tell as she clutched at his hands her time had come. "Stay with me, Elizabeth," his voice willed her to him as she leaned forward in the bed. He pulled her to his chest and held her there until the pain subsided.

"You are doing well, Mrs. Darcy." Mrs. Reynolds came around the other side of the bed to wipe Elizabeth's face.

It was still almost a half hour before the baby's head crowned, but one final excruciating pain brought Elizabeth relief at last. "It is a girl, Mrs. Darcy," Mrs. Reynolds said as she hustled to wrap the child in the swaddling cloth, while the midwife tied the cord after cutting it. A whimper of a cry echoed through the room as Elizabeth finally collapsed back against the bed.

Exhausted, she looked at Darcy to see if a daughter disappointed him, but all she saw was total contentment. He watched everything Mrs. Reynolds did with the child, trying to finally see the baby. Eventually, the housekeeper brought the child to him and placed his daughter in his arms.

Darcy held the baby, and his life changed instantly. "She is beautiful, Lizzy." He laid the child in the cradle of Elizabeth's arm where they both could see their daughter. Elizabeth turned back the cloth to see a petite face plastered with auburn curls. Darcy touched the child's hand, and its palm instinctively wrapped around his finger. "I told you, Mr. Darcy, your child loves your touch."

Darcy smiled at Elizabeth. "She is so small."

"She will grow soon enough, my Love," Elizabeth assured him.

"Mr. Darcy." The midwife touched his shoulder. "Why do you not take your daughter for her first walk through Pemberley? You should not be here for what comes next. We need to clean Mrs. Darcy after the birth."

Darcy nodded. "I will be back soon, Elizabeth." He kissed her lightly, taking the baby into his arms. Elizabeth found it amusing that a small bundle fascinated *the tall, proud Mr. Darcy.*

Darcy could not have been to the lower floor when the pain struck Elizabeth again. When it came, she smothered her cry with a pillow. The afterbirth should not be so painful, and even the midwife seemed surprised the pain did not subside.

Elizabeth finally gasped, "What is it?"

Mrs. Reynolds hurried to the edge of the bed. She shoved a cloth into Elizabeth's mouth to muffle the sound.

"It is another baby," the midwife shouted as the head showed itself.

Elizabeth's eyes went wild, and Mrs. Reynolds quickly rang for Hannah. "Hannah, go tell Henry to keep Mr. Darcy downstairs as long as possible, and then bring me another cloth."

Hannah rushed away, returning at a trot. They bolted the door, and Hannah took Darcy's place on the edge of the bed. In only a brief moment, Elizabeth knew another child was imminent. "Mrs. Darcy, I need you to push again," the midwife ordered.

Elizabeth took several deep breaths, and when the pain came, she bore down hard, using the last of her energy to push the baby's head clear.

"Once more, Mrs. Darcy," the midwife barked. "You are almost there."

This time the cry could not be muffled, but Elizabeth sustained the effort until the child slid out onto the preparation cloth. She collapsed back against the pillows as Hannah bathed her face with a cool cloth.

The midwife cut a second cord, and Mrs. Reynolds went about cleaning the child. Elizabeth waited for what seemed to be a lifetime to hear the weak cry burst forth.

"Is it all right?" Elizabeth called out as they heard Darcy's footsteps outside the chamber.

"Let me in, Mrs. Reynolds," Darcy's voice demanded when he found the bolted door.

"In a moment, Mr. Darcy," the woman called, but her attention was on the child she held in her arms. "Come on, Sweet One," she coaxed as she rubbed its back and feet. Finally, a deep intake of air came, followed by a loud cry. "Thank God," Mrs. Reynolds said a little too loudly.

Elizabeth started to weep with relief; her shoulders visibly shook.

"Hannah, let in Mr. Darcy," Mrs. Reynolds said calmly as she wrapped the child in its cloth.

When Hannah unbolted the door, he literally shoved the maid out of the way as he rushed to Elizabeth's side. "Lizzy?" He searched her face to see if she was all right.

"I am fine, Fitzwilliam." She looked past him to see Mrs. Reynolds approaching with another child. "It is a boy, Mr. Darcy," Mrs. Reynolds placed his heir in his arms with a certain amount of reverence. "Pemberley has waited so long." The woman could say no more; she was overcome with her emotions.

"Let me see," Elizabeth demanded.

Again, Darcy turned the child so his wife could see her son. The baby had Darcy's long torso and black hair. "He is definitely your child," Elizabeth teased. "By the way, where is your daughter?"

"I did not forget my little princess, if that is what you mean, my loveliest Elizabeth. I placed her in Henry's very able hands before I rushed to your side."

"She is here, Mrs. Darcy," Hannah called as she entered the room.

"Well, I certainly hope that is all," Elizabeth laughed nervously.

"Elizabeth, you are the most amazing woman." Darcy leaned down to kiss her. "Who would think we would have twins?"

Once again, Mrs. Reynolds made Darcy leave the room. This time he only agreed to go as far as their joint sitting room. The midwife massaged Elizabeth's stomach, and they placed damp warm cloths on her to help her pass the afterbirth. Mrs. Reynolds, with Hannah's help, cleaned the room as well as the Mistress. Then they allowed Darcy back in the bedroom.

The picture of Elizabeth and his children together in her bed seemed part of a "perfect" plan. Elizabeth slumbered as their son nursed so Darcy picked up his daughter. He walked about the room, holding the child, cuddling her close to him, his life finally framed in squares of practicality. Eventually, Elizabeth's eyes fluttered open as the child pulled away from her breast. Seeing Darcy enthralled with their daughter sent sweet sensations through her. "Are you happy, my Love?" she said sleepily.

"I spent a lifetime preparing for this moment. That is what my father said when Georgiana was born. I understand now what he meant. They are perfect, Lizzy; you are perfect. Like you promised, I will no longer have to work so hard at being happy. Everything I need is in this room."

Darcy handed her their daughter, and he took their son. She adjusted the child to her other breast. "This could be a full-time job," she laughed.

"I will bring in an extra wet nurse tomorrow," Darcy said as he rubbed his son's back, waiting for the burp to come. He looked back to Elizabeth. "It is amazing, Elizabeth, how this immense love sweeps over a person when he holds his child for the first time."

"A baby is a testament to love."

"In that case," he teased, "we must be twice as much in love as everyone else."

"Is everything well with Georgiana?" Elizabeth felt ashamed for not asking sooner.

"My sister will marry Mr. Harrison," Darcy said at last. "He saved her from Captain Rutherford. Edward and I decided our story would be she came to Hines Park to announce her engagement, and the storm delayed my arrival."

"You do not intend to tell me what happened?"

"Tomorrow, my Love, I will tell you everything. Edward will bring Mr. Harrison here, along with Georgiana. We need to discuss several things regarding Georgiana and Kitty, but you must be exhausted this evening. My sister and Mr. Harrison are safe; that is what is important."

As he walked toward the window carrying their child, Elizabeth asked, "Have you considered names for our children, Mr. Darcy?"

"You know me too well, Lizzy." Darcy laughed at himself. "Before I heard your screams, I took our daughter into my study. I stood at the French doors, and I foolishly showed her the gardens when a thought came to me from my tour on the Continent. In Italy, I discovered the phrase *Dare alla Luce,* which means *give unto the light.*"

"Like in the well dressing mosaic?" she teased.

Darcy graciously ignored her taunt. "At first, I considered the name *Lucy,* as a reference to the *light,* but with a son, too, I have come upon a different idea. Traditionally, I should consider naming my son after my father, but our Pemberley breaks with traditions. *Dare alla Luce—give unto the light.* What do you say to Ella and Lucas?"

"Ella Darcy—Lucas Darcy—not traditional names, but I believe they suit our children." Elizabeth eased Ella from her breast. "May we put the children safely between us and rest together, Fitzwilliam?"

"Of course, Lizzy; you must be exhausted. I cannot wait for Georgiana to see the babies; she will be so happy." Darcy looked pleased again.

"You realize, Mr. Darcy, we are likely to be descended upon by various relatives over the next few weeks. When we next have a child, my Love, let us do so in the dead of winter when the roads will prevent travel, then we will have the child to ourselves." Elizabeth looked about her. She moved Ella next to her in the bed, caressing the baby's face. "Lucas, my son, you must protect your sister." Elizabeth teasingly rubbed the boy's stomach.

Darcy sat down on the edge of the bed. "Ella, my daughter, you must teach your brother some of your mother's sensibility and your father's foolishness."

"We will have quite a household," Elizabeth snickered.

"A year ago there was only Georgiana and I in this house. Now we have added so much more. I have you and the twins. Georgiana will have Mr. Harrison, and we can even consider Kitty and Mr. Ashford." Darcy stroked Elizabeth's arm as he spoke. Her curls spread out over her pillow, and Darcy enjoyed the intimacy of the scene.

"Then you regret nothing about our life, Fitzwilliam?" Elizabeth asked nervously.

"Regrets, my Elizabeth, are the past crippling a person in the present. They are a waste of time." Darcy caressed her face. "I regret nothing about us, Elizabeth. Nothing at all."

CHAPTER 28

*"Pride relates more to our opinion of ourselves,
vanity to what we would have others think of us."*
Jane Austen, *Pride and Prejudice*, 1813

Darcy told Elizabeth all the details of Captain Rutherford's attack on Hines Park, including his intended conquest of Georgiana. "Mr. Harrison used the last of his energies to save Georgiana. They beat the man nearly to death, but his only thought was to save my sister."

"Captain Rutherford hated Mr. Harrison that much?" Elizabeth readjusted her position in the bed.

"When Mr. Harrison became a designee for Parliament, Captain Rutherford felt the need to step up his resistance. From what I heard from the captain's cronies, they planned to burn Hines Park to the ground, but the storm delayed their efforts. If not for the storm, we may have found the estate in ruins and Mr. Harrison dead. The delay made it easier to overcome the captain's forces because they partook of Harrison's wine cellar too much."

"Shall the constable take offense?"

"As Edward is the son of the Earl of Matlock, Mr. Harrison headed to Parliament, and Georgiana my sister, I doubt it."

It actually took Edward an extra day to return to Pemberley. The constable had numerous questions, and Chadwick Harrison took a turn for the worse, but they managed to roll into Pemberley early in the morning. Georgiana supervised when the staff took Mr. Harrison into the house. She gave orders to Mrs. Reynolds about his care. "I expect someone to tend to Mr. Harrison's needs immediately."

Mrs. Reynolds laughed with amusement. "Yes, Miss Georgiana," she said while thinking how grown up the girl suddenly became.

Georgiana knocked on Elizabeth's door, excited about the news of the babies. "Come," Elizabeth called, knowing her sister would visit immediately upon her return.

"Elizabeth." Georgiana came rushing to her side. "I missed you so."

They embraced as Elizabeth took in the confidence the girl showed. "I missed you also." She touched her sister's face. "Did he hurt you?" Elizabeth asked tentatively.

"I was frightened, but I knew somehow Mr. Harrison would come for me. The captain, I believe, was surprised by my resourcefulness. I do not think he ever judged me to have any grit." Georgiana seemed proud of herself.

"Then he did not know the true you," Elizabeth added with a smile. Hannah and one of the wet nurses entered, carrying the twins. "Now, my dear Sister, let me introduce you to your niece and nephew." Georgiana giggled with anticipation. Hannah placed the girl in Georgiana's arms. Her son became Elizabeth's. "Georgiana, may I introduce Ella Jane Darcy and Lucas Edward Darcy."

"I love the names," Georgiana squealed. She turned back the blanket to look at her niece, gently touching the fuzzy soft baby hair. "She looks like you, Elizabeth."

"Then let me show you your brother reincarnated." Elizabeth seemed pleased when she turned back the blanket on her son. "Fitzwilliam can never deny this child."

Georgiana stepped over to the bed to see her nephew up close. "An heir for Pemberley," she said softly as she touched the child's head. "Fitzwilliam must be ecstatic."

"Your brother does seem quite pleased with himself—as if he planned it this way. I believe Fitzwilliam discovered love is not thunder's flash but something more subdued and mellow."

"A melodious harmony," Georgiana finished Elizabeth's thought.

"Exactly," Elizabeth added, "one logical progression."

Darcy and Edward met in the study. "The constable finally questioned Mr. Harrison. His retelling of Rutherford's attack coincided with what I told the man earlier, and no legal action will be taken against us. Rutherford's men are a different story. Harrison's servants are restoring the house; two of his staff were laid to rest yesterday. Unfortunately, Mr. Harrison had some complications due to the number of times Rutherford beat him so Georgiana and I attended the rites in his place. I thought it best for Georgiana to be seen taking on the responsibilities as mistress of the estate."

"As usual, Edward, you are thorough in your assessment of the situation." Darcy showed his disapproval.

"Accept it, Fitz," Edward offered a gentle warning. "You may insist on a longer engagement, but Georgiana chose Mr. Harrison for her own, and like you with Elizabeth she is determined to have her way. It is one of those damnable Darcy traits in which you so often take pride."

Darcy shrugged his shoulders as if he did not like relinquishing control of his sister's future. "I suppose I have no choice."

"Good," Edward added with finality. "I do have other news."

Darcy seemed less interested. "And that would be?"

Edward slid Darcy's insignia ring across the desk.

Darcy picked it up, examining it closely. "Where did you get this?"

"From off Captain Rutherford's finger." Edward hoped to solve the mystery. "Georgiana says you never take it off; you had the ring on when you left for Hull, but I do not recall seeing it when we found you in Brigg."

Darcy leaned back in his chair, holding the ring close where he could see it. Images filled his eyes.

A fourth well-dressed man bent over him. "You will not need these items, Sir." The man hissed as he took Darcy's walking stick and diamond stickpin. "Nor this." The man ripped the ring bearing the family crest from Darcy's finger.

"No," Darcy moaned loudly, trying to resist the man's thievery.

Then the filcher strode to the horse awaiting him. Mounting, the man looked back at Darcy lying on the ground and tipped his hat to him. The man's blond, tight curls glistening in the late afternoon was all Darcy could decipher; the man took the lead, riding tall in the saddle.

"Rutherford was one of my attackers!" Darcy's voice held confusion. "He planned my attack."

Edward continued with the mystery. "Do you remember what the captain said when we forced our way into the bedchamber?"

With disbelief laced through his voice, Darcy whispered the words reverently. "Mr. Darcy, you are a hard man to kill." He shook his head in bewilderment. "*Honi soit qui mal y pense.*"[5]

"Evil to him who thinks evil," the colonel translated. "Very appropriate. Thank God the man failed in both his attempts."

"Yes," Darcy spoke quietly. "Now both Mr. Harrison and I have a chance for a brighter future." Both men sat contemplating what might have been. Eventually, Darcy changed the atmosphere found in the room. "Before you leave for Bath, Edward, you must come to the nursery and meet *my future.*"

"I told you Elizabeth would make you happy, Fitz."

"All right, Edward," Darcy warned jokingly, "I will learn to listen to your advice. I bow to your intuition. Now, come and see how I polluted the shades of Pemberley."

"You remember, Darcy?"

"I remember, Edward. Most of it came back over the last few weeks. I sat watching Elizabeth, worrying about her—learning to love her again, and the memories came sneaking back in. At first, I thought them to be my dreams, but later I knew otherwise."

Edward embraced his cousin. "You deserve happiness, Fitz. Now, I must see these children. It will bedevil Lady Catherine when I rant and rave about them."

"Have you made arrangements to send her Ladyship away?" Darcy asked as they crossed to the doorway.

"When my commission expires next week, I will make arrangements for Anne and me to holiday in Italy. While there, I will let a small villa for our aunt. Do you suppose Italy to be far enough from Rosings?" Edward's sly smile lit up the room.

"Maybe you should consider India or even China." Darcy's mood improved. "In a little over a fortnight you will be married as well, and then you may begin your own family."

Edward laughed, "You have a head start."

"It is not a competition," Darcy reasoned.

Edward placed his arm around Darcy's shoulder as they climbed the staircase. "Everything we ever did was a competition, Fitz. Do you suppose we could change our stripes?"

"Tigers never do," Darcy laughed.

Edward laughed, too. "No, tigers never do."

Georgiana snuck into Mr. Harrison's room in the late afternoon. "Mr. Harrison," she spoke quietly as she came close to the bed. "I brought something for you to see." Georgiana sat on the edge of the bed.

Harrison's eyes slid open; he tried to smile at Georgiana. "Miss Darcy," he said through the laudanum, "you should not be here unchaperoned."

"I brought my own chaperone." Georgiana leaned down closer to show him the bundle she carried in her arms. "This is my niece Ella Jane Darcy. Is she not beautiful?"

It took a few seconds for Harrison to refocus his eyes on the child. "She favors Mrs. Darcy," he said at last. "Is Mr. Darcy disappointed not to have a son?"

"That is the beauty of it all; Elizabeth had twins. I will bring Lucas to see you later." Georgiana's eyes danced with happiness.

Harrison tried to tease her, "Do twins run in the Darcy family?"

"We will have to wait and see," she whispered close to his ear.

"I am sorry," he said quietly, "my troubles forced you into an engagement you did not want at this time. Please know I will do the honorable thing, Miss Darcy."

"Mr. Harrison, do not apologize. I chose to come to Hines Park. I could have sent a post to warn you, but I knew whatever happened to you, I must be a part of it. Are you sorry to be saddled with me after all?" Georgiana needed his assurance.

"God, no," he nearly exclaimed. "I thought of nothing but you for months now. In fact, if I had not been thinking of you, I might have been more aware of the captain's impending attack."

"It seems you hold me to an impossible standard." Georgiana playfully moved the hair away from his face. "First, you say you enjoy thinking of me, and then you blame me for your current pain."

"Miss Darcy, I assure you, I would do it all over again for the opportunity of being alone with you like this."

"Then, Mr. Harrison, do you ever plan to ask me to marry you, or do you expect me to walk down the aisle without ever receiving your proposal?"

Harrison found his condition mortifying. "I planned to wait until I did not look so bad, and I was not lying here like a broken twig."

Georgiana put the sleeping Ella on the end of Mr. Harrison's bed. She stared down at him. "Do you suppose, Mr.

Harrison, I am so shallow I would only love you when you are perfectly coiffed? Could I not love you in times of trouble—in sickness and in health? Do you think so poorly of me?"

Harrison did not like the gist of this conversation. "Miss Darcy, please listen to me." He reached out for her. "I want everything to be perfect for you because I love you desperately. An edict from your brother is not what I call a moment to remember. I want a romantic moment when I can ask you to be my wife. I want to be able to take you in my arms and claim you as mine."

"Mr. Harrison, why can this not be our romantic moment?"

"You deserve so much better than a beaten man and a darkened bedchamber. You are the most exquisite person I have ever known," he pleaded.

"Mr. Harrison, do you not think we are beyond a proposal in the garden? Captain Rutherford took us to another level of intimacy. What I deserve is a man who accepts me for who I am, who loves me for my strength and for my vulnerability." Georgiana's voice rose in anger.

"Georgiana," he started, but her irritation reached its breaking point. She picked up the sleeping child and left him struggling to get out of the bed.

A few hours later, Harrison heard a light knock on the door. "Yes," he called.

"Mr. Harrison, you wished to see me?" Georgiana voice still reflected her contempt from earlier.

"Come in, Miss Darcy." When she opened the door, lighted candles peppered the room, and vases of flowers filled every corner. Georgiana's eyes sparkled with surprise. "My garden awaits you, Miss Darcy. Will you not join me?" Seductive overtones laced his voice.

"Mr. Harrison, what a surprise!" Georgiana's eyes did not move from his face.

Harrison offered a gesture of his hand. "I am afraid I must ask you to come to me, Miss Darcy. It took several robust men to prop me up in this bed. I cannot offer you a proper bow or a proffered arm."

Georgiana still stood barely inside the door. "What do you plan to offer me, Mr. Harrison?" She took a few small steps toward the bed.

"Unfortunately, Miss Darcy, you already own my heart. I believe I may be running out of things of worth to offer." He patted the edge of the bed, indicating she should join him there.

"There is only one thing of which I wish you to speak." Georgiana moved closer to the bed but did not sit.

Harrison reached under his pillow and withdrew a small box. Then he made a point of looking deep in Georgiana's eyes, willing her to sit beside him. "Miss Darcy, from the time I came here in December, I have been unable to repress my feelings for you. I love you most ardently. Earlier today you expressed a like regard, and I pray with all my heart your affections and wishes are unchanged. I would consider it a profound honor if you would accept my hand in marriage."

Georgiana's eyes misted over; this was the moment of which she dreamed. "I receive your proposal with gratitude and pleasure," she began. "To be known as Mrs. Harrison would honor me."

"Say it again, Georgiana," Harrison teased.

"I want to be your wife—the mother of your children—the mistress of your estate. Is that not enough, Chadwick?"

"I could listen to those words all day. Yet, I suspect we should make this official." He opened the box and removed a diamond-encrusted ruby ring. Slipping it on her finger, Georgiana leaned down to kiss his lips tenderly. Harrison slid his hand to the back of her neck and held her lips to his when she started to withdraw. "So perfect," he moaned.

"Perfect," she whispered.

Harrison returned to her lips one more time before he released Georgiana. "Would it be too much to ask you to stay with me for a while? I do not want to be without you this evening."

"Fitzwilliam will not be happy, but I will have cook send us both up a tray. I will leave the door open," Georgiana reasoned. "I shall return in a few minutes."

"You will not be gone long?" Harrison asked, a certain amount of longing found in his voice.

"Not long, my Love." Georgiana caressed his chin line. "May I bring Lucas for you to see?"

"Babies give me wanton ideas," he joked. "Wanton ideas of your being the mother of my children."

"So we are back to the forwardness, are we?" Georgiana giggled.

Harrison asserted, "You like me that way."

"True—truly I do. I will return soon." Georgiana squeezed his hand.

Georgiana rushed to Elizabeth's room to show her sister the ring and to share her happiness. "I feel changed somehow," the girl gushed with excitement.

"You have changed, Georgiana. You are no longer a shy, young girl; you are a confident woman. I am so proud of you." Elizabeth hugged the girl she learned to love. "However, like your brother, I will miss you when you leave us."

"Thank you, Elizabeth, for listening to me and hearing what I had to say. You gave me my voice and my confidence."

"Like my darling Fitzwilliam, the person you are now is who you were always meant to be."

"May I take Lucas to see Mr. Harrison?" Georgiana rushed about the room, trying to focus her excitement.

"I always welcome the praises of others for my children so, of course, you may. However, do not start thinking of your own family too soon. Your brother is having enough trouble picturing you as a bride and wife without picturing you as a mother, too."

"Fitzwilliam, I have an idea of which I wish to speak." Elizabeth cornered him in the dining parlor. It was her first evening downstairs since having the twins.

"Yes, my Love." Darcy took her arm to lead her to his table, a very symbolic act in his estimation, a confirmation of Darcy's "refound" devotion to her.

"When my parents and the Bingleys come to Pemberley, I would like to have a tenant celebration."

"Of what do you have in mind?" Darcy held the chair for Elizabeth and then took his place at the head of the table.

"After Edward's wedding, my parents and the Bingleys wish to follow you back to Pemberley to meet the twins. Kitty will remain with us. The tenants are anxious to meet your heirs also; they anticipated the births for a long time. I thought a day of celebration would be appropriate—maybe something similar to an extended family picnic. We could share Mr. Harrison's engagement to Georgiana, as well as Mr. Ashford's to Kitty. The community needs to see the stability Pemberley offers, and I wish my family to see how proud I am of being your wife."

How could Darcy refuse such a request? Elizabeth recognized the requirements of being Pemberley's mistress. "Elizabeth, I do not object to the idea, but I do not want you to overextend yourself after having the twins."

Elizabeth squeezed his hand. "I promise not to overextend my energies. I will rely heavily on Mrs. Reynolds and the household staff. I seriously believe the tenants need to see us together as a family. After your attack, rumors flew about whether Pemberley would survive; the Derbyshire community needs to know we are united with the children, and we will be here for a long time."

"You are so amazing, Elizabeth. I have said it before, but my words cannot do you justice." Darcy's eyes locked onto hers. Elizabeth simply shrugged her shoulders, not accepting his praise. "Do as you think best then, Mrs. Darcy," he added with a sense of contentment.

Over the next few weeks, Pemberley returned to a state of normalcy. The twins consumed much of Elizabeth's waking hours. Mr. Harrison recovered from Rutherford's attack; the bruising went away, and the wounds healed. Darcy and Georgiana traveled to Kent for Edward and Anne's wedding. They attended the ceremony and the breakfast; then they took their leave. Darcy delivered from Elizabeth a handwritten note of thanks to Charlotte for her loving friendship. The note also told Charlotte of Elizabeth's joy with parenthood.

On the return trip, Darcy stopped in Hertfordshire. The Bingleys and the Bennets would join the Darcys for a few days at Pemberley. The Darcys stayed at Netherfield because Darcy wished to renew his relationship with Charles Bingley. Some of his memories of Charles's friendship also resurfaced. "I found a property an hour away from Pemberley if you are still interested, Bingley."

"Maybe we can see it when we come to Pemberley."

"I assume the Bennets know nothing of this," Darcy added.

Jane looked about nervously. "I do not wish my mother to suspect our plans, Mr. Darcy."

"It would please Elizabeth to have you so close, especially after Georgiana's wedding."

"That means a great deal to me also, Mr. Darcy. Family is important to all of us." Jane squeezed Bingley's hand and gave him a slight nod.

"There is something else we have not told the Bennets. My wife is with child." Bingley beamed as he said the words out loud.

"Then it is important to find you the perfect estate, and that is exactly what we will do."

"He filled the room with candles and flowers," Georgiana gushed. "It was perfect."

"I am most anxious to see Mr. Ashford; it has been nearly two months. I worry he forgets me." Kitty needed Ashford's pledge. "The wedding is six weeks away, and we have discussed nothing. I am afraid, Georgiana, he no longer loves me."

"Oh, Kitty, if you could just see how miserable the man is without you at Pemberley, you would never question his regard. His sermons have lost their passion. Mr. Ashford goes through the motions, but, you, Kitty, bring life to the man's existence. Mr. Ashford offered to give up the living from my brother for you. What other proof do you need of his affection?"

"I hope you are right, Georgiana; I am just worried I may lose him." Kitty dropped her eyes and bit her lower lip. "May I tell you something, Georgiana?"

"Of course, Kitty."

"I let Mr. Ashford kiss me on several occasions. Could he think less of me because of it?" Kitty looked worried.

"Kitty, I guarantee the man loves you. If you allowed him some liberties, they have not lessened his desire to marry you. In fact, you may have increased those desires. I guarantee it, and in two days' time, you will guarantee it also."

★ ★ ★

Elizabeth walked about the lawn of Pemberley, overseeing the festivities. She became quite adept at supervising several activities at once. Pockets of people stretched out on blankets, enjoying the late afternoon sunshine. Her parents visited at Pemberley for nearly a week. The Bennets would remain with the Darcys for three more days before returning to Longbourn.

Mrs. Bennet barely spoke the first two days at the house, too enthralled with her surroundings to dare speak to Mr. Darcy about his home. "Oh, Lizzy, bless me, I never imagined Pemberley to be such a great estate. I cannot wait to tell my sister Phillips and Lady Lucas how important you really are. You were so smart to give Mr. Darcy an heir right away. These great men expect it, you know, my girl."

"Yes, Mama, I know." Elizabeth's eyes rolled in exasperation.

Mr. Bennet liked hiding himself in Darcy's library. "I could spend a lifetime in that room, Lizzy."

"Mr. Darcy does share your love of books, Papa." Elizabeth hugged her father. "Come play with your beautiful grandchildren. Mrs. Reynolds and Hannah are bringing them down from the nursery." Elizabeth led her father to some chairs scattered under a large Spanish chestnut.

"Mrs. Darcy." A woman rushed over to speak to Elizabeth. The woman made Elizabeth a perfect curtsy. "We be thankin' ye Mistress for thinkin' of us in yur time of happiness. I brung ye somethin' for the babes." She thrust two wooden rattles in Elizabeth's hand. "Me son carved 'em himself."

"Thank you for your goodness, Mrs. Fleming. Mr. Darcy and I are pleased you are here today. Enjoy the activities." Elizabeth touched the woman's hand before moving on. She placed the rattles on a blanket holding various gifts designed for the children.

Darcy came up behind her and lightly touched her waist. Elizabeth turned to look up at him; she caressed his jaw line as she gifted Darcy with a gigantic smile. "Mrs. Reynolds is bringing the children down from the nursery, my Love."

"Everyone seems to be enjoying themselves." Darcy scanned the area.

"The day is perfect."

"I am pleased to see you wearing my mother's necklace; you have not worn it since our wedding." Darcy's eyes drifted down Elizabeth's body. "You are very beautiful today." He whispered in her ear.

"Mr. Darcy," Elizabeth leaned in close and lowered her voice, "if I did not know better, I would think you had unchaste ideas."

Darcy gave her a mysterious smile. "I miss you, Mrs. Darcy."

"And I you, Sir." Elizabeth blushed with her boldness as she examined his physique closely.

His breath came shallower. "Then maybe. . . ."

Elizabeth touched his lips with her fingertips. "Not maybe," she whispered again. "Definitely."

"I love you, Elizabeth." Seeing her wearing his mother's necklace made Darcy feel very possessive, and a surge of need rushed through him.

"Shall I expect this reaction each time I wear this necklace?" Elizabeth smiled, watching his eyes fill with desire.

"Definitely," he teased.

Elizabeth taunted, "Then I will wear it and nothing else."

"Not fair, Lizzy." Darcy nearly moaned.

She pursed her lips. "Touché, my Love—*definitely* not fair."

Mrs. Reynolds and Hannah brought down the children and handed them to Darcy and Elizabeth. They took a dominant position on a slight incline. Standing very close to each other in a show of solidarity, they waited for the crowd to gather around. Georgiana helped Mr. Harrison, who still struggled, although his progress was evident to everyone. Elizabeth motioned for Kitty and Mr. Ashford to come forward also.

Darcy cleared his throat as the gathered masses moved even closer. He hated speaking at any type of gathering beyond one of a few close friends. Elizabeth, sensing his discomfort, edged closer, allowing her fingers to caress his arm in the guise of shifting the baby in hers. Darcy glanced down at her when her touch awakened a knowledge he was no longer alone.

Clearing his voice a second time, Darcy began to speak. "Friends and family of Pemberley, Mrs. Darcy and I welcome you today, and we appreciate your sharing in our happiness. As many of you know, Pemberley has been blessed of late. We are blessed to have Mrs. Darcy's sister, Miss Bennet, accepting the hand of our own Mr. Ashford." The crowd acknowledged the happy couple as Ashford brought Kitty's hand to his lips.

Darcy continued, "The Pemberley family and I have been blessed to have my sister Georgiana Darcy with us for these many years. Her goodness and generosity is well known among you. Now, Miss Darcy has accepted the hand of Mr. Harrison and will split her time between his estate in Dove Dale and in London, as Mr. Harrison will serve county Derby in Parliament." The crowd took great pride in their connection to the new PM and showed it with cheers and applause.

When the commotion settled, Darcy prepared to raise his voice again, but before he could express the words in his heart, he gazed into Elizabeth's eyes. Finally, he turned back to the faces he knew as the Master of Pemberley. "I am blessed to have found an incomparable woman who in a short time made Pemberley her own. Mrs. Darcy loves this estate as I love it, and this remarkable woman has given me—given us—the greatest gift of all. She has given Pemberley a future. Help me to welcome my daughter, Ella Jane Darcy, and my son, Lucas Edward Darcy." With that, Darcy and Elizabeth turned back the blankets and allowed those gathered that day to view the heirs to the land. A tumultuous roar burst forth, and both parents reassured their children all was well.

Elizabeth placed Ella in her mother's arms and took Lucas from Darcy. Cradling her son close to her, Elizabeth began to circulate among the clusters of people anxious to see the heir to Pemberley. Darcy, Georgiana, Mr. Harrison, Kitty, and Mr. Ashford were immediately surrounded by well-wishers.

After a few minutes, Darcy rejoined Elizabeth among the crowd. "Mrs. Darcy, your father wishes to hold his first grandson," Darcy spoke authoritatively, but Elizabeth knew he wanted to relieve her of her duties to his tenants.

"Of course, Mr. Darcy." She excused herself from the group and thankfully placed Lucas in Mr. Bennet's waiting arms. To her father Elizabeth whispered words of endearment, and Mr. Bennet returned her sentiments. "I miss you at Longbourn, Lizzy," his eyes misted as he spoke to his favorite daughter, "but it is quite evident your place is here with Mr. Darcy."

Elizabeth looked up, catching Darcy's gaze across the lawn. "It is, Papa. Coming to Pemberley, I found myself. I belong at Pemberley because Mr. Darcy is here."

It was the Bennets last night at Pemberley. Mrs. Bennet took stories of Elizabeth's success as the estate's mistress and mother of Darcy's children to Hertfordshire to share with any who might listen. Mr. Bennet took memories of his first grandchildren, knowledge his Lizzy found happiness, and a stack of Darcy's books to read. He would return the books at Kitty's wedding.

"Mr. Bennet." Clayton Ashford approached where the older man stood with Darcy.

"Mr. Ashford." Mr. Bennet turned toward the young vicar.

Ashford looked a bit backward. "May I speak to you, Sir?"

"Of course, Mr. Ashford."

"If you will excuse me." Darcy started to take his leave, but Ashford asked him to stay.

"I have some news which I feel an obligation to tell both of you," Ashford began. "I lately received a letter from my father's uncle. Unfortunately, the man recently lost his only child—his son. As I am the next male in line, his estate will fall into my hands upon my relative's passing."

Ashford said the words so solemnly, Mr. Bennet knew not whether the vicar looked forward to the event. "Well, young man, it seems your potential is more than I anticipated." Mr. Bennet thought the situation to be amusing.

"Thank you, Sir. Of course, I wish no harm to my relations. I simply chose to make you aware one day I will be able to give Miss Bennet a nicer home. I believe your daughter deserving of more than I am currently able to give her."

Mr. Bennet teased, "You believe our Kitty to be deserving?"

Mr. Ashford looked a bit askance. "Most definitely, Mr. Bennet."

Mr. Bennet gave Darcy half a wink. "Mr. Ashford, I once thought my Kitty to be one of the two most foolish girls in the country—her sister Lydia being the other. However, if she earned the regard of a landed gentleman, I may have to change my estimation of her."

Darcy picked up on Mr. Bennet's teasing nature. "Maybe, Mr. Bennet, we should ask the size of Mr. Ashford's estate before we offer our congratulations or extend our approval."

"I believe you are correct, Mr. Darcy." Both men took Ashford into their gaze, leveling a serious stare on him.

Ashford began to stammer. "I believe, Sirs, it has an income of a little less than three thousand pounds per year."

After an exceedingly long pause both Darcy and Mr. Bennet began to laugh. Darcy slapped Ashford on the back. "We apologize, Mr. Ashford, for taking our pleasure at your expense. Although I would hate to lose you from our community, I am sure both Mr. Bennet and I extend our sincere congratulations. We are pleased for your beneficial situation. Where might the estate be?"

Ashford still appeared confused, but he relaxed some. "Near Bedfordshire, Mr. Darcy."

"Well, we will pray for your relations' continued good health," Darcy added with a smile.

"Considering my wife's nerves can tolerate no more than the splendor of Pemberley right now, I will spare you, Mr. Ashford, by not sharing your news with Mrs. Bennet until we are well on our way to Longbourn." Mr. Bennet patted Ashford's shoulder and strolled away.

Ashford looked bewildered. Darcy took it all in before trying to assuage Ashford's qualms. "Do not fear, Mr. Ashford, Mr. Bennet only finds those amusing whom he believes to be the most worthy. You will get used to the man's sense of humor; even I once feared asking for Mrs. Darcy to become my wife."

"How could Mr. Bennet consider you to be unworthy?" Ashford thought this to be an amusing possibility.

"The man may appear indolent, but he cares dearly for his daughters. I am sure your news pleased him thoroughly." Darcy led Ashford back toward the gathering. "When will you tell Miss Bennet?"

"Soon—I wanted to give Miss Bennet more than simply my love; it appears God answered my prayers, but I will sorely miss my time tending to my congregation." Ashford's eyes affectionately drifted to where Kitty stood talking to her sisters and Georgiana.

"I am sure your Lord will not turn his back on your service in his name," Darcy assured him. "When the time comes, you will find God has bigger plans for you."

Ashford asked in all honesty, "Do you truly believe as such, Mr. Darcy?"

"There was a time, Mr. Ashford, I thought my destiny to be decided by my birth right. However, since meeting Mrs. Darcy, I have been persuaded to see God places a person on the path, but his destiny is still in his own hands."

They joined the four ladies, and Elizabeth stepped to Darcy's side, intertwining her arm through his. "May I, Fitzwilliam?" she asked as he nodded in agreement.

"Kitty." Elizabeth's eyes sparkled with excitement. "Mr. Darcy and I have news for you and Mr. Ashford. Lord and Lady

Haverty called upon us last week to pay their respects and to meet the twins. While here, I showed Lady Haverty to the nursery; your design impressed her Ladyship. She offered to pay you two hundred pounds to redecorate two rooms at her estate."

"Elizabeth," Kitty gushed, "tell me you do not jest."

"We do not jest, Kitty," Elizabeth confirmed what she said. "If Lady Haverty is pleased, you could earn additional funds for your talent."

"Did you hear, Clayton," Kitty bubbled with laughter, "I could earn money just like an independent woman might do."

"I heard, Miss Bennet." Ashford barely acknowledged Kitty's enthusiasm.

CHAPTER 29

"It is a truth universally acknowledged, that a single man in possession of a good fortune must be in want of a wife."
Jane Austen, *Pride and Prejudice*, 1813

As the evening progressed, Kitty finally cornered Mr. Ashford alone for a few minutes. He pretended to read, but Kitty knew his attention to the book to be a sham. "Mr. Ashford," she spoke softly, hoping to relay a sense of intimacy, "have I offered you some offense?"

Ashford brought his eyes to meet hers. "No, Madam, I find little fault with you."

Kitty, who had grown wiser in the past year, knew just what to say. "My dear, Clayton," she whispered, "we each have one fault: I keep no secrets, and, you, my Love, conceal everything. Please tell me what displeases you."

Ashford looked deeply into Kitty's eyes, holding her gaze before he spoke. "Miss Bennet, when one first meets you, he finds you to be a little rough around the edges, but on closer examination, he cannot help but see you are absolutely beautiful."

Kitty blushed and looked away briefly, but, finally, she returned his gaze once again. "Mr. Ashford, you try to distract me from my pleas with your words of flattery. Please, Clayton, I beg you not to shut me out."

"If you insist, Miss Bennet, but it will seem foolish," he began slowly. "Although I applaud your ingenuity, I fear your abandoning me for the fame you may achieve as an *independent* woman. I know your preference for balls and parties, and I can give you none of that—at least, not in the near future."

Against propriety, Kitty took his hand in hers. "Clayton, I love you." She paused before continuing, hoping to find the right words. "May I tell you something? Last winter when I traveled to Nottingham with my sister and Mr. Darcy, I went for many long walks across the Pennington and the Matlock estates, and on those walks, I found myself. I found I am not my sister Lydia; I am more like Elizabeth. I have a certain resolve to prove myself better than the station in life which defines me, and although balls and socials once were my entertainment of choice, I am no longer that foolish girl; I would prefer the company of well-informed people and good conversation. That is the person I have become, and that person loves you. I would like the opportunity to earn part of my own money; my father can give me very little as part of my dowry, and I want to bring something to this marriage besides my regard for you. We may use the money I receive to purchase the extras for the parsonage, to buy books for the school, or even put the money away for our children." Kitty dropped her voice on the last line.

Ashford looked at Kitty as if seeing her for the first time. "Our children?" he stammered.

Kitty released Ashford's hand after spotting her father's intense stare in her direction. "Do you not want children, Mr. Ashford?" Kitty's voice held hurt, and she bit her lower lip to force back the tears welling in her eyes.

"Of course, I want children—our children." Ashford's words demanded her attention with the urgency in his voice. "I just never suspected you held such thoughts."

"Every woman dreams of her husband and her family," Kitty whispered so only Ashford could hear. "Every woman needs to feel the warmth of the man she loves—to share her intimate self with another. A woman dreams of a man who offers her both love and respect; she dreams of his accepting her for her strength and her vulnerability. A woman does not wish to always conceal her mind in deference to her husband's." Kitty meant her words to let Ashford know she expected to be treated with some equality although the British laws did not demand he do so.

Ashford's eyes filled with love. "Miss Bennet." His voice was laced with desire. "It will be a very long wait until I may call you my own."

"I feel likewise, Sir." Kitty looked about nervously, knowing the conversation turned more intimate.

Ashford cleared his throat. "Miss Bennet, I have something to tell you about our children's futures, but I must ask your forbearance and not to become too excited until it happens."

Kitty seemed confused. "Yes, Clayton?"

"When I sought another position away from Pemberley, I contacted several family members. In my correspondence, I learned a small estate in Bedfordshire is entailed upon me—upon our family in the future." Ashford's voice came soft and comforting.

Kitty's eyes flashed with surprise. "Clayton, this cannot be true."

"I am afraid, Miss Bennet, it is not in my nature to exaggerate the truth. It may be many years before the property becomes mine; you must be patient. Your father prefers to tell your mother upon their return to Longbourn. Therefore, I must ask you to keep this to yourself this evening."

Kitty started to giggle. "You are sincere, Sir?" Ashford nodded in affirmation. "May I not tell anyone?"

"Tonight you must tell only your dreams. Tomorrow you may speak the words out loud."

"How large? I mean, how large an estate?" Kitty could not hide her excitement.

Ashford looked pleased. "From what I know of it, I understand it to be a little larger than your home at Longbourn. My father's uncle is a respected man in the community, and we shall assume his place upon his passing, although I do not wish any harm to the man."

Kitty checked her enthusiasm, not wishing to sound greedy, but the thought of assuming the position of mistress of even a small estate thrilled her. At one time she thought marrying Clayton Ashford was "settling"; now, all her dreams came true. She learned to love him, and now he would give her a position in society. It was the best of both worlds. Kitty realized she would not have the life Elizabeth or Jane did, but she had been right to follow their examples. Kitty would do everything she could to make Ashford a good wife and to make a valued life. Automatically, Kitty thought how jealous Lydia would be of her good fortune. Finally, she redirected her attention to Mr. Ashford. "We will administer to those surrounding Pemberley until our time comes to be elsewhere. Possibly, if we are successful with the village school here, Clayton, we might replicate it in Bedfordshire. You will know how it might be done; it will not be new."

"You speak my ideas out loud, Miss Bennet."

"In the meantime, I hope, Sir, you will see your way to give me permission to pursue any connections my sister may provide me. I will not *advertise,* but I would like to prove my worth to you, to my family, and to myself. I never felt myself worthy of anyone; Clayton, it is important to me." Kitty's eyes beseeched his.

"I wish we were alone, Miss Bennet," Ashford whispered, "so I could show you your worth to me. I can no longer imagine my life without you in it. If decorating rooms makes you happy, my sweetest Katherine, then I will be satisfied to have you happy."

Kitty looked about mischievously before speaking. "Let the husband render unto his wife due benevolence: and likewise also the wife unto the husband."[6]

Ashford chuckled. "The first bond of society is marriage; the next, our children; then the whole family and all things in common."[7] He spoke the words seductively, and Kitty giggled nervously.

In revenge, Kitty pursed her lips, letting Ashford know she would meet his challenge. "Hail, wedded love, mysterious law; true source of human offspring."[8]

Ashford nodded in agreement. "I see, Miss Bennet, you learned your lessons well. Yet, may I add Plutarch's advice to a bride, 'A good wife should be as a looking glass to represent her husband's face and passion; if he be pleasant, she should be merry; if he laugh, she should smile; if he look sad, she should participate of his sorrow.'"[9]

Kitty found this verbal exchange with Clayton Ashford stimulating. She used to observe Elizabeth and Mr. Darcy fence verbally, but she never understood the allure until now. She stood and looked down enticingly at Ashford before saying, "You forget, my dear Mr. Ashford, the old proverb says, 'If you want peace in the house, do what your wife wants.'"

The man laughed out loud. He stood and offered Kitty his arm. "I could never refuse you, Miss Bennet," he said invitingly into her ear as he led her back to her family.

★ ★ ★

The Darcy party finally arrived at his London townhouse. Traveling with the twins presented their own challenges. They came to London from Hertfordshire, having stayed a few extra days at Netherfield following Kitty and Mr. Ashford's wedding. This allowed the newlyweds the opportunity to use Kensington Place for their first few nights of marital bliss. Lady Haverty would meet Kitty tomorrow in the afternoon to choose fabric and furnishings for the rooms at her Ladyship's estate, which Kitty would redesign.

"Mrs. Darcy, we are pleased to see you again." The butler took their outer garments.

"Mr. Thacker, we apologize for bringing you a house full to which to attend." Elizabeth shot a quick glance at Darcy; they had not been in London together since the initial days of their marriage.

"The staff is ready to serve you, Madam, and we are thrilled to finally be able to see Mr. Darcy's children for ourselves. We arranged the nursery per your instructions." Darcy noted the ease with which his staff addressed his wife.

Elizabeth smiled with the reference to the twins. She became accustomed to the reverence with which the Derbyshire community treated her children, but she had not anticipated how the same feelings would, naturally, permeate the London staff. "Is my sister about, Mr. Thacker?" Elizabeth looked around expecting Kitty to greet her.

"Mrs. Ashford is in the drawing room along with the young vicar. They have been quite pleasant guests, Mrs. Darcy. The staff enjoyed serving them."

"Thank you again, Mr. Thacker. May we have some light refreshments brought to the drawing room?" Elizabeth offered the man a smile and a light touch to his arm to let him know she was glad to see him again.

"I anticipated your needs, Madam. They will be there momentarily." He made a quick bow and exited toward the kitchen.

Darcy leaned in to speak to Elizabeth privately. "It appears, Mrs. Darcy, you won over my London staff as well." He smiled down at her.

"My Husband, what I know of interacting with your staff, I learned from observing you, Sir. I profess no real knowledge of any of this." Elizabeth gestured to their surroundings. "Prior to my marriage to you, I held no point of reference to this lifestyle. If I am successful, it is a compliment to your patience and understanding. I cannot imagine how you must have felt assuming all this on your own; I am thankful for the model and guidance you gave me this past year."

Many of Darcy's memories returned, but Elizabeth adopted the habit of acknowledging what all Darcy went through when he first became the Master of Pemberley. Her sentiments seemed to provide a transition between Darcy's former life and the one they shared. "I am pleased you find contentment in these duties, Mrs. Darcy." He continued to whisper to her as he led Elizabeth through the main hallway.

"Fitzwilliam," she confided, "I find contentment in being your wife. I would be content to be in a tenant's cottage if you were there. The house means little without you. Some day I hope you will believe those words; I never fell in love with the wealth—I fell in love with an honorable man."

Darcy paused, allowing the others to enter the room ahead of him. "Elizabeth, I served you poorly as a husband in this past year; yet, you continually accept me back into your loving heart. I do not deserve your regard, but I thank God you still wish to share my life, my home, and my bed."

"Your bed, Mr. Darcy?" Her eyebrow shot up with a teasing gesture.

"Your bed or my bed or our bed," Darcy picked up on her tone, "as long as we are there together."

Elizabeth touched his jaw line. "As long as we are together."

Darcy stood at the door to Elizabeth's dressing room; his wife luxuriated in her bath, unaware of how closely he watched her. His affection for Elizabeth Darcy continued to grow; he allowed himself to respond to her both emotionally and physically, and Darcy often found himself thinking of her when he should be attending to other issues. Today, memories of the passion they shared repeatedly in his Kensington Place townhouse flooded Darcy's sensibilities. He excused her maid, and now Darcy patiently waited for his wife to finish her ablutions.

"Hannah, I am ready," Elizabeth called without looking around. She rested against the back of the tub, eyes closed, letting the water seep around her body.

Darcy paused before answering her, amused by the delight she took in everything she did. Finally, his resonant voice responded, "I sent Hannah away, Lizzy."

Elizabeth rolled on her side and peered over the lip of the tub. A smile overspread her face. "Mr. Darcy," she teased, "has the Master of Pemberley chosen to take on the position as my handmaid?"

He approached her, sauntering over to where Elizabeth laid in the water. "A handmaid," he taunted, "would help you *get dressed*, Mrs. Darcy. That was not what I considered as my duties as the Master of Pemberley."

Elizabeth's eyes sparkled with anticipation. "And what, pray tell, would you consider to be one of your duties as the Master of Pemberley?"

Darcy took a large towel from the shelf. He held it open to her, bidding her with his eyes to step out of the tub. She did as he suggested, and Darcy encircled her wet body with the towel, while lightly kissing her forehead. He whispered in her ear as he trailed kisses down the dampness of her neck, "As the Master of Pemberley, I consider it my *pleasure*, never a duty, to love you as a husband should, Mrs. Darcy."

"Then I may depend on you, Mr. Darcy, to keep the chill away." Elizabeth went up on her toes to nibble on Darcy's lower lip.

"I guarantee you will not feel a chill, my Dearest One." Darcy kissed along Elizabeth's neck and collarbone. She lolled her head back to allow him easier access; Elizabeth moaned as Darcy pressed his need. "Lizzy," he whispered seductively, "I must have you. I thought of nothing else today." Darcy kissed her, quickly deepening the kiss. Finally, he cupped her chin and looked deep into Elizabeth's eyes. "I do love nothing in the world so well as you. Is not that strange?"[10]

Elizabeth laughed lightly. They spoke lines from Benedick and Beatrice before. It was a favorite play of Darcy's. "As strange as the thing I know not. It were as possible for me to say I loved nothing so well as you, but believe me not, and yet I lie not, I confess nothing, nor I deny nothing."

Darcy pulled her closer to him, needing to feel the softness of her skin along her back and hips. Her response made him smile, and before he spoke again, he partook of another kiss. "I swear by it that you love me, and I will make him eat it that says I love not you."

"You have stayed me in a happy hour. I was about to protest I loved you." Elizabeth snaked her arms around his neck and pulled Darcy's mouth to hers once again.

Even with the closeness and the return of Elizabeth's desire for him, Darcy wondered if she forgave him for all the pain of this first year. "And do it with all thy heart?" he asked the question through the play, not willing to sacrifice his feelings to her in any other way. The memory of his prejudice still haunted him.

Elizabeth knew exactly what he needed at that moment. He needed her pledge that they would survive. "I love you with so much of my heart that none is left to protest."

Darcy swallowed hard as she arched toward him. "Come bid me do anything for thee."

Elizabeth pulled his head down to hers once again, kissing him with all the passion she felt whenever in Darcy's arms. "Make me yours, Fitzwilliam; I want to be your wife in every way."

He picked her up in his arms and carried Elizabeth to her bed. "Elizabeth, I will spend my life trying to make you happy." He laid her back on the pillows and began to kiss lightly down her arms and torso.

"I am happy in your arms, Fitzwilliam." Elizabeth kissed behind his ear and along his chin line. "I am happy right this moment because I see the man with whom I fell in love; my life is complete with you and the twins."

"I will live in thy heart," he spoke softly as he set to proving his desire. Elizabeth smiled at Darcy's unexpected vulnerability. He wondered for a moment if he would ever deserve her love. Then he allowed himself the pleasure of enjoying the warm fragrance of Elizabeth's skin. Elizabeth arched against him, and Darcy lost himself to her. "Lizzy," he moaned.

Darcy led Elizabeth and the rest of his party to the private box for the theatre production. Mr. Harrison and Georgiana sat together; initially, they would live at Kensington Place when they were in London. Darcy reasoned it would be more *comfortable* for his sister to be in her "home" while learning her duties as Mr. Harrison's wife with all his new responsibilities. Kensington Place already had a trained staff capable of handling the type of entertaining the Harrisons would need in those early days of their marriage. Eventually, Harrison would take his own place for the two of them. It would be another two months until their wedding. Georgiana *insisted* on coming to London with Mr. Harrison after the first of the year. Darcy *insisted* she spend the Festive Season at Pemberley.

So, they compromised. Georgiana and Mr. Harrison would marry in mid-November. They would spend the Festive Season at Pemberley, helping Elizabeth with the tenant celebration. Although not married, Harrison, with Georgiana at his side, would offer his tenants a similar gathering for All Hallows Eve. Elizabeth and Darcy would serve as their mentors in this matter. The Bishop at Matlock would marry Georgiana. The wedding breakfast would take place at her uncle's estate; the Matlocks planned an elaborate affair for her. Matlock would be closer to London, but Darcy felt she should be at Pemberley, although the small church could not hold the anticipated throng who would attend.

Lady Haverty, still chattering on to Kitty and Mr. Ashford, joined the Darcys as a revered personage. The seven of them sat comfortably in Darcy's box. Lady Haverty became a staple at Pemberley over the last few months. Initially, when she came to the estate, she showed Darcy her disdain for his choice of a wife, but Elizabeth made inroads into her Ladyship's regard that first day, although, in reality, Elizabeth cared not for the woman's manners. Then she reasoned Darcy lost his mother and his Aunt Catherine; if she could build a relationship with Lady Anne's childhood friend, then maybe Darcy would see his wife differently.

That was when Darcy had no memory of Elizabeth, but even with the return of his husbandly attentions to his wife, Elizabeth continued to cultivate a positive relationship with Lady Haverty. The woman, lonely for her own family, happily embraced the young couple, listening to the opinions of Lord and Lady Pennington and the Matlocks rather than Lady Catherine. Now, Lady Haverty deemed it her responsibility to Lady Anne's memory to serve as a "sage" to the young Mistress of Pemberley. Elizabeth listened to the venerable older woman and then did what she deemed best for her family; yet, Lady Haverty never considered Elizabeth's independent mind a slight to her Ladyship's position in society. Instead, the woman learned to enjoy the new life springing from Pemberley. Now, her Ladyship thought helping Kitty Ashford to be the perfect way to enjoy the Darcys' company while building herself a reputation for innovation in her home—a friend of young designers.

"You will love the performance," Lady Haverty invoked as she took one of the lower seats in the box.

Kitty gushed, "This is magnificent! Look at the chandelier, Clayton." She pointed out the obvious with her eyes and the tilt of her chin.

Darcy, Elizabeth, Georgiana, and Chadwick Harrison took the seats behind them. Although not raised in a life of opulence, Elizabeth knew what was expected of her: The constant gazes of others who came to the theatre to be seen and those who came to the theatre to look at the rich and the famous were to be ignored. Polite indifference was the rule, and Elizabeth lightly touched Kitty's shoulder to reel in her sister's enthusiasm.

Watching the stage with polite attention, Elizabeth realized many of the stares were directed toward her. She turned to look at Darcy; his handsome profile brought a smile to her face. Instinctively, she rested her hand in the crook of his arm. Darcy looked down at her hand, took it in his, brought it to his lips, and returned it to his arm. Elizabeth gave him the slightest purse of her lips, and Darcy's eyebrow shot up with the provocation.

A hard stare brought Elizabeth's attention back toward the stage and the audience. An attractive woman sat with a small party in a private box across the way. Elizabeth became acutely aware of the scrutiny in which she found herself. "Fitzwilliam," she whispered as she leaned close to him so as not to disturb the performance, "who is the striking lady in the box on the right?"

Darcy dreaded the question; he hoped Elizabeth did not notice. They spent two exquisite days at Kensington Place rekindling their love, and now his response could destroy those moments. "No one of any consequence." He tried to avoid the inevitable.

Elizabeth felt his body stiffen under her light touch and noticed how Georgiana shifted her weight away from where Elizabeth sat. She raised her eyes once more to the woman, and she knew even without her husband's confirmation; Elizabeth looked into the steady gaze of Cecelia McFarland. Her eyes misted over, as she fought back the tears. She looked at Darcy again, silently demanding he acknowledge her question. Darcy took her hand into his lap and began to stroke her inner wrist with his fingertips. He dropped his chin and mumbled softly, "I am sorry, Elizabeth, for hurting you. Please know I love you more than life."

He did not raise his head again until Elizabeth touched his chin with her index finger. Darcy looked up at his wife, and she held him there with her gaze. The music swelled behind them, but neither of them turned away. He let his gaze run over her. A jumble of memories rushed at Elizabeth, but she gave Darcy a nod, stating she knew her position as his wife. He squeezed her hand as she leaned in to say, "I adore you, my Husband."

Relief flashed across his eyes; Elizabeth would not turn him away. He read her answer in the silence which coursed between them. Finally, Darcy mouthed the words, "Thank you."

Cecelia McFarland carefully watched this interplay between husband and wife. For someone of such low connections, Elizabeth Darcy carried herself well. It almost explained why the haughty Mr. Darcy married her. The woman affected his heart, and the right woman could capture even the crustiest man's heart. Yet, in Miss McFarland's twisted opinion, this pert young woman corrupted the Darcy bloodline; Fitzwilliam Darcy needed to purify his name. By the time the curtain came down, Miss McFarland convinced herself, despite his earlier cut, Darcy still deserved something better than Elizabeth Darcy. Cecelia McFarland decided she would confront the Mistress of Pemberley and make her stand for Darcy's attention one last time.

Elizabeth watched as the spectators made their way toward the exit. "I will fetch the wraps," Darcy whispered in Elizabeth's ear, while motioning to Mr. Ashford to join him.

Lady Haverty took Kitty's arm, joining the throngs working their way through the vast interior passages. Her Ladyship took up a position on the staircase's vast landing where those stiffly bowing to one another could admire her. She introduced Kitty to various friends and pointed out several dignitaries to the young girl's delight.

Finally, Elizabeth and Georgiana stepped through the draped door to the box and into the busy corridor. Mr. Harrison led Georgiana a few feet away to introduce her to some members of the Parliament.

When Miss McFarland stepped casually in front of Elizabeth, the woman's appearance took her by surprise. Elizabeth wanted to turn away, but there was nowhere to which to run. Miss McFarland closed the trap. "Mrs. Darcy, I presume," the woman's voice nearly purred with perfection.

Cecelia McFarland, by all standards, easily portrayed a woman of social standing and position. Her well-bred manner seethed with ambition. Elizabeth felt a bit intimidated; yet, she would not give Darcy up without a fight. She squared her shoulders and lifted her chin. "The purloined author Miss McFarland, I assume?" Elizabeth's voice matched her enemy in false sweetness.

"Where is your husband?" The woman moved in closer to tower over Elizabeth.

Elizabeth wanted to take a step back to open up the sightlines, but instead she used one of Darcy's tricks and stepped up to be within inches of the woman's face. "Mr. Darcy, unfortunately, has no time to continue your relationship, Miss McFarland. I thought he made the point clear previously. I would suggest you seek your interests elsewhere." Elizabeth watched with delight as the woman flinched with her words.

"Should we not allow Mr. Darcy to make that decision? In what world do you believe you could compete with me? No matter what you do, Mrs. Darcy, you will always be found wanting. With whom do you believe your husband spent his time before he was called home for your lying in?" A sneer curled the edges of the lady's lips.

Elizabeth's voice dripped with sarcastic sweetness. "Mr. Darcy and I spent the weeks before my lying in with his cousins in Bath. So, if you wish to insinuate otherwise, Madam, it will be my pleasure to call you out as the liar you are. Check the social registry; you will find us there." Elizabeth purposely turned her back on the woman and began to put on her gloves.

Miss McFarland's temper steamed; she deluded herself into thinking Fitzwilliam Darcy cared for her, and the woman would not be defeated so easily. "This is not over, Mrs. Darcy," she said to the back of Elizabeth's head. "The game is not yet won by you."

Elizabeth turned slowly to look at Cecelia McFarland once again. "Do you play chess, Miss McFarland?" Elizabeth plastered on her face the fake smile she often used with Lady Catherine.

Miss McFarland looked taken aback. "I despise the game." Her voice held pure contempt.

"That is too bad, Miss McFarland. It is a favorite of my husband's; yet, that is neither here nor there. If you knew the game, you would know the king is useless without his queen. That is called *checkmate*." With that, Elizabeth walked away to join Georgiana. She never looked back to see the woman's look of utter bewilderment.

"Who is that attractive woman speaking to my sister?" Kitty whispered into Lady Haverty's ear.

"I believe it to be Miss McFarland," the older woman shared before greeting an acquaintance moving down the Grand Staircase.

"Excuse me, Lady Haverty." Kitty dropped a quick curtsy and started to leave, wishing to be at Elizabeth's side.

At seeing the girl's obvious distress, Lady Haverty clutched Kitty's arm. "What is wrong, Mrs. Ashford?" her Ladyship hissed into Kitty's ear.

"Miss McFarland played poorly by my sister; I must go to her." Kitty confided.

"Played poorly how?" Lady Haverty demanded.

"I am not at liberty to say," Kitty added quickly, trying to make her exit, "but let us just say if the woman were successful the Darcy name would be tainted with scandal."

As Kitty ascended the stairs to be by Elizabeth's side, she saw the woman in question turn to leave Elizabeth's company. Miss McFarland unceremoniously raised her skirts enough to descend the steps quickly. She bumped into several slower theatregoers exiting the building. Kitty stepped to the side to allow her to pass, never looking again at the woman who nearly destroyed all their lives.

Just as Kitty reached Elizabeth and Georgiana, a scream of surprise echoed through the rafters of the hallway. They all jumped from the sound; spinning around, they caught only the commotion of bodies bumping into each other and sprawling at the foot of the Grand Staircase. The crowd pressed forward, including what was left of the Darcy party, bending over the railing, everyone anxious to see the source of the hubbub.

Leaning awkwardly against a column support post of the staircase reposed Miss McFarland. The hem of her gown was torn and her dress askew. Blushing, the woman quickly pulled herself to a standing pose, recovering her demeanor and straightening her dress. However, the snickers of the crowd did not stop even when she restored her bearing, and she looked around nervously for some explanation.

The crowd froze in some horrid montage. Miss McFarland stood alone by the support post, trying to determine how to extricate herself from an obviously embarrassing situation, and, momentarily, she locked eyes with Elizabeth Darcy, noting a look of amusement on the woman's face. The crowd continued to stifle twitters and guffaws. Finally, someone in the back could be heard plainly in the silence of the hall. "My God, the woman's bald!"

A look of horror overcame Miss McFarland's composure as she automatically reached for the wig she wore, finding it setting awry, covering her head but not in place. Tears filled her eyes as she looked into the faces of all those who would now shun her. With her hand trying to adjust the wig as she ran, the woman, who only moments ago commanded the room, now fled from it in alarm. The titters became full out laughter as she streaked past the members of the *ton*.

Kitty buried her face in Georgiana's hair, trying to stifle the laughter which shook her shoulders. Elizabeth and Georgiana schooled their countenances and forced back their desire to join in the crowd's taunt. "Poor woman," Kitty said sarcastically.

"The encore was as entertaining as the actual perform-ance." Elizabeth's tongue-in-cheek comment bubbled out as she fought hard to regain her equanimity.

Georgiana could barely force a straight face. "I am sure tomorrow's reviews will say the performance was so powerful, it caused the hair on one's head to stand on end." All three of them nearly lost it with that comment. Each had to look away and cover their faces with their hands.

Finally, Elizabeth took a deep breath to steady her compo-sure, trying to control her natural tendency for mirth. She allowed her eyes to scan the others on the staircase, and then gasped at seeing her Ladyship being helped to her feet. "Lady Haverty," she called as she pushed her way through the crowd to the woman. "Lady Haverty, please tell me you are unin-jured." Elizabeth quickly moved to support the woman.

"My pride might be a bit injured, Mrs. Darcy," her Ladyship intoned in her best attitude, "but I am well otherwise. Did you see what happened?"

"No, your Ladyship." Elizabeth dropped her eyes, hoping no one realized she had a confrontation with Miss McFarland before the woman tripped on the staircase.

"Then you did not note how I shamed myself by accidentally stepping on the hem of Miss McFarland's dress?" Lady
Haverty forced Elizabeth to look at her. With a nod of her
head she continued. "I am getting up in age and must have
taken a misstep."

Elizabeth stared at this woman who once spoke out against
her. Now, as she gazed at Lady Haverty, the corners of Elizabeth's mouth turned up in a smile. With the realization of what
the older woman just confessed, Elizabeth pushed the laughter
deep within her. "Lady Haverty," she chuckled lightly, "you must
be mistaken. I believe you are known for your lightness of foot."

"Am I really, my dear Mrs. Darcy? Then you will not think
poorly of my mistake? Rumors may hurt one's reputation, and
I would not wish to bring shame to your family through association." Those few knowing seconds established an understanding. Lady Haverty protected Elizabeth from the rumors
following Darcy.

"Your Ladyship will remain a treasured acquaintance of the
Darcy family as long as I am the Mistress of Pemberley." Elizabeth locked arms with the woman and led her to where the
others stood.

★ ★ ★

The cathedral at Matlock glistened as the early winter sun
flickered through the stained glass windows, shimmers of rainbow colors dancing across the faces of those in attendance.
Darcy prowled the recesses of the church, dreading the prospects of giving his sister away in marriage. On one level, he
knew Georgiana would be happy with Mr. Harrison, but
Darcy had not come to complete acceptance that Georgiana
had grown into a competent woman. In his mind's eye, Darcy
saw his sister as the little girl for whom he was responsible.

Everyone he knew sat in the cathedral awaiting Georgiana's appearance. Although his parents would thoroughly approve, he thought he preferred the relatively simple ceremony he shared with Bingley. The wedding breakfast would occur at the Matlocks' estate. Several tenants from both Pemberley and Hines Park journeyed to Matlock as a sign of respect; they waited patiently outside the church to offer well wishes.

"Mr. Darcy, you must wipe that gloomy countenance away." Elizabeth spoke softly to him alone.

Darcy turned to look closely at his wife. "How is my sister?" Darcy's thoughtful attitude relayed his need for assurance of Georgiana's will to go through with this.

Elizabeth considered teasing him but then thought better of it. "Like any woman truly in love, Georgiana glows. The only *cloud* overshadowing her day is she feels she displeases you somehow, my Husband." Elizabeth touched his sleeve, drawing attention to what she said. "Can you not give Georgiana the comfort she seeks on this, her wedding day?"

"I do not wish to lose her, Elizabeth." The words hung in the air.

"You can never lose Georgiana. She carries you with her in every step she takes. You, my Love, are more than a brother; you are Georgiana's parent, guardian, role model, and friend. You treated her with respect and taught her what you value. The magnificent woman she has become is because of you. Please give her your blessing and not just your consent."

Darcy touched Elizabeth's chin with his index finger before moving away. Her words made what he had to do easier. He tapped lightly on the door where Georgiana awaited him. When he heard her acknowledge his entrance, Darcy took a deep breath before entering. He stood mesmerized by the image of the woman she had become. "You remind me of our mother." His words told the secret he felt in his heart.

"Do I really?" Georgiana's nervousness crept into her words.

Darcy walked over to where she stood; he took her hands in his and spoke to her from his heart. "You, Dearest One, are so much like her; I find I do not wish to lose you. I withheld my support for this union for selfish reasons. Losing you to Mr. Harrison is like losing our mother once again."

Expressing such needs cost Darcy greatly, and relief rushed through Georgiana in knowing he did not disapprove of her actions after all. She reached out and caressed his face with her palm. "Fitzwilliam, we each must find the path which makes us happy; Elizabeth is your path, and Chadwick is mine. Yet, Brother, we are always—always connected; for so many years there was just us two. Please be happy for me."

"I am happy for you, Georgiana; although being the selfish man I am, I put my own happiness above yours. Forgive my obsession of trying to protect you when you no longer need protection. It might take me some time to adjust to your not being at Pemberley any longer, but I do love you, and I do give you and Mr. Harrison my blessing."

"Thank you, Fitzwilliam." Her eyes misted with tears.

Darcy cleared his throat, forcing back the sadness he would not show her now. "There are two days in a woman's life which should be perfect—her wedding day and her child's birthday. Ignore everything else today and concentrate, Dearest One, on the happiness you will feel once you are Mr. Harrison's wife. This is your perfect day." He brought Georgiana to him and kissed her cheek. "You are as beautiful as I ever saw you. Now, let us go and hypnotize Mr. Harrison with your beauty. When Elizabeth came down the aisle, I knew if I died that moment, I would be happy for I looked upon the most beautiful woman in the world. Mr. Harrison is in for that same exquisite moment when he sees you." Darcy watched as a light blush overtook her body, but his sister took his proffered arm as pure bliss covered her smile.

Sporting the fashion of the day, Mr. Harrison wore a dark brown embroidered silk satin suit. He paced the front of the church waiting for Georgiana's entrance. A stir at the rear told him the time arrived. When he took his place and turned to behold Georgiana, her appearance on Darcy's arm took his breath and replaced it with a longing he did not know existed.

There she stood in all her glory. Georgiana wore a silver matte satin gown with flecks of gold threading throughout and overlaid with gold embroidered English net. The gown laced up the back with silver and gold alternating silk ribbons; the bodice gathered at the center, emphasizing her blossoming bosom. Although most women chose a bonnet to wear as part of their wedding attire, Georgiana wanted Mr. Harrison to remember her beauty on this day. So, instead she chose a scalloped edged lace, which she attached to a jeweled comb. Accenting her blond curls draped loosely at the nape of her long slender neck, the lace, draped down her back, hung to the floor.

Harrison stumbled back a few steps upon seeing her; she, literally, looked like an angel, and for a moment, he thought his heart stood still. Then Georgiana Darcy began her procession down the aisle toward him, and the man's happiness could not be contained. He considered shouting for joy, but instead he let the smile on his face and the tears welling in his eyes speak of his exhilaration.

Georgiana took her place beside Chadwick Harrison, and the words he longed to hear began. "Dearly beloved, we are gathered together here in the sight of God. . . ." The rainbow of light from the stained glass window danced about Georgiana in a mystical benediction. Harrison forced himself to concentrate on the words of the service, but the words could not calm his racing heart. Only Georgiana's countenance gave him comfort.

"Who giveth this woman to be married to this man?"

Darcy's voice rang clear. "I do." He lightly kissed Georgiana's cheek and then placed his sister's hand in the bishop's. The clergyman placed that same hand in Mr. Harrison's and then continued with the vows. Harrison's heart swelled as he spoke the words which would bind him to Georgiana Darcy forever.

"...to love and to cherish, till death us do part, according to God's holy ordinance, and thereto I plight thee my troth." Chadwick Harrison fell in love with Georgiana nearly a year earlier; now, he could create a future for them. ". . . with my body I thee worship and with all my worldly goods I thee endow." Never abandoning looking deeply in her eyes, Harrison slipped the ring onto Georgiana's hand.

"Forasmuch as Chadwick Harrison and Georgiana Darcy have consented together in holy wedlock and have witnessed the same before God and this company, I pronounce they be man and wife together, in the Name of the Father, and of the Son, and of the Holy Ghost. Amen."

★ ★ ★

Elizabeth turned over in the bed she shared with Darcy to find his side empty. Reluctant to give up the dream she had of him, she eventually opened her eyes to find him standing silhouetted in front of the bedchamber's window. Smiling, she knew his thoughts without asking. Quietly, Elizabeth slipped out of the bed to join him. She encircled his waist from behind, and Darcy reached out to pull her to him, holding her tightly.

"Will you not return to our bed, my Love?" she whispered softly as she caressed Darcy's jaw line.

Several minutes passed before he spoke the words identifying what really bothered him. "Do you believe Georgiana to be happy?" His doubts about serving his sister's future laced Darcy's words.

Elizabeth resisted the urge to tease him; Darcy needed a different comfort this evening. "Our sister found happiness." The answer spoke the simple truth.

"What if Mr. Harrison hurts Georgiana?" Darcy protected his sister for so long, he could not relinquish the need to do so now. Elizabeth realized his tendency for self-censure so she tried to choose her words well.

"Mr. Harrison loves Georgiana most ardently."

"How do you know, Elizabeth? How can you be so sure?" Darcy turned to face her, but he did not withdraw from his wife's embrace.

"The man literally stumbled back upon Georgiana's entrance today. The love he feels for *our* sister could not be hidden."

Darcy seemed surprised. "Did he really?"

"Mr. Harrison is violently in love with Georgiana. He physically protected her twice. You said so yourself, my Husband, the man was single-minded in Georgiana's defense with Captain Rutherford. He would allow Rutherford's men to burn the estate or even take his life, but protecting Georgiana was a different story."

"That does not mean he will not hurt her; I ardently love you, but I hurt you." Darcy looked in Elizabeth's eyes, seeking the forgiveness she already gave him, but which Darcy did not fully give to himself.

"Our trials were not of our own making, Mr. Darcy; you cannot compare what happened to us to the normal relationship between a man and a woman. However, even with everything, we found our way back to where we belong. You, Fitzwilliam Darcy, are my dream—my destiny."

Darcy could not resist kissing her lightly; Elizabeth's words moved him. "I remember our wedding; you were so beautiful. It was all I could do not to run to you and take you in my arms. You, however, were all calm and innocence."

Elizabeth brushed her lips over Darcy's before speaking. "Mr. Darcy, I am so pleased my acting skills improved to such a degree; I assure you, my Love, calmness was not part of what I felt standing next to you."

Darcy's breath became shallow as he asked, "Then, pray tell, what did you think?"

Elizabeth flashed him a quick smile; she kissed him lightly, allowing her lips to linger close to his. "I kept thinking, oh, please, Reverend Woodson, hurry and make me this magnificent man's wife before he changes his mind."

Darcy chuckled, "Magnificent?"

Elizabeth gave him a little growl in his ear, and then accented each of her words with a kiss along Darcy's chin line. "Magnificent . . . superb . . . handsome. . . ."

Darcy allowed his hands to drop to Elizabeth's lower back after pulling her hips to him. "I will again surrender to your charms," he gasped as Elizabeth continued to distract him with her closeness. Darcy lost himself to his wife's body for a few minutes, his interest in Elizabeth's intimacy increasing rapidly. Then a thought crossed his mind, and Elizabeth felt Darcy's body stiffen. He blushed when he asked, "Did you speak to Georgiana about what she should expect tonight?"

Elizabeth could not completely stifle her amusement as the "prideful" Mr. Darcy asked about his sister's wedding night. "I spoke to Georgiana," she gave him at last. "I told her the same thing I told Kitty—what my Aunt Gardiner shared with me."

Darcy's eyebrow shot up. "Mrs. Gardiner? Not your mother?"

Elizabeth laughed out loud. "Trust me, my Love, if I listened only to my mother's advice, I still would be denying you my bed."

"I always respected Mrs. Gardiner." Darcy's smile turned up the corners of his mouth as he returned to kissing Elizabeth deeply.

Finally, she asked, "Will you not come back to bed, my Love?"

He paused in his need to kiss Elizabeth's neck and shoulder. "Soon, Mrs. Darcy." He withdrew from her a few steps and tried to settle his emotions. "I believe I want to stay here for a few more minutes. As tempting as you are, Elizabeth, I fear I am missing my sister this evening a bit more than I reasonably should."

"Do not question whether you did your duty to Georgiana, Fitzwilliam." Elizabeth stepped up behind him and lightly touched Darcy's back. "She could not be more prepared for the life she chose. The only thing more surprising than the chance Georgiana is taking is where that chance is taking her."

Darcy kissed Elizabeth's cheek. "I know you try to ease my mind, my Love, but I still question whether I did well by Georgiana."

Before she could answer, a light knock came at the door. Darcy strode quickly to the opening. He found Henry standing outside. "I beg your pardon, Sir," the valet stumbled over the words, "but a late post came a few minutes ago. I thought it might be important."

"Thank you, Henry." Darcy took the letter from the silver salver and closed the door. With shaking hands, he crossed to sit in a chair close to the candle where he could read. "It is from Georgiana," he said distractedly. Darcy broke the seal and unfolded the paper, reading the words out loud.

14 November

My dearest Brother,

I realize this is highly unusual, but I insisted Chadwick stop on our journey and allow me to post this letter to you. I should have said these things in person, but I could not do so without the emotions overcoming both of us. Fitzwilliam, how may I thank you for giving me everything worth having in life? I speak not of Pemberley or the wealth. I speak of the freedom you gave me—the freedom to be me.

Darcy's words drifted off as tears welled in his eyes, and Elizabeth slipped out of the room to allow him some privacy. Darcy continued to read his sister's missive, only now, he did so silently.

512

A young girl has so many questions, and you, my Brother, never thought any of mine to be foolish ones. You encouraged me to pursue what I love—my music, allowing me the freedom to develop my skills. You valued me enough to trust me with the knowledge of Pemberley. You taught me not to accept the attentions of a man who did not recognize my wit and my intelligence to be equal to my beauty and my wealth. You could have sent me away to school—an unhappy defection—but instead you kept me close and showed me love. Then you brought Elizabeth into my life at just the right time, teaching me that marrying for affection and respect to be superior to marrying for practical purposes. Luckily, with Mr. Harrison, I married for all three.

Fitzwilliam, I will miss your calling me "Dearest One," your tap of my chin with your index finger, and your loving glance across a crowded room. You gave me unconditional love and the confidence to be my own person. Although I look forward to being the mistress of my own estate, I dread being away from you, my Brother, but I go to Hines Park knowing your love goes with me.

Your affectionate sister,
Georgiana Harrison

Darcy swallowed hard, fighting back the emotions. Georgiana knew he needed her tonight, and his sister answered his silent call. He watched as Elizabeth slipped back into the room; she carried Ella, sleeping quietly in her mother's arms. Elizabeth came to where Darcy sat; she placed the sleeping child in his arms and seated herself on the floor at his feet. She leaned against his knee, stroking the back of Darcy's calf while he held the child close, lightly caressing her face with his index finger.

Finally, Elizabeth spoke tenderly, but with passion. "Ella needs the same kind of love you always gave to Georgiana. She needs to know what to value in this world. Ella will need to make good choices; as a woman, she will need a strong man who will help her find her worth. Your daughter needs the same lessons you gave to your sister; it should be easier this time, my Love; you learned well with Georgiana."

Darcy directed his attentions to his wife. With a smile he asked, "If it is to be so for Ella, what should I teach Lucas?"

"His family duty," she teased.

"Never, Mrs. Darcy." His humor returned. "My son must learn to value the women in his life."

"Even if they are progressive in their thinking?" Elizabeth got on her knees and moved in closer to where she could touch him.

Darcy met her taunt by looking deep in Elizabeth's eyes. "Especially if they are progressive in their thinking—they are the most difficult to understand but are the most worth knowing. Maybe my princess needs to return to her crib," he smiled, "and we need to return to our bed, Mrs. Darcy."

"I was thinking something similar. Is it not wonderful we two think so much alike?" Elizabeth took Ella from him. "Warm the bed, Mr. Darcy; I will be right back."

Elizabeth headed back to the nursery. Returning a few minutes later, she found Darcy already under the counterpane. She slid in next to him, warming herself against his body. She encircled his neck with her arms and began to kiss along Darcy's neck. "I love you, Fitzwilliam."

"Both you and Georgiana knew what I needed tonight." He raised his chin to allow Elizabeth access to the indentation at the base of his neck.

"All I did, Mr. Darcy, is remind you others need you as much as Georgiana." Elizabeth now kissed along his collarbone, and Darcy felt the warmth spreading through his loins.

He cupped her chin and brought Elizabeth's mouth to his. "My dearest Elizabeth," he said, his voice taking on a seductive huskiness, "thank you for reminding me what I want and what I need lie in you and the children. A dreamer is protected by the security in being home."

Elizabeth kissed him deeply. "Life offers each of us a thousand chances; I am pleased I am the one with whom you chose to spend your life. Love comes gently when we least expect it—like walking in a dream."

Darcy pulled Elizabeth as close as he could, pressing her body to his. He kissed her passionately while touching her intimately. "I love you, Lizzy," he whispered into her ear.

"Umm," she moaned, "perfection lies in those words." Elizabeth draped her leg across Darcy's body.

"Lizzy," he murmured as he directed kisses to her neck and chest. "I must have you."

Elizabeth touched him in the way she knew would enflame his passion further. "Where you are, my Love, is where I intend to be. I surrender to your charms; I want to be where no one will dare to interrupt us."

"Then it is a good thing, Lizzy," he teased, "you lie with the Master of Pemberley."

"It is an *excellent* thing to lie with the Master of Pemberley." She gasped with Darcy's assault of her sensitive spots. "In fact...."

Darcy put his fingers over her mouth. "This is not the time to demonstrate your wit, my Love."

A teasing smirk flitted across her face. "What should I demonstrate, Mr. Darcy?"

"How much you love me, Mrs. Darcy." His kiss this time left Elizabeth gasping for air. "Tell me you want me, Lizzy."

Her fingers tugged at the curls along the nape of his neck. Darcy met her eyes with an intense rush of desire. "I want you, Fitzwilliam."

"Kiss me, Lizzy," he demanded as he began to take pleasure in the love Elizabeth freely offered him.

Resources

Austen, Jane. *Pride and Prejudice*. Clayton, Delaware: Prestwick House Literary Touchstone Press. 2005.

Cressbrook Multimedia. "Well Dressing." *Peak District Multimedia Guide*. 1997.
{http://www.cressbrook.co.us/features.wellhist.htm}.

Decker, Cathy. "Images of Real Regency Clothing." *University of California at Riverside*. April 20, 2004.
{http://hal.ucr.edu/~cathy/rd/rd.html}.

"Gunter's Tea Shop." *Georgian Index*. August 2006.
{http://www.georgianindex.net/Gunters/gunters.html}.

"Hannah More (1745–1833)." *British Abolitionists*. February 2001. BrycchanCarey. November 17, 2007.
{http://www.brycchancarey.com/abolition/index.htm}.

Mactyre, Shelley Chrystal. "Regency Hero." 2002. *Shelley Chrystal Mactyre*. January 18, 2008.
{www.mactyre.net/archives/regency/}.

Myretta, Barbara, et al. "Pride and Prejudice." *The Republic of Pemberley*. 2004–2005.
{http://www.pemberley.com/janeinfo/pridprej.html#Toc}.

"Olaudah Equiano (c.1745–1797)." *British Abolitionists*. February 2001. BrycchanCarey. November 17, 2007.
{http://www.brycchancarey.com/abolition/index.htm}.

Overton, Mark. "Agricultural Revolution in England 1500–1850." September 19, 2002. *BBC*.
{http://www.bbc.co.uk/history/british/empire_seapower/agriculture_revolution_01.shtml}.

Ross, David. "English History: Georgian England." *Britain Express*. Little Rissington, Gloucestershire, England. {http://www.britain.express.com/ Histor/Georgian_index.htm}.

Shakespeare, William. *Much Ado About Nothing*. Edited by David Bevington and David Scott Kastan. New York: Bantam Classics. 2005.

Waugh, Joanna. "Historical Factoids." *Factoids*. 2005–2007. *Jaleroro*. January 18, 2008. {http://www.joannawaugh.com/Factoids.php}.

"William Wilberforce (1759–1833)." *British Abolitionists*. February 2001. BrycchanCarey. November 17, 2007. {http://www.brycchancarey.com/abolition/index.htm}.

"Women's Legal Position in Regency Times." *Regency Life*. January 18, 2008. ihug. {http://homepages.ihug.co.nz/~awoodley/regency/legal women.html}.

[1] William Shakespeare, *The Tempest,* Act IV, scene 1, line 156.

[2] Michel de Montaigne, *Essays.*

[3] Madame de Staël, *Corinne.*

[4] William Shakespeare, *The Tempest,* 1.2.

[5] Motto of the Order of the Garter, Edward III (1327–1377).

[6] *New Testament,* I Corinthians, vii, 3.

[7] Cicero (106–43 B.C.), *De Officiis.*

[8] John Milton (1608–1674), *Paradise Lost.*

[9] Plutarch (46?–120?), *Moralia: Advice to a Bride.*

[10] William Shakespeare, *Much Ado about Nothing,* 4.1.

OTHER ULYSSES PRESS BOOKS

DARCY'S PASSIONS: *PRIDE AND PREJUDICE* RETOLD THROUGH HIS EYES
Regina Jeffers, $14.95

Profound and amusing, this novel captures the style and humor of Jane Austen's novel while turning the entire story on its head. It presents Darcy as a man in turmoil. His duty to his family and estate demand he choose a woman of high social standing. But what his mind tells him to do and what his heart knows to be true are two different things. After rejecting Elizabeth as being unworthy, he soon discovers he's in love with her. But the independent Elizabeth rejects his marriage proposal. Devastated, he must search his soul and transform himself into the man she can love and respect.

MR. DARCY'S DECISION: A SEQUEL TO JANE AUSTEN'S *PRIDE AND PREJUDICE*
Juliette Shapiro $14.95

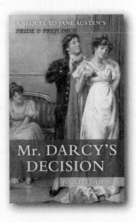

Newlyweds Mr. and Mrs. Fitzwilliam Darcy begin their married life quite blissfully, but it is not long before the tranquility they seek is undermined by social enemies. Lady Catherine de Bourgh makes little attempt to hide disdain for her nephew's wife. However, Elizabeth has more pressing matters on her mind—carrying the Darcy heir being the most pleasant of them. Concern mounts with the sudden return of Elizabeth's sister Lydia. Alarming reports of seduction, blackmail and attempts to keep secret the news of another's confinement dampens even Elizabeth's notoriously high spirits.

The Lost Years of Jane Austen: A Novel
Barbara Ker Wilson, $14.95

There was an interval in Jane Austen's life, before any of her novels were published, when she disappeared from sight. This book seeks to fill those missing months with a visit from England to the colony of New South Wales. It is a fact that Austen's aunt, Mrs. Leigh Perrot, was brought to trial on a shoplifting charge. Botany Bay, Australia, was where Mrs. Perrot might have been transported as a convict. Jane Austen and her uncle would have had good reason to visit the unfortunate woman in Sydney Town, where the dashing Mr. D'Arcy Wentworth has settled at Homebush, a convict revolt is brewing at Castle Hill, and no one is quite certain whether the Napoleonic War has ended or not.

Mr. Darcy Presents His Bride: A Sequel to Jane Austen's *Pride & Prejudice*
Helen Halstead, $14.95

When Elizabeth Bennet marries the brooding, passionate Mr. Darcy, she is thrown into the exciting world of London society. She makes a powerful friend in the Marchioness of Englebury, but the jealousy among her ladyship's circle threatens to destroy Elizabeth's happiness. Elizabeth is drawn into a powerful clique for which intrigue is the stuff of life and rivalry the motive. Her success, it seems, can only come at the expense of good relations with her husband.

To order these books call 800-377-2542 or 510-601-8301, fax 510-601-8307, e-mail ulysses@ulyssespress.com, or write to Ulysses Press, P.O. Box 3440, Berkeley, CA 94703. All retail orders are shipped free of charge. California residents must include sales tax. Allow two to three weeks for delivery.

About the Author

—◦◦◦—

Regina Jeffers, an English teacher for thirty-eight years, considers herself a Jane Austen enthusiast. She is the author of several novels, including *Darcy's Passsions*, *Wayward Love: Captain Frederick Wentworth's Story* and the upcoming *Vampire Darcy's Desire*. A Time Warner Star Teacher and Martha Holden Jennings Scholar, Jeffers often serves as a consultant in language arts and media literacy. Currently living outside Charlotte, North Carolina, she spends her time in the classroom and with her writing.